Bouquets of Bloom

Danita J. Snulligan

Dedication

This book is for the youthful individuals who think their grand ambitions are too surreal to come to fruition and for the educators who gift them with words and deeds of encouragement to believe otherwise.

Table of Contents

Part I

Part II

Part III

Part I

Chapter One:
Croix-des-Bouquets

Like a mischievous cat moving in a clandestine manner, she navigated her way from the kitchen and tiptoed onward through the living room. Cristal's heart raced excitedly as she carefully floated into the bathroom and stood anxiously next to the sink. *'All I need are three capfuls,'* she whispered to no one. Each intentional effort would move her closer to her goal, another artistic creation of a new bottled treasure. Cristal understood the risks involved in her actions to follow. The possibility of getting into big trouble again was great, especially if too much of her father's rubbing alcohol was poured and wasted. She couldn't bear the thought of disappointing him again. But still, she pressed on.

After retrieving the rectangular container beneath the cabinet, Cristal poured some chemicals into a small capsule. She then returned the larger container to its place and gently closed the door. Her mother had taught her the art of organization early. 'Everything has a place, everything in its place.' Careful not to let it all splash away or capsize, Cristal swallowed hard, bit her bottom lip, and cautiously leveled the capsule onto the tray. 'It's *a really important ingredient for my new perfume,*' she convinced herself, '*even if I do get a spanking, it's worth it.*' Without incident, the girl who could not see navigated around bulky collections of living room furniture with her tray and returned to the kitchen to extract the precious liquid with an eye dropper.

At age five, Cristal became adventitiously blind years before her spirit was quelled by the powerful earthquake that hit Haiti, a country in the Caribbean Sea. Gradually, after the loss of her sight, she began getting her days and nights confused. When other members of the Duvernay family were fast asleep, Cristal lay restless in bed for hours, listening to nocturnal animals at a great distance from her bedroom window. The sounds of barred owls and coyotes were her favorite. But, on this particular sizzling summer night past one o'clock in the morning, Cristal busied herself at the kitchen table. She was on the verge of designing the latest version of what she believed would be an exceptional perfume.

Careful not to wake her father, mother, and brother, Cristal sidestepped lightly through the crowded space between the kitchen cabinet where stacks of old newspapers rested near the plastic trashcan just below the windowsill. She contorted her body into a position where she could press her nose against the dusty metal screen to whisper to her great-grandmother. Granny Lou had fallen asleep hours before on the outside porch.

"It's almost ready, Grandma," Cristal spoke eagerly.

The elderly woman had fallen numb in her antique slated rocking chair under a calm, starry night sky. She blinked hard awake with a grumble and a cough at the sound of her granddaughter's voice. Granny Lou fumbled and searched for a pair of glasses that had fallen off her face and onto her lap. After a few more rapid blinks and wiping of the eyes, she turned and put into focus a silhouette on the opposite side of the screen. Her great-grandbaby's cute little diamond-shaped face glowed like a ray of light. "Here I come, Moonbeam."

Dried floral tops from wild lavender plants were crumbled and crushed between the palms of Cristal's hands as she rubbed them rapidly together. They, too, were inserted into the miniature bottle.

She then used a funnel to scoop from a battered bucket of fresh rainwater to fill the small bottle halfway. An eyedropper made it difficult for Cristal to achieve the desired results for the following two ingredients. '*If I use a spoon, it will be worse,*' she thought. So, to the best of her ability, Cristal also injected drops of lemon juice and one drop of vanilla extract into the glass container's narrow opening.

As quietly as possible, Cristal crushed a round mint candy in a plastic bag with the heel of her shimmering black patent leather church shoe. The sweet-smelling particles were sprinkled into the container to mingle with other ingredients. A small amount of oil was left from the hibiscus petals she and her little cousin, Mikaela, picked in early spring.

Weeks before, under the watchful eye of her Aunt Rachelle, Cristal and Mikaela picked flowers near the gates of their city, Croix-des-Bouquets. The girls aimed to capture the flowers' fragrances at their peak, just before blooming. Granny Lou taught them how to extract fragrant oils methodically.

"After plucking the petals from the stems, put 'em in these zip-loc bags." Moments passed.

"Like this, granny?"

"Yes, now get my two wooden mallets out of that drawer on the left, tap the bags, and bruise the petals."

"Ohhh, this is fun," the girls chuckled as they banged and hammered away as instructed.

"That'll release them oils inside," proclaimed Granny Lou.

The girls poured a smidgeon of olive oil and almond oil into bags before shaking them hard and dynamically. The mixture was then spooned into a glass jar and covered tightly.

"Now, don't y'all bother 'em. Leave 'em on the porch and let 'em sit for a spell," their great granny demanded.

For over 48 hours, the girls exhibited an impressionable amount of patience by occupying themselves with jump rope competitions, water gun fights, and their favorite game of rock school.

In the final step, Granny Lou commanded, "Now drain the oils into this second jar through a layer of cheesecloth like this."

Mikaela watched closely as Granny Lou put her hands over Cristal's hands to manipulate and demonstrate. The wilted and battered petals that had taken three weeks to transition from buds to bloom were abruptly discarded.

Cristal poured the oils from the hibiscus flowers into the bottle. She liked creating with these blossoms because her father, Jesse, told her they were Haiti's national floral emblem. '*Awww... geez,*' she murmured when several droplets of the valuable oil dribbled down her arm, '*now it's probably gonna be less than two ounces.*' After screwing the lid tightly, the young creator vigorously shook the bottle's content exactly fifty times. That was the last and final well-executed step of her most superlative perfume to date.

The eighty-one-year-old woman's aching joints actively protested as she pulled to a stand like a thirteen-month-old baby, ready to take their first independent steps. A couple of bone-popping sounds signaled to Cristal that her granny would be inside shortly. The old woman grabbed her support cane and hobbled inside at her great-granddaughter's exuberant request. Although it was way past her bedtime, she was happy to observe her little Moonbeam engaged in something that brought her absolute joy.

"Smell this and tell me what you think." Granny Lou's fingers, stricken with rheumatoid arthritis, trembled.

She reached for Cristal's latest "secret" potion but feared she might drop and break the small receptacle. Granny Lou held it close to her nose and deeply inhaled as best she could without signaling a bout of excessive coughing.

"Oh, my goodness, this is quite impressive," she responded warmly and genuinely. "I think this might be your best one yet!"

Granny Lou's thoughts flashed back to her teenage years when she used to put dabs of vanilla extract behind her ears before going on dates with suitors. She couldn't afford the price of fresh and velvety-smelling perfumes.

It was Cristal's sixth creative scent. "Really?" She responded in a high, shrilled voice. The young designer squealed, jumped up and down, and grinned widely with sheer delight.

"Shhhh, don't you go and wake the others. And yes, I do," Granny Lou confirmed. Cristal radiated with pride.

"I did just like you told me, Granny. Yesterday, I used the bucket to capture the rainwater early, right before noon. After that, I let it sit an extra hour longer to capture rays from the sun. It might've absorbed all seven colors of the rainbow this time!"

With a look of intense love, Granny Lou examined Cristal's funny animated expressions. Wiry sprigs of hair escaped and freed themselves from her high and messy ponytail. Lightly with trembling fingers, the girls' great-grandmother tucked them back under a scarlet red scrunchy. Granny Lou's mind began to drift and reflect on the life-altering changes that would soon affect the entire Duvernay family. She loved her grandchildren and great-grandchildren so much. She hoped that Cristal's new life would be one full of promise. *'She deserves a fresh start,'* Granny Lou muttered under her breath, *'and so does her poor mother and little Wilky.'*

"What you say, what's that granny?"

"Nothing, baby, nothing. That's real good, real good. Now, it's late-early. Go on and get to bed because tomorrow will be a long, hectic day for everybody," revealed her granny.

Cristal laughed, "How late-early is it?"

"It's 2:30 in the morning."

Cristal couldn't resist. Just once more, she held the liquid jewel close to her own nostrils and took a whiff, "Ummm," she moaned. She, too, was pleased with her latest captured innovation. Ever so slightly, Cristal tilted the bottle for a dribble on two of her fingers. She then stood on tippy toes and placed the fragrant dabs generously behind each of her grandmother's ears.

"Granny Lou, what's the name of a person with a bunch of money?"

"Umm…Rich?"

"No, not that word. I want another one."

"Well, I don't know," Granny gave a long pause. "How about fortunate, a person with a great fortune?"

"Fortune…fortune," Cristal repeated and pondered. "Yeah, that's it. Granny, do you really think there is a pot of gold at the end of every rainbow like the ones in those fairy tales you read to me?"

This ever-present show of idealism and innocence seemed to tug at Granny Lou's heart each and every time.

"I believe so, but I don't really know. Your granny ain't never been so favored to find out. You and your little brother are about the closest thing to a treasure I've ever had."

"Hmmm…just in case it is true," Cristal responded, "I think I'm gonna name this new fragrance *"Fótin Bon"* – *"Good Fortune."* Anybody that wears this will feel so, so lucky!"

Although Cristal had never been to school, Granny Lou was convinced that her eleven-year-old great-grandbaby was a very clever little girl. "That's a good name, sweetie. Santi bon koute che," the old woman muttered.

Baffled best described Cristal's feelings when her great-grandmother spoke in proverbs like her father often did. She tried with mental agility to decipher the phrase 'Smelling good is expensive.' With creased eyebrows and a questionable shrug of the shoulders, Cristal screwed the lid on the bottle and placed it in the top pocket of her flannel pajamas. Prudently, she was determined to get it to her room safely.

Granny Lou's lower back pinched and ached terribly, but the six-foot woman tried to bend downward and kiss Cristal's forehead. "Ahhh," she said as her nostrils engulfed the sweet, blended fragrance again. "That strong smell of lavender should carry your little behind right to sleep. Now git." Cristal was slow to respond. A glance at the old grandfather clock standing tall in the corner prompted the belting of orders once more. "Go to bed, Cristal. It's a couple of hours before dawn. And don't forget to say your prayers!"

Chapter Two:
Rainbows

Just two months prior to creating her sixth fragrance, Cristal revealed her last visual memories to her younger brother, Wilky, and his friends. "I remember rainbows," she said as they sat eating thick slices of warm potato bread dipped in glasses of coconut milk. "I remember feeling small under a big blue sky. I saw the bright yellow sun peeking behind puffy clouds resembling fat, funny faces." Cristal's descriptive narrative continued as the boys fixed their gaze in her direction. "The hills and mountains were covered in green. I remember Momma's look, too." Mystified expressions ricocheted between the boys. "Her face was kind and pretty. Her skin was the color of caramel candy, and her lips were shaped like a heart." Stunned by Cristal's vivid recall after six years, everyone sat enchanted in a silence that seemed just short of infinity. Ever so sly movements were used to wipe two tumbling tears with the collar of his shirt, and no one noticed; Wilky could only hope.

The Doctors never provided Jesse or Dahlia with a definitive diagnosis or reason for their daughter's vision loss. It occurred one unsettling night when Cristal became violently ill. "What's the matter, baby cakes?" her mother asked.

On that rare occasion, Cristal climbed into her parents' bed that night, waking them from a deep slumber.

She whined and winced like never before, "My head hurts, mommy."

Dahlia knew that her baby girl had to be in intense pain. Cristal was usually a cheerful and healthy child with no more than a cough or sore throat during the island's mild winters. Unlike her son, Wilky, her daughter rarely complained. Dahlia first took Cristal's temperature with great concern and gave her a cherry-flavored chewable tablet for toddlers.

Dahlia rolled, dipped a small towel in cool water, and placed it on Cristal's forehead for possible relief. Next, the young mother boiled grated ginger, a white onion, a clove of garlic, and turmeric roots for a cup of tea. She let it simmer for a few more moments before removing the brew from the fire. The last step was to add a touch of cream with two hefty tablespoons of honey. Dahlia picked Cristal up from the sofa and hoisted her baby girl onto her lap. She blew on the brew until it was lukewarm, bringing the medicinal tea to Cristal's puckered lips. Slowly, she began to sip her mother's special tea. Dahlia tried comforting her child for over an hour by humming and singing soothing lullabies. Back and forth, she rocked her child until she fell asleep. Dahlia then carried Cristal to bed and wrapped her in a plush indigo blanket.

The following morning, Cristal awoke, but her ability to see things clearly vanished. When she opened her eyes, nothing but darkness with specks of light presented itself. "Mommy, I can't see."

Granny Lou yelped, stomped her feet, and clapped her hands in fear. Vehemently, she began to shout and pray for her granddaughter's health. Jesse and Dahlia rushed their daughter to St. Francis de Sales Hospital with as much speed as the timeworn family van could muster.

A team of doctors took turns using their ophthalmoscope to peer at the fundus, the retina, and the optic disc at the back of Cristal's eyes. A scan using a computed tomography of her brain was also conducted. The older and more experienced Dr. Bernard Abloh concluded, "Based upon Cristal's symptoms of a headache, jaw pain, and fever, she may have retinal arteritis." He couldn't be sure. "It is unusual for such a disease to occur so rapidly and result in total blindness for someone as young as Cristal."

Dahlia pleaded, "What do we need to do?"

"How can you help her?" Jesse asked.

"I'm going to write a prescription for something to ease her pain. Could you bring her back here in a week? I want to examine her again." The mystified doctor moved closer to the inconsolable young parents and shook their hands goodbye.

Jesse and Dahlia took Cristal back to Dr. Abloh every week for a month. At their fourth office visit, he reluctantly announced to the grief-stricken parents, "The findings from my ongoing evaluation and research have revealed that your daughter's pupils do not consistently constrict and dilate in the presence of light. This poor reaction indicates damage within the visual pathway to the brain. As a result, she is legally blind with no certainty of a prognosis for improvement. I'm so very sorry, but this is a serious impairment that is not in my hands to heal."

For months, the entire Duvernay family sulked, sobbed, and mourned. They felt betrayed and abandoned. Moving through the five stages of grief from the loss of Cristal's vision occurred at different rates and intervals for each person in the household, including little Cristal. One Sunday morning, before heading to church, Papa Jesse slammed his fist on the breakfast table, upsetting the salt and pepper shakers. "Enough!" he commanded. He had decided for everyone that it was time to accept the change in circumstances. From that moment on, nothing more was said in despair about Cristal's blindness, at least not until approximately five years after the big 2010 earthquake.

Understandably, when Cristal first lost her vision, everyone was overly attentive and consumed with worry for her safety. They stressed over the possibility that their baby girl could get severe injuries while moving erratically about the house. For months, Cristal remained under a watchful myopic eye. The family wanted her in close proximity, morning, noon, and night. They chose at any cost not to rearrange the furniture. They wanted Cristal to be familiar with the layout of her home and move about safely and freely.

One morning, Dahlia's close friend, Zoe, stops by during a routine visit. They enjoyed a fresh pot of bold, full-flavored mountain-brewed coffee. Zoe brought a dozen moist, to-die-for homemade blueberry muffins as an apology of sorts for a wounding remark she made during her previous visit. "You don't think your father asked a shaman to put a voodoo curse on you when you were pregnant with Cristal, do you?"

Haitian Vodou, an African diasporic religion that developed in Haiti between the 16th and 19th centuries, was practiced by many citizens in the country. Dahlia was hurt and felt terribly offended by such an insulting question.

"Despite the fact that my father disagreed years ago with who I chose for a husband, I believe he still and always will love me and wants the best for my children. How could you ask something like that?"

Zoe's attempt to avoid passing judgment had failed yet again. Only a few of her relatives knew that her name was the anglicized variant of the word zo, Haitian Creole for 'bone.' Members of the Zoe Pound street gang were known to be *'hard to the bone'* during historical times when conflicts against Haitians arose. Zoe's pressuring personality didn't depart much from its origins, but she and Dahlia had established an unlikely friendship.

During another casual midweek visit, Zoe observed Dahlia and Granny Lou's constant hovering and smothering behavior when caring for Cristal. Zoe's outspoken personality flickered through as soon as Granny Lou left for the bathroom. "Chile, y'all need to lighten up and let that baby figure out how to maneuver by herself. Since the beginning of time, blind folks have traveled independently without needing somebody to tell them every step of the way. They used sticks, boards, geese, and all kinds of things to get around. It's in the Bible." Zoe stopped lecturing, only to take another sip of coffee. "The rest of Cristal's senses will kick in and take over. She'll learn. You'll see. Stop crowding that baby and give her room to breathe," she spouted.

Dahlia nodded, "I guess you're right. I just don't want her breaking any bones or getting that pretty angelic face of hers all scarred up."

Eventually, the well-meaning adults in Cristal's life did begin easing up. They gradually allowed her to move around the house several feet beyond arm's reach. It appeared Cristal had also started adjusting quite well to her permanent disability. As family members and friends observed her confidence growing daily, an uneasiness subsided among the adults. She started traveling from room to room with ease and played in the front yard with her toys under an acceptable watchful eye like any other child. Now, whenever a bump or misstep slightly injured Cristal, the Duvernays agreed that it was best not to make a big deal of it.

Now Wilky, their son, whose visual acuity was sharp as an eagle's, was forever bouncing around in a red and blue cape. It seemed he kept this favorite birthday present tied around his neck from sunup to sundown for years. The little daredevil frequently attempted to fly, tuck, and dive off anything taller than himself. Because of his rambunctious and boisterous nature, he was the one his parents really should have been bracing themselves for and worrying about. Because of his love for the game of football, they feared breaking bones, concussions, or worse, were inevitable. But at the end of the day, the young, hands-on parents understood that minor accidents were bound to happen to any growing child, whether they could or could not see.

Chapter Three:
Spice Girl

By age eleven, Cristal had become increasingly competent at using her sense of smell, hearing, and touch to accomplish many daily living skills. She would make discoveries independently by putting together pieces of her tiny world like a giant puzzle. But the morning after creating *Fótin Bon,* Cristal wasn't sure if the yummy smells of freshly baked biscuits and fried plantains were what actually awakened her. Or maybe it was the competing sounds of her mother's faint whimpering from the kitchen that was very near the bedroom she shared with her rumbling, snoring little brother. It was hard to detect which sensation was culpable.

Cristal's father spoke against the clattering of porcelain cups placed atop matching floral saucers in a low, calm tone. The blustering sobs from her mother grew louder with every passing second. Those eerie cries sounded familiar, and Cristal became frightened. Feelings of anxiety flooded her brain. 'There's *no way that Wilky and I both slept through another horrible disaster like an earthquake,*' she assured herself in a muted voice. But she did wonder if some other ruinous and wretched event on another level had occurred. Cristal hoped not. Her mother had suffered enough hardship.

A little over a year and a half ago, on January 12, 2010, approximately 220,000 people were killed when an earthquake hit the country of Haiti. Thousands more were seriously injured on the mainland of Hispaniola. The optics from an aerial view were massive and utter obliteration. Such a horrific misfortune it was for all who survived. Although the Duvernays lived thirty-one miles from the epicenter, tragedy made a rushed and deliberate journey directly to the core of their family as well. Dahlia lost both of her parents that dreadful day. Her mother's body a few days following was buried in a mass grave. However, her father's body was never found. Dahlia's oldest sister, Mariah, died five months afterward of injuries from infection, broken bones, and internal organ and nerve damage. Poor medical attention, or lack thereof, was the primary problem.

Psychological first aid was unavailable for Dahlia or others who lost family members and friends on the island. Like a poisonous vine winding itself around her entire body, Dahlia felt bound by severe bouts of depression as a result of the very personal and horrendous tragedy. The aftermath of the earthquake affected her ability to feel, think clearly, and behave in her usual good-natured and nurturing manner. She experienced everything at once and, in an instant, became paralyzingly numb. Often, Dahlia cried and seemed to wither like a beautiful spring flower that sprouted before an extended frost. So fragile she had become. Stress hormones surged through her body, impacting one of the most vital organs, her heart.

Weeks passed when Dahlia refused to get out of bed only to milk the goats. "I'm not feeling well," she'd whimper like an undisciplined and unprepared student wishing to skip school. "I just need to stay in for a few more days." Months passed. Cultivating and selling fresh vegetables and fruits from a once viable community garden was a job Dahlia used to enjoy with neighbors and members of her church, but not anymore.

Granny Lou consistently tried to coax her daughter-in-law to get up and sit on the porch to soak in some sun and drink a cup of blue lotus tea. The effects of the organic tea were known to relax the whole body and promote a euphoric or joyous feeling. Dahlia's mother-in-law even baked a rum cake. It was her favorite, but trying to lure Dahlia out of bed with the tasty dessert was unsuccessful. Consistently and adamantly, she refused social invitations from neighbors and church members. Dahlia could only manage to lift and shake her head 'no' from under an Egyptian goose-down comforter that became her haven. Granny Lou refused to serve her meals in bed. So, Dahlia stirred like a sloth to do nothing more than go to the bathroom and sit at the table to twist and poke her fork at the meat and vegetables served on a plate set before her.

In due course, the change of seasons painted an emotionally different canvas, and sunlight became the disinfectant. Although Dahlia continued to sulk and brood, her time in bed began to diminish. As a consequence of the fallout from the natural disaster, the family income, like so many in their community, began to decline. But instead of going back outside to help cultivate and then sell what remained of the produce in the garden, Dahlia decided to get busy baking. Her recipe for a lemon-flavored pound cake with a praline filling was quite a delectable treat. Granny Lou suggested that she add a combination of condensed milk and some inherently sweet and clean-tasting goat's milk to the batter instead of buttermilk. It made all the difference. The recipe was never written down but scripted to heart.

With Granny Lou's assistance, Dahlia calculated the call for specific ingredients, "You need a hint from here, a pinch there, a dash of this, and a dollop of that." This secret mixture was the ingredient that made this cake superior to any others sold throughout the vast miles along the island coast.

While cakes baked in the oven, Cristal relished the infrequent opportunity her mother allowed. She flipped, uncorked, and unscrewed lids to various spices and seasonings organized in a kitchen cupboard. She recognized many basic ones: thyme, cinnamon, cumin, oregano, ground ginger, chili powder, garlic powder, rosemary, and smoked paprika. They all smelled so fresh.

"Momma, where do these spices come from, a farm?"

"Yes, they are harvested from a farm. I get mine at the market, where they arrive in shipping containers from Central and South America."

"Mmmm…this one smells like licorice. What is it?"

"That's anise."

"Oh, this smells fruity; what's this?"

"That's amchur powder. I use it in chutneys and soups."

Cristal continued digging deeper and deeper through the assorted pouches, canisters, and jars on three separate shelves. "I like this one too!" She held the round metallic container close to her nose and deeply inhaled the contents.

"And this one?"

Dahlia, feeling a bit exasperated by the constant interruption from her ever-so-curious daughter, looked up from a newspaper article. "Cristal, that's enough for now, okay honey? That's saffron, part of a flower. Go ahead, put it back on the shelf, and don't spill any of it. It's too costly to waste."

She was such an obedient little girl. "Okay, mommy." Sensibly, Cristal climbed down the 2-tier ladder and sat quietly beside her mother at the kitchen table to wait. Once cooled, she assisted in packaging the mini-size delicacies into baggies with twisty ties for closure. Her Aunt Rachelle would transport several dozen of Dahlia's little cakes to markets to sell along with her very own handmade souvenirs.

Chapter Four:
Krik? Krak!

Cristal and Wilky's Papa Jesse was a skilled construction worker and professional painter by trade. In the past, he worked with a crew hired for business and personal projects. A friend who was a licensed electrician taught him tricks of that trade as well. However, because of the tragedy that shook the land and shuddered the spirits of many, Jesse answered a higher call and developed an unwavering commitment to his new job. During these times, he routinely left home five days a week in the early morning hours for civil service work with American Red Cross volunteers. As a supervisor working in food delivery and logistics, Jesse was responsible for facilitating the sorting and packaging of nonperishable food items to families and individual citizens in need throughout Haiti.

The compassionate men and women arrived from all over the United States. They helped victims still living in haphazard campsites in wide-ranging capacities under tattered green tarps pitched along buckled and broken roads. The wearied and tossed earthquake victims lost just about everything. Their previous homes were reduced to a landscape of dust and rubble that was now surrounded by fetid trash and dangerous jumbled debris. Even the St. Francis de Sales Hospital, where Cristal and her little brother Wilky were born, was demolished.

Her mother's sobs and cries continued in what seemed to be a rhythmic timing. Cristal strained her ears harder to hear the conversation between short guttural gasps. Frozen like one of the statues in the town square, she heard only bits of secret chatter.

Cristal grimaced at her brother's grizzly sounds from the other twin bed just feet away from hers. Her frustration grew because Wilky made it difficult to discern any part of Granny Lou's and Papa Jesse's conversation. Her great-grandmother once told her she had 'ears like a hawk.' Wilky said Granny Lou meant to say she had 'ears like a bat.' Either way, at that moment in time, Cristal's dainty pierced ears failed to inform her brain about any details entombed by current events.

She tossed the smooth linen sheet lightly to the side and tiptoed towards the bedroom door. Waking Wilky was something she did not want to do. But of course, the unexpected happened. 'Ouch!' she screeched. This time, she stubbed her big toe on a large wooden crate parked in the middle of the floor. She even thought she might have collected a nasty splinter from this fiasco. *How in the world did I miss bumping into this sneaky rigid beast last night?* she wondered. The crate was filled with some of Wilky's most valued wooden toys and included hundreds of colorful Legos. As Cristal bent down to massage a throbbing toe, her forehead sharply struck the corner of a dresser drawer she shared with her brother. The harm was afflicted just above her left eye. 'Ouchie!' she cried out in the most excruciating pain. Once again, Wilky had failed to close the drawer completely shut. Now, Cristal was beyond furious. She couldn't see, and he was habitually careless. One could not be changed; Wilky had to do better.

It seemed that Wilky was forever leaving obstacles in Cristal's path. She knew he didn't do it intentionally but hated sharing a room with him again. She wished her brother would return to his mission school in Port-au-Prince, Haiti's capital, and continue living with her father's sister, Rachelle. At least then, Wilky and his junk box would be out of her way. And she wouldn't have to inhale his smelly, bugle-sounding toots throughout the night, either. Unfortunately, Cristal knew she'd have no such luck. Wilky wouldn't be going anywhere anytime soon. After that horrible day when the earthquake struck, only a few schools on the island remained safe. Her father reported that many stores, the new government building, and even the men's and women's prisons had perished.

Several days after the geological disaster struck, the ground continued to shake in Croix-des-Bouquets, where the Duvernays resided. The after-shock rippled towards the northern suburb located eight miles northeast of Port-au-Prince. Croix-des-Bouquet was once a city located on the shore but was relocated inland after the 1770 Port-au-Prince earthquake. Legend has it that the town takes its name from a tradition of the Spaniards passing through to deposit bouquets at the foot of a large cross on the land where the city was built. Subsequently, Croix-des-Bouquets extends a tradition of beauty through the sculpture of iron at the gates in an ode to very talented Haitian artists and sculptors.

Papa Jesse said that the original quake registered 7.0 on the Richter scale.

Curious, Cristal asked, "What does that mean?"

She grumbled when Wilky blurted out the answer before her father could respond. "It's a measure of the sudden release of energy within the earth's crust."

Without real intent, Cristal was naturally inclined to roll her eyes and frown in tandem with irritated sighs. Wilky was such a smart aleck. Sometimes, he got on his sister's last nerves with quick, brainy responses. But as annoying as her little brother could be, her love for him was over the moon. Forever grateful she was when he'd gently shake her awake from realistic nightmares of ferocious hairy monsters growling and chasing her with clubs down a rocky hill. Night terrors involving thundering avalanches that crushed people as they screamed, trying to run chaotically for refuge, were the worst. Those types of images haunted Cristal more frequently. "It's just a dream, Cristal," Wilky repeated with warm, empathetic words of comfort. "Wake up. It's just a dream," he would whisper while gently shaking her shoulder. The cries of panic soon subsided, and Cristal would eventually drift back to sleep.

"Geez, what's wrong with you?" Wilky asked with one eye squinting open when he heard Cristal's loud cry of pain. At first, he thought she might have had another pensive hallucination.

"You are the most inconsiderate little brother a sister could ever have!" she shouted. "I wish you knew what it feels like to have somebody around who's so inconsiderate. I wish you'd think twice about leaving stuff lying all willy-nilly over the place."

Cristal had recently learned that phrase from her Aunt Rachelle and thought it was the perfect context to use it. Wilky was shocked and dismayed so early in the day. He cringed, seeing his big sister crouched like a tiger near the door. The palm of her hand pressed firmly above her right eye, where a spot of blood emerged from it. Wilky felt terrible. Sadly, he watched the twisted expressions of exasperated anger on his sister's doll-like face.

Wilky thought about the Saturday afternoons when he would hold Cristal's hand and guide her through the crowded shops at the Galerie Marassa market in Port-au-Prince. Strangers sometimes pinched Cristal's plump cherub cheeks. They complimented her on a big, bright, toothy smile framed by deep-set dimples. Although she loved receiving compliments, Cristal hated the startling, uninvited touches. Wilky knew his sister was pretty and cute, even with the small scar on her chin. That flaw was insignificant to anyone who knew and loved her.

Cristal favored her Aunt Rachelle, who had many old and young male admirers. Wilky recalled a little over a year ago when he and Cristal joined their aunt and cousin at the market. The four shoppers weaved in and out of souvenir stalls amidst a swell of tourists seeking something special for Dahlia's birthday. Out of nowhere, a six-foot-three-inch tanned man with an unbuttoned Hawaiian shirt appeared. Wilky heard him tell Aunt Rachelle how beautiful she was. "You must be an angel with your wings clipped. I've never seen such gorgeousness and sophistication here on God's green earth." His conversation was smoother than silk and sweeter than sugar cane.

The hairy-chested man with a struggling beard and receding hairline continued to ogle and flirt, keeping up with Aunt Rachelle's escalating fast pace. "You look like a young Chaka Khan," he told her.

Aunt Rachelle giggled and blushed. "You've got to be kidding me," she stated with disbelief.

Wilky felt somewhat embarrassed for the guy when a horizontally challenged woman with a rubbery and wrinkled scowl suddenly appeared. She grabbed the charismatic rake by the arm, jerked, and spun him around, clear away from Aunt Rachelle. "Chester, what the heck do you think you're doing?" she yelled. "I am so sick and tired of your darn mess!"

Immediately, Aunt Rachelle swerved and ducked to the back of the next souvenir stall. The unhappy couple could be seen wildly gesturing by nosey onlookers and were heard belligerently arguing as they reversed directions to head back toward the tour bus. "Eeeww," Cristal quipped, "he smelled like alcohol mixed with cilantro and nutmeg." Aunt Rachelle and Cristal had great trouble controlling their laughter.

Wilky made a beeline for the media center the following Monday when he returned to school. He could hardly wait to research the singer Chaka Khan on the computer. The media specialist had to help him with the search because Wilky kept spelling the name with a '*Sh*' instead of a '*Ch*' and found nothing. The foolish young man was right about one thing, Wilky concluded. His aunt did resemble the American singer. Although he didn't have the vocabulary to articulate it, he saw the image and aura of a celestial and natural beauty on the cover of one of Chaka Khan's top-selling albums.

Witnessing Cristal balled up on the floor in the present upset Wilky to no end. He hated thinking his big sister might get another jagged blemish on her face. And if it never went away, he'd forever be reminded he was responsible. By the time he mustered up enough courage to say, "I'm sorry," it was too late.

Cristal had already picked herself up and limped towards the door. Before crossing the threshold, she returned to check and ensure her treasure trove of six miniature glass bottles hadn't wobbled from the dresser and shattered. "Thank goodness," she voiced in anguish.

Wilky eased the cover back over his head and tightly shut his eyes. Desperately, he tried to go back to sleep - back to that victorious and lofty dream of his team, the Stingrays, winning the national football tournament. Of course, he would be the story's hero who saved the day by scoring the goal-winning point, catapulting the ball swiftly past the goalie and into the net.

By age six, Cristal began making natural accommodations to protect herself from most obstacles above her waist. It became an excellent habit from muscle memory to keep her arms extended in front of her body. When she walked past large pieces of furniture traversing from room to room, she managed to avoid severe injury from sizeable things in her path. Wilky would tease her and say she walked with her arms stretched like the Bride of Frankenstein.

Cristal believed that the moment she walked into the sitting room, she heard her father say something like, "You cannot heal in the same place where you hurt." But he got quiet the moment she appeared before them. "Bonjour," piped Cristal with false cheer as she gingerly approached to greet everyone.

The aroma of Brazilian nut coffee filled the air. "Bonjour Mademoiselle," replied Aunt Rachelle.

Cristal's arms stretched wide as she traveled about five steps towards her aunt's voice. They engaged in an affectionate embrace. "Oh, you smell like magnolias and tangerines," Cristal announced.

"It's a birthday gift from Mikael," Aunt Rachelle shared proudly. "It's *Fenty Bleue Eau De Parfum*,"

"It's nice!" Cristal complimented.

Cristal continued to move clockwise around the table to kiss her papa next. She then landed a kiss on Granny Lou's cheek. At last, Cristal reached out for her mother and made a real effort to climb onto her lap. To no one's surprise, she was softly pressed away. "What's wrong, Momma? Why are you crying?" Not knowing what the matter was, she sincerely and affectionately was ready to reassure her mother that everything would be okay.

Dahlia purposely ignored the floating question and planted a kiss on her daughter's forehead instead. "You know you're too big to sit on my lap."

There was a time before the devastating earthquake when Dahlia was much more compassionate towards her son and daughter. They used to laugh, sing, and have good old-fashioned fun under the warmth of the Caribbean sun. One of Cristal's fondest memories was when her mother let her sit on her lap in the rocking chair and would read to her and Wilky just before dusk. They'd eat one of Granny Lou's raspberry-flavored iced treats while listening intently to their mother read. She used a variety of animated voices when reciting Aesop's fables. The tales delivered value-driven lessons about life, nature, and friendship. Aunt Nadine, who lived in the United States, sent Cristal the book for her eighth birthday, hoping that someone would read to her often. At the end of each tale, Dahlia would have Cristal and Wilky attempt to explain the moral of the disarming lesson. Each child had their best-loved stories.

- The Tortoise and the Hare: *Never give up!*

- The Ants and the Grasshopper: *Work hard and play hard!*

- The Dog and the Shadow: *Be happy with what you have.*

- The Bell and the Cat: *Ideas are good, but execution is better!*

One evening, after reading a fable, Dahlia explained to Wilky and Cristal that Haiti is a country of incredible beauty and suffering. During the Haitian Revolution, a series of conflicts between 1791 and 1804, enslaved Africans overthrew the French regime. Centuries of relative isolation resulted in great poverty, but an enriched and unique culture emerged, as evidenced in the Haitian language, music, and religion.

Papa Jesse would sometimes join them on the porch, and as a local storyteller, he was frequently invited to participate in the Krik? Krak! Festival. It is a familial celebration and folkloric storytelling event in which evenings are full of music and stories. Jesse always wanted to take advantage of every opportunity to educate Cristal and Wilky about their heritage.

"Your ancestors gave you more than wounds to bear; you each have an enormous capacity for strength and intellect to claim." Hearing her husband speak blessings over her children made Dahlia glow with pride. His stories usually ended in Haitian proverbs that matched ethical principles as well.

- Tanbou prete pa janm fe bon dans: *A borrowed drum never makes good dancing.* Tic hen gen fox devan kay met li: *A little dog is really brave in front of his master's house.*

- Woch nan dio pa konnen doule woch nan soley: *The rock in the water does not know the pain of the rock in the sun.*

- Bay kou blye, pte mak songe: *The giver of the blow forgets, the bearer of the scar remembers.*

In the spring of 2011, Dahlia presented a mere shadow of her affectionate self. On singular occasions, she would share any natural joy locked inside. It pained Jesse to witness the distance growing farther between his wife and their two beautiful children. He felt guilty at times, too, because, by the end of a long physical day, he was exhausted and emotionally drained and had little to offer in the way of spirited interactions. Jesse knew he had to do something drastic to try and save his family from further neglect. Night after night, he knelt on his knees to pray. Relief flowed over him early one Sunday morning. Jesse had come to terms with the decision to be made, and he knew then without a doubt that it was the right one.

"Sweet Pea, your mother and I have something important to tell you and Wilky when I return from the city later this evening. For now, go wash up. It's time for breakfast," her father instructed.

"What is it, papa?" Cristal pleaded, "Tell me. I wanna know what's making everybody so upset?"

He patted the mound of soft curly hair piled on his daughter's head and gently pulled a tuff of collective strands. Stretching about thirteen inches with a quickness, it sprung back upon release. "Later, baby girl," he stated, "I'll tell you later. Go wash up and get ready for breakfast."

At first, no one acknowledged the wee 'boo-boo' above Cristal's right eye. "Wait a minute," her mother said. Cristal stopped and turned in her direction. Dahlia leaned back in her chair to reach and open a cluttered junk drawer. She fiddled and found the first-aid baggie. "Come here," Dahlia commanded softly. She grabbed a paper napkin from the table, dipped it in a half-filled glass of water, and blotted the blood spot on her baby girl's face. "After you wash your face and brush your teeth, come and let me put some aloe vera gel on your scrape and apply this bandage over it."

Cristal felt loved and gave a quick snuggle, "Thanks, Mommy."

Granny Lou handed Jesse his sack lunch filled with a tasty egg and onion sandwich, a ripe ma'ammee apple, and the last thin slither of banana bread. She watched with sadness as her strong, silent grandson trudged with heavy steps and an equally heavy heart towards the door. The roundness of his slumped shoulders was burdened with great emotional weight. Granny Lou thought her grandson was far too young to deal with such struggles. Jesse removed his late father's favorite Panama hat from a wobbly peg and headed out the door. But not before he kissed his grandmother goodbye. By the time Jesse stepped off the porch, Granny Lou had reached the door and loudly spoke through the screen a redacted quote she remembered from C. S. Lewis, a British literary scholar. 'Remember, baby, it's not the load that will bend and break you. It's the way you choose to carry it. You'll get through this.'

On this day, Jesse and other workers would unload and distribute several boxes of food, clothing, and shoes that arrived by a United States plane from thirteen churches in the East Baton Rouge Parish of Louisiana. In August of 2005, over 1,800 lives were lost in several southern states in America due to the Category 5 hurricane named Katrina. The pastors and empathetic members of their congregations wanted to extend their gratitude and help others in need, just as they had been covered and blessed. It would be a long and tiring day for Jesse. He and fellow coworkers needed to drive the shipment to the border near Comendador, a western city near the Dominican Republic.

Chapter Five:
Dagnabbit

Cristal sat at the kitchen table, eating her breakfast alone. Still tossing and turning was Wilky in his bed while his scrambled eggs with cheese cooled to room temperature. Cristal decided to quench her thirst with one more tall glass of milk. She figured she had enough time before leaving the porch to wait for her Aunt Rachelle and cousin Mikaela to arrive. She stood and headed to the refrigerator, but after opening it, Cristal became disappointed. Quickly, she detected that the big metal pitcher was filled to the brim. Cristal knew it might be too heavy to hold steady and balance. But this was an excellent time for her to select and repeat one of the most applicable upbeat and optimistic mantras her father taught her to voice whenever she faced minor tests. 'It's *gonna be alright. I am capable. I can do it!'*

"I got this," Cristal said aloud as her bottom lip shivered. She struggled to transfer with a cup in one hand and the cumbersome pitcher in the other. When she started pouring a liberal amount of the chilled chunky beverage from its' large container into a smaller one, it proved far too challenging to stabilize in mid-air. Great splashes of milk spilled out. Cristal lunged forward in an attempt to place the pitcher on the counter. Within a few hasty seconds, all went 'splat' and then 'clang' onto the linoleum floor. "Oh no!" Cristal cried out. From the back bedroom, her mother responded in a slightly delayed unison but louder.

Cristal was afraid that a terse swat on her backside would undoubtedly follow. "Thank goodness," she prayed under her breath when she recognized the distinct audible sounds of shuffling footsteps and her grandmother's cane pounding. Granny Lou came to her rescue. "No need to cry over spilled milk, my child." The old woman's knees creaked and cracked as she knelt to wipe away the wasted milk. Desperate to help, Cristal only made a much bigger mess by swishing a tiny dishrag around and around in overlapping circles. An untypical frustration suddenly rose in Granny Lou, and she gave a rare scolding. "Just go sit down, Cristal… sit down."

Saddened and embarrassed, Cristal garbled under her breath, "Not being able to go to school and learn new things is bad enough, but not being capable of cleaning up my own mess just stinks!"

Friday mornings during summer months were always full of high energy and activity around the Duvernay home. Everyone had something that needed to be done. Wilky and his Stingray teammates had one final practice before the big tournament the following day. Before he could clean his plate, he heard his name shouted from the front yard. Wilky hurdled outside, letting the screen door slam. With a mouth full of buttered biscuit clumps and a bowl of cereal in hand, he stretched and yawned while taking in the early morning sunshine. Wilky accidentally dropped the spoon without care, but instead of picking it up, he decided to eat and drink the rest of the cereal right from the bowl. Ubiquitous excitement saturated the air. Endy and Marjon, his best friends, had been yelling and beckoning him to come outside for a while. The Duvernays' dog barked excessively. He scampered about chasing nothing but happiness and mosquitoes.

Wilky stood entertained by all the commotion brought about by his two teammates clowning and teetering on a deflated tractor tire in the yard.

Since sunrise, Cristal has been on the porch helping her Aunt Rachelle and cousin Mikaela. "Papas' got some important news to tell us later today," she told Wilky.

"What is it?" he asked.

"I don't know, but it's really something big." she shrugged in response.

"Well, what's it about?"

"I'm not sure."

"Well, dadgummit, why say anything at all, dodo brain?"

"Oh, shut up, you big Willy Wonka screwball," cracked Cristal.

"Alright, alright, stop that. Be nice to each other," chided Aunt Rachelle. Endy and Marjon chuckled at the siblings' friendly banter. They laughed harder when Cristal stuck her tongue out behind Wilky's back and dipped her head cattywampus.

"Let's go, Wilky. Coach Reno will be mad if we're late," urged Endy.

So thrilled and hopeful they all were for the chance to become first-place winners. Wilky zoomed into the house to put on his socks and cleats, then kissed his mother and great-grandmother goodbye. For a few moments, the three friends played in the front yard. They kicked the soccer ball, practicing a series of roulette turns and spins. Next, the close friends worked on the elastic move, which required a player to roll his foot over the ball and then bring it down to the other side, just past his opponent.

Today, Coach Reno needed everyone to brush up on the rainbow move. It was a toughie, and only three out of ten of Wilky's teammates seemed to master it. This move involved using one foot to swiftly move the ball up the back of the other leg and flick it over an opponent's head before collecting it on the other side. Endy tried it and accidentally kicked the ball onto the porch where Aunt Rachelle, Mikaela, and Cristal sat. After bouncing twice, the ball's trajectory targeted Mikaela's glass of juice.

"Hey, watch it!" she screeched. "Ain't none of y'all got skills." Cristal laughed hard.

"Sorry," Endy shouted back.

Mikaela turned to Cristal and announced, "They play like squirrels running scared from spikey giant falling pinecones." Aunt Rachelle and Cristal burst into laughter.

"Who's the cutest," Cristal asked Mikaela. "Endy or Marjon?"

Aunt Rachelle interjected with her own opinion, "Wilky."

"Nah," Mikaela sounded in objection. "Endy is."

The young boys, feeling confident, punctuated the air with the Stingrays' chant:

'*We are the mighty, mighty Stingrays heading your way,*

Gonna bend the ball with an unstoppable play.

Eyeball outgoing man to man,

We'll sting with flapping tails and interrupt your plan.

We are the mighty, mighty Stingrays heading your way,

Getting you out of formation will make our day.

At the goal mouth with a righteous fake over,

We'll confuse you to think we're playing Red Rover.'

With arms pumping hard, the three amigos raced down the hill, heading east for about a quarter of a mile to a makeshift soccer field. Cristal had grown tired of twisting and twirling the dried banana leaves, jute, and sisal between her nimble fingers. She really did enjoy helping Aunt Rachelle make woven nesting baskets to sell to wealthy tourists. Before the earthquake hit, her aunt worked as a clerk at a mission school. But now, she traveled twice a month to barter, sell her in-demand handmade souvenirs, and fill in as a math tutor for elementary students living nearby. Cruise ships docked on the sandy beaches of Punta Cana in the Dominican Republic on the first and third Saturday of every month. The sale of Aunt Rachelle's items generated rewarding profits.

Cristal decided to take a break from singing and working. She probed, "Auntie, is it good news or bad news that Papa has for Wilky and me?"

A carefree response from Aunt Rachelle revealed nothing. "Don't worry your pretty little head. Be patient, and you'll find out soon enough."

"Awww, Auntie, c'mon and tell me," Cristal groaned with disappointment.

"You do know it is not my place to tell, right?" pronounced Aunt Rachelle firmly. "The goat's business is not the sheep's business."

Respectfully, Cristal responded, "Yes, ma'am."

The two proceeded in silence, committing to the task at hand. Neither felt like singing in harmony anymore. Instead, they pretended to listen to Mikaela nearby, carrying on with made-up jingles while she created flowery bracelets.

Startled and interrupted by her daydream, Cristal snapped her body around toward a steel bell ringing with a deep resonance. From a far distance, the familiar noise was actually expected. Rising from the low, rickety stool, she was determined to avoid a catastrophic airborne transport from point A to point B. She was never sure if or what Wilky may have left haphazardly lying on the porch. Just as Cristal reached for the handle of the prickly screen door, she stepped on a spoon and made it bend and crunch. "Dagnabbit," Cristal fumed while kneeling to pick up the crushed utensil. She then entered the house and headed towards her bedroom to obtain a couple of necessary items. "Ouch," she winced for the third time on the same suspense-filled morning. Bumping her right thigh on the corner of two stacked, sturdy luggage pieces hurt. Thoughtlessly, Aunt Rachelle sat them down randomly in the center of the living room. '*Maybe Auntie is getting ready to go on another cruise with her fiancé,*' Cristal surmised. She spat on two fingers and then rubbed them across the minor scratch. Stored under her bed were a pair of sneakers. Cristal slid her feet inside and eased toward the dresser. She then retrieved a pair of shabby suede gloves from the bottom drawer. Granny Lou's hearing was failing, but she knew when she saw Cristal enter her bedroom it was time for her to take a hike.

"Prese! Prese!" she shouted. "Don't keep Mrs. Rosie waiting. She's one of my best customers. And don't forget to put on some sunscreen!"

"Okay, granny. I'm moving fast."

Cristal was used to this outburst because it was repeated frequently, like a refrain in a poorly written poem every Friday morning. She hurried to slather Hawaiian tropic sunscreen on her arms, legs, face, and hands. Granny Lou stepped out onto the porch and traveled a short distance in the grassy gravel to pull a cord to ring her own secured buoy bell three times. It was a signal to Mrs. Rosie that Cristal was on her way.

For the past eight years, Granny Lou's childhood friend rang a durable bell on most Fridays. Her other customers could drop off and pick up their own laundry midweek. However, Mrs. Rosie had severe arthritis in both of her hips, too. The job of climbing the hill to get and retrieve her laundry used to belong to Aunt Rachelle when she was younger. But now, it was her little niece's responsibility. Mrs. Rosie would stand resting against a split wooden post after pulling a cord that she rang to signal her presence. This clever idea of communicating in such a manner on the hill near the Duvernay home was the brainchild of Granny Lou's late husband, William. On this particular Friday, a not-so-full basket of dirty laundry sat at Mrs. Rosie's feet while she waited patiently for Cristal's arrival.

The Duvernay family was one of only a few families near the foothills of the mountains that owned a full-size and working washing machine. William had purchased a high-priced appliance for his wife's 50th birthday, and it was hauled to Jesse and Dahlia's home when Granny Lou and Papa William came to live with them. This luxury appliance allowed Granny Lou to earn money by washing a few neighbors' clothes. William declined a passioned request to buy his wife a dryer the following Christmas. "Fresh air is free," he said, "clean clothes can be hung out on a line to dry beneath the warmth of God's magnificent sun." However, William and Jesse did construct a shed to hang wet clothes in, but those aromatic results paled compared to sun-dried clothes. That being the case, Granny Lou planned to save some of the money she earned to buy herself a dryer because business always lagged during the rainy season.

After two years of effort, she did save enough money to buy herself a new 7.0 cubic foot dryer. Conversely, Granny Lou never made the big purchase. It seemed that after her husband passed away, her grandchildren and great-grandchildren were forever in need of something, and they were always her priority.

As early as Cristal could recall, somewhere around the age of four, her first chore was to help her grandmother with the laundry. While gripping Granny Lou's apron, she would sidestep down the angle of the clothesline. Wooden clothespins taken from inside an old, dented coffee can exchange hands one by one. It was an easy task and a great sensory experience for a young child. Cristal delighted in breathing in the honeysuckle scent of clean, wet laundry, especially when it blended with the distinctive aroma of fresh grass after rain. She enjoyed the feel of the cool and damp, brightly colored cotton fabrics softly flapping against her face and arms amidst a gust of air. In a lazy, fluttering way, the sheets appeared to wave to the high hills with the help of balmy trade winds from the sea. And Granny Lou had definite rules for hanging her clothes:

Granny Lou's Rules for Hanging Laundry

1. Hang all shirts by the tail and not by their shoulders

2. Line up the clothes so that each one shares a peg with the next piece of clothing.

3. When taking clothes down from the line, the pegs should be collected and returned to the can.

4. Socks are always hung by their toes.

5. Hang all clothing in the order of their color– whites with whites, blues with blues, etc.

Cristal recalled her great-grandmother's interesting memory about her mother and their laundry chore. "When I was a little girl," Granny Lou said, "I helped my momma with the laundry. She'd boil our dirty clothes in large pots, and then we'd scrub them by hand and beat them with sticks to get them clean." Cristal was thankful those days were over. "Hurry up, Cristal. Rosie is waiting!" Granny Lou yelled in a loud, stern voice.

"Don't make me take a switch to your narrow little behind!"

"I'm on my way!" she yelled back with a tone of politeness.

Chapter Six:
Cheerio and Lila

Cristal placed the tattered glove on her right hand on the porch and shoved the other in her back pocket. She prepared herself for the 150-yard trek up and down the steep hill to make the exchange with Mrs. Rosie. The five-foot-long, two-inch diameter walking stick that her Papa Jesse whittled and sanded splinter-free awaited her. Cristal named the tree limb Lila. Lila was the name of a famous Reggae singer in a band from Saint Kitts, an island in the West Indies.

Cristal was seven years old, and Wilky was six when the family took the majestic Princess Lee cruise liner on a fantastic vacation voyage for the very first time.

She swiftly snatched Lila from her corner home on the porch before Granny Lou had a chance to snatch a switch of her own and land a few swats. Cautiously, Cristal stepped forward, allowing her helper, Lila, to contact one of the largest trees near their home. It was located about fifteen yards west of the house. A taut rope was secured around its trunk and tethered to the post all the way up the hill where Mrs. Rosie would be waiting. Cristal laid Lila at the tree's base and grasped the taught line with her gloved right hand. She began the hike up the narrow dirt path. The young and healthy girl understood why she was needed for this particular chore and didn't mind. It was a difficult journey for people afflicted with joint pain. Gone were the days when she tugged on Granny Lou's apron and reached up to pass her clothespins. That job was passed along to Mikaela a few years ago, but only during the summer months when she was out of school. This trekking job offered Cristal a stint of freedom and independence. It allowed her valuable time with nature and prized moments of solitaire as she traveled alone away from home.

Mrs. Rosie lived alone, although she had four children and seven grandchildren spread about the island. Behind her back, Wilky and his friends called her Witch Rosie. She scared them because of her hunched posture and lined skin, wrinkled and cracked like old leather.

"Her face looks like a big smushy raisin," Marjon divulged.

"Like a thorny dragon lizard," Wilky blurted.

"She probably eats beetles and grasshoppers for lunch," remarked Endy. The boys bowled over in amusement.

"I bet she tucks that scaly articulated tail inside her briefs," joked Wilky. Uproariously, the boys rolled in the dirt, coughing and cackling with rowdy laughter.

"Stop it!" Aunt Rachelle scolded after overhearing their snide remarks. She walked closer, pointing at each boy and dispensing a condescending look. "What a mean thing to say. She's somebody's mother, grandmother, and great-grandmother," Aunt Rachelle snarled. "If she really were a witch, she would've conjured up a magical voodoo spell on all three of y'all by now." With that final remark, the laughter instantly came to a screeching halt. Seemingly the joy swooshed and was sucked up into the stir of a dusty funneled wind. Marjon pondered the thought that his recent string of bad luck resulted from a spell by Mrs. Rosie. Aunt Rachelle continued, "Keep it up, and she'd have y'all quacking like ducks every time you try to open your mouth and talk." Apparent terror rushed through their impressionable minds and over their terrified faces.

Now, Endy was hesitant to speak. With caution, he enunciated the phrase "Let us play," stretching out the word 'play' as if it had two syllables, *'puh-lay.'* No one heard an echo of quacking. Aunt Rachelle giggled.

Moments passed before the boys resumed their competitive game of marbles at full tilt. Cristal smiled when they commented negatively, but she didn't think it was that funny. "She smells like cinnamon and gives me a piece of gum or candy whenever I see her. She's nice," Cristal admitted. The boys said nothing.

Over the past two years, Granny Lou always managed to pay Cristal a small allowance for helping her gather and fold the laundry. She was wise enough to know that allowing her granddaughter to earn her own money helped instill pride and self-worth, which Cristal seemed to need. Aunt Rachelle taught Cristal how to count her earnings on Mikaela's large toy abacus, which displayed colorful fruit-shaped beads. "Move two beads over to the left, then place a finger after those beads and add three more. Now, what's your answer?"

Cristal responded successfully, "Five."

"That's good. You're a fast learner." When time permitted, Aunt Rachelle worked harder to teach Cristal how to manipulate the sliding beads on different columns by adding and subtracting more significant numbers. And sitting beside Mikaela while she studied her multiplication facts aloud helped Cristal learn hers. It wasn't long before Cristal could compute her savings accurately and quickly.

Sometimes, when Cristal became nervous trying to recall facts or speak in the presence of strangers, Aunt Rachelle noticed that she would wave or flick her hand and fingers in front of her eyes. She mentioned this atypical behavior to Dahlia and confirmed that she noticed it, too.

"Because the doctors said Cristal has some light perception, her repetitive hand movements in front of her face would provide some visual light stimulation. It's odd behavior for certain, but it does appear to calm her down," explained Dahlia.

"Oh, okay, maybe we can come up with something so she doesn't bring uninvited attention to herself," Rachel said to her sister-in-law. Dahlia agreed.

On Rachelle's next trip to the cruise port, she stopped at a souvenir shop and purchased an inexpensive folding floral-painted fan for Cristal. She also bought a lanyard to attach the fan to a metal ring. This fantastic idea allowed Cristal to wear the fan around her neck, and instead of light flicking with her hands before her eyes, she could fan herself as an inconspicuous alternative. Cristal liked the fan and enjoyed the breeze emanating from it. Aunt Rachelle and Dahlia liked how dainty and demure Cristal appeared when fanning herself in public places, especially on those few occasions when she found herself nervous amongst strangers.

***

Soft rain on the previous day resulted in a rugged and somewhat sticky path of mud. Cristal loved the feel of warm earth squishing onto her flip-flops and oozing between her toes. But for this chore, she knew wearing closed-toe shoes with a firmer sole was wiser. Not long ago, Cristal attempted to navigate the path without any accommodations but without success. Before her papa cleverly constructed the twine as a lead to guide her along the trail, Cristal convinced him to let her try and walk the uneven terrain while holding onto her dog's leash. She planned to do both, holding onto

Cheerio and Lila while balancing the laundry on top of her head. Papa Jesse didn't think it was a good idea, but he liked that his daughter was willing to take risks. Her father decided to let her try, but only if Wilky shadowed her by walking a few feet behind. But it didn't take long before Cristal realized Cheerio wasn't dependable enough to guide her safely. He barked and jumped while tugging wildly on the end of the leash, and Cristal quickly discovered the hard way that her dog preferred being free rather than harnessed. He loved to chase chickens that escaped the coop to search and peck for food at numbered grassy patches. Cheerio's natural urge to scamper and play caused Cristal to stagger.

"Wilkeeee!" she cried out. Her little brother couldn't move fast enough to prevent his sister from stumbling. Thank goodness a nasty tumble was avoided. The adventurous young girl managed to recover her footing and control her descent, although it took her breath away. At that point, her confidence was completely shaken. She decided it was best to return home with Wilky's hand in hers and let her father construct something special just for her.

Over dinner that evening, they discussed the incident. Jesse shared an ancient proverb meant to lift and encourage. "A stumble forward is not a fall. What does that mean?" he asked Cristal and Wilky. Cristal kept chewing with a shrug of her shoulders.

Wilky answered, "I dunno."

"There is always something to be learned from your mistakes, Cristal. And that goes for you too, Wilky!" Papa Jesse boomed. From then on, Cristal relied on her grip, connecting her to the taut rope as a lead while Cheerio ran happily ahead with no restraint. The mixed-breed hunting dog would dart about and circle back to check on Cristal for brief periods during parts of the hike.

Wilky was the family member who named Cheerio. It seemed forever and a day before their father finally bought them a dog that had already been vaccinated for rabies.

"What's he doing now?" Cristal questioned when they played, patted, and tried to get to know their new pet.

"He keeps turning in circles. I think he's chasing his tail," Wilky narrated.

Because the dog was light brown or beige in color, he appeared as a blur when he whirled in concentric circles. Wilky thought he looked like a Cheerio. And because he loved eating Cheerio cereal as much as his sister did, they agreed that Cheerio was his perfect name.

A good and faithful pet he had become even when he dashed ahead. Cheerio would break from play, occasionally turn, and observe whether Cristal could safely negotiate the rocky incline. Instinctively, she knew that her dog did just that. "Good boy, Cheerio…good boy," she praised.

Finally, Cristal reached her destination, where the tethered twine was attached to the wooden post where Mrs. Rosie sat waiting. Politely, she greeted her, "Good morning, Mrs. Rosie."

"Morning, Sugar Plum. Are you excited about your big trip? You know, I'm sure gonna miss your big bright smile." Perplexed, Cristal staggered backward; her body grew rigid. Mrs. Rosie puffed when she saw an astonishing look wash across the girl's face.

"What trip, Mrs. Rosie?"

The kind and elderly woman realized that she may have disclosed something that was probably supposed to be a surprise. She withdrew her talon-like fingernails, accidentally dropping a piece of butterscotch candy to cover her mouth. In haste, Mrs. Rosie made an about-face, slightly twisting her ankle on a snarly weed underfoot. Her only reply was a brusque charge, "Tell your grandma I should be back home around 5:00 tomorrow."

"Yes, ma'am." Cristal could hear slow, scuttling footsteps taper off the main trail. With a carved walking stick of her own, Mrs. Rosie slouched behind a deserted shed and clambered back to her one-room home constructed of concrete blocks and steel. Cristal shrugged and nodded in bewilderment. "What do you think that's all about, Cheerio?" The blended breed looked up, tilted his head, opened his mouth, and grunted with inflection before scampering away.

Cristal stepped off the beaten path a few yards in a northeasterly direction. After removing her glove, she picked a favored fruit that was round and about the size of a tennis ball from one of the few remaining damsel trees in the area. She then returned to the path and sat in the basket on top of Mrs. Rosie's soft pile of dirty laundry. Under the simmering sun, Cristal peeled the ripened, glossy, rough skin to devour the sweet white flesh. Without warning, Cheerio zipped towards her, panting heavily. He rested two great paws on Cristal's lap. Patting a wisp of his hair and plucking dirty matter from his eyes, she ever-so-lightly began to pull one long, floppy ear and then the other. To her adored puppy, Cristal started singing two verses of a popular kid's song that Mikaela taught her.

'Do your ears hang low?

Do they wobble to and fro?

Can you tie 'em in a knot?

Can you tie 'em in a bow?

Like a continental soldier,

Do your ears hang low?

Do your ears stick out?

Can you waggle them about?

Can you flap them up and down?

As you fly around the town?

Can you shut them up for sure?

When you hear an awful bore?

Do your ears stick out?'

Cristal never shared this secret with anyone, not even her little cousin and best friend, Mikaela. Cheerio's doggy breath was her most beloved scent in the whole wide world. And she liked that his licked paws smelled like Fritos. She even fancied her furry four-legged friend's long, wet tongue, especially when he let it slurp across her face. It tickled and made her force breaths and chuckles. Cheerio barked in rapid succession, beckoning Cristal to stand. He was getting thirsty and ready to return home.

Up on her feet, she jumped and then slipped on her left glove before delicately balancing the broad plastic basket on the crown of her head. Positioning the base of the laundry basket an inch before her tightly secured ponytail took only a brief second. With a firm right-hand grip, the determined girl held onto the brim of the basket and used her left hand to clench the twine. As she began the trek down the known path, the sun beamed brightly from overhead. Its hot rays could be felt on Cristal's neck, arms, and shoulders. She was so glad she obeyed Granny Lou's command to apply a generous amount of sunscreen. She and Wilky had been sunburned before, and the aftereffects really hurt. At that moment, she realized it was almost noon and time for lunch.

About a year before he passed away, Grandpa William taught her how to tell the approximate time of day when the sky was clear day. It was all based on the sun's position.

Halfway along the route, Cristal reflected on what Mrs. Rosie said. She began to worry, and as she often did, she engaged in self-talk. *'Is Papa going to deliver good news? Maybe he was planning a long family vacation to a beautiful beach somewhere, and momma cried because she didn't want to spend so many days and nights away from home.'* Cristal's mood changed from worry to bliss. In small light hops, she began skipping. One darned sock from the soiled load glided up and out. Cheerio barked twice, circled into a blur, and then leaped to snatch it mid-air as it fluttered toward the ground. The intelligent dog brushed the fabric on Cristal's leg to alert her of its escape. "Thanks, little buddy," she said, scratching behind his ears. She pushed the sock deep inside the frumpy pile. "Awww shucks, I forgot to get a piece of gum from Mrs. Rosie," she told Cheerio. He yapped twice in a show of empathy.

Cristal lowered the dirty load onto the ground near the tree and picked up Lila. On the porch, she opened the screen door. "We're back, Granny Lou. Mrs. Rosie told me to say 'Hello' and that she'd be ready for it tomorrow around 5 o'clock."

"Well, alright. Thanks, baby," Granny Lou yelled from the kitchen, where she had just placed a savory pot of squash soup on the stove to simmer for lunch. Cheerio lapped tepid water from a bowl in the corner, quenching his thirst with a tongue curled backward. The pair then walked to the back of the house, where the bleating sounds of Fi, Fo, and Fum could be heard. The family goats roamed inside the square wire fence where they were securely contained. Cristal and her mother used to check on them together daily to ensure the kids didn't get their heads caught in the four-inch squares. But now it was a daily added chore just for her and Cheerio. Wilky was honored to name the three older goats, and Cristal gave the others their names. Sometimes, the siblings thought they made strange noises like a chorus of infants crying for bottles of warm milk.

Before the earthquake, Papa Jesse sold Fee. He needed to pay tuition and the cost of textbooks and supplies for Wilky's education. Some of the money was also used to purchase the compulsory uniforms – navy blue or khaki pants and white shirts. Last week, their father sold Miny and Moe. Cristal didn't understand why but certainly wouldn't ask. Dahlia once told her and Wilky, "Children are supposed to stay out of grown folks' business. You don't get to count other people's coins." Neither Dahlia nor Jesse would have talked to their children about struggling financially.

The stench at the south end of the fence reeked with the nasty smell of manure. Cheerio huffed and barked in a high-pitched agreement of discontent. "Let's get out of here! It stinks," Cristal bellowed, releasing a tight pinch of her nostrils. "See ya later…," she yelled, calling all the farm animals' names, including the youngest kids, Eeny and Meeny. Robust winds carried an unrecognizable scent as the duo turned the corner and walked through a field. Her nostrils flared. "Hmmm… I'll have to ask Mikaela to come with me tomorrow and explore this area; maybe plumerias are starting to grow again." She and Cheerio returned to the porch, where Cristal chose to sit on the rocking chair to rest and relax. Without warning, Cheerio swept a wagging tail against a dangling leg. For that act of love, Cristal serenaded her faithful canine companion with a beautiful love song.

Chapter Seven:
Papa's Big Reveal

Dinner consisted of white rice and spicy black beans served with fried red snapper topped with a glazed tomato sauce. "This is a delicious meal, Momma Louise. Thank you, I really appreciate it," Jesse commented. Cristal and Wilky gulped their food down so fast that it pirouetted right off their taste buds and straight down the shoot to their tummies. Too eager they were to hear high-priority news. Granny Lou hastily cleared the table, knocking a few dishes together with a nervous racket.

Before her husband unveiled his plan to their little ones, Dahlia teared up yet again. "I need to go lay down," she mumbled and brusquely left the table, not bothering to pick up the cloth napkin dropped to the floor.

Cristal and Wilky's papa turned in their direction. "I want to do what's best for this family," he paused, "I've thought about it long and hard, and I've had to even get on my knees and pray about it." A clearing of the throat extended the pause. "I need to send the two of you and your mother to live in the United States. You'll be staying with your Aunt Nadine and her family in Georgia."

An awkward and temporary silence blanketed the room. Then, audible gasps from each child siphoned the air and hijacked it from the room. Cristal tried hard to untangle what her father had just said mentally.

"What do you mean?" Cristal asked.

"Live with who?" questioned Wilky.

Cristal perceived nervous tension in her father's voice for the first time. He coughed, cleared his throat again, and coughed once more. "Nadine, my sister. My youngest sister who lives in Atlanta, Georgia. She's the one who sends the two of you birthday presents every year. She and her husband, Isaac, were kind enough to invite y'all to stay with them for a while. That's what a close and loving family does in a time of need. They look for ways to help."

Papa Jesse grabbed Cristal's hands and pulled her close just as she began to cry. "Isaac has a daughter. I think she's about a year older than you, sweet pea."

Cristal bit her top lip, and in a quivering voice, she had an important question: "What about you and Granny Lou? Won't y'all come with us?"

Before he could speak, Wilky interrupted. "What do you mean to go and live in the United States? That's way across the Atlantic Ocean! What about football? I need to stay here and play for the Stingrays. I'm one of the best players they got,"

With a whine of her own, Cristal peeped, "Don't you love us anymore? Are we getting on your nerves?" She once overheard her mother say those same exact words while talking to her friend Zoe, which hurt a lot. After that biting remark, Cristal tried to stay out of her mother's hair as much as possible. Now, she wondered if her father had also felt like that.

Jesse knew it wouldn't be easy breaking the news to his children. He struggled to hold back his painful emotions and dropped his head in both hands. "Granny Lou and I will come later. I have work to do here. There are a lot of people who still need my help." He spoke more rapidly, "Your mother must leave this place. There are too many bad memories for her here, and those memories are making her ill. She needs a change of scenery—a place where she has a chance to heal and be whole again. It will be a very long time before things are back to how they used to be in Haiti before the quake hit. And the two of you need to go to school."

Cristal froze in disbelief. She could not imagine life beyond her beloved home near the mountains and the sea. She sprung to her feet to head for the door but suddenly halted dead in her tracks, feeling dizzy and dazed.

Wilky jumped to his feet, too, and with a feral snarl, he yelled, "I have a football tournament tomorrow. I ain't going to no Georgia, and you can't make me!"

If Granny Lou could, she would have shuffled fast on her feet and swatted Wilky on his behind for talking disrespectfully to his father, her loving grandson. Luckily for Wilky, he won the race. "Let him go," her grandson waved on. Wilky took off, purposefully slamming the screen door as hard as possible in his wake. After booting the rickety stool off the porch, he clutched a fistful of marbles from his pocket and flung them far into the yard. Poor Cheerio howled feverishly at the disruptive chaos that jarred him from a needed nap.

It was a while in time before the conversation in the Duvernay home resumed—Cristal's sudden burst of actions expelled the mad silence. She probed, jumping and swaying from side to side while flapping her hands. "What do you mean we both need to go to school?"

Weeks before, during a lengthy, long-distance phone call, Nadine told her big brother that the Garland County Public Schools (GCPS) was the largest school system in the state of Georgia. It consisted of 120 schools, with over 188,000 students enrolled. After conducting some research, Nadine discovered that GCPS had a highly acclaimed vision department consisting of nine exceptional teachers of students with visual impairments (TSVI). The team often referred to themselves as the VIPs (Vision Important Professionals) and included four certified orientation and mobility specialists (COMS). Last year, they served 139 students with total blindness or those with low vision.

Nadine continued to share more specific information with Jesse. "The TSVIs' expertise is to teach students how to read and write using those dots that make up the braille code and to use Nemeth code to complete math assignments. They also teach students activities of daily living and provide training in innovative technologies."

Papa Jesse could not contain his excitement, "That's gonna be real good for Cristal. She wants to learn to read and write. And just like Momma Louise said, with all of her natural curiosity for learning, my baby's direction in life can soon be crystal clear."

Nadine continued, "I talked with the principal, and she told me that an O&M specialist will be able to teach Cristal age-appropriate skills that will enable her to use a long cane independently to travel safely in the school and community."

Cristal could hardly believe her ears when Papa Jesse shared the details. "Really, papa?"

"Yes, Sweet Pea."

"You mean I will be able to go to school with other children…even those who can see?"

"Yes, baby." He grabbed a handkerchief from his back pocket and dabbed the tears from Cristal's eyes before drying his own.

Granny Lou also used a corner of her worn linen apron to dry her eyes as well. Pure adoration was written all over her face as she witnessed this portrayal of tenderness between her grandson and his daughter. Never would she be blessed with such an endearing likeness again.

Jesse kissed his daughter on the forehead and left her to check on Wilky. He understood his son's pain and wanted desperately to provide his much-loved flesh and blood with some level of comfort to try and ease the sting.

Outdoors on the porch, the dejected father stood tall beside a son engulfed in despair. Jesse got down on his knees in an attempt to reconstruct a stronger bond. For Wilky's sake, a more personal rationale for the shunned decision was warranted. "I know it will be hard at first, but you must go. I want a better future for you and your sister. You can't spend all your days swimming, playing football, and shooting marbles with Endy and Marjon."

Wilky said nothing. He refused to engage in a respectful exchange of eye contact that a father deserved at such a hollow moment.

Jesse began speaking with a slight stutter, "Don't you want to be an architect one day?" Wilky's face contorted with a questionable movement of his head. An intense silence followed, and the question was left unanswered. "Beyond mountains, there are always more mountains, son. But there is peace in the valleys and hope in the hills. Life is full of tough choices." Papa Jesse continued his appeal, "Have faith that I'm doing what is best for you, your sister, and your mother. Since you were put on this earth, I've wanted nothing more than to protect you from evil and dangerous things."

With a mouth drawn down and eyes welled with water, Wilky frowned. His self-absorbed level of immaturity won the inner battle that triggered the inevitable desire to leap clear off the porch. The boy's muscular, small-scaled soccer legs surged to top speed, kicking up a fury of dirt and gravel. Like a blaze of light before the onset of a violent thunderstorm, he bolted up the steep hill, continuing to run until he was out of his father's sight.

Cristal crawled into her mother's bed and snuggled beside her. Over and over, she sympathetically stroked Dahlia's long French braids and then spoke, "It's gonna be okay, Momma."

In a shallow declaration, her mother replied, "I know, baby. I know." Dahlia pulled her sweet and precious daughter close and placed her head on her chest. Cristal laid still in the warm embrace and eventually fell asleep listening to the soft beats of her mother's broken heart, yearning desperately to heal.

Chapter Eight:
Stingrays vs. Manatees

On Saturday morning, after Jesse finished burning the weekly trash in a bottomless outdoor pit, the family ate a hardy breakfast. Granny Lou decided to make Wilky's favorite pancakes and Haitian omelets called "ze fri ak banann bouyi." She prepared them with fresh eggs, minced garlic, onions, and cheddar cheese. When the last bit of food was relished, Dahlia told Wilky that because the big trip was only a week away, she and Granny Lou needed to take the van into town to buy several things for their journey ahead. Dahlia's excuse was partly valid, but she honestly did not want to be surrounded by a cheering and laughing crowd.

"I won't be able to make your game, Wilky. After I return from the store, I need to start packing us up. I'm sorry, baby, but be sure to take all that good juju with you." Dahlia spoke with only a hint of enthusiasm. Wilky said nothing.

"You don't get to ignore your mother; you heard what she said," His father reprimanded. Wilky raised his head and saw his father's piercing gaze.

"Yes, sir." He then turned to his mother, "I'm sorry, momma. It's okay if you can't make it." Jesse was relieved he didn't have to punish Wilky for being obstinate. As any empathetic parent would, Jesse needed to find a solution to cheer up his son.

"What do ya' say, eh? I'll take you, Cristal, and Endy, on my mobylette instead of riding the slow and crowded tap to the ballpark."

"Yes!" shouted Cristal, raising both fists and punching the air.

"Alright then," Wilky sullenly replied.

Cristal and Wilky had always been thrilled to ride on the back of their papa's mobylette. And Jesse loved to hear them squeal with glee like little chipmunks. But it had been long since they enjoyed that super cool fun. The children would hold firmly onto each other and their father as he dashed through paved and unpaved streets, bouncing high like a flying squirrel. Skillfully, Jesse would lean to the right and then to the extreme left. Like a magician or superhero, their father dodged and weaved around other risk-taking motorists. Usually, he never allowed more than two additional riders, but he wanted to make this last time memorable. Cristal was disappointed that Wilky showed no sign of excitement or appreciation. Her brother often played a stubborn and ornery game of silence whenever he didn't get his way. "You're being mean, Wilky," she told him later in their room.

Wilky's team, the Stingrays, had made it to the football finals by competing with other young players aged 8-10. The teams competing were from leagues in Haiti and the Dominican Republic. Although Wilky was a scrawny ten-year-old, he was one of their best players. He and Endy played the position of forwards, standing on the field in front of their teammates. Wilky was better with chip and bending shots. Endy had almost mastered the headshot. Marjon's ability to dribble and move the ball down the field with increased speed and control had dramatically improved. The Stingrays didn't even make it to the finals last year, so winning the tournament this time was a real possibility.

Like the end of a magic carpet ride, the mobylette floated and sailed safely with its passengers to their destination. Jesse turned off the ignition and let down the kickstand. Wilky and Endy vaulted off like Olympic gymnasts. "Good luck, boys! Show 'em what you got!" his father yelled.

Endy turned and waved in a merry voice, "Thanks, Mr. Duvernay. We're going for the big 'W'."

Wilky didn't bother. He sprinted fast and furiously towards Coach Reno, who was handing out fresh jerseys. Marjon and his family arrived a little earlier. The three friends and their teammates used every bit of time to participate in a few practice drills before the tournament began.

The crowd of spectators began pouring in for the long-awaited event. Since the quake, very few community events brought everyone together for fun and games. Cristal and her father hurried to the shortest line to buy two bags of boiled peanuts. Without Lila, Cristal held on even tighter to her father's hand as they navigated the wooden bleachers where men were blowing swirls of smoke from rolled cigarettes.

Small groups of wives and girlfriends set a short distance from the men, huddling close to engage in small talk peppered with hot gossip. Jesse found a spot where Cristal could sit next to some girls who used to be in Wilky's class.

"Oh, you look so pretty, and you smell nice," one of the girls complimented.

"Thanks!" Cristal responded enthusiastically, "It's one of my own perfumes." She offered the girls some of her salted peanuts, and without hesitation, they shoved their hands into the small bag and ripped it.

From two bleachers up, Papa Jesse watched and shook his head in displeasure. His little girl was too naïve to know about the 'give before you take' principle of power, but he hoped the compliments given to Cristal were genuinely from the heart. The bag's contents were devoured almost instantaneously before attendees stood to sing the national anthem of Haiti, 'La Dessalinieene.'

The announcer ended his speech with a redacted quote from Nelson Mandela. 'Sport has the power to change the world. It has the power to inspire. It has the power to unite people in a way that little else does. It speaks to youth in a language they understand. Sport can create hope where once there was only despair.' Athletes and spectators alike exploded with cheers and waved miniature flags of horizontal red and blue coloring.

The love and comradery from his old high school buddies Ricardo, James, and others bestowed the welcome relief Jesse needed from the ugly and physical demands of the week. A rolling ritual of complaining from other fathers launched. They spoke of their frustrations with the slow flow of money Haitian government officials were reluctant to release to rebuild Haiti.

"I read that over a billion dollars was donated from countries from all around the world. What happened to that money is what I want to know. Where is it?" asked Marjon's father.

"Yeah, our president claims that the money pledged was never received," another father barked. The men grunted and groaned, complaining and nodding in agreement.

"I don't know what to believe," said Jesse. "After Baby Doc got charged with embezzlement, corruption, and crimes of torture, you'd think there would be greater accountability from our public officials."

Endy's uncle shook his head angrily, "Haiti is the only country in the world where, for generations, descendants of enslaved people were forced to pay reparations to descendants of their masters."

"Such a blatant shame," Ricardo replied. The swap of griping and grumbling continued until a referee made a bad call, and the spectators' boos and hisses took over. Old friends sat reminiscing for relief from their troubles by laughing and teasing each other between fouls, scores, and penalties. They shared bonded memories - talking about the good old days when life, in hindsight, was simpler and more carefree.

The Stingray's opponent, the Manatees, dominated the first half of the match with prowess moves early on. When a key player for the Manatees was carried off the field due to a torn meniscus, the Stingrays only rallied for a remarkable comeback. Unfortunately, by the end of the first half, Endy received a yellow card from the referee for unsportsmanlike behavior. Cheers and boos from Stingray supporters came in waves. Wilky did his best to shield the ball from defenders. Coach Reno lost his cool during the second half. When Marjon fouled out, gloom and doom like a dark thunderous cloud engulfed the Stingray's spirits. "Keep your heads! Look where you're dribbling! Get the lead out of your behinds! Add the umph to try!" But it was all to no avail.

Honestly, the Manatees' offense was better adept than the Stingrays. They demonstrated remarkable skills at faking a pass and controlling the ball. And many of their players were quite dexterous at using both feet and both sides of their feet. Wilky was the most valuable player on his team, scoring two of the Stingrays' three field goals. At the end of the day, Cristal went home hoarse from yelling, and Wilky and his teammates went home with long, melancholy faces and second-place trophies.

After a late meal, Papa Jesse spoke, "You made me proud, son. Kudos to you and your teammates for making it as far as you did."

Sarcastically, Wilky quipped, "You were there, right? You know we lost."

"Wilky, you stop that right now!" shouted Dahlia. "Did you give it your best?"

"Yes, ma'am."

"Then that's what matters; we're both very proud of you."

Dahlia calmed down.

"Now, it's getting late, and tomorrow is a big day," her sniffles began again. "Everyone is rising early to get dressed. We are going to church. It will be the last time we all attend together, at least for a while." With a well of tears, she exchanged a loving glance. Simultaneously, from across the table, Dahlia and her husband reached for each other's hands.

Wilky and Cristal lay restlessly in their twin beds. Both were absorbed with feelings that weighed heavily on their minds. "I've never been to school before, Wilky. I don't know much of anything. Everyone will laugh at me. I don't even know how to make friends." Cristal lamented.

Wilky said nothing. He pretended to be asleep and even faked an expanded snore. Patiently, he waited for his sister to doze off. When she finally did, like a sly and mischievous fox, he climbed out of the window with something he grabbed from the crate of miscellaneous collectibles and ran away deep into the night.

Chapter Nine:
Buckle Up

One week later, the two little members of the Duvernay family were ready to take their first flight on an airplane. An announcement blared over Toussaint Louverture International Airport's loudspeaker: "Passengers at gate five traveling to Atlanta, Georgia, please prepare for boarding." Dahlia and her husband stared deeply into each other's eyes and spoke in whispers. Jesse glanced over at his children and watched tears flow down their faces. Their heightened sadness caused his heart to skip several beats. "Se La Pou'w Lai!" he shouted in a high-spirited tone. "Experience it!" he said again, repeating the motto of Haiti in English.

"Ai yai, yai," sighed Wilky as he clapped his hands on the side of his head. Everyone laughed, including a few bystanders. Like his granny insisted the night before, Wilky moved forward first and hugged his father. Cristal stepped up next and gave him his second sincere embrace. Papa Jesse planted a kiss on both of his children's foreheads, then positioned a plum-colored hibiscus behind Cristal's ear with a steady hand. The message her father spoke only to his daughter was never forgotten, "Your joyous spirit shines brightly, my princess. I want you to uphold and guard this natural gift like a precious stone."

"Okay, daddy. I will."

"And remember," her father's voice quavered whilst quoting an African proverb, "a diamond doesn't lose its value due to lack of admiration."

In line for the airstair, the three hopeful travelers turned and waved before ascending a small flight of stairs leading into the plane's cabin. The rumbling and roaring just before takeoff inspired a range of emotions for Dahlia, Cristal, and Wilky. Dahlia wasn't too fond of flying; this was her third trip by plane. She shut her eyes tightly and said a prayer. Her appeal to God ended after a request to dismiss any chance the plane would take a sudden nosedive. 'Please spare my children and me from a deadly fiery crash.' Involuntary cremation was not in her plans. The Boeing 737 Max rocketed down the runway at the speed of light and bounced twice before charging high into the sky. Jesse's children and his wife were oblivious that he stood waving goodbye with both arms stretched long after a giant cluster of billowing clouds swallowed the airplane.

Cristal tugged and tightened her seatbelt. She reached for her fan and began fanning for several minutes. Dahlia noticed the distress on her daughter's face and grabbed her hand to help calm both of their nervous energies. Cristal clenched Wilky's hand on her right with a firmer grip. "Tell me what you see!" she shrilled with edgy excitement.

He matched her exuberance with a face pressed against the window. Wilky announced, "Everybody looks like army ants!" A few seconds later, "I never knew the island was so long, narrow, and green. Wow, the sea is a swirly turquoise blue. It looks like one of my agate marbles!" Wilky writhed and wiggled, rapidly verbalizing multiple adjectives to describe the shrinking images below. Cristal got the gist of only chunks of his rambling. The plane reached cruising altitude within twenty minutes, and most passengers began to relax.

Inside her new beaded purse, a gift from Aunt Rachelle, Cristal pulled out three round and wrapped pieces of hard candy. Mrs. Rosie had given her a mixed bag of treats that included butterscotch, cinnamon, and peppermint sweets. Cristal offered one to her mother and one to Wilky. She sucked and chewed on a piece of candy herself and then removed and fingered the trumpet-shaped hibiscus her father slipped behind her ear.

"Hey, those are cirrus clouds and cirrocumulus clouds over there!" Wilky pointed out to no one in particular.

"My, my, my, you're a smart little boy," declared a male flight attendant passing out peanuts and sweet wafers from a rolling cart.

A big smile highlighted Wilky's face. Within fifteen minutes, he grew bored staring into the abyss and slowly drifted off to sleep with his head resting on his sister's shoulder. A precious clambroth marble in Wilky's right hand, gifted by his dear friend Endy, held steady. Dahlia glanced over at her sleeping children before reclining her chair and closing her eyes. Their dreams were whimsical and suspenseful all in one. She reflected on the days leading up to their departure from Haiti.

Like a loyal and dutiful pet, Cheerio efficiently guided Jesse and Dahlia to Wilky's hiding place early Sunday morning. He was sniffed out from an old abandoned shed high in the mountains. Reluctant to follow even though he was hungry, thirsty, and filthy, Wilky walked behind in his father's footsteps. Despite that distressing incident, on Sunday evening, Duvernay's home at sunset was full of sentiment and festivity. Hours after Cristal and Granny Lou returned from church, the pastor joined them at their home and said grace in the presence of family and friends who assembled to indulge in a culinary feast. It included a slow-roasted pig served with costly delicacies. Aunt Rachelle had organized a magnificent celebration with people from the community who were thrilled to participate in a warm and elaborate send-off for Dahlia, Cristal, and Wilky.

All were astounded when Mrs. Rosie stood to speak with a wave of one hand. Mikael, Aunt Rachelle's fiancé, immediately turned off the music when she gestured for him to do so. Mikael handed Mrs. Rosie the microphone. Those guests who danced the merengue stood to the side or took a seat when Aunt Rachelle shushed the small crowd of adults and children in attendance. "To Dahlia, change starts in your thinking. When you go through hardships, you must choose not to surrender; that is strength. I wish you great perseverance to master the power you have within to let your light shine again and be a beacon that enthuses others."

Mrs. Rosie pointed to Cristal with an index finger affected by firm nodules at the joint. "My dear little Cristal, unlike the evening primrose flower that only blooms in darkness, I want you to know that in my eyes, your sweet and charitable nature blossoms as lovely as the rising sun. Rarely will the paths you follow in life be a straight line, but may you continue to walk with grace and confidence no matter where your travels take you."

"And to Wilky," everyone angled closer, "Your ancestors were proud, brave, and intelligent warriors. As you venture out into an unknown world, never let others tell you where you belong or place limitations on you. You get to decide the heights you want to climb, and I believe you will reach the pinnacle of success. And if you don't, you will be hunted down and spanked with my jointed grey and scaly tail."

Laughter followed by a round of applause and nods of affirmation and appreciation. For a fleeting moment, that inside joke appeared in Aunt Rachelle's eyes to transform Wilky, Endy, and

Marjon into grotesque wax-like figures. The faint quacking sound similar to that of a mallard duck made Marjon panicky. He looked around for Endy, but he had ironically ducked under a table in fear. Just to be certain he wasn't stricken with a curse, he whispered to his mother and asked if he could have another slice of double fudge chocolate cake. "No, you've already had two." Marjon didn't mind that his request was denied; he was just happy to know his speech was discernable and his vocal cords worked properly. The night ended perfectly with family and friends bestowing their blessings and dispensing unique gifts to the departing Duvernay members.

Granny Lou called Wilky and Cristal out on the porch the day before their sentimental journey. Dahlia stood at the screen door as her grandmother-in-law gave a serious talk to her great-grandchildren. "I expect for you two to represent the Duvernay family name well. Keep your chin up and shoulders back, and carry yourselves like you are loved because you are. Be patient with your mother as she works to heal from her trauma. Reach out to connect with your father often. He's going to be very lonely without you. I realize that y'all may be too young to understand everything that's going on, but one day, I promise you, you will be grateful for his sacrifices." They squeezed in close and hugged her. Later, Granny Lou instructed her great granddaughter to leave Lila behind. Cristal couldn't imagine how she'd get along safely without her. '*Oh well, I guess I'll be able to find another strong branch somewhere in Georgia,*' she convinced herself. Dahlia witnessed Cristal bending down to deeply inhale Cheerios' gamey-smelling breath for the very last time. At that moment, Dahlia wished she'd had a camera to capture Cristal's smile.

A wind current causing slight turbulence redirected Dahlia's thoughts to the present day as she moved to get more comfortable in the narrow airplane seat. So proud she was of her husband, Jesse. He had taken care of everything all by himself. Jesse's close relationship with key employees at the United States Embassy in Port au Prince made it all possible for it to happen rather quickly. During a short window of time after the earthquake struck Haiti, the Brazilian, Chile, and U.S. governments offered humanitarian visas to certain Haitians displaced by the quake. Many migrated for economic reasons due to lack of jobs. The documents and exams required Jesse secured, including medical records needed before arriving in the U.S. The passports in Jesse and Dahlia's possession were obtained years before when Rachelle invited them to go on a cruise and meet her boyfriend, Mikael. He was a drummer in a popular band that traveled with the Princess Lee cruise line. Although he was Mikaela's father, Rachelle kept him a secret from the family for quite a while.

Despite suffering significant losses, Dahlia knew she was blessed to have a God-fearing husband like Jesse. His undying love, dedication, and commitment to her and the children were the catalysts for all positive things to come. Dahlia prayed that Jesse would be able to join them sooner than later if only he could persuade his grandmother to move to the United States. Dahlia was wise enough to know that if she insisted, her husband would not be happy if he folded to her pleas and made the journey with them. His love for his grandmother and his country was also paramount. Dahlia was determined to be optimistic. A bible verse echoed in her mind. '*There is a time for everything and a season for every activity under the heavens.*' She needed to believe it may be possible for her husband to visit them during the winter holidays.

Part II

Chapter Ten:
Georgia on Your Mind

Eight hours later, the landing gear unfolded with exact precision beneath the plane's wings. The tires touched down on the runway with a heavy bounce at the world's busiest airport, Atlanta Hartsfield Jackson International Airport. Dahlia held Wilky and Cristal's hands as they followed a stream of fellow passengers through the crowded terminal. Brimming backpacks filled with sentimental gifts jiggled with every quick step. Their mother paused only to read the sign 'Baggage.' The trio headed to the baggage claim area as the arrow directed. Between the three of them were six overstuffed pieces of checked luggage that rose from the baggage carousel to begin their first rotation before they all could be removed. A plethora of unidentifiable sounds and peculiar smells circulated throughout the enclosed atmosphere.

Cristal breathed deeply, "I can't believe we're in America!"

"Yeah, me either," Wilky brooded.

Although it had been at least seven years since Dahlia had seen her sister-in-law, Nadine, she recognized her immediately. Her pecan brown complexion matched her brother Jesse's. The similarity of their strong, dimpled chins was a feature that genetically linked them as sister and brother. Nadine and Isaac greeted the new arrivals with open arms, hugs, and kisses. Raeni stood several feet away, listening to them shout and jump about as they greeted each other. She initially frowned at the bright, vivid color combinations on Cristal. For Raeni, it was too much. But Raeni knew from a few humiliating experiences of her own that first impressions could be misleading. She told her dad that she would try hard not to pass judgment on her relatives and extend the warmest of welcomes.

As the steel-wheeled commuter train pulled away from the airport, it gained a speed of almost 70 miles per hour. Isaac explained to Wilky that his family often used the MARTA train as an easy way to get around many parts of the city. He liked to try to avoid sitting for hours in congested traffic. Isaac continued to share, "In 2009, Atlanta ranked eight out of the top ten cities with the worst vehicle queues in the U.S. It's a cultural hub attracting those who work in the music and movie industry."

As the train charged ahead, making several stops along the redline. Raeni looked at Cristal out of the corner of her eye. She had never met someone who couldn't see before and wondered how her cousin did everyday things. Raeni watched Cristal open her backpack and remove something from a small plastic bag. It was brown and shriveled. Raeni watched as Cristal broke off several small pieces and placed them in her mouth. Gesturing with the bag, Cristal turned towards Raeni, offering her some of the bag's contents, "You want some?"

"What is that?" asked Raeni.

Wilky turned around, "It's papita, a fried plantain mixed with salt."

"No, thanks," Raeni responded.

Cristal shrugged and snacked away. She enjoyed the comfort of the cool air circulating from within the train.

Raeni leaned forward and exchanged a quick glance with Nadine from across the aisle. She then sat back and began to ponder the depth of her new role as a big cousin to Cristal and Wilky. Raeni removed the headphones from around her neck and placed them snuggly over her ears. Immediately, she began swaying from side to side, singing along with one of her favorite artists. Cristal listened to the sound of her cousin's choppy singing and talkative passengers filing on and off at each rail station. A few moments passed before Cristal decided that she did like the sweet citrus scent of her cousin's perfume; she passed the smell test.

"How old are you?" Cristal asked. Raeni pulled her headphones off as if bothered.

"What?" she questioned with a peculiar high pitch.

With the increased volume, Cristal repeated herself, "How old are you?"

Raeni shrugged her shoulders and said nothing because she didn't understand what Cristal was asking. The rate at which Cristal spoke and her heavy accent made it difficult for Raeni to decipher. Wilky interrupted his conversation with Uncle Isaac and turned around again. He made certain to speak slowly and in perfect King's English, "She wants to know how old you are."

"Oh," said Raeni, "I'm fourteen."

Wilky translated, "She's fourteen."

Surprised and disappointed, she was that her father had gotten the age part wrong by three years. Cristal slumped in her seat. What was even more startling was that Raeni couldn't decipher and understand the weighty accent of Haitian Creole. After all, Cristal could hear her mother and Aunt Nadine speaking the native language of Haiti fluently. 'So *why doesn't Raeni speak the language?*' Cristal thought. She listened more intently to her mother's conversation with her aunt and recognized a peppering of English interjected in their rapid-firing conversation. She used context clues to fill in the meaning of certain words she simply didn't have as part of her repertoire at the time.

At the Brookhaven Park and Ride lot, Isaac loaded the luggage in his black seven-passenger 2011 special edition Range Rover. "Oh, I like this car," declared Dahlia.

"Wow, this is dope!" gushed Wilky.

"Thanks," Isaac replied cheerfully.

"I told him we didn't need all of this space, but he insisted we needed it to chauffer Raeni and her gaggle of friends around," grumbled Nadine. Isaac chuckled, and everyone piled in.

"Fasten your seatbelts," commanded Nadine looking back.

"My goodness, look at all these cars! How does anybody get to where they want to go and be on time?" Dahlia said, gawking at the bumper-to-bumper traffic.

"These roads are like tangled noodles going every which way!" shouted Wilky.

Rude or distracted drivers ignored Isaac's left turn signal as he tried to procure a slot in the middle lane of Interstate 285. Under his breath, he mumbled a few obscenities, then continued talking about how the highways were always under construction to expand and accommodate people moving to Atlanta. "People move here for better job opportunities and better pay. The city is full of young entrepreneurs. There are a lot of great colleges here, too."

"What's entrepreneurs mean?" asked Wilky.

"People who aren't interested in working for others choose to start their own businesses selling products or providing some type of desired commodity or needed service."

"Cool. Maybe I could do that." Wilky replied.

Cristal liked the new car smell from the leather upholstery and enjoyed the air blowing from the vent overhead. However, she was anxious to hear the sounds and smells of the city. She whispered something into Wilky's ear. "Uncle Isaac, can you let the window down?"

"Sure, just as soon as I reach the exit ramp ahead," he cheerfully responded. As they slowed to exit and merge onto city streets, Isaac spoke into a device on the dashboard. "Rear windows down." A massive gush of hot air rushed in to engulf the vehicle and stir the passengers.

"Alright, alright!" said Wilky with an echo from Cristal. Wilky stuck his head out the window, straining to peer up at an extraordinary skyline. Cristal reached in front of her brother and held her hand out of the window to feel the pressure of the wind blowing against it.

"Wilky, get your head back in this car! Cristal, keep your hands inside." Demanded their mother.

"The city boasts at least 39 skyscrapers at heights above 400 feet," informed Nadine. The Range Rover slowed, sped up, veered, and swerved in and out of traffic.

"Hey, that's my song!" yelled Isaac, bobbing his head in rhythm and jabbing the air with his right index finger. Isaac immediately pressed a button on his steering wheel to increase the volume from the premium Bose speakers. In amusement, Dahlia, Cristal, and

Wilky smiled as Isaac and Nadine belted out the lyrics to a country song - something about a fighting soldier in a civil war going bang. In unison, the duet sang all the words to the next country tune by Diamond Rio.

About three miles from their destination, the car stalled in traffic one car lengths away from a truck with maintenance men treating a paved road with tar and gravel. Cristal shuddered and rushed to cover her mouth and nose. She thought she might choke on the obnoxious-smelling toxic fumes. Louder than intended, she complained, "Air is different in the Caribbean." Raeni looked up from her phone and chuckled. Isaac rolled up the windows.

The Willow Woods gated community consisted of 22 spectacularly constructed exterior townhomes. The builder was a descendant of old money who was raised in the Upper East Side of New York. He designed the multi-level terrace housing development to emulate the historic 19th-century brownstones in the neighborhood where he grew up. The common area, exclusively for residents, was modern and sprawling. The playground, tennis court, and swimming pool completed the property. Tall Georgia pine trees lined the perimeter, and a well-maintained landscape with trimmed bushes and squares of flowery plants dotted the inside area.

"We don't have a beach nearby, but we do have a nice large swimming pool and a playground in the back," said Nadine.

"This is real nice, Nadine," expressed Dahlia.

Isaac hit a few buttons on an electronic display and eased his new and glistening motorized toy into the two-car garage next to his wife's green Toyota Camry. Between Isaac and Wilky, four trips were made from the car to get the luggage. The ladies gathered inside. Cristal held onto her mother's hand to follow close behind while Nadine gave them a brief tour of their new residence.

Raeni grabbed a juice box from the fridge and ran upstairs to beat Cristal to the bedroom. She flopped down on her bed with striped patterned comforters that matched the curtains. It was a girly room painted cotton candy pink with a tall five-foot shelf bookcase filled with books, trophies, and stuffed animals. A cello sat in the corner next to a computer desk. A 32" smart screen TV was mounted on the wall above two adjacent dressers. Raeni waited for the arrival of her new roommate and could hear them climbing the stairs. Nadine put her hands on Cristal's shoulders and gently walked her forward. "Sweetie, this is where you will sleep." She continued by guiding Cristal with a hand on her elbow. She physically prompted Cristal to touch the bed with her hand. "For you and Raeni, I bought matching sheets, covers, and throw pillows. Your bed is positioned in the corner to the left of the window, and you and Raeni each have your own dresser," she said with a smile.

Dahlia glanced around the expansive room, "I like this setup. There is so much space. This rug in the middle of the floor," Dahlia patted it with her foot, "will help Cristal establish her whereabouts. Thank you so much, Raeni, for letting my baby share your space. Cristal is a sweet girl, and I hope you won't feel like it's too much of an inconvenience."

Nadine quickly interjected, uncertain how Raeni might respond. "Raeni is used to having someone frequently share her bedroom. That's why we got rid of her queen-sized bed and bought her these full-sized beds. She has sleepovers often."

Raeni commented, "It's okay. I hope that Cristal likes it here."

Nadine continued, "Show your cousin where the bathroom is and then help unpack her things. Dinner will be served in about an hour."

"Yes, ma'am," said Raeni. Nadine and Dahlia turned and walked down the hall to a slightly smaller bedroom.

"This is where you'll sleep," Nadine gestured to Dahlia. Dahlia looked around at the freshly painted white walls with soft lilac-colored curtains hanging at the window. The white and delicate eyelet bedspread and pillowcases adorned the queen-sized bed. A beveled glass vase filled with fresh white lilies, yellow roses, and blue delphiniums was on the round bedside table next to a bowl of chocolate mints. A stack of wellness books about 'reclaiming your life after difficult times' was arranged on top of a vintage deep purple dresser.

Dahlia looked up at her reflection in a gilded mirror and witnessed the effects of her fluctuating emotions. "Awww…thank you so much," she communicated between sobs.

The best place for Dahlia to be at that time was inside an embrace. She and her sisters-in-law hugged for a long time. "I love my big brother; you are his wife, and I love you too. We are family, and that's what family does; we look out for each other," Nadine said with a few rolling tears of her own.

After a long pause, Nadine asked, "Do you think it's alright for Wilky to sleep out here on the sleeper sofa in this loft area?"

"Yes, yes, yes. He'd love to have more space for himself, especially where he can be right in front of that big TV screen. How big is that thing anyway?"

"It's a 64" screen. Isaac bought it last Christmas to watch the Superbowl once he discovered that the Pittsburgh Steelers were playing the Green Bay Packers. Chile, he loves him some Steelers."

Dahlia shook her head, "Girl, I don't know anything about that. Wilky likes football, but I think you all call his type of sport soccer."

"Yeah, you're right," Nadine nodded as she moved across the room. "I hope this is enough closet space for you and Wilky's things."

"That's plenty," Dahlia commented. A slight feeling of guilt washed over Dahlia. "Nadine, when Raeni is ready to invite one of her friends for a sleepover, Cristal can come and sleep with me."

"She'll be fine. We'll work it out. I'll leave you to get settled and relax a little before dinner."

Looking around the room from the edge of the bed, Dahlia felt grateful for such a cozy and impressively decorated space. But with the few comforts of home within reach, a wave of sadness crept inside her. Before Dahlia laid down to rest, she gripped her purse from the top shelf of the closet and withdrew two cherished items. Close to her nose, she held the white cotton handkerchief her husband had pulled from his pocket to wipe her tears as they said farewell at the airport. Dahlia deeply inhaled Jesse's resplendent masculine scent for a moment, then gently unfolded a letter he had written to her only weeks after they met. It was a benchmark in time when she was a young and innocent teenager. 'My Sweet Dahlia... with all my heart and mind, I promise you that whatever obstructions life puts in our path, as long as you are willing to clasp your hand tightly in mine, we will navigate around them and live our tomorrows with no regrets. I promise you.'

Chapter Eleven:
Shared Space

As soon as her stepmother left the room, Raeni exhaled a long, weary sigh before addressing Cristal. "Come on, let me show you the bathroom. Follow my voice, cross the hall, and turn left." Cristal reached a bathroom that smelled like linen and sky. "Here it is," said Raeni as she tapped on the door twice before wheeling quickly to return to her room. Wilky witnessed it all with a grimace but was satisfied and turned away after his sister entered the bathroom without incident.

"Ahhhh," Cristal sighed upon entering and respectfully closing the door behind her. Immediately, she began familiarizing herself with the expansive bathroom that seemed to echo even when she spoke softly. Marveling at the smooth touch of the hourglass bathtub with jacuzzi jets, Cristal soon discovered that you must enter the shower separately through a sliding door and then step up. She continued exploring by touching the knobs and the rainfall showerhead with a wand. "Wow, this is fancy. I'm gonna ask momma to show me how to take a shower," she spoke out loud.

Cristal lingered, exploring every inch of the bathroom. She twisted the caps off two body washes and deeply inhaled each before returning them to their nook. An extra fluffy bathmat rested on top of the baked earth tile. Kneeling, Cristal fanned her hand, moving it left and right, then systematically up and down across the non-slip glazed surface. She liked the texture of the terracotta floor. The adjacent room within the bathroom contained a V-shaped toilet seat with an attached remote. "I wonder what these buttons are for?" she questioned aloud but dared to push them. Later, she would discover with her mother's help that a bidet with a dual nozzle spray and warm hand dryer was a special feature of the commode.

Wooden, hand-carved oriental bookends supported several small inspirational books on a shelf above the tank. Above that hung a great rectangular framed picture that Cristal made a mental note to ask Wilky about. She took longer than usual to inhale the decorative soaps that sat like multiple scoops of ice cream in a ceramic bowl near the basin. To the left of the luxury oval-shaped mirror was a rack with neatly rolled plush terry towels. Cristal continued her exploratory escapades in the double cabinets beneath the sink. One by one, she lifted to smell a bevy of fragrances from at least eight items in plastic, aluminum, or glass containers with unique tops and lids of their own. The most pungent smells, she surmised, had to be for cleaning and not for bathing or shampooing your hair. Without warning, an intense knock greeted the door.

"Hurry up, Cristal. I gotta use it!" Wilky crowed. He wriggled and danced about, believing that he might not make it downstairs to the powder bathroom in time.

'*Not just yet,*' Cristal decided. She had to let her fingers and hands follow the contours of the faucet and handles. They were far different from the simple round ones in her bathroom at home that required one to twist and turn for the water to flow. These required her to flip the hot and cold levers up and down and shift to either side for graduated temperature changes.

"Hurry up!"

"Okay, I'm washing my hands. Here I come," she asserted.

"Girl, here she comes. Let me call you back," Raeni whispered to a friend before clicking off the phone. Haphazardly, she began unzipping Cristal's suitcases and pulling clothes and other personal items out to put them away. Cristal stood on the oval rug, listening to Raeni open and close drawers from the dresser near her bed. She quickly discerned her cousin's fitful actions. Raeni was grabbing Cristal's things and hastily shoving them inside drawers. Cristal took a few steps forward and reached out to touch her cousin. Very slowly, she did her best to pronounce her words clearly in English. "I can do it." Raeni turned around, taken aback by this tiny voice making an independent declaration. She backed up and sat on her bed. Raeni watched her little cousin, who could not see, move with self-reliance to complete certain tasks.

In a bottom drawer, Cristal put away four new neatly folded pairs of jeans she received as gifts. She put five pairs of shorts in the same drawer. Next, Cristal unfolded and refolded several random tops and placed them in the drawer above the other. Then she put two new pairs of pajamas and a robe next to her tops. The third drawer was where she stored her delicates.

"Hangers, do you have?" Cristal politely asked while gesturing and holding up a dress. She decided that she might be better understood if she slowed down when speaking and didn't let the words tumble out so quickly.

"Ummm, sure." Raeni grabbed some padded hangers from the closet and gave them to Cristal. "Over here is the closet," she said while tapping on the door with a hanger. One of Cristal's satin dresses slid off the bed and onto the floor. Raeni picked it up.

"I'll hang this red dress up for you, okay?" Cristal reached out to touch the fabric.

"A Sunday dress," she shared.

"It's pretty," Raeni commented.

"Merci beaucoup."

"Oooh... okay, little French girl," Raeni joked, and Cristal giggled.

After hanging up seven dresses, Cristal methodically emptied special items from her backpack and organized them nicely on top of her dresser. She placed the plastic bottle filled with Caribbean rainwater gifted by Mikaela first. Next to it, Cristal put a small hand-held abacus and two beautiful silk fans from her Aunt Rachelle on the dresser. She placed a velvet jewelry pouch containing a crystal charm necklace from Granny Lou inside her top drawer. Finally, Cristal clustered the six bottles containing her very own perfumes in a special arrangement. Raeni sat astonished, watching her cousin move so gracefully. She admired the meticulous way Cristal completed personal tasks and the actions she demonstrated so responsibly.

"What are those?" Raeni asked, pointing to the bottles. She immediately caught herself and felt foolish for pointing. "What's in those?" Cristal turned in Raeni's directions, unsure exactly what was being asked of her. Raeni traveled to the dresser and tapped a bottle on the dresser.

"What's this?" asked Raeni.

"My perfumes," replied Cristal.

"Perfumes?" Raeni questioned, wondering if she had heard Cristal correctly.

"Yes."

"Can I smell?" Raeni asked while proceeding to open small vessels one by one. She inhaled each carefully. "I like this one the best." She touched Cristal's hand with the bottle. "What's in it?" Raeni asked.

Cristal explained her process using a combination of English and Haitian Creole. She spoke about collecting various flowers and combining them with alcohol, Caribbean rainwater, and other modest ingredients. Raeni understood some of the information, and she didn't. "Uhhh...I think a few things are missing in these. Something else should be added."

"Eh?" said Cristal.

"Here, smell my favorite perfumes." The girls sat on the bed, and Raeni handed Cristal one expensive bottle at a time.

"This is Coco Mademoiselle."

"Ummm…ki jan bèl bagay!"

"You like?" asked Raeni after reading Cristal's facial expressions.

"Oui, oui," Cristal replied in excitement.

"This one here is Light Blue by Dolce and Gabbana."

"Ahhhh…smell of lemons."

"And this is my favorite one of all. My mom sent it to me for my fourteenth birthday."

"Mom? Nadine?" Cristal questioned.

"No. My mother lives in Europe. Nadine is my stepmother. I call her 'MaDine,' short for Momma Nadine. I'm her bonus daughter."

"Oh," Cristal didn't quite understand, but she planned to ask her mother to explain it further. She removed the top from the third round 3-dimensional bottle. "I like. What is it?"

"Yes, it's really nice, right? I love it. It's *First* by Van Cleef & Arpels. I only wear this perfume on special occasions because it's really expensive," Raeni boasted. Cristal caught the word 'expensive' and remembered Granny Lou's comment about someone smelling good. "You feel rich, eh?" Cristal asked. She thought about her conversation with Granny Lou that one night in the kitchen.

Raeni chuckled, "I guess so. I'm gonna look on the computer and see if I can find out what they put in colognes and perfumes. Maybe you can start adding some of the same stuff to yours!" Raeni hopped up and walked to her desktop computer to Google, '*What are most perfumes made of?*' The rapid clicking and clacking of the computer keys got Cristal excited and perplexed at the same time. She got a positive vibe from Raeni's voice inflections and energy. Cristal waited eagerly while choosing to sit on her own new bed. In the corner against the wall, she found a stuffed teddy bear propped on top of a velvet throw pillow. She searched for the furry creature's eyes, nose, and mouth and then began tugging and looping the ears of her new bedtime companion. A dash of sadness clouded her thoughts. She missed her Cheerio.

Raeni continued her search. "Okay, it says here that most perfumes have the following ingredients: essential oils used for scenting, acetone, linalool, camphor, formaldehyde, and methylene chloride," she reported.

Cristal sat quietly for a few seconds. She didn't understand most of the items that Raeni said. "Ok," she responded. Raeni watched as a strange expression etched across Cristal's face. There was an awkward pause.

"Get Wilky, please," Cristal told Raeni. Raeni summoned Wilky as requested.

"What y'all want?" Wilky asked with a stitch of irritation in his voice. An all-day marathon of the Three Stooges was playing on cable TV, and Wilky didn't want to miss one of their hysterically funny antics.

In Haitian Creole, Cristal asked Wilky to have Raeni repeat what she said about making perfumes. Raeni understood a tad of their exchange and shared her computer screen with Wilky. He moved in close to read the information. Wilky pronounced the words as best he could but didn't know precisely how to interpret the ingredients in another language. But he had no problem deciphering Raeni's last comment.

"Raeni said you could buy some of the oils at a store nearby. She will ask her dad to see if he can find her old chemistry set stored somewhere amongst all their access furniture and junk stored upstairs on the third floor. She thinks it has some of the stuff you could use to improve your perfumes."

"Ohhh, nice, okay, nice," replied Cristal, "thank you." Raeni smiled; she liked her new younger cousin. She liked her humble and pleasant demeanor. Wilky did a 360-degree turn around the cotton-candy-painted room and was fascinated by the different possessions that filled every inch of it.

With gawking eyes, he asked, "Why did you get all these trophies?" Eleven awards varying in size crammed the shelves between books and antique dolls.

Before Raeni could answer, Nadine called up from the bottom of the stairs, "Time to eat, guys, come on down."

"I'll tell you later," said Raeni. "I'm hungry. Let's go eat!"

"Me too," chimed Wilky. The three stood at the bathroom door, taking turns to wash their hands.

Raeni walked backward in front of Cristal, "follow my voice," she commanded. Cristal reached her hand out to the right to locate the wall, then brushed against it with her forearm and elbow for a line of direction.

"You're almost at the stairs," Raeni informed, "they have carpet on them, so you're not going to slip or slide easily," Cristal understood, and Wilky appreciated how his cousin was looking out for his sister. He realized he didn't need to worry about Cristal falling on the descension, so Wilky barreled down the stairs and hurried to the kitchen table. Cristal touched the wall with her hand and cautiously moved her right foot forward to locate the top step. Raeni gently brought her hand forward to position it on the railing. Cristal detected the depth of the first riser by sliding her heel up and down it and then began her descent to the first floor. She wasn't used to navigating such a long, uninterrupted flight of stairs, but she managed it well. The sounds of laughter, affirmative chatter, and clamoring dishes in the kitchen were just the auditory information she needed to continue confidently the rest of the way.

Chapter Twelve:
Table Talk

After saying grace, Wilky scrutinized all the food on his plate. "What is this?" He continued poking his fork into a lumpy mound of something yellow and red piled high on his plate.

"It's my award-winning lasagna," Nadine said proudly.

"Oh…well, what are these?" he asked after sliding his fork into a clumpy mixture of green and slimy-looking vegetables.

"Wilky, stop it and eat your food," Dahlia demanded with a look of embarrassment.

From across the table, Raeni watched Cristal's every meticulous move. Cristal carefully unfolded the paper napkin and placed it on her lap. She located her utensils to the left and right of her plate. She was able to identify the different foods named by lightly probing them with a knife. Using the fork as a cutter, Cristal took a small bite of lasagna. She then used her knife as a pusher to help load the vegetables onto her fork. A twist of the lips accompanied a slight frown when Cristal tasted the mashed potatoes. She thought they were way too bland. "Excuse me, eske ou pase m 'sel la ta tanpri?" Dahlia passed the saltshaker by letting it touch Cristal's left hand. Raeni, Isaac, and Nadine stopped chewing and tilted forward for better optics. Cristal tenderly shook sprinkles of salt into the palm of her cupped right hand and then flicked the tiny granules onto the potatoes with her thumb.

The sounds of munching and chewing and lively kitchen table conversations resumed. But Raeni continued to study Cristal as she curled her fingers on one hand and slid them forward along the table to locate her drink. Raeni was impressed that she did not knock it over. Dahlia was the one who had set the table, and just like the hour hand on an analog clock, she placed Cristal's drink at the one o'clock position like always. Isaac noticed the mutual look of surprise on Raeni's face. They both were impressed with Cristal's dainty and precise table manners.

"Time to eat! Pass the peas, please! Get your popcorn and peanuts; it's time to eat!" Those short, quirky phrases came from a place beyond the kitchen. Dahlia, Cristal, and Wilky were startled. All three turned in the direction of the weird, squawky voice.

An uncharacteristic look of surprise appeared on Dahlia's face. "Who is that?" she asked.

"Oh, that's my parrot, Sudoku," answered Raeni.

"Your parrot?" Wilky asked with an elevated voice.

"Yeah, my African Grey parrot. He's in the screened-in sunroom."

Cristal shouted, "Kisa li ye? Kisa li ye?"

"It's a talking bird," Wilky translated. He jumped up from the table to go and see for himself.

"Careful, Wilky," Dahlia warned after he almost toppled everyone's water glasses. Behind the heavy gold drapes were glass and a screened sliding door slightly ajar. Sure enough, a beautiful silverish-grey bird with scalloped pattern plumage, orange eyes, and a bright red tail sat flapping its wings. Wilky stood in awe, watching it fly and glide from perch to perch. Sudoku's decorated home was a 61-inch wrought-iron cage.

Nadine felt compelled to explain, "Sudoku can probably say about 200 words. He can't add or anything like that, although he can count to ten. Raeni just likes the popular puzzle game and its name. She got him three years ago for her birthday."

"My goodness," said Dahlia. "Ain't that something? You all have a live talking bird living in the house."

Isaac and Nadine laughed. "We thought it would be good fun for Raeni," said Isaac. "You know, ornithologists say that some species of birds are brilliant and are known to soothe their handler through emotional episodes."

Dahlia added, "Kind of like a dog, cat, or any other support animal, huh?"

"Yes, exactly," Isaac replied. "She used to spend a great deal of time playing with Sudoku, training it to learn more words. But, she's seemingly lost interest and neglects the poor thing now."

"Awww... Daddy," Raeni twittered, "he's too high maintenance, and I got a lot of other stuff to do."

It had been an incredibly long and tiring day for everyone, and dining together for the first time was a great way to wind down. In a circular motion, Isaac rubbed his pooched belly and expressed a garish yawn. As typical, after a big meal, he retired to the bedroom to watch the evening news. Dahlia helped Cristal start her bubble bath and returned to the kitchen to help Nadine with the dishes. After Wilky bathed, he and Cristal sat on the porch wearing their newly gifted pajamas and slippers to play with Sudoku. They watched the bird master swooping dives using his strong muscles and fluttering wings to fly from a swing to a ladder. He had lots of toys to discourage boredom and alleviate stress. When he looked in the mirror and whistled before saying, "Pretty bird," the siblings laughed hard. They persistently tried for over an hour to get Sudoku to talk in English first and then Haitian Creole, but the mulish bird said nothing.

After washing dishes and tidying up the kitchen, Dahlia stepped out onto the porch to be with her children. "It's late, time for bed," she told them. They chatted a little longer, recalling special memories of their own pet, Cheerio, who was sadly left behind. Wilky wondered and asked his mom if he'd ever see his pup again. "I don't know, baby, but let's be glad he's there as good company for your dad." Wilky and Cristal nodded their heads in agreement.

"Oh, my," uttered Cristal when she stepped away from the sunroom and back through the sliding door. She had tried safely navigating around an artificial palm tree with hanging branches. She wanted to avoid having the huge leaves brush against her face. Cristal ambled towards the center of the room and contacted the glass coffee table. Cristal thought she was following a clear and direct path to the stairs. "Tomorrow, I'll ask momma to guide me through the house at least twice so I can learn the layout real soon." Cristal wanted to know where all the glass furnishings and delicate figurines were located. It would be awful, she thought, to break valuable items in her aunt and uncle's home.

Nadine and Dahlia sat at the table, drinking a cup of evening tea and eating what remained of the sweet potato cake that Granny Lou made. With everyone else in bed, they felt relaxed talking openly. Dahlia was curious. "Isaac seems like a really nice guy. He appears to be a happy and very content man. How did the two of you meet?"

"It's funny that you say that. His older brother Barry told me that their mother gave him the name 'Isaac, the one who laughs' or 'the one who rejoices' because he practically came out of her womb laughing."

Dahlia cackled loudly – a departure from her usual feminine laugh. "Now that is funny. Actually, it's hilarious!"

Nadine sustained, "Girl, we met one night at a salsa event at the Fern Bank Museum. Isaac and his brothers Barry and Ricky, 'The Granger Boys,' stepped in wearing cowboy hats, tight blue jeans with big silver belt buckles, and cowboy boots. All three are over six feet tall, so they stood out in the crowd, garnering a lot of attention. When the disc jockey played Bachata music, Isaac asked if I wanted to dance. Neither of us knew what we were doing, but we had a ball trying." Nadine continued recalling the romantic details, "We talked all night. I was attracted to his quick wit and unrestrained laughter. Isaac was most definitely a perfect gentleman. He walked my girlfriend and me to our car, and that's when he and I decided to exchange numbers. The rest is history."

"Cowboy hats and boots? He's a country boy!" Dahlia exclaimed. "That's why he likes country music so much, huh?"

Nadine nodded, "Yes, indeed."

"I was wondering what that was all about," Dahlia admitted.

"I got me a good old country boy. We even go line dancing on the first Saturday of every month. You should come and join us sometime."

"I don't know about that, but thanks for the invite. How old was Raeni when you met him?" she snooped.

"Raeni was seven at the time. Isaac and her mother had been divorced for three years when I came into the picture." Nadine felt comfortable talking and bonding with Dahlia. They were only two years apart; Dahlia was the older of the two. Nadine was confident that her brother, Jesse, had shared some of her personal stories but didn't mind repeating them or filling in the details. Although both ladies learned English as young girls in their private school upbringing, it had been quite a while since Nadine had a lengthy conversation in the language of their shared birthplace, and she relished it.

"It was a bitter divorce and a nasty custody battle. Farrah got a big job promotion at an international bank and expected the family to move to Belgium. Isaac had no interest in relocating and leaving Georgia or the US, for that matter. Neither would budge from their stance, so the divorce proceedings ensued. Isaac's parents helped him pay for an experienced family law attorney from a prestigious firm. After that mighty aggressive team of lawyers dug up nasty and inappropriate comments Farrah posted online, including some objectionable pictures from her college days, it was enough for the judge to consider both sides seriously. The judge didn't think it was in Raeni's best interest to remove her from the love and nurturing upbringing bestowed upon her by her father and both sets of grandparents. As a result, full custody was awarded to Isaac. Should Farrah decide to return to the States, Isaac is more than willing to acknowledge her visitation rights."

"How much do you think, if any, cultural differences contributed to the problems they faced and the decision they made to file for a divorce?" Dahlia probed.

"I'm really not sure, who knows," answered Nadine. "Isaac would probably never admit it. But I believe that some of it did have something to do with their mixed marriage and the pressures and demands he and Farrah experienced from their superiors on the job.

Each of them had their sights on reaching and climbing for higher rungs on the corporate ladder."

Dahlia nodded. "Well, does Farrah call or have any contact with Raeni?"

"Isaac said that she called frequently for the first couple of years. Farrah's been to the States only twice since she moved to Belgium. Raeni hasn't seen her in three years. Understandably so. My bonus daughter is a little salty behind it all. Farrah has since remarried and started a whole other family, and Raeni has a half-brother, Colton, whom she's never met."

"That's got to be hard for her, knowing that her mother is on the other side of the world and not knowing when she'll ever see her again.'

"I believe she feels abandoned by her mother, although it's never been expressed in those terms. As a precaution, Isaac ensures she gets a monthly wellness counseling visit. He doesn't want to miss any signs that she might plummet into a state of depression. She's experienced a level of unhappiness that no child should deal with. At her previous school, Raeni had to deal with that whole 'mean girls phenomenon'," Nadine shared while making air quotes with her fingers.

"What do you mean by that, teasing and name-calling?" Dahlia asked.

"Yes, Raeni struggled with handling taunts and teasing for being a bi-racial child. Once she entered sixth grade, Isaac enrolled her in a fine private school with diversity, equity, and inclusion at the center of their mission. Students who attend the school come from seventeen different zip codes in Georgia. It's a little pricey, but the grandparents on her mother's side asked to share in paying for her tuition."

Dahlia reflected on the benefits she received from attending a private college-preparatory school in Haiti. She and her sister, Mariah, were blessed to have such a privileged upbringing, but neither pursued education beyond high school. "Well, that is a real blessing for her, but how sad it is that she doesn't have a stronger bond with her mother. Does she FaceOff or FaceTime, or whatever the kids call it, to better connect with her mother and little brother?"

Superfluous laughter followed. "It's called FaceTime, and it's kind of funny that you mentioned that. Her therapist made an astute observation, noting that it appears whenever Raeni does FaceTime with her mother, she seems to experience a negative emotional spiral. Isaac and I aren't sure why it creates such strong melancholy feelings. We were thinking it would have the opposite effect. He had a difficult talk with Raeni and let her know that he doesn't recommend or want to encourage that kind of interaction with her mother anymore, especially if she feels worse after the connection."

"Ummph, Ummph, Ummph," Dahlia expressed as she shook her head in empathy.

Nadine continued, "We've only been married for three years, and Raeni and I have finally begun to develop a close bond. I refer to her now as my 'bonus daughter'. I have to admit, it was tough initially because she was so used to having her father all to herself. As you can probably tell by the décor in her room and the contents of her closet, Isaac spoils Raeni rotten. He feels a little guilty about how things turned out, and I think he tends to overcompensate. He plans to buy her a pony for her birthday in November," Nadine stated with eyes rolling in objection.

"A pony? Why a pony, and where in the world is she gonna keep one?" Dahlia questioned.

"We had a destination wedding on Mackinac Island in Lake Huron. Our honeymoon was actually a big family affair," Nadine shared with a roll of her eyes.

"Most of Isaac's family from Georgia were present. Remember I sent Jesse an invitation to share with you and Rachelle?" Dahlia felt a little embarrassed that neither she nor Jesse made an effort to attend, but at least they did send a lavish gift in their absence. "Yes, I remember getting an invitation; I just forgot about the location - exactly where the event was held."

"That's okay. I wasn't expecting you all to make it, honestly. Girl, his mother sprung for us all to stay at the famous award-winning Grand Hotel."

"Wow! I've heard of that place. And isn't that the resort where the movie *Somewhere in Time* was filmed?" Dahlia asked.

"Yes, it is." Dahlia didn't mean to be impertinent but had to ask, "So tell me, Nady, what does your honeymoon have to do with Raeni getting a pony for her birthday?"

"Oh no, not at all. I did get a bit sidetracked," Nadine giggled. "Isaac chose the resort location because he wanted to ensure that our wedding was an amazing experience for Raeni as well. Her first horseback ride occurred there, and that's when she fell in love with horses. We practically toured the entire 8.2-mile long island by chauffer drawn carriages or bicycles."

"That's right, there are no motorized vehicles allowed on thisland, right? Do you have some pictures I can look at?"

"Yes, of course." Nadine walked to a corner table in the living room and grabbed an 8 x 10 wedding photo in a silver brushed metal picture frame. She then collected a silver engraved photo album from the bottom drawer of the coffee table. Dahlia slowly flipped through it with an immense interest in the details.

"Your dress is simply gorgeous, and I love that pearl and crystal hairpiece!"

"Thank you. I saw a similar gown in a magazine and knew I wanted to see more styles from the designer. So, I decided on a road trip to New Orleans with two of my girlfriends. We visited the designer's bridal boutique for a private showing, and that's where I found exactly what I wanted."

"Girl, that's the way to do it! For such a special day, you deserve everything that your heart desires. Look at Isaac's smile. The photographer captured the expressions of one of the happiest men on the planet." Nadine chuckled.

Several pictures had been taken of the happy couple standing in a beautiful garden or riding in the back seat of an authentic horse-drawn carriage. Raeni was seated in the front, holding onto a spray of fluffy multi-petaled white and pink roses. Isaac's brothers and a friend, his groomsmen, were decked out in slim-fit three-piece paisley tuxedos. A snapshot was also taken of Nadine and Isaac riding a tandem touring bike. Before the lovebirds rode off to enjoy the island referred to as a National Historic Landmark, Isaac's sister-in-law, Phyllis, decorated the back of the bike with pink and white streamers that read, 'Just Married.' In jest, she also attached a sizeable hand-printed sign in bold black markers, 'and Already in Cycle Therapy'. Dahlia smiled. She started reminiscing about her and Jesse's small and simple wedding. It was a joyous, celebratory day for sure, but one occupied with a tinge of disappointment.

Moments of sentimental reflections from her past ensued as Dahlia turned page after page of the lovely couple's album. "I remember my first horseback ride. It was an amazing equestrian experience in the countryside of Santorini, Greece," Dahlia announced.

"What you say! I didn't know you had traveled internationally," declared Nadine.

"Yeah, I did. But that's a long ago bittersweet memory now." Dahlia sullenly confessed, accompanied by a depressed chin drop in a deliberate attempt to avoid eye contact. The sensitive and caring sister-in-law decided not to press since Dahlia didn't go into any detail. Especially after seeing that cheerless look on a face that should have been excited to share in what most would consider a magical once-in-a-lifetime experience.

"Isaac's family has some land a few counties over from here," Nadine stated. "He'll keep Raeni's pony there. His oldest brother Barry and his wife Phyllis breed greyhounds. They recently started leasing part of their land to horse owners and trainers needing stables to board their horses. Each spring, Barry and Phyllis participate in the Bill Pickett Invitational Rodeo when it comes to town. They both like to ride. You and the kids will enjoy it, too. Y'all should plan to come."

"Well, I'm up for new experiences. I'm already out of my comfort zone, plus, I'm sure Cristal and Wilky would enjoy all the competing sights, sounds, and smells."

"Good. Now, don't say anything to Raeni because she doesn't know she's getting a pony yet."

"Oh, I won't. That secret is safe with me."

"One reason he's buying such a grand gift is that Isaac hopes it will keep his only child close to home when she graduates from high school. He'd like Raeni to attend college locally so he can be close by if she should ever find herself in a toxic situation or if she needs him in the event of a serious emergency."

"Well," Dahlia commented, "she seems to be a sweet and pleasant girl. Doesn't her name stand for *Queen*?" Dahlia asked.

"Chile, yes. She really is sweet and remarkably gifted," replied Nadine. "Raeni is the second chair to the principal cellist in the orchestra at her school." Raeni's bonus mother bragged a little more about her bonus daughter's accomplishments. "Last summer, she and one of her best friends, Marsha, signed up for a teen writer's camp, and Raeni entered a contest and won the first place prize of $300.00."

"My lord! That's a lot of money for a young lady her age," replied Dahlia while taking another bite of the moist cake. "What in the world did she write about?"

Nadine explained further that *Rock, Paper, Scissors* was the title of her short story. "It's about a widowed father having to decide late in life which daughter he wants to live with instead of being put into a nursing home. His freedom to move about is severely limited to the length of his oxygen tube, and there are many other factors the family must consider. Despite their professional successes and unbeknownst to their father, each daughter has peculiar and eccentric habits. Rock, the oldest one, is a minister. Paper, the second daughter, is a corporate lawyer. And Scissors, the baby of the family, is a political science teacher and activist. The father spends three consecutive months with each daughter before making the ultimate decision as to where he will live." Nadine took the last sip of tea and continued. "The camp's purpose was to teach the participants how to actively research a topic instead of just Googling for background information. It was essential for the participants to conduct interviews or even get help setting up focus groups with people in the community." It was Raeni's support from Nadine that proved priceless. "I must admit," Nadine boasted, "with my networking skills, I helped her make some exceptional connections for her research."

Dahlia was intrigued. "So, who did the father wind up living with and why?"

"I'm going to let her tell you. Or better yet, she'll probably appreciate it if you take the time and read her story."

"Well, it will give me something else to think about instead of wallowing in all this grief. I can't seem to move past the point of pain. Sometimes, it feels like I'm holding on to life by a fine thread, a real frayed one. The Lord knows I need to pull it together to be a better parent to Wilky and Cristal. They are good children who don't shirk their responsibilities. They even brush their teeth twice a day without being told. My love for them and their father is the only thing that keeps me holding on," Dahlia confessed.

Nadine watched as a curtain of sadness veiled her sister-in-law's face. She couldn't fathom the nature of the pain that comes from losing a father, mother, and sister in succession. "Dahlia, you've been through so much. No one would fault you for taking all the time you need to recover. You may even want to consider talking to a counselor." Nadine carefully avoided potential missteps in demonstrating sympathy and support for Dahlia. While some people are uncomfortable witnessing another person's pain up close,

Nadine was not one of these individuals. She knew grief was not contagious and genuinely wanted to help.

"I'm just glad Jesse reached out to Isaac and me to ask if it was okay for you and the kids to come. I told Isaac I'd do anything for my brother because if it weren't for Jesse, he and I would never have met. Of course, he laughed at my persuasive tactic but didn't hesitate to grant my request. Honestly, Jesse is the reason Granny Lou and Grandfather William let me come to the United States to attend the University of Georgia. UGA is in the top 10% of the country for journalism. Although I received a full-ride scholarship from the Worldwide Village organization, my grandparents were adamant about me not leaving Haiti. They were afraid I would be too far from home alone. But thanks to Rachelle and Jesse - especially Jesse for making it happen. He advocated strongly on my behalf for weeks. And here I am with a Master of Arts in journalism and an editor for the Atlanta Journal-Constitution newspaper."

Dahlia enjoyed talking to Nadine. She felt uplifted, even if just for a moment. "Yes, Jesse is a real good man. I know I'm blessed. And, of course, the whole family is very proud of you. Your academic achievements are to be commended." Nadine blushed.

"Isaac has experienced loss as well," Nadine divulged. "His mother lost her fight with cancer three years ago, and he's still grieving for her. Isaac was a momma's boy, for sure. But I will say that he and his brothers are quite fortunate. Mr. and Mrs. Granger left their sons 178 acres of land. That land has been in their family since Reconstruction. At one time, it was used primarily for farming. They grew a variety of crops, such as tobacco, oats, and rice. His grandparents also had numerous livestock, including chickens, cows, pigs, and ducks. The brothers recently sold a third of it and got a pretty penny. Barry and his family live on the grounds of the same house where they all grew up. They've renovated it and added a few rooms to it, though. Now Isaac and Ricky are talking to builders. They plan to build homes on their own parcel of land."

Dahlia was a bit shocked and, at the same time, concerned. "So, you all will be moving into a new house by this time next year, huh?"

Nadine was candid, "Yes, but don't worry. Isaac and I paid off this townhome. You and the children can stay here as long as you want. "But," Nadine added, "I'm going to apologize in advance, sis. Sorry, I'm taking most of the furniture with me," she teased.

"Girl furniture is the last thing on my mind right now," Dahlia said with a chuckle.

Nadine revealed more, "I know Jesse told Isaac that he plans to send money once a month on behalf of you and the kids. It will all work out," Nadine assured her.

Dahlia began to cry. "God is good." She shook her head and covered her face with both palms in relief. "Granny Lou," Dahlia admitted, "gave me a little of her savings she'd set aside for emergencies. The totality of her gift and some money from our own savings adds up to a little over six thousand dollars. The kids and I are off to a good start. But I know I will need to get a job, some type of a job. I just don't know what kind or where."

Nadine reached out and patted Dahlia's hand, reassuring her sister-in-law. "Take your time and get settled in. Everything will work out. I'm claiming it."

Chapter Thirteen:
Sweet Dreams

"Good night," Raeni whispered.

Cristal lay thinking about how her life had changed so quickly from one day to the next. It had been some time since she had gone to bed with optimistic thoughts for her future. Snuggling up with her plush new bedtime companion, she whispered, "Good night, Raeni."

The day was long and arduous for the Duvernays and the Grangers. The only person still awake after midnight was Cristal. She simply could not go to sleep and thought about tiptoeing downstairs to the kitchen to sneak inside her aunt's kitchen cabinet to check out the spices. She concluded that the risk of waking someone and getting them upset wasn't worth it. Because of the central air that quietly cooled the entire home, she couldn't even listen out the window for city sounds or those of coyotes or barred owls. Cristal was anxious and overly thrilled about the opportunity to attend school. Indeed, that was the very reason she couldn't fall asleep that night. A reference to her as a student had been her deepest longing desire. Cristal could hardly believe it was going to happen.

After much tossing and turning, her mind drifted to a vividly painful memory. She recalled that one sunny afternoon, while rocking on the porch in her grandmother's favored chair, a heated argument ensued between Wilky and Marjon. The two quarreled with rising voices about where to place a draw bridge for the medieval castle they were trying to erect with Lego pieces.

"I told you that it doesn't make sense to put it right here," argued Marjon. He began jerking the plastic interlocking bricks apart.

"Hey, leave that alone!" Wilky yelled at his friend, then snatched and knocked pieces out of his hand. "If you're gonna try and keep your enemies out, then it needs to extend beyond the dry moat, dumbo."

"Dumbo?" Marjon shouted. "How can you call me a dummy when you didn't even know what a murder hole was?" The boys volleyed insults back and forth and continued their clash of ideas for a while. Each young up-and-coming architect disputed the other's position while building and rebuilding their intricate masterpiece.

Cristal enjoyed the banter, but she hoped Wilky and his long-time friend's dispute wouldn't lead to a fistfight. Suddenly, argumentative voices from inside the house grew louder. Cristal overhead her mother's shouts, "I will not be looking for a job. I'm gonna stay here and bake my cakes!"

Papa Jesse commented, "The products you're using to make these specialty cakes are too expensive. And you're practically giving them away. The profits from selling them don't add up. You do the math. We can't make soup out of water, Dahlia."

"I know, I know. I just can't."

"There's very little work coming in from any direction right now. I don't want to dip into our savings if we don't have to, Dahlia. It just wouldn't be smart if we had other options. You know I never wanted or expected you to go to work." After a sustained period of silence, Jesse's voice softened. "I see you're in a lot of pain. Believe me, I do. But our recent medical expenses…"

"Then sell Fo and Fum," Dahlia interrupted.

"Are you for real? We get a steady income from our goats' milk and their fibers every three months," Jesse exclaimed. The fallout from the earthquake put just about everyone on the island in poor financial straits, even those who used to living comfortably on a decent income.

Dahlia shared with her husband something oddly offensive, "Zoe was here the other day, and she suggested that maybe Cristal could earn a little money at the port when the cruise ships come in. She could probably get a good sum of change."

In sheer dismay, Papa Jesse and Granny Lou shouted emphatically, "No!"

"Absolutely not," Cristal's father held firm, "There will be no beggars in this family." Granny Lou was so upset she wanted to swear. She looked at Dahlia and wagged a crooked finger, "You must have lost your dadgum mind! Just because somebody throws you something doesn't mean you have to catch it. You need help!"

"I didn't say that's what she should do. I'm just telling you what Zoe said!"

"Lord, you know we got enough on our plate now. Please protect this house from negative outside energy and forces," prayed the family matriarch. Because of Zoe's flagrant disregard for Cristal's well-being, Granny Lou's 'Mal De Ojo' or 'evil eye' never made her feel nearly as welcomed as before.

Marjon and Wilky were so uncomfortable with what they heard that the dueling boys recklessly abandoned the partially assembled castle and left the porch in a hastiness to kick around a soccer ball. Cristal was sick to her stomach. She reached for the folding fan around her neck and began flicking and fanning exceedingly. Disheartened, Cristal needed to move about and release nervous energy. So, she grabbed Lila and started doing laps around the yard. Cheerio was close on her heels. She could never imagine asking someone she didn't know for money in a million years. As her middle name may have implied, Cristal Shyana was a very shy girl but one with a lot of pride.

Cristal was afraid to talk to strangers and had several other social concerns. Her only real friend was her younger cousin, Mikaela. Not only was she fearful of people she didn't know, but Cristal was scared to try something new and fail at it. More than anything, she was bothered and agitated at the thought that her little brother would one day surpass her in knowledge. The Haiti Deaf Academy was for children who could not hear. The St. Raphael Center was a healthcare center that provided recreational activities for those who were deaf, blind, and physically challenged. However, they had limited resources to teach a curriculum for birth to high-school-aged children in braille reading and writing, technology, and travel skills.

Once upon a time, when feeling despondent, she confessed something heartfelt to Mikaela. "Wilky's going to grow up to learn so much more than I ever could."

Mikaela squeezed her cousin's hand and shook her head. "Don't worry, I'll teach you everything I learn. By the time you're a teenager, you'll know just about everything he knows." Cristal hugged her favorite cousin tighter than ever before.

It was such a painful memory for Cristal that day on the porch. Her mother never apologized for such an outlandish and cynical remark because she was unaware that her daughter had overheard the argument. But now, in a totally different place, in a land of more significant opportunity, Cristal eventually fell asleep and dreamt of a future where diamonds dotted the sky.

Chapter Fourteen:
Super Shoppers

Wilky knocked on the girls' door to tell them it was time for breakfast, and Cristal opened it. She and Raeni were already dressed and ready for the day. Wilky stepped inside, gawking once more at the trophies. A burnished 18" purple and gold sculpture of a wing-spread angel standing on a marble pedestal caught his eye. It was so heavy when he grabbed it with one hand that it almost fell to the floor. Raeni gasped and lunged quickly to catch a toppling possession. She rolled her eyes and sighed before gently returning it to its original location.

"Who are these people?" Wilky asked Raeni as he held up a large picture of a little boy with blonde hair and blue eyes wearing orange swim trunks and smiling for the camera. Colorful plastic shovels, buckets, and toys surrounded him. It looked like the happy little guy was trying to bury a long-legged lady with sunscreen smeared on her face in mounds of fine white sand.

"Put that down. Be careful, and don't drop it! That's my mom and little brother, Colton."

"You have a brother? Where is he?"

"He lives in Burgess, Belgium, with my mom." Before Wilky could ask a follow-up question, Raeni lifted another glowing trophy off the shelf. "I got that one two years ago. My team is called Fly Girlz. My friends and I, Marsha, Cynthia, and Angela, won first place in a Double Dutch jump rope competition." Raeni then reached for another trophy, a sparkling gold cup with wide handles.

She held it for Wilky to see but not for him to touch. "This one is for the solo jump rope competition I won all by myself," she said proudly.

Cristal sat intensely listening on the edge of the bed with her teddy bear, Ginger. She listened to the conversation and was able to comprehend some of it. Wilky glanced over and read the bewildered look on his sister's face. Raeni continued in a sing-songy voice describing the competition, "With increased acceleration, I had to perform three basic steps for the judges: the two-foot bounce when both feet jump over the rope together, the one-foot bounce - repeated jumps on one foot, then the other, and the alternating foot or 'boxers' step' - running in place while stepping over the rope."

Wilky interpreted this as the best that he could for his sister. Cristal went to her top drawer and pulled out a rope made of tightly braided twine Aunt Rachelle had made for her. "I can jump rope, too," said Cristal proudly. Raeni looked at the frayed intertwined string knotted at both ends. She glanced at the wall at her collection of multi-colored ropes made of sturdy, durable plastic. Her cords had thin handles that provided a comfortable grip, making for a smoother and more consistent rotation.

Raeni looked back at her little cousin's toothy smile and dimpled cheeks, "Sweet!" she said enthusiastically, supporting Cristal in giving a high five. Raeni turned and winked at Wilky. Within that moment, Wilky's heart warmed, and he decided he could grow to like and even love his new cousin.

"I spoke to your father this morning," Dahlia said. "He misses the two of you terribly and can't wait to hear about your new school."

"Awww, I wanted to talk to him," whined Cristal.

"Me too," exclaimed Wilky. "He told me to hug you two, and he's going to call back in a few days."

"Ok," the siblings replied in unison. Dahlia walked over and gave them individual bear hugs. The cereal's name brand wasn't familiar to her, but Cristal decided to try the same one that Raeni was eating. She was glad that her mom had helped pour milk inside her bowl. Cristal was too afraid that an accidental spill might occur, and Nadine or Raeni would think of her as a clumsy klutz. "Mmmm...it tastes like chocolate chip cookies," she happily announced with both feet kicking in delight.

"Which type of cereal would you like, Wilky?" asked Nadine as she placed two more boxes on the table.

"Oh, I want this one." With grand excitement, Wilky snatched up a yellow box with a picture of a dinosaur juggling assorted colored balls. He munched on a few fruity-tasting morsels before emptying them into a bowl. "Mmmm...these are so good!" Wilky poured his milk into a bowl for the first time without carefully splashing it on the table. Dahlia was impressed with her little guy. He dipped his spoon and scooped a pile of crunchy morsels into his mouth wide open. "Eeeww... this milk tastes nasty!" he blurted. Colorful pieces of cereal and milk spewed forcefully across the table. "Yuk," he snorted.

"Eeeww, that's nasty!" said Cristal. She worked to remove bits of grain from her hair and her arm. Raeni burst into laughter, and Cristal joined.

"Wilky, that is enough. My goodness!" Dahlia scolded. "Go upstairs right now and sit your behind down, and don't you dare turn that TV on." For the next hour, Wilky sat sulking and looking out the window while tossing a miniature soccer ball from one hand to the other. It was a gift from his former teammates, with all their names written in permanent marker. His thoughts coasted back to Haiti and the times spent with his best friends Endy and Marjon, kicking a soccer ball along the shores of a sandy beach. A cycle of emotions seemed to capsulate his aching heart with feelings of cresting joy, only to be displaced by the lowest point of pain. Breakfast that morning for Wilky consisted of two dirty Oreos, an angular piece of beef jerky, and some watermelon-flavored bubble gum, all found at the bottom of his backpack.

Later that morning, Raeni requested, "MaDine, may I show Cristal and Wilky the playground and the big kidney-shaped swimming pool?"

Good naturally, Nadine replied, "That's a good idea, sweetie, but I'd rather you wait until we get back from Super Shopper. Your Aunt Dahlia wants to buy groceries. We're in for a treat tonight because she's going to cook a special meal this evening. We also need to buy some school supplies."

Cristal danced and twerked excitedly when school was referenced again, "Lekol...' ecole"! They laughed at her poorly executed 'Grand Jete'. The word 'school' was one of the first nouns in English that Cristal learned at an early age.

After hearing the laughter, Wilky came running down the stairs to see what was causing the jolly commotion. His mother gave him a stern look. Staring down at his shoelaces, Wilky addressed his Aunt Nadine, "I'm sorry. I shouldn't have spit out my food like that. I won't do it again."

She pulled him in tight and wrapped her arms around his shoulders, "That's all right." With puppy dog eyes, Wilky looked up and smiled. Nadine continued, "You two are attending school next

Tuesday, and we need to register you all. Your mom just spoke on the phone to the secretary at the school. When we return from the store, we will download and print the forms needed to register you two."

Dahlia announced, "Both of you need to get vaccinated before you can attend."

"Kisa?" Cristal asked. She wasn't familiar with the term vaccinated.

"I need to make an appointment with a doctor so that you and Wilky get the required shots. They will protect you from getting very sick," she told her children.

"Yikes! We already got three of those dip-something shots last year in Haiti!" Wilky cried out.

"The Diphtheria shots, I know, but here in the United States, they require more." Like her little brother, Cristal dreaded getting a series of painful shots. Nadine, Dahlia, and the two young ladies grabbed their purses.

"Oh, I forgot something," Cristal announced, "I'll be right back." Quickly, she ascended the stairs to get her handheld abacus off the dresser, then slid it into her purse. Once she returned, they all headed to the car parked in the garage.

Alone and on his highest perch, Sudoku chirped twice and squawked, "Super Shoppers rock, saving money around the clock. We're more than bread, milk, and honey; we can save you money. We're more than bread, milk, and honey; we can save you money..."

The Super Shoppers store was crowded with customers buying everything from fresh cranberry scones to camouflage hunting gear. Wilky was fascinated by the many aisles and the outlandish items along the perimeter. He'd never been in a store that large. Spinning around and around, he belted, "This store is huge!" Cristal wrapped herself in a hug, *Li nan frèt!* – It's freezing in here!"

Before Nadine and Dahlia turned towards the grocery department to shop for items on their list, including more soy milk and regular milk for Wilky, Nadine handed a second list to Raeni. "Raeni, will you take this and pick up the supplies Wilky needs for school?" She looked down at the list and then up at her aunt.

"We're not going to get anything for Cristal?" Raeni asked politely. Neither Nadine nor Dahlia knew what supplies to purchase for Cristal.

"We won't get supplies for her just yet. We need to meet with her teachers first." Dahlia answered. "But would you help pick out a couple of cute tops for Cristal? Wilky can get a t-shirt."

"Sure," Raeni responded cheerfully.

Dahlia gave Raeni a fifty-dollar bill, two twenties, and a ten. Raeni was keen on being treated like a responsible teenager. "And get yourself something, a new backpack if you want," Dahlia suggested.

"Thanks, Aunt Dahlia!" The women proceeded to walk straight ahead in pursuit of their grocery items, and the young super shoppers grabbed a cart of their own and turned to the right. Raeni held Cristal's hand while looking up to read the aisle signs.

"Meet us at the snack bar by eleven o'clock, and stay together," Nadine directed before walking out of earshot.

"Yes, ma'am," the threesome replied.

"Won't I need to buy some uniforms?" Wilky asked Raeni.

"Nahhh… you're lucky not to have to wear those ugly things in the Garland school district. It sucks that they require them at my school." Raeni replied. Wilky recalled his father saying that wearing uniforms to school enhanced school pride and community spirit. Puzzled by Raeni's comment, he shrugged his shoulders and hitched a ride on the end of their shopping cart. Cristal released her grip from Raeni's hand to hold onto the front end of the cart. Raeni struggled to push in a straight line. Cristal narrowly missed getting grazed by an extended clothing rack. Slowly, the team zigzagged past blinking blue super-sale lights on columns near different aisles, carefully dodging a frenzy of customers snatching up sale items everywhere. An upbeat song by Gloria Estefan – a Cuban-American singer, played on the intercom system.

After getting Wilky's supplies for school, Raeni made a detour to the beauty and bath department. "Why are we over here?" he asked.

"I want to show Cristal some oils she might want to use to make her perfumes," Raeni answered.

"Oh, ok," Wilky nodded. Wilky explained to his sister the department they were now standing in.

"Ohhh, Thanks! I have money to buy some." Cristal stated. Raeni let Cristal feel an essential oil kit with eight bottles. She turned to her left and asked Wilky, "What kind of scents are in there, and how much is it?"

"It's only $12.88," Raeni answered. Wilky read and translated from the labels. "True lavender scents help with sleep and relaxation. Patchouli has a rich aroma that opens your psychic abilities. Rose oil is considered the flower of love and the queen of oils. Wild Orange has a zesty freshness and promotes awareness and spiritual well-being. Lemongrass – has a fresh, lemony, grassy, and sweet fragrance. Jasmine has a floral scent that is rich and fruity. Peppermint oil helps relieve aches and pains. Tea Tree has a clear, clean smell." Wilky was exhausted.

"This is good," said Cristal as she pulled the abacus from her purse. Raeni watched with great admiration. Cristal engaged in self-talk, subtracting the cost of the oils from the savings she'd earned from helping Granny Lou with laundry and Aunt Rachelle with her baskets. Displaying a huge smile, she placed the kit in the cart. "Yes, I will get this."

The next stop was the boys' clothing department. A cool turquoise blue Bart Simpson tee with a crew neck caught Wilky's eye immediately. "That's it. I want this one." He handed it to Raeni to place it inside the cart.

"That was super-fast!" she exclaimed. Raeni found a cute button-up scarlet top with tulip sleeves for herself. She and Cristal sorted through several racks of clothing. They eventually chose a denim blouse with a pocket and rainbow applique heart for Cristal. A t-shirt with rhinestones against a soft cotton material was also placed inside the cart. Cristal could feel the difference between them, and she liked them both. She thought about what the other girls at her new school might wear, especially if uniforms weren't required. Cristal would have to rely on Wilky to update her with their latest fashions. '*Maybe mom will let me buy some more clothes when she starts working. I'm gonna ask her,*' she decided.

"Wilky, do you like these tops?" Nothing was said. "Wilky?" Cristal repeated. Raeni looked around but didn't see the hide or hair of her little cousin.

"Wilkeee, Wilkeee!" she yelled louder and louder. Cristal and Raeni alternated, calling his name. Raeni's mind began to go wild and crazy with fear, "I hope nobody kidnapped him!"

"What?" Cristal asked.

"I hope nobody took him and left the store."

Cristal was scared and wanted to cry. Michael Jackson's 'Beat It' hit was suddenly interrupted by an anonymous voice, "Attention Super Shoppers – Attention Super Shoppers" blasted through speakers. "The parents of Wilky Duvernay, please come to the customer service desk immediately!"

Irresponsibly, Raeni began pushing past racks and racks of clothing, bumping into columns, and averting other customers. Cristal narrowly avoided a minor scrape on her arm by a chest-high display. Lightweight coats and puffer jackets jostled off wire hangers before parachuting to the floor.

At the customer service desk, they met up with Nadine, Dahlia, and Wilky. With shaky knees, Wilky wore a painted expression of embarrassment. He stood holding onto a fluorescent green glow-in-the-dark soccer ball that he bounced on a raised knee with both hands. A smirky-looking assistant manager stood as customary beside the lost child now claimed. Wilky had gotten disoriented between the automotive and sporting goods department at the very west end of the store. Although he was never in any imminent danger, he knew at that space and time, he had become an overwhelmed Super Saver shopper.

Chapter Fifteen:
Knuckleheads

Raeni walked stiffly like a robot, leading Cristal along the cobblestone pathways surrounding the Willow Woods Townhomes complex. Wilky rushed ahead, too excited to wait; he wanted to locate the playground on his own. "Long sticks tree limbs here?" asked Cristal.

"No. Why?" asked Raeni.

"They help me not stumble into holes."

"Oh, I know what you're talking about. I saw people on TV walking with long, skinny sticks. I'll keep my eye out for a branch or something that might help."

"Some flowers here?"

Raeni did a 360-degree turn, "No, I don't see any. There are some pretty ones up front at the main entrance by the gate. I can't remember. But there might be some around by the pool."

It was a hot sweltering day, '*No breeze?*' Cristal wondered. She fanned herself for a few seconds before the duo continued walking.

"Oh, oh… sorry," said Raeni after causing Cristal to almost stumble at the curb's edge. She felt bad that she hadn't been more focused. In those few short moments, Raeni was learning that guiding a person with no sight required concentration. Guides need to horizontally shift their eyes to ensure that the person being guided is free from obstacles on both sides of the body, objects that might cause harm on a hard and solid impact.

There were bands of kids hanging out in groups on the playground. All were desperate to have fun and soak up every last minute of their summer vacation. Some kids hung around near the swing set. Impatiently, they waited for their turn.

"Hurry up and get off… you've been on too long!" yelled a tall, chubby girl with square Coke bottle glasses and coarse yellow hair.

"Wait your turn, Big Bird," shouted the more petite freckled face girl with short red curls. A few kids began to laugh, but when the girl with the yellow hair shot a mean mug with a balled fist, grins were erased as steps backward were taken.

Wilky looked around at the island of green grass. *'There's enough here to kick around a soccer ball,'* he imagined. The area was furnished with tall slides, long curvy tunnels, sit-and-spins ladders, and monkey bars. There were more than enough structures for Wilky to climb on, hang from, jump over, and climb through. Far more equipment was available in that location than the new playground built at his private school in Haiti. That is before it was all wrecked by the powerful earthquake.

Finally, it was Wilky or Cristal's chance to swing. The spoiled brat of a brother secured the empty swing first. With fast and desperate speed, he pumped his legs back and forth harder and harder. He swung so high that his body lifted right off the seat. 'Ooohs and Ahhhs' were uttered by some nearby boys and girls. Raeni guided Cristal to the next available swing, placed one of her hands directly on the swing's chain, and then pushed Cristal gently forward on her back several times. Raeni wasn't sure what to do next. She figured Cristal's muscles would instinctively figure it out.

"With your feet on the ground, push off, and then keep straightening and bending your legs," yelled Wilky from two swings over.

Had there been a large tree in their front yard back in Croix-des-Bouquets, their father would have certainly made a swing for them to play on.

As Cristal swung forward and backward, Raeni stepped several feet away. Two little girls with blue popsicle stains coating their lips and tongues ran up to Raeni. These curious onlookers, along with others, launched a series of questions.

"Her eyes are open. Can't she see?"

"Can she hear?"

"Does she talk with her fingers?" asked one of the older kids.

Raeni was a little uncomfortable with the unwanted attention. "No, she can't see. And yes, she talks, just like you and me."

"Was she born like that?" asked a little boy with a mullet haircut.

"She's fine. Okay?" Raeni subconsciously tried to present a carefree, nonchalant demeanor.

"I was just askin,' gee wizz."

Raeni moved to the shade just as Cristal's gross motor movements accurately kicked in. She began pumping her legs to swing independently. Raeni thought about the new experiences Cristal would embark upon as a first-time student and was wishful her little cousin would make friends. The high school sophomore started thinking about her own upcoming school year. She made a personal commitment to practice more on the cello to move to the highly-coveted first chair position. *'Last year, I barely made the 'A' honor roll, but I'm gonna do what it takes to be first this time around*!' Raeni's most pressing concern was really whether or not she would be lucky enough to share at least one class with her first schoolboy crush.

Daxton was someone the teenager had become infatuated with ever since a long-term substitute teacher switched him with another student to be her biology lab partner. The pair had loads of fun and laughter dissecting a frog's eye and then a cow's eye with a slight lack of precision. She liked Daxton's deep baritone voice, comparable to the vocal sounds of the country singer Josh Turner, who her father loved to imitate. Daxton's polished confidence, Raeni thought, was similar to a first-draft baller's swag. His initial conversations presented a charming and laid-back personality.

Last May, on 'Yearbook Day', each and every time, Raeni was elated to be in his presence. However, her best friend Marsha told her not to show it so much 'and bring your giddiness down a few notches.' She was grateful for the advice because, without a big sister around, Raeni wasn't certain how to act around boys. At least one hundred times, Raeni read what Daxton wrote on the inside cover of her freshman yearbook, 'Ur2Cool2Be4gotten'. The love-struck teenager even sniffed his signature, hoping somehow the black ink captured the smell of his spicy wood-fragrant cologne.

"We'd better head back," Raeni told Wilky and Cristal after glancing at her watch. "It's almost time for dinner, and I still want you all to see the swimming pool." Raeni felt terrible that she often used the word 'see' in front of Cristal. "Oops, I mean, I want to show you the swimming pool…oops, sorry! I mean, check it out."

Wilky laughed and responded in French, "*Pas de soucis* – no worries." Raeni chuckled with a sigh of relief after witnessing a smile on her cousin's face.

"What's the noise?" Cristal asked.

"I don't know," Wilky answered with matched curiosity. As they walked closer to the pool, three boys about Wilky's age yelled and bawled. Pounding and thud sounds waved through the air as they approached the boys' activities. Everyone's upward focus was on a 17" wide dried clump of mud attached to the side of a garage.

"Oh, oh…those knuckleheads are always up to something. Stop, don't!" Raeni warned. But it was too late. "Let's get out of here," Raeni said as she grabbed Cristal's hand. Wilky grabbed the other hand, and they ran fast away towards a bench.

One boy had the half-baked idea to throw a huge, jagged rock at a target. It took only one perfect aim to bring the creepy brown thing smashing to the ground. Like fighter jets headed for combat, a horde of angry wasps circled and bobbed, seeking out the perpetrators. Those feisty insects wasted no time delivering sting after sting to Darius, Jeremy, and Zach.

Wilky narrated the chaotic activity, and all three sat bowling over with laughter. Each held their panged stomachs while whooping in amusement. Faint cries and howls from the reckless boys could be heard in the distance.

"I bet those are the same boys that made the people who work on the landscape and manage these townhomes drain the pool and close it two weeks ago!" Raeni declared.

"Why would they need to drain the pool?" Wilky asked.

"Well, it's kind of funny. At least my Dad and I thought it was, MaDine, but not so much. A woman was swimming laps in the pool early one morning when she saw what she thought was a pile of feces in the deep end of the water. But it wasn't that. It turns out that somebody threw in about five of those bite-size Baby Ruth candy bars."

"What's feces, and what kind of candy is Baby Ruth?" Wilky asked Raeni.

"Feces is what your body excretes after eating food, and a Baby Ruth is a candy bar made of dark lumpy chocolate with nuts."

"I don't get it."

Raeni realized she needed to water down her response because she was talking to a third grader, after all. "It looked like somebody had taken a dump, a number two dump, in the pool."

Wilky thought about it for a hot second and then began laughing so hard that Raeni thought it might throw up.

"Tell me what's funny, Wilky." Cristal pleaded after he finally picked himself up off the ground, almost peeing in his pants. It was Cristal's turn to laugh uncontrollably.

"The next time we go to Super Shoppers, I'll get some Baby Ruth candy bars. You'll understand exactly what I'm talking about."

"Ewww...Okay," Wilky replied between breaths.

"Ohhh, there are some flowers mixed in with weeds right behind this bench," Raeni told Cristal.

"What color?"

"Some of them are yellow and white; they kinda look like daisies. And I see some purple ones back by the fence."

"Help me pick for bracelets?" Cristal asked.

"Oh, sure."

After assisting Cristal with gathering flowers mixed with colorful weeds, Wilky swiftly vacated the area to run a safe distance after the knuckleheads just to see what bizarre event might happen next. The boys had jumped the fence and plunged into the artfully shaped pool, disrupting a pair of innocent twins wearing 'Baby Shark' life vests. Little did they know that the angry wasps would wait until the boys re-emerged from the water. To avoid possible anarchy, the toddlers' swim lesson with the young girl-dad ended almost as soon as it started. But one thing was inevitable, and as fate would have it, Wilky was destined to become close friends with at least one of the unlucky blokes.

Chapter Sixteen:
Ready, Set, Go!

Unfortunately for her children, who were eager to be students, Dahlia could not get them an appointment with a pediatrician before the beginning of school. On the day Cristal and Wilky got their vaccination shots, the Garland County Public Schools were in session for a week. And because she was a foreigner in a new place, Dahlia had her own trepidations about going to the doctor's office to speak on behalf of her children. She was very aware of the customs and etiquette surrounding communicative exchange compared to that in Haiti, which may be different under professional circumstances. Fortunately for her, the visit for her and her children was an amicable one. Dahlia was very impressed with Dr. Brooks. She liked her pleasant and professional demeanor.

Taking Nadine's suggestion, Dahlia asked the pediatrician how she could help Cristal sleep throughout the night now that Cristal was required to get up early on weekdays. "She needs to abstain from unscheduled naps at any time of the day," Dahlia told the doctor.

Dr. Brooks suggested that Dahlia purchase strawberry or cherry-flavored melatonin gummies from the downstairs pharmacy. "It's a natural sleep aid and will help fix Cristal's circadian rhythm. It's okay to let her take two about an hour before bedtime for at least the first couple of months. Then stop, and we can monitor her to see if she starts drifting asleep naturally once she's established a daily routine," Dr. Brooks suggested. Dahlia was grateful for the recommendation, and so was Cristal.

"I don't want to sleep in class. I want to learn everything my teachers want to teach me."

"That's right, baby. I'm glad that you want to be a good student. And from now on, you and Wilky will have an 8:30 curfew. I expect you to stay in that bed, too. No more getting up in the middle of the night to creep around in the kitchen trying to make colognes!"

"Awww, okay." Cristal pouted.

"That's not fair that we have to start school later than everybody else," complained Wilky. "The other kids will already know the routine, the rules, and everybody else's names and stuff."

"I know Wilky, but I can't do anything about it. We probably could have been here a week or two earlier, but your father wanted to wait until after your soccer tournament. He knew how important it was to you."

"Oh, yeah." Wilky reacted with a nod. He knew that any further complaints just weren't warranted.

On the way to work Monday morning, Nadine dropped off enrollment papers and the required health forms at the school. In the afternoon, the assistant principal scheduled two meetings back-to-back. The first was an initial eligibility meeting so that Cristal could receive special education services because she had the medical diagnosis 'legally blind'. The second meeting was an Individualized Educational Plan (IEP) to put goals and objectives for her in place. This plan held teachers accountable for teaching specific skills to help Cristal succeed academically. They would also be designed to improve her independence in other compensatory areas like daily living skills, social skills, and technology.

Because Dahlia had no transportation of her own, she couldn't attend the meetings in person but chose to participate via phone conference. The regular and special education teachers introduced themselves and proceeded to talk about their areas of study and expertise. A school psychologist said she would conduct the necessary assessments for Cristal once specific forms were signed. It was a blizzard of information. Dahlia didn't understand it all, primarily because the team at the table talked fast while using innumerable acronyms: AT, ESY, FAPE, LEA, LRE, and PLAAFP. She couldn't decipher their meanings and would try to remember to request a detailed printout of the acronyms with definitions. However, Dahlia agreed to review the paperwork and sign the IEP the following morning, so there would be no further delay in enrolling Cristal.

Nadine accompanied Dahlia, Cristal, and Wilky on Tuesday morning to their new school. As guests, they sat in the front office as the receptionist instructed. "Good morning," asserted a tall, muscular man greeting them with a booming voice. His dark blue Polo shirt was tucked neatly in a pair of belted khaki pants for a dressier look. Everyone stood. "My name is Brick Macklberg. I'm the assistant principal here at Azalea Grove Elementary – Home of the Cobras and one of the best schools in the nation." Dahlia and Nadine shook his hand and introduced themselves.

"I'm sorry that Dr. Simone Martin, the principal, is not here to greet you. She's attending a leadership conference at the Georgia State Capitol today and tomorrow."

"That's fine," Dahlia responded, "here are the completed forms you need." Dahlia handed him shot records and other completed forms. He then gave them to a lady waiting in the wings.

"Thank you," said Mr. Macklberg. "This must be Cristal and William. I am so glad to have the two of you join us." He extended his right hand to shake Wilky's hand, which he returned with the clasp of a limp noodle. The assistant principal grinned and then patted Cristal on her shoulder, causing her to jump in surprise. "Would you ladies like for my secretary to get you a cup of coffee or tea?"

"No, thank you," both ladies chimed.

"Well, please join me in the conference room down the hall. I can answer any questions you may have regarding yesterday's meetings, and I also need you to sign a few more papers. We'll discuss the class schedules for our bright new pupils, too," said Mr. Macklberg with a wink and a smile directed at Wilky.

"Mr. Macklberg," began Dahlia, "I know that you and a team of teachers met yesterday to discuss the best classroom setting for Cristal because she can't see, but I'm also concerned because she is not quite fluent in English yet. She understands more of it than she actually speaks and is pretty good at ascertaining meaning from a certain context." Mr. Macklberg gave a north and south nod of the head and allowed Dahlia to continue. "I learned to speak English because I attended a private school from the very beginning. We had an exceptional dual language curriculum." She looked at Nadine, and she agreed with a complimentary nod. "Wilky also learned to speak English at his mission school, and my husband speaks some as well. But in our home back in Haiti, we primarily spoke Haitian Creole and some French because their great-grandmother did not speak it."

Wilky interjected to add a comment he'd heard from somewhere, "My daddy speaks fluent facts, though." Nadine chuckled and made a mental note to tell her brother of his son's praise.

Mr. Macklberg, a first-year assistant principal, gave a perfunctory signal of understanding. "Yes, Dr. Martin and the team discussed some of those exact concerns. It is best practice to consider every aspect of Cristal's needs and all that her school day should encompass. Because of your daughter's chronological age, the team feels confident placing her in a fourth-grade class for now."

Wilky frowned. His thoughts questioned their judgment, "How could Cristal be in the same grade as me? She's never even been in school!"

Dahlia reached out and patted him on the shoulder. "Just hold on, Wilky."

Mr. Macklberg continued, "She'll have three main teachers. Mrs. Lovelady will be her homeroom and science teacher. Cristal will be in Mrs. Tubilleja's Social Studies and ELL class and have two periods with Ms. Saunders, a Teacher of Students with Visual Impairments."

"Oh my, that's a lot of people with most likely different styles of teaching to get used to," stated Dahlia.

"Ms. Saunders will teach Cristal to read and write using the braille code and will also teach math assignments using the Nemeth code. Our district has purchased some of the most innovative technologies to convert information formatted in print to auditory output. And I believe there's some device with an internal camera that's used to take a picture of just about anything and give descriptive information about an object or activity."

"Now that is impressive!" said Nadine.

"And, of course, Cristal will go to PE, Art, and Music on alternating days with her homeroom class."

"I'm sorry, but what exactly is ELL?" Nadine asked.

"Oh, my apologies," said Mr. Macklberg, "it means that Cristal will be in a classroom with other students who are also learning to speak and improve their English. ELL stands for 'English Language Learners'."

Dahlia and Nadine glanced at each other with a gesture of agreement, "That's good," Dahlia commented.

Mr. Macklberg continued to explain, "We have eleven returning students with low vision or total blindness. Two of those students are in the ELL program as well. Your daughter will be in good company, trust me."

Although she didn't understand the entire explanation, Cristal capitalized on the pause generated from all the mental processing going on around her. She tapped her mother's shoulder and leaned in to whisper into her ear. The assistant principal was eager to know what the young girl wanted to contribute to the conversation. Dahlia immediately relayed her daughter's concerns.

"How is she going to get around without a stick? Should we buy her something more sturdy and sophisticated, or will somebody lead her to her classes for now?"

A confident smile appeared on Mr. Macklberg's face as he rested back and swiveled from left to right in a fancy cushioned chair. All new faculty members, including himself, received professional development training during an in-service prior to the first day of school. The training focused on the general needs of students with visual impairments, including training by an O&M

specialist to teach students how to use their remaining senses to travel with purpose and confidence.

The assistant principal answered, "Mr. Nick, our Certified Orientation and Mobility Specialist, will conduct an ongoing assessment to identify the skills he'll need to teach Cristal. He will initially focus on protective techniques and teach her to walk safely with another person in the halls. At some point, he will also instruct her on how to use a long cane, one specifically chosen to meet her needs. She'll receive training to travel as safely, efficiently, and as independently as possible."

"Cristal likes spending time exploring the outdoors," Dahlia explained, "will his training be for just inside, or can he help her get around with some degree of safety outside as well?"

"Good question," Mr. Macklberg stated. "Yes, he'll first start training inside the building to address common daily routes. Next, he'll work in the immediate outdoor area of the school. Eventually, Mr. Nick will provide instruction in the community as well. But he'll give you a permission slip to sign to take her off-campus. It will include dates and times throughout the school year when she will be riding on a school bus to various sites."

"Alright then. I like that plan," said Dahlia. She interpreted everything for her daughter, and Cristal scooted comfortably in her seat. She swung her feet back and forth, bobbing her head slightly in excitement.

"What about me? Who's gonna be my teacher?" Wilky asked after sitting uncharacteristically patient.

"William, you'll be placed in Mrs. Collier's third-grade class."

"What? I already did third grade! I should be with fourth-graders." Wilky was downright furious. "I had good marks on my last report card!" he asserted.

"Calm down, Wilky," Nadine advised while his mother grabbed his whirling hands and pulled them together on the table.

Mr. Macklberg testified, "William, it's because your studies were unfortunately interrupted due to the earthquake in the middle of your third-grade year."

He turned to his mother before shooting a look of contempt and refusing to let the assistant principal form his lips to speak another dadgum word. "But momma," Wilky began protesting, "I studied just like you and Granny Lou told me even after my school was destroyed. I kept reading my books and worked on some tough math problems."

Dahlia looked at her son and acknowledged his assumption and his hurt. Wilky had continued his studies as best he could under her own tutelage. Jesse even tutored him in math when he had the time. She squeezed Wilky's shoulder to let him know that she understood the anguish.

Macklberg felt bad for Wilky, too, but stuck to his guns. "Mrs. Duvernay, if Mrs. Collier finds that William exceeds his peers across the third-grade curriculum, she can recommend that he get evaluated for the next grade. This test may even determine if he'd be eligible for an after-school program with a gifted and talented math and language arts curriculum. It is specifically geared towards students with high IQ scores in certain areas of study."

"Well, that sounds fair," Dahlia reluctantly agreed. "My son is naturally smart. I'm certain his teacher will discover this rather quickly." She then reached out and pulled Wilky in close to kiss the crown of his head. In a New York minute, the first school bell rang, activating a soft cascading sound like a harp. Although it wasn't the same resonance, Cristal's thoughts immediately raced back to the sound of Granny Lou and Mrs. Rosie's clanging bell - their personal signaling method. For the first time since leaving Haiti, she fretted about who would pick up and deliver the laundry for Granny Lou's best customer. *'Maybe Mikaela will do it since she's still not going to school.'*

For the silent thrill, Mr. Macklberg pushed back from the conference table, letting his chair roll several feet. "I'm going to get Mrs. McCallister, the office assistant, to walk these two young scholars to class because as soon as the second bell - the tardy bell rings, I have to make the morning announcements," he stated proudly.

"Oh, I almost forgot, there's one more thing." Dahlia noticed his facial expression change, with a furrowed brow and a searing look. "I need to give you a copy of the parent handbook. Please become familiar with it because you'll find the information extremely valuable. It will answer many of the commonly asked questions parents and students have about our school's rules and expectations, amongst other things." He opened the sizeable double file cabinet but couldn't seem to locate even one copy of the green paperback book. He noticed a box nearby, walked over and pulled out a fifteen-function Swiss Army knife from his back pocket. Skillfully, the administrator opened the multiple-bladed object with the fingers from the left hand and bent low to slice the packing tape. The swift and sudden movements caused his Polo shirt to become untucked. It furled upward, exposing part of the man's lower back.

"OMG! That is so cool!" Wilky blurted while pointing to Mr. Macklberg's backside.

"What, what is it?" Cristal asked fervently.

"He's got a mean tattoo all over his back!" Wilky relayed in Haitian Creole, "What is it about Mr. Macklberg? What does it mean?" he asked with an overabundance of zeal. The young assistant principal snatched a parent handbook from the stack and quickly moved to an upright and vertical position.

"Oh, uhm… it's a Native American tribal tattoo," he replied while tucking his shirt back inside his pants.

"What's the name of your tribe?"

"The Creek Indians," he turned and informed everyone present.

"That is so dope!" Wilky reached forward with his fisted right hand for a bump. Mr. Macklberg obliged by completing the two-part action with his fist. The little architect growing inside of Wilky drew from his memory bank. "I remember reading that their houses were made of plaster and rivercane with thatched roofs. The Creeks were known for their burial mounds, too! Are there some here in Georgia?" Mr. Macklberg was quite impressed with the little boy's knowledge. The bond of mutual respect formed between the two was instantaneous.

"Well, there is a historic mound in North Carolina," he answered, glancing at the clock on the wall.

"That's lit!" Wilky stated.

Nadine stood silently admiring the handsome man and his tattoos. Dahlia cut in, "Okay, Wilky, that's enough. Calm down," she added with a slight chuckle, so enthralled by her son's intellect. Mr. Macklberg cleared his throat, rubbed his nose, and handed Dahlia the handbook,

"Tear out the last page and sign after reading everything, please. Wilky can give it to Mrs. Collier to turn it to me."

"Alright, will do," Dahlia agreed after tucking it away with other papers in her purse.

A proud mother and devoted aunt gave two eager children tight hugs. Big kisses were planted on their cheeks and foreheads. Dahlia's eyes welled with tears while reading over Cristal's face, a face filled with unbridled joy and anticipation. Wilky noticed her watering eyes, and before turning away, he made a quick Dougie hip-hop dance move that he learned just yesterday. Dahlia and Nadine gave a hearty laugh. They watched Mrs. McCallister adjust Cristal's grip to slide and place her hand just above Mrs. McCallister's elbow. The twosome proceeded to travel briskly down the hall with Wilky close behind. Cristal leaned over to smell her guide's scent, "First, by Van Cleef & Arpels?" she asked with a rise in her voice.

"Oh my goodness, yes!" Mrs. McCallister was flabbergasted. "How did you know? My husband purchased this for me during our summer vacation in France, and it's authentic. The real deal it is!"

Cristal chuckled and replied in her best French accent, "Oui je sais, Madame." Mrs. McCallister slowed her pace. "Yes, I know, Madam," Cristal repeated for her in English with her non-Haitian accent. So impressed Mrs. McCallister was that she made a mental note, vowing to check in on Cristal whenever possible.

"Cristal, I will walk you to your class first and introduce you to your homeroom teacher. William, if you hang back for a minute, I'll get you to your class soon," Mrs. McCallister instructed. Small clusters of students brushed past, hurrying to reach their rooms before the second bell.

Mrs. McCallister stood at Mrs. Lovelady's classroom doorway with Cristal on her arm. "Your new student has arrived. Here is Cristal Duvernay," Mrs. McCallister announced with an air of haughtiness, making Cristal sound like a person of celebrated status. Wilky pushed between the adults, twisting and oscillating his neck up, down, and all around. He marveled at the colorful walls decorated with posters, banners, and students' constructed artwork. He saw a solar system model, a fish tank, a half dozen plants along the windowsill, and a life-size plastic skeleton sitting at a corner desk.

"Welcome, Cristal. My name is Mrs. Lovelady. We're so glad to have you join us. Class, say hello to Cristal."

"Hi, Cristal."

"Hey, Cristal."

"Welcome, Cristal."

"Hola."

The sing-songy greetings continued to circulate amongst 17 students. Wilky broadcasted a little too loudly, "This class is proper. It's got everything!"

Mrs. Lovelady looked down at the observant admirer. She appreciated the compliments because extra effort was made to create such an inviting learning environment for three whole days over the summer. Mrs. McCallister outwardly rotated her arm, and Cristal automatically released her grip. "Have an awesome day, mademoiselle."

Cristal displayed a nervous smile before timidly reacting, "Merci beaucoup," She listened to the abandoning sound of Wilky's squeaky new tennis shoes escorted by fading clicks of Mrs.

McCallister's kitten heel pumps signal the direction of their footpath.

Left alone and standing poised in the doorway, Cristal presented on her first day of school as a pretty girl in a stylish outfit. She wore a new pair of black jeans, neon pink tennis shoes, and a white t-shirt with a glittery unicorn rising on two legs. Before Raeni left for school that morning, she slipped a silver rhinestone headband on Cristal's head and positioned it perfectly in front of her two fluffy ponytails. It resembled a crown. "Now, you look like a trendy fourth-grade student."

"Thanks." Cristal replied, assuming correctly that 'trendy' was an awesome thing.

Mrs. Lovelady guided Cristal to a seat up front and near the door. She provided light physical support and demonstrated hand-over-hand how to hang her backpack on the back of the chair. "We're all waiting for the morning announcements, Cristal. Then you will walk next door to your first academic class."

Cristal smiled nervously in response to something she wasn't exactly sure of. She fingered the iridescent stone on the necklace Granny Lou gifted her and fidgeted with other miscellaneous items inside her purse. Cristal decided to let her fan remain unseen for the first time in a long time.

Chapter Seventeen:
Introducing William DeMarco Duvernay

"Have a great first day, William," Mrs. McCallister voiced after ushering him to the front door of his classroom. "Please pardon the interruption, Mrs. Collier; our new student is here."

Unfortunately for Wilky, the tardy bell rang before he could be properly introduced. Feeling a little awkward, he leaned against the wall with his arms akimbo near what he assumed to be the teacher's desk. He stood wearing red high-top tennis shoes, khaki cargo shorts, and a white short-sleeve T-shirt with a colorful patch of the Haitian flag on the pocket. Wilky shifted and panned his light brown eyes with unusually long eyelashes around the room to find the person in charge. 'Oohhs and ahhhs' flowed from the mouths of several girls as they laid their eyes on the new student. It was almost as if Wilky was a famous front-and-center artist ready to perform for a select live audience full of groupies.

This unexpected reaction caused Wilky to subconsciously reposition his whole body and cross his arms and legs for some kind of physical barrier. Nervously and impatiently, he continued to wait in this radically unfamiliar environment. '*Where is the teacher?*' he griped. His eleven-inch reddish-brown locs swung in the air as he swiftly turned to run through the open door, but that liftoff didn't happen. A prompt and delicate little hand of an older woman, approximately four feet nine eleven inches tall, grasped Wilky firmly on his right shoulder.

A booming and buoyant announcement commenced over the intercom, rousing rooms full of little people throughout the school who were ready to learn.

"Good morning, Azalea Grove Elementary students! Welcome back once again to one of the greatest schools in the nation – the home of the mighty Cobras." Mr. Macklberg spoke with the zest and enthusiasm of a sportscaster ready to call plays instead of an administrator addressing students with the same daily proclamations. Before handing the microphone over to hyped little ones, he reminded everybody interested in participating in the after-school Cobra Clubs to turn in their forms. "Your parents need to use the yellow envelope provided to include a check or cash. You should return it to your teacher by next Friday."

A third-grade student followed that announcement by introducing herself first before reading the lunch menu. A fifth-grade student took the microphone next to read the thought for the day after her animated introduction, "If you are not willing to learn, no one can help you. If you are determined to learn, no one can stop you, a quote from Zig Ziglar."

The last student, a 4th grader from Mrs. Lovelady's class, told the joke for the day, "Why don't clowns eat cannibals?" There was a slight pause, "Because they taste funny!" Laughter echoed down the halls of learning.

Mr. Macklberg ended the announcements with his charge to the entire faculty and student body. "Love yourself. Be kind to each other and take care of your school. Remember, this place where you sit today is directly connected to the stance you will take tomorrow. Now go forth and have an incredibly awesome day!" With that charge, highly qualified teachers began instructions for the first academic subject of the day.

"William, we're so happy to have you as a new addition to our class," voiced Mrs. Collier. Wilky was stunned when he realized that the petite lady standing before him was his teacher. Her silvery grey hair was pulled into a tight, impenetrable doughnut bun. His teacher's glasses sat perched on a nose that resembled a pair of Aunt Rachelle's favorite stilettos, "Please come and take the empty seat between Kenny and Michesly."

Incensed for being left to stand vulnerable for so long, he murmured in a low voice, "Wilky is my name." He then slumped past several cohorts and seated himself in his assigned chair. After Mrs. Collier took attendance, she summoned Wilky from behind her desk.

"William, please come here." All eyes tracked Wilky negotiating his way around the horseshoe layout of desks until he reached Mrs. Collier. "Would you prefer that I call you Willie?" she asked hushedly.

"No, ma'am. I want to be called Wilky."

"Well, that works for me!" she stated in a sunny tone, gesturing to give Wilky a fist bump. Wilky chortled before letting his knuckles tap Mrs. Collier's miniature knuckles. "One more thing, Wilky. Would you please introduce yourself to the class and tell us a little about yourself? It's important that we all get to know each other because, for one year, we're like a family of many cousins, with one Aunt at the helm. And you've probably already noticed that you've got a few starry-eyed fans." she winked.

Wilky smiled, "Yes, ma'am." He liked Mrs. Collier – she's 'prime,' he later told Cristal. As instructed, Wilky stood in front of the class to introduce himself.

"My name is Wilky Duvernay, and I'm from Croix-des-Bouquets in Haiti. It's located in the Caribbean. My family and I are lucky to be alive. Thousands of people were killed or badly injured when the earthquake hit on January 12, 2010. The city of Port-au-Prince, Haiti's capital, was almost totally obliterated. The main soccer stadium, Stade Sylvio Cator, was partially destroyed, and hundreds of people experienced homelessness and had to pitch tents in the muddy fields. My father sent me, my mother, and my sister here to Georgia so we could go to school because my school had extensive damage. About a hundred books were all salvaged and confiscated from the rubbish."

Wilky paused for a few seconds, realizing his mouth was drying. He was talking with intensity and nervousness. After examining his new classmates' faces, Wilky thought he recognized a fair-skinned boy with curly black hair sitting on the room's left side. The boy had several reddish-colored puncture wounds scabbed over his face and neck. Wilky later learned his name was Jeremy. Jeremy was one of the three boys Wilky saw diving into the swimming pool at the Willow Wood Townhomes who tried desperately to avoid an injection of venom from a hoard of wasps.

Mrs. Collier was impressed with Wilky's rather large vocabulary and communication style. *'Such a loquacious little guy, so refreshing.'* The veteran third-grade teacher wanted to hear more, so she cleared her throat and nodded to encourage him to continue speaking.

Wilky did but was uncertain how much more to share. "Math and Science are my favorite subjects. Soccer, or football as you Americans would call it, is my favorite recreational activity, but I like constructing things with Legos, too. I want to be an architect when I grow up. Umm, and I guess that's it." Wilky looked over his shoulder at Mrs. Collier, and he could tell she was pleased. Several students shot their hands up high in the air.

"Wilky, do you mind answering a few questions?" Mrs. Collier asked.

"Uhhh…No, ma'am," he replied respectfully. No doubt, Jesse would have been pleased with his son's distinguished representation of the Duvernay name.

A tall girl named Brianna, with a black and white polka dot dress and a purple sash, stood up after Mrs. Collier called her name. She tugged her hair to ensure soft, toppled ringlets with a plum-colored bow moved and bounced like large Slinkys. In a gentle whispery voice, she declared, "I like your hair, Wilky." He smirked with tons of embarrassment. Nervously, Wilky rubbed his hands from the crown of his head to the very end of his locs. A couple of the girls giggled. Trevor, a boy sitting up front, snapped a pencil in half over his extended leg. He was feeling a bit salty by all the attention the new kid was starting to get.

"Brianna, do you have a question? Because if not, you need to take your seat," commanded Mrs. Collier.

"Oh…alright." Brianna glowered as she fluffed and patted her posh taffeta dress with a noisy rustling petticoat underneath.

Mason, an active empath, stood when called and questioned with deep concern, "Did you see people get crushed in the earthquake?"

Wilky grimaced, thinking about his mother's parents and sister who were killed. "No, but my mother and father drove around and saw bodies crushed in the aftermath of all the destruction." Sympathetic groans overcame the room.

Andrew asked, "Why do you talk funny?"

"Huh…what?" Wilky responded with an uneasy frown.

Mrs. Collier interjected in quick defense, "He speaks with an accent, Andrew. It is a manner of pronunciation specific to the Caribbean Islands where he was born. The primary language in Haiti is Haitian Creole and not English. I imagine we all probably sound different to him as well."

"Oh, I guess so," the curious student responded.

Dmitry, who his peers often characterized as a nerd, expressed something that Wilky found very troubling. "I heard once on the news that there are no trees in Haiti, and people get sunburned easily from lack of shade. They said that children ate the trees. Why would somebody want to eat trees? Was there no food around?" he innocently asked.

Wilky was baffled, "Aww, naw. I don't know anybody that eats trees."

Mrs. Collier cut in sharply, "I heard a similar story on the news as well, Dmitry. That is an example of false reporting. It is simply not true. However, the word 'Adirondack' means 'they who eat trees or bark eaters', which originated as a derogatory term given to the Algonquin Indian tribe by the neighboring Mohawk people."

"Oh, ok." uttered the studious boy.

"What grade is your sister in?" asked a student named Cameron.

"She's in fourth grade," replied Wilky with relief and gratitude for the simple question.

"Time for one more question," directed Mrs. Collier. "There will be plenty of time during lunch and recess to get to know Wilky." The teacher surveyed the remaining hands, which were waving high. She decided to call on a sweet-looking girl named Autumn. A huge grin veiled Wilky's face when Autumn, sporting a boy bob haircut, stood wearing blue shorts and a yellow t-shirt. A soccer ball was on the front of her tee with the lettering '*Just Kickin' It*' written across the top. Through Wilky's eyes, a radiant, all-consuming glow emanated from Autumn.

"Is there a McDonald's in Haiti?" she asked.

He chuckled, "No, but I ate my first McDonald's cheeseburger last week. And I wouldn't say I liked it. It was almost inedible. It tasted kinda rubbery and yucky; Wilky stuck out his tongue and shook his head with a look of displeasure. His locs swung in an artful motion. Most of the students laughed. "But my sister and I love their French fries," Trevor grunted and mumbled something under his breath when Wilky rushed past and headed to his seat.

As soon as Wilky sat down, a student named Kenny turned around and placed a folded piece of paper on his desk. Wilky opened it and saw a caricature drawing of a boy with airborne locs on a distorted head and a little body. His arms were stretched wide, all while surfing on a board in the ocean. Wilky laughed hard. "That's cool, that's what's up," he said, giving Kenny a big nod. The promising sketch artist returned the gesture, and an immediate rapport originated between the two.

Mrs. Collier instructed everyone to begin working on a social studies research project from the tablets at their desks. She moved around the room, hovering over hunched shoulders to help the students get started. Wilky was relieved when the teacher made it to his desk because Michesly was beginning to become annoying.

She leaned forward to ask one question after the other while pushing her desk closer. Wilky started to feel that his personal space was being violated and taken hostage. Michesly munched on some trail mix from a napkin inside of her desk. She tapped Wilky on the shoulder.

"You want some?"

"Umm…no thanks," Wilky replied.

"It's got M&M candies in it." Wilky scanned the rules on a poster near the door again and read #3, '*No eating in class*'.

 He debated it but once more repeated, "No thanks."

"You'll need to create a password that won't be easy for others to guess," Mrs. Collier told Wilky, "and it needs to consist of at least seven letters and two numbers." Wilky contemplated his options for a couple of seconds and came up with the letters C-H-E-E-R-I-O and the two-digit number from his Stingray jersey, '23'. '*No one will ever guess this*,' he concluded.

Lunchtime rolled around fairly early for all third graders. Mrs. Collier glanced at the clock, stopped teaching two-digit multiplication, and instructed everyone to close their math books. "Finish up where you left off for homework," she said, "and we'll go over it tomorrow."

Wilky was glad that he only had four more problems to solve. His stomach rumbled and grumbled. He could hardly wait to see what foods would be served in the cafeteria. He hoped it was something like red beans and rice with a spicy ackee fish like Granny Lou made.

After shoving the math book inside his desk, Wilky lined up behind Kenny. He looked around the room, hoping to get an up-close glimpse of Autumn. "Ouch!" he yelled suddenly when a bundle of his locs was yanked. The hard pull made his head lurch backward. Wilky touched the back of his head near the sore spot and turned around with an excruciating look of pain. Standing behind him was Trevor, a stocky boy who was a little big for his age. He wore an oversized red and black plaid shirt with baggy jeans. '*He looks like a lumberjack*,' Wilky thought.

On Trevor's face was a wicked and clownish grin, which he had completed by tailing it with a maniacal snicker. Bending low, he whispered in Wilky's ear, "You look like a little sissy in those dreadlock thingies." Wilky's eyes and mouth opened wide in dismay. For a dramatic moment, he felt shocked and discombobulated.

As the class snaked left and right down the halls toward the cafeteria and past the media center, the clinic, and the front office, Wilky wished he had thought to inform and educate Trevor right on the spot. He was willing to tutor free of charge whoever else was in earshot by starting with a quote from his Aunt Rachelle, '*From the perspective of the Haitian people, this style of hair, letting it grow naturally, is a connection to Africa and a rejection of western cultures' standard of beauty*.' Wilky followed in a line behind his peers, reflecting on a time when his father and grandfather engaged in folkloric storytelling at a festival. They informed the spellbound crowd, '*Use the word locs to describe your hair instead of dreads or dreadlocks*.' Papa Jesse preached to the captive gatherers, '*The origin of those terms goes far back to the slave trade when enslaved people couldn't groom their hair properly. They no longer had the time or access to the personal tools and cleaning solutions they were accustomed to. Enslavers would call their hair nauseating and 'dreadful', hence the word 'dreadlocks'.'*

Wilky was disappointed that his lunch choices consisted of only three entrees: a chicken Caesar salad, a vegetarian hot pocket, or something crumbly that looked like lumps of fried nuggets. The salad with two vegetable sides was the winning choice. Wilky spoke kindly to the cashier and told her his student number, which he had already memorized. He then walked quickly to sit next to Kenny and across from Jeremy after seeing this new crew gesturing wildly to get his attention. "These vegetables hardly have any taste to 'em," Wilky complained aloud after a few bites. He watched his new friends ravenously gnawing and swallowing their hard, round nuggets between big chocolate milk gulps. Wilky ate his salad and a few kernels of buttered corn and green beans. He listened as his classmates talked about new video games they had recently acquired or desired.

Wilky was really mad about the incident between him and Trevor. He knew Trevor was way too big to try and fight, and he had never been in a real brawl anyway. Wilky was confident that he would lose. His imagination began to get the best of him. What if Trevor learned to fight from one of his uncles, who was an ex-convict, and fought other inmates daily just to survive?

Back in Haiti, his best friends Endy and Marjon always had his back, and vice versa. They were like brothers, and he was already missing them, especially now. Everything was different, and Wilky knew that he'd have to figure out something fast, or his troubles would soon escalate. In some way, he'd have to devise a strategy and confront 'Trevor the Bully' all by himself. Wilky looked up and saw what must have been 4th graders filing into the cafeteria. Cristal was guided by a teacher to the food service line. He hoped her first day at school was going much better than his. "There's my sister," he pointed out to Jeremy and Kenny.

"Your sister is blind?"

"Yep," answered Wilky.

Kenny stated, "My great-grandfather went blind, and they gave him a cane. Is she gonna get one?" "

I think so," answered Wilky.

"Cool," Kenny and Jeremy responded in unison.

Wilky looked to his right, and Autumn and Brianna leaned forward at the other end of the lunch table. He heard giggles from several girls. '*What the heck was that all about?*' Wilky wondered.

Everyone's recess was held indoors due to a light rain shower. The students in Mrs. Collier's class voted to play a game, 'Heads Up, Seven Up,' in their room instead of watching thirty minutes of cartoons in the gym. However, Wilky was unfamiliar with the game and was happy to sit and watch. He thought it was funny when some of the boys thumped other boys hard on the back of their necks and then tapped their thumbs when Mrs. Collier wasn't looking.

On the third round, he decided to put his head down with his thumb up and eyes closed, too. Wilky thought it would be fun to try and guess the mystery person who'd tap him if he were fortunate enough to be picked. Luckily for him, his thumb was tapped, and he wasn't thumped hard on the back of his neck either. After hearing the refrain, 'Heads up, seven up,' Wilky stood for his turn to take a guess. He studied closely the faces of the remaining six classmates standing against the chalkboard. Wilky noticed them all unsuccessfully attempting a stoic, uninvolved look, trying not to give themselves away. He exercised logical deduction.

"Autumn?" Wilky inquired hopefully.

"Yes," she responded coyly.

Chapter Eighteen:
Introducing Cristal Shyana Duvernay

Mrs. Lovelady guided Cristal to her first academic class next door. When Cristal entered, Mrs. Tubilleja, her ELL and Social Studies teacher, was busy placing various magazines on the student desks. The teacher introduced herself and led Cristal to a little cubby area. "This is your personal space to place your books and other school items."

"Okay," Cristal replied. Mrs. Tubilleja bent over and used a hand-under-hand method to demonstrate to Cristal how to hang her backpack on a hook. Then, the teacher opened a door and indicated that Cristal could also place some other things there. "Ummm," Cristal said under her breath after smelling Mrs. Tubilleja's hair infused with the scent of green apple shampoo. Cristal was unaware that she made Mrs. Tubilleja blush.

The teacher placed her hand on the back of the chair and said, "Your desk is directly across from your cubby, okay?" Cristal understood her frame of reference.

"Yes, ma'am." Mrs. Tubilleja arranged for Cristal to sit adjacent to another student. Most of her students sat in pairs, and the others sat together at a round table.

Nevaeh, one of the more advanced English-speaking fifth-grade students, sat beside Cristal. The girls were given supplies: poster boards, bottles of glue, coarse-colored papers, pipe cleaners, foam shapes, and yarn. "I want you to create an interesting collage," directed Mrs. Tubilleja.

From the look on Cristal's face, it was apparent that she didn't quite understand the instructions, so Mrs. Tubilleja beckoned her young teacher intern, Ms. Camling. She was happy to assist the girls with their projects. Ms. Camling was a zealous and detail-oriented college student. She had already gained a lot from watching the interactions between the teachers of students with visual impairments in the VI resource class. In just one short week, Ms. Camling was inspired and wanted to learn all she could. She knew not to move, tug, or pull a person's hands in a surprising or unwelcoming manner. While speaking first using simple instructions, Ms. Camling gently touched Cristal's hand with scissors, positioning the blades closed and away.

"Can we use a little hamster grain and get pom-poms and popsicle sticks from the art drawer?" Nevaeh asked.

"Of course," answered Ms. Camling. Nevaeh hurried to obtain all the items she thought Cristal might like to put on her collage.

For the next thirty minutes, Nevaeh talked to Cristal in English and used only a few Spanish words. Ms. Camling encouraged Cristal to repeat the names of the items she used on her project. Cristal was happy to learn new English words on her first school day.

When the timer went off, Mrs. Tubilleja clapped her hands twice and strummed a xylophone. "Time for clean up." She walked over to Cristal and Nevaeh to examine their collages. "Bella, Bella! "Beautiful, Beautiful!" she commented. Cristal's smile was broad. With Ms. Camling's help, she carefully placed her artwork on a table in the back of the room and independently reversed the route to her desk. The following day, Ms. Camling showed Cristal that her artwork was displayed on the wall with other classmates.

Many other students sat on a large throw rug, chatting about the people in the magazines and creating a dialogue based on actions depicted in the pictures. Some sat on fake grass in a teacher-made tree house in the corner. They read from picture books.

"Please, everyone, return to your seats. Let's review our first dialogue-based lesson from last week. I want you to practice introducing yourselves to Cristal. Speak loud and clear," Mrs. Tubilleja instructed. "One at a time, I want you to walk up, shake her hand, and tell her your name. Next, tell her positive personal information about yourself, including where you were born. Then, tell Cristal your favorite food and anything else you want her to know about you."

Nevaeh was first and said, "Hi, my name is Nevaeh. I am from Guatemala. My favorite food is pork roast with vegetables. My favorite thing is swimming. I like school."

"My name is Alfredo. I am from El Salvador. My favorite food is ceviche. I play softball."

"My name is Elise. I was born in California. My favorite food is enchiladas. I like to play games with my little sister."

"My name is Joshua. I am from Myanmar. I like hto-hpu nwe and buthi kyaw. I play the trumpet."

"My name is Camille. I am from Mazatlán, Mexico. I like corn dogs. I am good at hula hoop and jump rope." Cristal was excited to get to know Camille because she was fond of jumping rope, too, and always wanted to learn how to hula hoop. When her cousin Mikaela got one for her birthday just days before Cristal moved to the United States, she never got to try it out.

When Yehoon stood and walked toward Cristal with a broad smile, and two projected front teeth, someone yelled, "Don't do it, Yehoon. Don't do it!" Yehoon avoided eye contact with Mrs. Tubilleja. Instead of reaching to shake Cristal's hand and proceed with the usual introductions, he announced, "My name is Yehoon. I am from South Korea. I like hamburgers with cheese." He extended his index and middle finger in a nanosecond and pressed them against his thumb. He flung his forearm towards Cristal's right ear to make a buzzing sound like an aggressive honeybee. "And I like to make sound effects," he said, chuckling.

The class roared with laughter as they watched Cristal jump and squirm - using both hands to try and bat away an invisible insect. "Not cool," Cristal responded sheepishly in English.

"Okay, Yehoon." Mrs. Tubilleja said calmly, "It's silent lunch today." Yehoon went out of his way to kick the tall rubber trashcan near the door before returning to his seat.

"It's silent lunch and no recess now," the teacher scolded.

"That should be just one warning. I was funnin' anyway," he responded in a ruffled tone.

Mrs. Tubilleja stood at her desk and walked to the behavior bulletin board titled 'Soaring High'. She removed Yehoon's decorative cardboard spaceship from the high troposphere layer for 'outstanding'. His rocket traveled past the exosphere layer to the 'carbon footprint', indicating a need for severe correction and disciplinary action. If it went beyond the crust of the earth's layer to the core, he'd have to spend the next day at in-school suspension. It was uncommon for any of Mrs. Tubilleja's students to behave obnoxiously and reach that low. If they were lucky enough to remain at the top of the ozone layer at the end of the day on Friday, her students could visit the giant jawbreaker machine that only cost a penny. Mrs. Tubilleja had to admit that she'd been fortunate to have an exceptional group of students over the past seven years.

One by one, Cristal's new classmates continued to greet her. There were so many that she worried she might not remember everyone's name or recognize their voices. Finally, it was time for an introduction of her own. Mrs. Tubilleja said, "Cristal, it's your turn." Her teacher walked over and waited a few seconds. She then repeated herself after gently touching Cristal on her shoulder. "Cristal, stand up and tell us a little about yourself."

With shaky legs and all, Cristal stood. She grabbed her fan from her purse and fanned for a few seconds. Tensed, Cristal clasped them together with the fingers on both hands and held them under her chin. It looked almost like she was praying.

"My name Cristal Duvernay from Croix-des-Bouquets, Haiti. I like perfumes. I like eating poule creole and fried bananas. I have a brother, Wilky."

Mrs. Tubilleja paused and then gave Cristal a circular rub on her back. "Excellent, Cristal. We are so glad you're here." Cristal's dimples dug deep when she took her seat. Mrs. Tubilleja handed out a sheet of paper. "Take this home to your parents. It is a notice asking them to permit you to bring in a personal item you value for an assignment on Friday."

Mrs. Tubilleja continued explaining to the entire class as she helped Cristal fold the paper in half and place it in her backpack's front pocket. "I would like everyone to bring in an item for 'Show and Tell'. For the next two days, you will be working on an informative paper explaining the object and how it is designed to be used. Please consider bringing in something that is a favorite hobby or pastime that you enjoy engaging in, something that has your hands busy." She further explained, "For example, if you like to play hockey, then bring a hockey stick. You would describe the hockey stick by explaining what it is made of and how it is shaped. Next, you would write how to hold it and how to use it to play the game of hockey. Now, I would like for those who were in my class last year to re-explain this assignment in more detail to others." A slight grumble ensued.

"Go ahead and break into groups and discuss this amongst yourselves. Share some of the items that you remember from last year. If you need more help from Ms. Camling or me, raise your hand." Collaboration with the teacher of students with visual impairments occurred during early morning planning on the specifics of the assignment for Cristal and other students with visual impairments.

Mrs. Tubilleja turned towards Cristal. "Cristal, you will get more instructions later from Ms. Saunders, your VI teacher."

Camille and another student named Gabriella hurried to Cristal's desk. "Can she and Nevaeh sit with us at the round table to talk about the assignment?"

"Sure, why not." Mrs. Tubilleja answered.

It was time for Social Studies. Ms. Camling instructed the students to get their books and turn to page eleven. "Cristal, the orientation and mobility specialist, will be here soon. You can sit and listen as the other read aloud," Mrs. Tubilleja told her. Not certain what to do with her hands after sitting still for about ten minutes listening to her classmates, Cristal walked a few short steps to her backpack and pulled out a 24-count box of scented crayons and other items that Aunt Nadine had sent for her tenth birthday.

She loved using them. By positioning a thin, bumpy mat underneath a sheet of paper, Cristal could feel and then smell her waxy doodles. With raised eyebrows, Ms. Camling and Mrs. Tubilleja glanced at each other. They were impressed with Cristal's decision to engage in an acceptable independent activity. For the next half hour, Cristal rested her chin in her left hand with an elbow propped on the desk. She doodled while listening.

After Social Studies, Mrs. Tubilleja asked Cristal to put her things away and listen with the rest of the class as she showed the second half of the movie Charlotte's Web on the overhead projector. Afterward, the students were expected to review animal vocabulary and simple nouns by completing a worksheet and writing sentences and questions about the movie. Cristal liked the lively music that accompanied the animated characters and tried her best to comprehend the characters' actions. At first, she thought she heard something about a spider and a pig talking in a barn, but she wasn't sure. It just didn't seem to make much sense.

Cristal's daydreams began transporting her back and forth from her present situation to her past life in Haiti. Unbelievable, she thought. I'm a real student sitting in a classroom with students who want to learn.

Suddenly and without warning, a sneeze like a circus elephant sickened with a bad case of the flu blasted through the room. "Achoo!... Achoo!... Achoo!"

"Eeeww, stop it! You sneezed on my neck," complained Alfredo as he wiped away the glob of snot.

Keyon managed to speak between two more grunting pig sounds, "Sorry." Everyone laughed, including Ms. Camling.

The classroom door swung open. "Mrs. Tubilleja, I'm so sorry I'm late! One of my students broke his roller tip, and I had to run to the parking lot and get one from my truck to fix it." Cristal's desk was so near the door that her nose got a big wind of a woodsy aromatic scent. In a more modulated voice, the visitor announced, "I'm here to meet with Cristal Duvernay." Cristal was startled when the man spoke her name.

"Oh, yes. Good morning, Mr. Nick." Mrs. Tubilleja walked over and stood beside Cristal's desk.

"Cristal, Mr. Nick is here for you." She touched Cristal's arm, and when she stood, Mrs. Tubilleja draped Cristal's arm around hers and led her to the door. One of Mrs. Tubilleja's former students, Tiara Ayusar, stood waiting patiently in the hall. She was a 4th-grader from Gabon, Africa. Mrs. Tubilleja was happy that Tiara's teacher had released her from class to join Cristal and Mr. Nick's first lesson.

When Tiara first arrived in the United States two years ago, she primarily spoke French. She now speaks English well enough to no longer require direct instruction from Mrs. Tubilleja. Tiara was an ambitious student when she was in the ELL class. After she reviewed the enrollment papers that Cristal's mother had completed, Mrs. Tubilleja got the idea to mention to Mr. Nick about perhaps including Tiara in a few initial O&M lessons with Cristal. She hoped the girls might make a great connection in the process. The teacher drew from her training while pursuing a master's degree in Linguistics that Haitian Creole and the French language were quite similar. It was a plus that the girls were the same age.

Mr. Nick politely introduced himself in the hallway, articulating each word slowly. "I am an orientation and mobility specialist. I will teach you how to travel safely, efficiently, and as independently as possible to important places in the school and outdoors." Cristal smiled. Although she didn't clearly understand everything he said, Cristal knew he would help her travel. She liked the tone of his voice, and his breath smelled like spearmint.

Ms. Camling asked Tiara if she could try to explain to Cristal what Mr. Nick had said. "Yes, ma'am," said Tiara. She turned to Cristal and said, "*Yo apprendre à marcher en toute sécurité.*" In English translation, Tiara said, "He will teach you to walk safely."

Cristal's heart instantly felt relief and was filled with insurmountable delight. Wiggly fingers and a rocking shift in her weight let Mr. Nick know that Cristal was ready and excited to learn something new. He said, "First, I will teach you how to travel between Mrs. Tubilleja's class and the restroom. Then, I will teach you how to get from Mrs. Tubilleja's class to the Vision Resource room, where Ms. Saunders will provide instruction in braille and technology."

Tiara did her best to translate for the next hour. They began with Mr. Nick teaching a hand-over-hand method to introduce the skill of trailing the wall. He placed the back of Cristal's right hand against the wall in a forward position from her waist. He then used verbal and physical prompts to get her to bend her left arm and hand in front to protect her face. She walked several yards using this method until she reached a fire extinguisher. He emphasized the words "fire extinguisher" and asked Tiara to explain to Cristal that it is used to put out fires.

"Elle est utilisée pour éteindre les incendies," said Tiara.

"Aaahhh...yes," said Cristal.

Mr. Nick then proceeded to teach Cristal how to 'square off' by placing her back against the wall to establish a straight line of travel across the hall. Cristal crossed the hall safely and located a water fountain. She trailed to the girl's restroom. Mr. Nick asked Tiara to follow Cristal inside the bathroom and watch her familiarize herself by hand trailing the walls to locate the stall, sink, and hand dryers. "Make sure she washes her hands on the way out!"

The last O&M skill for the day was to teach Cristal how to travel using the basic human guide technique. Tiara had seen other children travel the halls using this skill, but never had she gotten the opportunity to lead another student. She felt proud that she was selected out of all the other kids in her 4th-grade classroom to be the first to assist someone this school year. Mr. Nick directed the pair to walk from the top of Stairwell B to the main office.

"C'est un parcours facile à retenir," said Cristal.

"What did she say," implored Mr. Nick anxiously.

"She said that that was an easy route to remember," Tiara repeated in English.

Cristal continued, "C'est un parcours qu'un chevalier voyagerait sur un échiquier."

Tiara looked a little puzzled, "I think she said something like that was a voyage for the knight in chess."

Mr. Nick was astonished, "What?" he asked with excitement. "She's absolutely right! That's called an 'L' route. Travel straight and then make one turn to the right or left." Mr. Nick was impressed. He looked at Tiara and said, "Do you play chess?"

Tiara answered, "No, I don't know how to play."

With a chuckle of embarrassment, Mr. Nick responded, "I'm sorry, but would you ask Cristal if she plays chess?"

Cristal replied, "Ummm, no. Je sais pas comment les morceaux se déplacent que. Mon grand-père m'a appris un an avant sa mort."

Tiara translated once more, "She doesn't know how to play, but before her grandfather died, he taught her how all the pieces move on the board." Mr. Nick nodded his head in approval.

"Cristal, I'm going to use my finger to draw a route on your back, and I want you to tell me what chess piece would travel in that manner." Mr. Nick drew an invisible diagonal line on Cristal's back from her left shoulder down towards her right side.

"Bishop," Cristal answered.

"Fantastic!" Mr. Nick declared. He watched as Tiara and Cristal traveled using the human guide method to the vision resource room. Mr. Nick introduced Cristal to Ms. Saunders, her teacher of the visually impaired, and prepared to leave.

"I'll see you tomorrow, Cristal." Mr. Nick and Tiara then turned down the hall and walked away.

Cristal called out before they parted to their respective places. "Thank you, Mr. Nick. Thank you, Tiara."

Those two felt oddly moved and lucky that they had the opportunity to meet Cristal Shyana Duvernay.

Chapter Nineteen:
Better Tomorrows

For the current school year, all announcements at the end of the day began with the song 'Tomorrow - A Better You, A Better Me' by Tevin Campbell. It was a comforting auditory prompt for teachers to wrap up their final lesson. Students would then start packing their belongings and prepare for bus numbers to be called. After reminders of upcoming events and forms needing to be signed and returned, Mr. Macklberg gave final directives for the day. "Complete your homework. Stay safe. Get plenty of sleep, and I'll see you tomorrow."

Although the assistant principal was new to the school, he was among the campus's most popular and favored staff members. From the students' perspective, he was a kind and inspirational role model. The staff respected Mr. Macklberg's integrity, gratitude, and overall vision for the school.

Dahlia stood outside the gates of the Willow Wood Townhomes with other parents, waiting for the Garland school bus #317 to deliver their precious cargo. "How was the first day of school?" she asked after bear-hugging her two little ones. Wilky hugged her tightly but didn't purposely mean to ignore his mother's question. He was intent on hearing a detailed explanation from Jeremy about a 'Back to School' scavenger hunt activity planned by parents at their clubhouse next week.

"Mommy, I love school. I am a student now. My teachers are so nice, especially my VI teacher, Ms. Saunders. She smells like sugar doughnuts. She showed me all of this electric stuff that's made for people who can't see. She will teach me how to use a tablet that talks and a braille thing that I can carry around my neck to read and do my homework. Mommy, did you know that the braille code was invented so that people who can't see could learn to read the bible?"

"No, I didn't," Dahlia interjected once Cristal took a couple of breaths.

The Duvernay triad stepped inside the house and into the kitchen, where Dahlia again donned her apron. She stirred the pot of stew minus the plantains and nutty-flavored malanga.

Raeni could be heard upstairs playing her cello. She was practicing a music score for the contemporary musical, 'The Addams Family'. It was one of two productions that the high school drama students would perform this school year. Raeni, the first chair cellist, was selected to play with other orchestra members in the pit. The classic 'Hello Dolly' musical will be performed in the spring.

"Don't disturb her right now; wait until she stops." directed Dahlia.

"Okay, Mommy, Here's a note from my teacher. I think you have to sign it."

Cristal unfolded the permission slip and handed it to Dahlia. Wilky gave her a pen from his backpack and handed her the yellow envelope about the Cobra Clubs. "I want to join the after-school Lego club. Can I?"

Cristal forgot about that envelope and gave hers to her mother, too. "At lunchtime, I sat with my new friend Tiara, who is from Africa and can speak a lot of French. Another girl named Ivanna from Ukraine speaks Ukrainian. I'm going to find out what clubs they will join."

Dahlia looked briefly at the paperwork and decided to review everything in detail later. She wondered if there was a cost for the after-school programs. Regardless, Dahlia knew she'd pay for it because her children deserved it after being uprooted from their homes and friends so abruptly.

"Let me look everything over, and I'll let you know tomorrow."

"Okay," chimed Wilky and Cristal. Dahlia wished that Jesse was there to see the look of complete joy on their daughter's face. It was a happy moment enveloped in her feelings of sadness. Perhaps Cristal's future would hold great promise as Granny Lou and her husband predicted.

Dahlia shuddered, thinking about the maniacal conversation she had with Zoe – suggesting that she and her baby girl travel a great distance away from home to beg for money in the crowded Dajabón market near the border of Haiti. A pang of guilt showered over her. "Come give me another hug, baby. I'm glad you are happy." Cristal wrapped her arms tightly around her mother's waist and then headed to her bedroom to share her joy with Raeni. Once the music stopped, she could hardly wait to tell her cousin she recognized the fragrance, '*First*', on a lady at her school.

After noticing Wilky's somber mood and unusual silence, Dahlia asked a question. "Tell me about your first day?"

Wilky was about to climb the stairs, drop his backpack, and plop in front of the TV. He didn't even look her way, "It was okay," he stated in a laidback manner. He hoped she wouldn't probe anymore.

"Just okay?" his mother asked. "Did you make some new friends? Do you like your teacher?" Dahlia continued to investigate.

"Yes, ma'am, Mrs. Collier is nice. She's a real short lady. She looks kinda like a Ti Kók, but she's cool."

Dahlia tried to contain a chuckle. "That's not nice to say your teacher looks like a bird."

Wilky chose not to tell his mother about his worries stemming from Trevor, the tyrant. He figured her best motherly advice would be for him to reveal the events to his teacher. She might otherwise say, 'ignore the bully and walk away'. Neither response would provide the best option or solution for dealing with Trevor. 'Mothers don't understand what it's like to be a smaller boy that a bigger person bullies,' Wilky conjectured. He was prepared to go low, real low and deep, in the Georgia red clay. Without being told, he unzipped his backpack and pulled out his math book at the kitchen table.

Nevertheless, he wanted to be near his mother but not bother her with his troubles. Wilky finished his four problems and then dashed upstairs to watch TV. He knocked, waited for the correct verbal response, and then poked his head in to say hello to Raeni before plopping down on the sofa. After spending several minutes searching for a remote deeply embedded between cushions, Wilky clicked on the TV. He hoped to find the Three Stooges because he wanted to laugh excessively and temporarily escape his anxieties and fears.

"I just got a call from Isaac, and he's going to be late," Nadine proclaimed to no one in particular. "He said we should go ahead and start dinner without him." One at a time, Raeni, Cristal, and Wilky went to the bathroom to wash their hands before bouncing downstairs and seating themselves at the table.

"I hope you all like the Joumou soup and cornbread," said Dahlia, "I didn't have all the items I needed to make it like I wanted. Hopefully, the alternate ingredients don't compromise the taste too much."

Nadine led grace and asked to bless the cook for the time spent in the kitchen preparing dinner. "It feels good to get off from work and come home to a nice meal made from scratch for a change."

"Ummm...this is delicious, Aunt Dahlia." Raeni slurped and scooped another big mouthful of the chunky potatoes, beef, squash, and other warm vegetables on her spoon.

"It sure is," said Nadine after a double bite of the jalapeno cornbread. "I know you want to start working somewhere soon," she said through a mouthful. "So, I'll be sure to ask around at work tomorrow to see if my coworkers know of any place that's hiring. What kind of work would you be interested in?"

"I don't know, but some place where I don't have to walk far to get there, especially not in this hot and sweltering southern heat."

Because Uncle Isaac wasn't at the table, Cristal spoke primarily in Haitian Creole. She didn't want to be rude, but for his and Raeni's sake, whenever they were present, Cristal used English words and phrases when plausible.

"I had a chicken Caesar salad for lunch. What did you eat, Wilky?" asked Cristal.

"Some nasty nuggets. That food tastes weak," replied Wilky. "Momma, can I take a small bottle of hot sauce to school with me? I can keep it in my backpack until lunchtime." Nadine and Dahlia chuckled.

"Sure, baby," his mother replied.

"Oh yeah, when I went through the lunch line, the lady at the register saw my t-shirt and asked if I was from Haiti. I told her, yes that I was from Croix-des-Bouquets commune. She said she lived in Port-au-Prince about fifteen years ago. And when I gave her my student ID number and my name popped up on her computer, she told me that she knows some Duvernays," shared Wilky matter-of-factly.

"What? Really?" Dahlia asked excitedly, "What's her name?"

Wilky took a long, tall drink of fruity red punch and replied, "Her name tag said Mrs. Plaizill."

"Hmmm…" said Dahlia, "I don't know anyone by that name."

"It sounds a little familiar to me, but I can't place anybody in my head," Nadine said.

"Oh, Momma," said Cristal, "my teacher, Mrs. Tubilleja, wants everyone's parents to sign up on a calendar to bring one of their favorite foods to share with the class on different Fridays during the year. The students get to ask questions about the meal and cultural traditions during interviews with the parents. Mrs. Tubilleja said she would send home more information about it. Can you come, and will you make some shrimp, Boulet?"

"I guess so," Dahlia answered with a little less enthusiasm than Cristal had expected.

"Raeni, how would you rate your school day on a scale from one to ten?" This question, amongst others, was part of a ritual that Isaac and Nadine started two years ago. Their intentions weren't to interrogate Raeni, but they were committed to keeping a finger on her pulse to ensure she was doing okay. They also engaged her by sharing snippets from their workday.

"I would rate it an eight." Raeni had a history class with Daxton this school year, but they sat on opposite sides of the room. He did manage to say 'hi' once the bell rang when they transitioned to their next class.

Nadine continued with the upbeat questioning, "Did you say thank you to anyone, and was there something interesting you learned today?"

"I did thank my psychology teacher for allowing me to come by at the end of her lunch hour to clarify a project. We have to create an edutainment board game that can reunite families and friends around the table once again for enjoyment. She said that families need to participate in meaningful connections that don't include electronics or social media."

"I like that idea. Let me know if you need some help with that project. It sounds like fun."

"Okay. And I got some new music in orchestra class. Right now, I'm learning to play 'Elegance' for the Hello Dolly theatre play."

"That's nice. I'm looking forward to seeing that production and hearing you play your cello."

"Thanks, MaDine."

"What about you, Wilky? How would you rate your day and tell us something you learned?"

Wilky hesitated, "I'd rate my day a five, and I learned that a 'bat in the cave' means that there's a big ugly booger in your nose." Raeni and Cristal burst out laughing. Nadine wasn't expecting anything like that for a reply.

Dahlia jumped in, "That's silly. Don't say things like that at the table. And why would you rate your day a five out of ten?"

Hesitant to tell the whole truth, Wilky answered, "I'm just not sure everybody likes me, that's all."

"Well, give it time, Wilky. It's only your first day. I expect you and Cristal to always be kinder than necessary to others, but I also want you to develop the courage to be disliked. Once you do, you will find yourself in life's winning lane."

Wilky shrugged, not fully understanding the last comment. "Yes, ma'am."

"Cristal, how would you rate your day?" asked Nadine in Haitian Creole. A more mature answer she expected from her young niece.

"Today was a terrific ten." Dahlia smiled at her daughter's choice of alliteration. "I learned that the little bumps on paper are for reading and writing in braille. My science teacher, Ms. Lovelady, told me it takes about 200 pounds of lavender flowers to make, I think, a pound of oil. I told her I like flowers, and the smell of lavender was one of my favorites. My friend Tiara is in that class, but not my VI class, and she likes flowers too."

"What happened?" asked Raeni. Wilky willingly translated for her.

"Cristal, don't forget to speak in English to the best of your ability when seated at the table," reminded Dahlia.

"Yes, ma'am."

Conversations continued between bites of the tasteful stew and cornbread. Raeni, Wilky, and Cristal shared more details about parts of their school day as Dahlia and Nadine engaged in adult discussions about stories from the local news. Sudoku clung to the bars at the top corner of his cage with his beak and feet, waiting to hear relatable conversations. Soon after that was the outburst, "Five alive, local news that changes lives, and that's no jive! Five alive…"

Just as everyone finished the scrumptious supper, the phone rang. It was Jesse. He had called only once since his family had moved away. It was costly to call more frequently, and his wife understood why her husband wanted to check on everyone, especially today. He needed to hear their voices. Dahlia stepped away from the table to speak to her husband in private. Several moments passed before Cristal and Wilky could talk to their father.

"Hey, Sweet Pea, I miss you."

"I miss you too, Daddy!" Cristal exclaimed, "I like school. My teachers are really nice," she conveyed with abundant vitality.

"Did you meet other students who can't see?" he asked.

"Yes, sir. I met two students in my grade and three in the fifth grade who are blind. They know how to read and write in braille, use a computer that talks, and do a lot of other stuff."

"That's wonderful," replied Papa Jesse. "Did you get a new walking stick?"

"Not yet. My O&M teacher, Mr. Nick, said he would teach me how to use a cane to get around. I think it's like a long metal or plastic thing or something."

Her father was relieved that his dreams for Cristal were being fulfilled. Based on the enthusiasm in her voice, he could tell that he had made the right decision – at least for her. "That's real good, baby. I love you; now, put your brother on the phone."

Before she handed Wilky the phone, Cristal had one more thing to tell her father: "I love you, Daddy. I met a girl who speaks French. I think she really wants to be my friend, and she can see." Cristal continued, barely stopping to catch her breath. "Her name is Tiara, and she's from Africa. She sat with me at lunch today."

"I'm glad, Cristal. I knew you would be able to make friends in no time. You're a sweet girl."

Wilky grabbed the phone, "Hi, Daddy, when are you coming here?"

"Hey, my lil' man, it's gonna be a while, but tell me how things are going. How was the first day at your new school?" For privacy, Wilky walked out onto the patio where Sudoku fanatically gnawed on a woven palm leaf. "I like my teacher, Mrs. Collier. She seems nice, but…." Wilky wasn't sure if he should tell his father about Trevor.

"What is it, son? What's wrong?" Like most good parents, Wilky's papa could easily detect the presence of misery in his child's voice.

"There's a boy in my class trying to bully me," Wilky quivered, "and he's much bigger than me." His father's heart sank. Jesse wanted to be there to talk to Wilky face to face, protect him, and rescue him from harm.

"Did he hit you?" he asked. Wilky hesitated to answer.

"Well, no, he just yanked my hair hard, but it only hurt a little."

Exasperated, his father responded, "Talk to me, son. What is his name?"

Wilky wanted to cry but refused. "His name is Trevor, and I don't know why he started picking on me. He's like a big, thawed-out caveman," he whimpered.

Sudoku sat on his swing, listening and pecking at a round dangling mirror. "Hello, how was your day? How was your day? Same old, same old. Good. How was your day?" The African grey parrot had lousy timing. Wilky decided against rattling the stubborn bird's cage to shut him up because he feared the creature would tattle-tale.

"Who was that?" questioned Papa Jesse.

"Oh, that's Raeni's parrot. He can talk."

"They have a bird living in the house?"

"Yes, he's in a cage, and I'm in the sunroom.

"His name is Sudoku."

"Anyway," Papa Jesse continued with a sigh of frustration. He was committed to conveying sage advice, "A person is more than one thing, Wilky. There's no telling what makes someone decide to act out in anger. Perhaps things aren't going so well at his home. But that is not an excuse to be mean to others. Usually, a hapless bully will pick on a person because they think they are weak or believe that a person is better than them in some way. Sometimes, they don't like how others love or admire another person. It's called envy, and the only way that they think they will feel better about themselves is by bringing a person down to their level. You understand?"

"Yes, sir. Were you ever bullied when you were a little boy in school?"

Papa Jesse confessed, "Well, yes. I did get into a few fights. I was teased and bullied some." Wilky knew his father sometimes stammered when he spoke, but it only happened when he was nervous. It wasn't that bad, he believed. Wilky couldn't imagine someone even attempting to make fun of his father. His Papa Jesse was a kind and generous man. His friends Endy and Marjon loved him like an uncle. Jesse continued, "After we had to go live with Momma Louise and Papa Will, times were bad. We were poor, but they did their best to raise us on meager earnings. As a teenager, my clothes were shabby hand-me-downs, and my shoes usually had holes in their soles, and they always seemed too big or too small. Other kids gave me a hard time for that, at least up until I grew taller and put on a little weight."

Wilky knew he and Cristal weren't rich kids, but he never considered them to be poor, either. They had clean clothes and even more toys and stuff than Marjon or Endy ever had. He recalled the Christmas before the quake when he got a video hand game, and Cristal received a music box with a dancing ballerina on top. Delicious meals that included desserts were served every day in the Duvernay household. Wilky couldn't imagine going to his private school with shoes that were too big or shoes with busted soles.

Jesse had the desire to go into a little more detail with the father-and-son conversation. "Momma Louise and Papa Will did spend a little more money on clothes for your Aunt Rachelle and Aunt Nadine. My sisters looked just as nice as the other girls in school," he said proudly. Jesse thought about a few boys he had a scuffle or two with for coming after his sisters and chuckled under his breath, feeling no need to share those times with Wilky. "As we grew older, we became happy and content with the love that was shown. And there was always good food on the table. It wasn't until I learned to fix things for other people and build things with my own hands that I gained respect because I had earned enough money to better myself. It turned out that I was doing better than many of those boys who used to give me a hard time."

"Wow, Daddy. I didn't know that." This was the first serious conversation Wilky ever really had with his father. He had quieted and positioned himself now to listen because he missed being in his presence.

"Yep. I saved the money I earned from working hard jobs by purchasing this nice little home for your mother and me. Your mom is a blessing. She's a smart woman. One day, after a trip to the market, she returned home with an idea for us to buy the goats and chickens for extra income. And that community garden was her idea."

Wilky never considered what his mother and father's life was like before he was born. He remembered hearing the sad story about his grandparents' death from smoke inhalation while they slept. By the time neighbors came to rescue Papa Jesse's parents from the burning house, it was too late. Wilky remembered overhearing Aunt Rachelle talk about how it was a miracle that she and her siblings were not home then.

The school was out, and they had begged their parents to let them stay miles away with Granny Lou and Papa Will for the first two weeks of summer. They loved going fishing with them, picking berries, and making homemade ice cream. Had it not been for their little vacation away from home, they might have also met their demise. Wilky knew his father as a hard-working and God-fearing man. His Papa Jesse prayed at the dinner table and before going to bed. Still, like most children Wilky's age, he took a lot of things for granted.

"Listen to me, son, I never, ever want you to start a fight. Your mother and I are raising you and your sister to be good people. What I want you to do is use your head. You are an intelligent boy, and I know you don't want to tell your teacher, but if he hits you again, do not accept his anger. You must defend yourself. If he hurts you and there is no adult around, do not run because that could make things worse later. Do you understand?"

"Okay, yes," said Wilky through sniffles.

"Wilky, you don't have to be tall to bring down a giant or a bully. Do you remember the story of David and Goliath from your Sunday school class?"

"I think so."

"David was able to slay Goliath, the giant, with only six stones and a slingshot."

Wilky interrupted, "But I don't know how to use a slingshot, Daddy, and I won't be able to learn before tomorrow. I wish you were here," Wilky confessed.

"Wilky," his father spoke sternly, "use your strength. Use your brain first; if you must, then use those strong legs to swivel and kick him in his knees. It will drop this boy Trevor down to the ground instantly and put him in a great amount of pain. Do you hear what I'm telling you?" Before Wilky could answer, his father continued his directives, "Then you yell, stop it right now! And don't you ever put your hands on me again!" There was a moment of silence.

"Okay, Daddy. I understand. I can do that." Jesse could only pray that his son, at one of the worst moments of his young life, would be covered by the grace of God.

"Alright, I've got to go now. Keep an eye out at school and look out for your sister. I will call you next week. I love you, son."

A reluctant tear dropped from Wilky's eye, "I love you too, Daddy. Kiss Granny Lou for me and Cheerio, too."

His father laughed, "I'm not kissing that mutt. Now, put your mother back on the phone for me."

Wilky chuckled.

Jesse wanted to share two additional fragments of information with Dahlia. "Rachelle and Mikaela will be moving in next week. Rachelle said it's just temporary."

"That will be good," Dahlia responded. "I'm sure it will save her a little money and help Momma Lou out when it comes to getting a few things done around the house."

"Yeah," uttered Jesse before clearing his throat. "Momma Lou had a few choice words for your friend Zoe before running her away from here for the second time."

"Why? What happened?" asked Dahlia.

"Well," Jesse hesitated, "She dropped off some baked goods and said y'all exchanged a couple of recipes a while back but didn't think you had a chance to fix them for me before you left. She said she wanted to do something to lift my spirits and put a smile on my face since you're not around."

Dahlia's jaw dropped. After saying her goodbyes to her husband, she remained stunned and hurt for quite some time.

No one was aware of the conversation that occurred between Aunt Rachelle and Zoe at the market the day that followed Zoe's unanswered flirtation. Dahlia's sister-in-law's verbal sparring cut like a sharp and jagged knife into Zoe's wicked being without drawing a drop of blood. "Your behavior is repulsive and despicable. Go find a man of your own! You were supposed to be Dahlia's best friend, but you're really nothing more than a hideous, ghostly-looking snake in the grass! Stay away from my brother!" Rachelle concluded in a threatening tone.

Until dusk, Wilky remained in the sunroom playing and talking to Sudoku, averting attention away from his problem. He knew that at some point, he'd have to pivot quickly to a solution. Wilky fed the hangry bird a few pieces of dried fruit and a couple of live millipedes. He tried to get the beautiful bird to talk, but it made only random sputtering noises and a few high-shrilled whistling sounds. And then Wilky got an idea – a perfect solution to his problem. He rushed back through the sliding doors and ran into the kitchen. Everyone else had gone to their rooms to relax, read, or watch TV. Wilky quietly opened and shut several cabinet doors and pulled a chair out from the table. He stood on top to search other areas for a small plastic bag or a little container. Once found, he rushed back out on the patio. *"Maybe tomorrow won't be such a bad day after all,"* he predicted.

Chapter Twenty:
Tap, Tap, Twirl

The student teacher greeted Cristal once she and Wilky stepped off a bus with other students from their neighborhood.

"Hi, Cristal. It's Ms. Camling. I'll meet you at your morning bus and guide you to Ms. Lovelady's class for the next few days or at least until you learn the route yourself."

Cristal softly replied, "Good morning, Ms. Camling."

Ms. Camling then tapped the back of Cristal's hand with the back of her own. Just as Mr. Nick, the O&M Specialist, had instructed her, Cristal slid her hand up Ms. Camling's arm and held her above her elbow.

"See you later, Cristal Shy," said Wilky as he and Jeremy headed into the building.

"Bye, Willie Wonka."

After the announcements, Mrs. Tubilleja stood at the door and cheerfully acknowledged her students by name. Almost every student entered the class with these items:

- Sculpted artwork
- Board games
- Sporting equipment
- Expensive electronic gadgets
- Musical instruments

- Styrofoam wig heads with neon pink and green synthetic hair, and more…

"Place the items in your cubby or on the back table if they're too large. Make sure your name is written or taped on the item," she instructed.

Cristal entered with a medium round red and black plaid carrying case that Nadine had given her. It was an old make-up tote that Nadine told Raeni to take from the back of her closet. It was just perfect for Cristal to store most of the items she used to make her perfumes.

Mrs. Tubilleja was curious about what was inside the smart-looking case but didn't ask.

"Good morning, Cristal."

Cristal released her grip from Ms. Camling's arm and greeted her teacher appropriately.

"Good morning, Mrs. Tubilleja."

"Place your item on the rectangular table along the wall in the back. Do you need some help?"

"No, ma'am. I can do it." With the back of her right hand, as Mr. Nick had instructed, Cristal systematically trailed the wall to reach her destination. She placed her make-up case on the table, reversed directions, and trailed the wall past the cubbies to square off the wall. Then she took a few steps to her desk and waited eagerly for another school day to begin. It was mandatory as part of the university standards for Ms. Camling, the young student teacher, to introduce at least three daily lessons to Cristal under Mrs. Tubilleja's supervision.

As Ms. Camling stood in front of the class, her voice was weak and scratchy. It cracked when she called for everyone's attention. Successfully, Ms. Camling announced the language arts objective for the day without a misstep. A few students ignored her requests to stop talking and continued chattering amongst themselves. They didn't realize Ms. Camling was the 'teacher' of the hour. Ms. Camling cleared her throat twice, but Mrs. Tubilleja used a louder-than-normal tone and began counting 'one-two-three'. She stepped to the corner of her desk, picked up a wooden mallet, and strummed a musical scale on her prized xylophone. It was a hand-carved souvenir purchased years ago on a trip to Brazil.

Mrs. Tubilleja pointed to the class rules posted by the door, which were established and discussed on the first day of class, and she issued a verbal reminder, "Remember rule number four, class. Anyone talking after hearing the musical scale of the xylophone will receive one verbal warning before dropping their rocket on the behavior board." Everyone hushed at the second strumming of the melodic percussion instrument. Ms. Camling proceeded to teach a language arts lesson on past, present, and future verb tenses.

Later, during independent work, Mrs. Tubilleja directed Cristal to join her at one of the computer tables near the back of the room. She opened a CD case and took out one of the fifteen disks. Cristal could feel the disk and used a hand-under-hand method to feel Mrs. Tubilleja's hand insert it into the computer disk drive. Then her teacher whispered low into Cristal's ear, "Cristal, I'd like you to listen to something." She presented Cristal with headphones and prompted her to place them over her ears. Mrs. Tubilleja put dual headphones over her own ears so they could listen simultaneously. Cristal had never used a computer before and had no idea what to expect. However, once the audio began, she was captivated by a conversation between two girls speaking amongst themselves in Haitian Creole. The discussion was immediately translated into English.

Mrs. Tubilleja taught Cristal how to turn the volume up or down and stop, pause, and rewind the CD. Cristal learned quickly. She listened intensely to two lessons for the next thirty minutes and played each lesson twice. Lesson One was 'Everyday Greetings and Introductions'. Lesson number two was 'Small Talk About the Weather'. Mrs. Tubilleja had Cristal practice the exact dialogue with her. Cristal's face beamed when she understood the words and could repeat the conversation. Mrs. Tubilleja felt blessed to receive the loaner set of CDs from a colleague who taught at the nearby university.

"Take this home with you and practice every night. Your mother indicated on the enrollment form that you have a computer at home." Mrs. Tubilleja handed Cristal a single disk in a case of its own along with a headset.

"Yes, ma'am."

Later that morning, Mr. Nick arrived with a long cane precisely the right size for Cristal. It measured 44" from her sternum to the floor. This new mobility tool was prescribed to equal two of Cristal's stride lengths and would provide her with enough information to react and avoid making body contact with large objects below her waist. Instead of Tiara, a student named Blaise was there to interpret for Cristal in French if needed. Mr. Nick continued to explain with verbal and partial physical cues.

"The cane will do three things: provide some measure of protection from obstacles at waist level and below, including drop-offs like a curb or stairs. It will provide information about things you may encounter with the cane based on sound or textured changes in terrain. Lastly, the red tape at the bottom of this long white cane helps to identify you as a person with blindness." Then Mr. Nick introduced the cane parts: *strap, grip, shaft, and tip.*

Cristal was required to repeat the names after exploring each piece. She thought that the tip felt like a hard marshmallow.

"You're right," said Mr. Nick, "It's called a marshmallow tip!"

Cristal liked it. It was very different from Lila, her old walking stick. She didn't have to worry about splinters, and the new cane was much lighter than the heavy stick she'd gotten used to in Haiti. The best part was that it folded, too. *'Maybe my wrist and fingers won't hurt as much holding this.'* Initially, Cristal named her new cane Blossom because she liked the sound and meaning of the name. However, later that evening, she showed Raeni her new device, and Raeni suggested a different name that was more applicable.

"Name it 'Jurnee' because this cane will help you travel to many places all around Georgia as well as other places in the world." Years later, when they were young adults, Cristal told Raeni that that was one of the sweetest, most inspirational things someone had ever said to her.

"Don't spell it J-O-U-R-N-E-Y; spell it like that young and pretty actress spells her name," Raeni advised.

"Okay," agreed Cristal. Blaise was expected to return to class after thirty minutes. He said goodbye to Cristal and Mr. Macklberg.

"Thank you," said Cristal. "I like your name," Cristal told the fifth grader.

"Thanks."

She then turned to her O&M Specialist, "Tiara's coming?"

"No, not for today's lesson. I think you will see her later at lunch. I've got a surprise I want to share with you."

On the previous night, Mr. Nick had paid a small fee from his personal funds to purchase a translation app on his smartphone. Every time he spoke, an automatic translation was created to produce speech in the Haitian-Creole language, and it worked in e-verse as well. Cristal was excited all over again. Mr. Nick began the lesson by reviewing the human guide travel. His hairy arm felt odd to Cristal. She imagined that hair grew all over his face. Later at lunch, Cristal asked Tiara if Mr. Nick had a hairy face.

"You mean like a werewolf? Nahhh." The girls laughed. Cristal told Tiara that she liked Mr. Nick's cologne, one with an aromatic tobacco scent mixed with cedar.

For part of the remaining lesson, Mr. Nick taught her how to use the diagonal cane technique so that she could safely move around inside the school building. They eventually took a break from walking the halls and sat in the media center to work on a tactile map. Cristal liked pulling the different shapes of Velcro pieces off the board and placing them along straight 'I' routes and 'L' routes. She understood that a circle, triangle, or rectangle could be an abstract symbol used to represent landmarks like the water fountain, bench, pencil machine, and trophy case along a given route. Cristal could tell that Mr. Nick was an outstanding orientation and mobility specialist. He talked with a lot of energy and asked simple questions using the translation program. She was learning a lot about how to move her body safely and gracefully in the school environment. The specialist requested that Cristal repeat each technique's name and that she demonstrate the skills and associated verbiage at least twice before moving on.

Mr. Nick summarized what they worked on at the end of the hour and told her what to expect for the next day's lesson. "I wrote a book called *The ABCs of O&M*. One of the lessons is '*The Environmental Alphabet*.' Whenever you encounter an obstacle, landmark, or important location, I will introduce its name. It may even be a nontangible concept that I'd like you to learn. Whatever it may be, we will eventually have to check off every alphabet letter by the end of the school year. And it doesn't necessarily have to be in order. Environments we travel in are often not considered organized and tidy."

The translation was long and seemed to garble or misinterpret some phrasing. Cristal's perplexed look prompted Mr. Nick to give better examples. *A* could be for the Art room, *B* for the bathroom, *C* for the Cafeteria, and *D* for Dr. Martin's office. Cristal now understood what to expect for the next day's lesson. Tomorrow's lesson, Mr. Nick decided, would be more pleasurable for Cristal if another O&M student could join them.

The day's lesson with Mr. Nick ended when Cristal traveled before him, walking the 'L' route from Mrs. Tubilleja's class to Ms. Saunders's VI room.

"I'm proud of you, Cristal," he announced when she arrived at her destination. "You are a quick learner and a smart traveler."

Without his app in play mode, Cristal knew he was complimenting her by the tone and inflections in his voice. Last night, she did role-play using greetings and common phrases in English with Wilky and her mother.

"Mr. Nick. You are a good teacher." He grinned and did a little Texas two-step shuffle before returning to his office.

When Cristal entered Ms. Saunders's classroom, two other students with visual impairments were receiving training on an electronic braille tablet. Ms. Saunders stopped her instruction and greeted Cristal. She asked Kaylan and Ciara to stand and introduce themselves. The two students extended their hands to shake Cristal's hand. Ms. Saunders touched Cristal on her elbow and prompted her to extend her hand to shake theirs. Cristal did her best to recall translation lesson number one and introduce herself properly.

"Hello, my name is Cristal Duvernay. It is nice to meet you, Kaylan. It is nice to meet you, Ciara. Isn't the weather nice today?" Cristal asked.

"Uhhh, yeah," Ciara answered with little knowledge of conversational threads often used to spark conversations with a stranger.

"Wow, your hands are rough," said Kaylan, swiftly withdrawing his hand from Cristal's.

Ms. Saunders quickly interjected and said, "Cristal, let me show you where you can hang your cane on a hook."

Minimal instruction was required for Cristal to independently familiarize herself inside the classroom. Just as she was taught, she began systematically exploring all four walls using protective techniques and hand trailing when appropriate. An unusual discovery was an oblong tatami mat with a rosemary fragrance in a corner near some bean bags. While Cristal explored the room, Ms. Saunders spent the next fifteen minutes teaching Kaylan and Ciara how to access the internet using their braille devices.

"Okay, Cristal. We've got a lot to do today, but first, let's get started by introducing you to the braille code." Cristal sat poised with a purpose. She was eager to grasp and absorb this reading and writing system. Ms. Saunders continued, "A braille cell is a group of six dots. Braille letters are made by raising one or more dots in the cell." The vision teacher then presented a six-cup muffin pan and six tennis balls to support the objective creatively. She let Cristal feel the recessed cups within the muffin pan and then placed a tennis ball in the top left corner.

"This represents the letter *a*." Ms. Saunders had Cristal complete the action and pronounce the first letter of the alphabet. She then showed her a braille index card with an 'a' in actual braille. "This is the letter '*b*,'" said Ms. Saunders after placing one tennis ball in the top left cup and another in the spot underneath it. The eager-to-learn students quickly comprehended the abstract representation using the tennis balls, and as a team, they continued going through the alphabet. Cristal had already learned the ABC song in English from Wilky early on, so it was much easier for her to understand Ms. Saunders's lesson.

"We'll review some more tomorrow, and then I'll show you how to write these letters on the braille writer," said Ms. Saunders.

A classroom timer went off, and Kaylan and Ciara grabbed their long canes and returned to their regular class. Shortly after they exited, two other fifth-grade students entered with an assistant. Seung and Kendall needed help on a math lesson using the Nemeth code to calculate the addition and subtraction of fractions. They introduced themselves to Cristal, and she returned the greetings. The assistant began working with Seung and Kendall at a long table in the back of the room. Ms. Saunders was anxious to see and help Cristal with whatever 'Show and Tell' project she brought for Mrs.

Tubilleja's class assignment. She decided to shadow Cristal by walking behind her when she traveled the route to Mrs. Tubilleja's room to retrieve her things. They returned to the VI room, where Cristal stood with the plaid makeup case on the table before her.

"Show me," requested Ms. Saunders.

Cristal then laid the round leather bag flat on the table and unzipped it carefully. She was glad her mother thought to give her the now wilted bouquet of mixed flowers from the nightstand. Nadine and Raeni agreed it would help add more zest to Cristal's project if she demonstrated how she pressed flower petals before placing them in bottles. Ms. Saunders watched with great intensity.

Cristal then placed the plastic bag containing wilted lilies, yellow roses, and blue delphiniums on the table with two small glass bottles. She also included bottles of essential oils she purchased from Super Shoppers and some chemicals from Raeni's chemistry set: linalool, ethyl acetate, methylene chloride, and limonene.

"I like to make perfumes. This Choublak dous (sweet hibiscus) and this one is Good Fortune." With graceful movements, Cristal opened the containers and offered them for Ms. Saunders to smell.

"Oh my!" she gasped in amazement. "You made these?"

"Uhhh…yes, ma'am."

"Alright then, let's get started. Tell me how. Tell me." Ms. Saunders repeated herself.

Cristal clicked a few buttons on a braille tablet and then turned on a speech application named *Talk and Translate.* She connected a microphone to the device and told Cristal to explain the step-by-step directions for making her perfumes.

"I can't speak English good," Cristal told Ms. Saunders.

"Oh, no, no, no, I'm sorry. I didn't explain it well. When you speak in Haitian Creole, it will translate what you say into English. It will then type it on a screen, and you can feel the refreshable braille at the very bottom of this device. I know that you can't read braille now. Still, I want to show you how it works."

Cristal had yet to learn what Ms. Saunders said and what was supposed to happen next, but when given a microphone, she knew from singing songs with Mikaela on a tape recorder that she was expected to talk. She lined up all of the contents from the case in sequential order. Cristal then began to speak the steps for making her perfumes into the microphone. She began, "I pick fresh flowers and use some dried flower petals. I get fresh Caribbean rainwater and let it sit in the sun under a rainbow for at least two hours..."

Ms. Saunders sat impressed as Cristal spoke of using an eye dropper, funnel, and an eye dropper to add just the right amount of liquids: rainwater, crushed peppermints, scented extracts, and other natural oils. Cristal demonstrated how to pour the mixture using an approximate measure for each liquid through different-sized funnels.

"Oh, oh, so sorry," she said when some spilled onto the table.

"No problem," said Ms. Saunders. She and Cristal jumped up together to get paper towels. The vision teacher paused and watched as Cristal tried to remember which wall had the sink and paper towel dispenser on it.

"Turn right," said Ms. Saunders as she gently tapped Cristal's right shoulder. Cristal located the paper towel dispenser and returned to the table to wipe the spill. She found the trashcan near the sink with her foot and returned to her perfume accessories. Ms. Saunders was amazed.

"This is excellent, Cristal. Now let's listen as I play your recording back in Haitian Creole, and then we'll hear it repeated in English."

They sat and listened to Cristal's step-by-step instructions. A tear welled up in Ms. Saunders's eyes as she watched Cristal sitting still and marveling at the translation of her work. Ms. Saunders ran Cristal's fingers across the bottom of the device and told her that the very same information was now translated into braille. Cristal's deep-set dimples reappeared as she felt the tiny, raised bumps representing her creative product.

For the first time, Cristal was mesmerized by the brilliance of technology and uttered, "Oh, my, my, my."

"Now, let me show you how I can print this for Mrs. Tubilleja to read," said Ms. Saunders.

Cristal sat as Ms. Saunders began connecting with a few more buttons on the device. Soon, she heard a funny whirring sound from across the room. Cristal now knew what that big square object was on a small table that she had bumped into earlier. Ms. Saunders jumped up, went to the printer, and returned to show Cristal a piece of paper.

"This is a printout of what you've said. It is a draft of what we will give to Mrs. Tubilleja. But it needs more work." Ms. Saunders was so excited that she stumbled and stuttered her words. "We need to include time-order words like *first, then, next, and finally*," she explained.

Cristal nodded and said, "Okay, more work."

It had been a busy morning for Cristal, and now, during lunch, she sat happily eating with Tiara, Kendall, Ivanna, and another student named Joy. The steady influx of over 200 students made the cafeteria super noisy. Tiara almost had to shout when she spoke. "I was placed in Mrs. Tubilleja's class in second grade," she told Cristal in French. "My family moved to the United States when I was eight," she continued.

"Do you have any brothers or sisters?" Cristal asked her.

"Yes, I have an older brother in middle school and a little sister in second grade," Tiara answered.

"I have a little brother in third grade," said Cristal, "His name is Wilky." Cristal turned to her right and asked Kendall, "How old you were when you went blind?" Tiara saw the puzzled look on Kendall's face and translated, although it wasn't needed.

"Oh, I was born blind. My mom said I arrived too soon. I came into this world at seven months and weighed less than four pounds. I guess that's why I'm kinda small now for my age. I have retinopathy of prematurity." Kendall paused, giving Tiara a few seconds to translate as best that she could. "That means something was wrong with the blood vessels in the back of my eye. I think I got too much oxygen or something," Kendall added.

"Oh," murmured Cristal. She liked the sound of Kendall's peep-squeaky voice.

In her later years as a young adult, Kendall's mother had the foresight to get her auditions for jobs seeking cartoon voice-over acting. With only two years of college, it became a lucrative career for her.

"Why can't you see?" Kendall asked.

"I don't know," Cristal answered. "The doctors don't know either. I went blind when I was five years old. My mom said one night, I had a real bad headache. I cried a lot. When I woke up the next morning, I couldn't see, so they rushed me to the doctor. He wasn't able to do anything." Cristal shared.

"Oh, wow…that sucks," said Joy.

There was a moment of silence before Cristal spoke cheerfully, "I remember seeing rainbows!"

"That's sick." Kendall complimented her with a bob of her head.

"That's slang for cool," Tiara quickly explained.

"Hey Cristal, are you signing up for an afterschool Cobra Club?" Kendall asked.

"Yes. I like the club for flowers and plants."

"I don't know about others." Tiara explained, "Last year, the principal asked the teachers to create fun activities representing the seven different learning styles." She prepared herself for a long-winded translation exercise as Joy interrupted with a descriptive list.

"The computer animation club is for the visual learner. Karaoke Kids club is for the auditory learner who likes music, and the 'Speak Spoke' drama club is for the verbal learner who likes to use their voice a lot. Ping pong is for the physical learner. Robotics and Legos are for nerdy students that are good at math and science and like to think hard." Joy recognized her need to slow down to give Tiara a few seconds to catch up. "Tap, Tap, Twirl is a ballroom dancing club for people who are sociable and like to connect with others for movement activities."

Kendall added, "And this school year, they changed the name, 'Botany' to 'Naturalist'. It is for people who like to work in a garden and learn to grow herbs, vegetables, and flowers. Some high school students came here for a project and turned an old school bus into a greenhouse. Last year, it was mostly about the memory garden, but it's going to be different now. If you choose that club, you have to do it for two nine weeks in a row. And you are also expected to work in the memory garden too. It has to be kept tidy and free from weeds, trash, dead leaves, and other stuff."

Cristal was intrigued by all the incredibly cool activities mentioned but had a question. "What's a memory garden?"

Tiara rushed to answer. "Our memory garden is a special place with lots of blooming flowers where students and teachers can sit and meditate. You can pray for students and staff members who are no longer with us, and you can also pray for our community. Maybe one day, Mr. Nick can let us go there and check it out during an O&M lesson."

"Where is it?" Cristal asked.

"It's on the east side of the school grounds," Tiara answered, "there's a little path made from crushed shells leading you to the benches, bushes, and flowers along the path. You can stop and smell the roses."

Cristal was excited about viewing the garden and knew that that was the club for her. "That's what I want to join first, and then the karaoke one next." Kendall added, "There are memory stones out there too, and every time a stone is added, Ms. Saunders gives us a braille print copy of what's written on the stones. My mom said that one parent wanted to donate a koi fishpond. But the PTO said no.

They were afraid somebody might try to hop the fence and take the fish on the weekends."

Ivanna said, "You can buy a T-shirt for the club you join. Last year, the 5th-grade art students designed the shirts as part of a contest."

"Last year, I was in the *Tap, Tap, Twirl* class with Ciara and Kaylan," said Kendall. "Mr. Nick, our O&M Specialist, and Mrs. Tubilleja teach ballroom dance lessons. It is so much fun! You get to hold the boys' hands," the girls giggled.

Joy chimed in, "And I heard some boys from my class talking about signing up for that one." Tiara and Kendall giggled some more.

Cristal thought about it for a hot second, "That's what I want to do, too. What did you pick, Kendall?"

"I chose the *Karaoke Kids Club* because I'm a pretty good singer. I like singing popular and old-school songs that my mother and father listen to on satellite radio. The same teacher in charge of the *Karaoke Kids Club* is also over the talent show at the end of the year in May. So it's a good chance you'll get picked if you join that club. Last year, I sang *Pocketful of Sunshine* by Natasha Bedingfield. Mr. Nick said it was okay if I twirled my cane while performing."

Cristal pondered the choices again, "That's good. I like flowers, and I like to sing too!"

Ivanna told the girls, "I don't think I'll be able to stay after school this year. I don't have a ride home."

Cristal didn't think about that. Her mother didn't have a car, and her Aunt Nadine worked somewhere far in downtown Atlanta.

Cristal trusted somebody would devise a solution for her and Wilky to join the afterschool clubs. Between bites of soft-shell tacos, refried beans, and slurps of strawberry milk, the girls enjoyed chitter-chattering on topics about almost everything under the sun.

Without warning, a high-penetrating scream within the cafeteria ricocheted from wall to wall. Teachers, kitchen staff, and all but one student froze.

"What? What is it?" Kendall yelled in her peep-squeaky voice. The girls were just as frightened as everyone else occupying the crowded area. Trevor continued screaming and twirling around like a drunken marionette with arms thrashing madly between tangled wires. A teacher's first thought was that the boy was on fire.

"Stop, drop, and roll!" she yelled, but that tip was irrelevant to the circumstances. Desperately, Trevor tried to shake and remove about a dozen small, flat, squirmy arthropods, each with a thousand tiny feet, from around his neck and inside his t-shirt. Horror and uncertainty took control, causing streams of screams throughout the cafeteria.

Shrieks and shouts echoed down the hall past the administrative offices. Mrs. McCallister poked her head out of the office door. Dr. Martin closed her door, locked it, and positioned her heavy leather chair under the knob. Mr. Macklberg panicked, thinking there might be a dangerous and threatening intruder in the building who was brandishing a weapon and causing fear and turmoil. He bolted into the cafeteria and looked around, trying to find the source of the chaos. His gaze focused on a frantic Trevor J. Irvin.

"What's the matter? What's going on?" Mr. Macklberg asked, rushing to stabilize the hysterical student by placing both hands on his shoulders.

"There are nasty crawly bugs all over. Get 'em off, get 'em off of me!" Tevor cried aloud. Mr. Macklberg bent down to look closely at Trevor's hair and shirt. He wondered if it was lice.

"Oh, I think those are millipedes. They're not poisonous, and they don't bite humans," he continued, "but let's get you to the clinic anyway and get you checked out."

Once everyone realized it wasn't a violent, life-threatening emergency, roaring waves of laughter commenced. "It looks like some boy went crazy," said Tiara with a delayed response to Cristal and Kendall's question. The secret was out. Tough guy, Trevor, was frightened at the sight of the tiny insects, so much so that he jerked and squealed at the top of his lungs like a five-year-old girl. Someone later reported that he sounded like Mariah Carey hitting one of her signature high notes after twirling and thrashing about.

Trevor's eyes darted around the cafeteria before lowering his head with shame and embarrassment. The bellows of belly laughing, and finger-pointing continued. A conscientious teacher sitting with coworkers covered his gluten-free lunch meal from home and ran to the microphone to subdue everyone. He recognized that a person of authority needed to re-establish some kind of order. Mr. Macklberg gave the teacher a nod and a thumbs up. "Everything is fine, students. There is no need to be alarmed." Although he didn't really agree with his following vehement request, he said it anyway, "Go back to eating your nutritious, delicious, and scrumdillyumptious lunch."

The crowd of students laughed more, but slowly, the uproar dulled to its typical noisy volume. As Mr. Macklberg walked Trevor towards the exit doors, Trevor's eyes locked in a cold stare with Wilky's. Without looking down at his plate and breaking the stare, Wilky shook an excessive amount of Tabasco sauce onto his spaghetti with turkey meatballs. Trevor was almost certain he saw Wilky sneer and mouth the word 'sissy'.

Chapter Twenty-One:
An Alarming Day

On Thursday, Ms. Camling greeted Cristal at the bus pick-up lane and did as Mr. Nick suggested once again. She shadowed Cristal ten feet from behind this time as she walked with her cane, Jurnee. Cristal was learning to navigate the outdoor route from her bus to the main entrance of the school building. She maintained a firm grip on the cane and tapped its tip in front and to the left. She continued performing the two-point touch technique, alternating a tap to the left and then to the right - making sure the placement of the cane tip was opposite to her forward foot like Mr. Nick had instructed her the day before. Cristal then switched to the touch-trail cane method to detect the boundary of the graveled sidewalk adjacent to the grass line on her right side. Once she made an approximate ninety-degree turn to her right, the noise from the traffic behind her on Heather Hill Lane became apparent. This auditory cue helped align Cristal directly in front of the main entrance.

Along the walkway on her right, Jurnee contacted a bench first. Cristal carefully continued traveling forward. She next discovered three clay pots that decorated the walkway with flowers thriving in favorable soil. They busied themselves by transforming light into chemical energy under an early morning sun. The lavender flowers were easy to recognize because of their sweet, clean scent, and the verbenas for their lemony fragrance. But Cristal didn't recognize a trace of musky smelling Marigolds.

"What kind?" Cristal asked Ms. Camling.

"Ummm, I'm not sure, but I'll find out." Continuing inside the building after manipulating the door handles, Cristal successfully arrived at Mrs. Lovelady's classroom. With less than a minute to spare before the second bell rang, she proudly seated herself with a sigh of relief. Only once had she hesitated along the Z route because of a table placed against the wall in the main corridor, one that wasn't there the previous day; Cristal briefly became disoriented. PTO moms had arranged a display on the table for Cobra Club t-shirts that would be available next week for purchase.

Mr. Macklberg began the announcements with his usual vigor. A student from a fifth-grade class read the menu, "Corn dogs on a stick, tater tots, spinach, and apple slices. Caleb's Country Kitchen donates large chocolatey chocolate chip cookies." Cristal had never heard of a corn dog on a stick and was eager for lunchtime to roll around. She felt proud that she had memorized her student number and was ready to punch it into the keypad all by herself.

One of Ms. Saunders's vision students, Hasan, was selected to deliver the thought for the day. Hasan was a boy who lost his central vision after getting hit in the head with a winged baseball bat during a little league game two summers ago. His ability to speak clearly was also affected by the traumatic brain injury. As a result, Hasan was taught to use assistive technology that required him to type into a device that would speak for him.

"It's okay not to know, but it's not okay to not try. The author is unknown," spoke the artificial voice from the assistive device.

A student in second grade followed up with a knock-knock joke. He fumbled during the second half of the delivery, but students could hear Mr. Macklberg over the intercom, helping the little guy recover the joke's punchline. Others near the microphone were prompted to laugh.

Wilky was confident that he would have a great day when Mrs. Collier took the class attendance moments after the bell rang. Trevor was absent. Wilky hoped the bully didn't get sick or anything worse from the millipedes. '*Suppose they were infected with some virus or something,*' he speculated. '*Oh well.*' Wilky eventually opened his English book to page seventeen as instructed.

About ten minutes into the lesson, a female voice over the intercom apologized for the interruption. "Mrs. Collier, would you please send William Duvernay to Dr. Martin's office?"

His classmates' 'oohs and ahhs' sounds were released like a blast of compressed air from a can. Mrs. Collier shook her head, simultaneously wiggling a curved index finger aimed at the entire group. "Yes. He's on his way," she replied before handing Wilky a paddle with a '*hall pass*' painted on it in red. Autumn looked at Wilky and offered a quick smile for a boost of support.

On the way to the office, Wilky felt sick to his stomach. A flood of thoughts rushed through his mind, '*Suppose Trevor and his mother are sitting in the front office, and maybe I'm going to get kicked out of school. Daddy will be so disappointed. Indeed, it isn't that serious,*' Wilky self-talked. Today was art day, and tomorrow, they will have gym class. Wilky didn't want to be sent home for the next few days. He was looking forward to healthy competition between him and his new classmates. Midway to the front office, he poked his head inside the gym. No students were present, but Wilky spotted climbing ropes hanging from the ceiling, a trampoline, a vaulting table, a balance beam, gymnastic rings, and parallel bars strategically arranged.

"This is mad crazy! This looks like a gym for the Olympics," he exclaimed out loud.

What caught Wilky's eye next was a wire basket in the corner filled with various balls; one in particular was a soccer ball. Procrastination was clearly at play on his walk to the principal's office. Wilky could only imagine what terrible fate awaited him for that foolish stunt he pulled on Trevor.

Inside the gym alone, he kicked the ball around a few times and then began keep-ups by juggling it while using his feet, lower legs, knees, chest, shoulders, and head without allowing it to bounce to the ground. His skills were quite advanced for a typical third grader, and the PE teacher, Mr. Oblinger, noticed this while standing in the doorway of his corner office.

"Excuse me, young man, what is your name?" Wilky halted the juggling act, letting the ball bounce to the floor, but stopped it from rolling with one quick foot move.

"Wilky Duvernay," he answered nervously.

"Whose room are you in, and where should you be?"

"I'm on my way to the principal's office. I'm in Mrs. Collier's room."

"You're in third grade?" Mr. Oblinger asked with disbelief.

"Yes, sir. I'm sorry for playing with your ball."

"Go where you belong. I'll talk to you later."

"*Shucks, I'm in trouble again,*" he whispered despondently.

Wilky sat at a student-size desk in the principal's office, watching her swivel back and forth in a leather chair. She sat behind a colossal ornate desk covered with stacks of papers and playful knick-knacks. "William, I'm Dr. Martin, the principal here at Azalea Grove Elementary. I'm sorry I couldn't meet you, your sister, and your mother when you enrolled on Tuesday." Wilky kept his head down, afraid to anticipate what she might say next. "You're here because I haven't received the last page of the parent handbook that Mr. Macklberg gave to your mother. It's critical that she reads and signs it as soon as possible. I need you to give her this letter."

Wilky was relieved, believing that that was all to the visit.

"Yes, ma'am. I will ask her to sign and return it tomorrow." He stood ready to exit.

"I'm not finished just yet. Please have a seat, William." Dr. Martin continued, "How you wear your hair violates the school district's policy."

"Huh?" uttered Wilky in bewilderment.

Dr. Martin continued, "Long hair on males is not permitted. It is printed in the handbook along with other violations such as crayon-colored hair, visible body tattoos, nose rings, tank tops, and short dresses on girls." Wilky thought for a second about Mr. Macklberg's enormous tribal tattoo.

"You mean I have to cut my hair? They're not dreadlocks; they're locs. It's how my hair grows naturally. My mom washes my hair every week."

Dr. Martin politely waited him out, "These aren't my rules, William. I'm sorry, but as the principal, I must enforce district policies. Please have your mother carefully read the information and return the signature page tomorrow. You have until Tuesday; otherwise, you will not be allowed on our school campus. And don't forget to give her the letter as well."

Wilky's heart seemed to sink all the way down to his pristine high-top tennis shoes.

"Yes, ma'am."

Wilky's day improved a little once he sat with his friends in the cafeteria. Out of nowhere, somebody proposed an earwax contest. All the boys in Mrs. Collier's class used their napkins to wipe impacted wax from their ears, and the one whose napkin came out the cleanest was the winner. Wilky's friend Kenny was king, and he won the loser's chocolatey chocolate chip cookie. All male participants cheered and clapped. For fun, the boys and girls from the third-grade class got the chance to fly paper airplanes that they made during a STEM activity. Everyone hoped that theirs would glide the farthest distance. Autumn and Wilky got to laugh and play together without others noticing that they were completely smitten with each other. He watched Autumn run with pure athleticism to chase down her airplane that glided beyond many others. He surveyed the active playground full of kids and realized that none of the boys had locs or shoulder-length hair.

Inside the cafeteria, Cristal experienced some difficulty balancing her tray evenly and had to get a second one when hers fell to the floor. A custodian waiting in the wings to mop up spills scurried to clean it up while a teacher walked Cristal to the table. She was okay with it all because she was happy to eat a corn dog with mustard for the first time. After lunch, Cristal and her friends played with jump ropes and ran with their partners around the track.

Later in the school day, Mrs. Tubilleja sent Cristal back to Ms. Saunders' VI class with her kit full of items to finish her project. The vision teacher showed Cristal a talking application that she could use on an electronic tablet. "It was invented to read aloud printed materials. I want to show you how this works so that you can also access print. But I don't think that you should use it during your presentation. Tomorrow, when you present, Mrs. Tubilleja wants you to speak in English as best you can."

They practiced the presentation for quite some time. Ms. Saunders was confident that Cristal would do well and receive a good grade. Cristal was sent back to Mrs. Tubilleja's room. However, instead of going straight back to class, Cristal stopped in the bathroom. And that's when everything hit the fan. A painfully loud alarm sounded, signaling a systematic and organized 'safety in place' drill as required by the district. All teachers had been briefed on the procedure. They locked their doors and pulled down the shades at every window.

The shrill, ear-piercing alarm was upsetting and confusing to Cristal. She didn't understand what was happening but washed her hands anyway and then grabbed Jurnee and her perfume case. When she stepped into the halls, they were empty. So, Cristal tried to manipulate the door handle to get inside Mrs. Tubilleja's class, but the door was locked. She pressed her ear against the door but could not hear anything. Confused and terrified, Cristal decided to return to Ms. Saunders' class. Her door was locked as well. The bright light emitting from the exit door drew Cristal towards it. The change in heat on her face from sunlight shining through the window above the latch became her guide. She pushed the bar and walked outside. "Maybe everybody is out here," she said aloud. But that hypothesis proved to be false. No voices could be heard. Uncertain of where she was on the school premises and what to do next, Cristal began traveling along the building line while tapping her cane.

"Hello, hello!" she yelled, but there was no response. Her nostrils flared. She could smell the stench of garbage from a school dumpster and a muddle of odors emitted from an exhaust vent. 'I must be at the back of the cafeteria,' she surmised.

She continued walking. Cristal smelled the hydrangeas' sweet and fresh aromatic scent and could hear beautiful tones drifting from aluminum wind chimes. *'Okay, I'm passing the memory garden now. I'm on the east side of the building.'* She continued to walk along the outdoor perimeter, selecting helpful cues to provide information about her current position in space. Suddenly, the traffic sounds from Heather Hill Lane were all the confirmation she needed. Mr. Nick was right when he said, "The sound of traffic can be your friend." When Cristal turned the corner, she and Jurnee recognized something familiar. She stood briefly next to the scent of the Marigolds; Cristal was now aware of her exact whereabouts and sped up to the school's front doors. She knocked and knocked and knocked. Frightened by her aloneness, Cristal began to cry.

***

Later in the evening, Isaac made a rib-tickling comment during dinner. "I think I married the wrong Duvernay," he joked, after absorbing another one of Dahlia's sensational meals. Nadine thumped her husband on his head. Raeni and Dahlia laughed.

"How would you rate your school day?" asked Nadine, directing her gaze at Raeni.

"A six; nothing good or bad happened. It was just a normal school day." Raeni was disappointed that Daxton didn't bother to stop and say 'Hello' when they passed each other in the halls.

"That's how I'd rate my workday too, nothing special," Nadine reported.

"My boss allowed everybody to do their work without interruptions for a change. Cheryl got upset because somebody took her peach yogurt from the fridge, but that's about it." Isaac rated his day a five.

"My buddy Brandon got fired for arguing with the new boss again. Who knew that the guy had a short fuse? If Brandon had just taken a stroll around the parking lot or even sat in our recently purchased high-powered massage chair in the lounge and chilled, it would have been a different outcome without a doubt."

"Oh, that's too bad," said Nadine. "Brandon is the one with the doughnut-shaped bald spot and piranha-like teeth, right?" A wave of background laughter rolled through the homey atmosphere.

"Geez, Nadine, that's a little harsh, ya think?" her husband commented.

Nadine tried shrugging off her goofy facial expression, "Aww, that's too bad. I like him. Brandon seems to be a nice and cordial individual."

Cristal began shifting in her seat. "You're pretty quiet this evening, Cristal. How was your day?" her mother asked. Cristal told everyone what happened to her during the safety drill as best she could in English. Dahlia and Nadine were shaken, and Isaac stopped chewing for a moment in disbelief.

"You mean you stood locked outside the school building all by yourself?" her uncle, Isaac, asked. Wilky translated, but it wasn't necessary.

"Yes, sir," answered Cristal. She began a more detailed account and nervously switched from English to Haitian Creole.

"Mrs. McCallister saw me on a camera, and that's how they found me. I sat on the bench with Jurnee, my perfume kit, and my fan."

Dahlia interpreted the account this time around and was beyond upset. "Something could have happened to my baby. Somebody could have snatched her. I need to call up to that school tomorrow to let them know what is not acceptable!"

Nadine agreed. "We can go up there together first thing in the morning if you want."

"No, I don't want to make you late for work another day this week. I'll call them and take care of it."

Everyone sat silent, eating fried pork, rice, gravy, and plantains. Dahlia almost forgot to inquire about her son's day at school. "Wilky, how would you rate your day? You're awfully quiet, too."

"A two," he responded with gloom.

"What happened to you?" asked his uncle.

Wilky looked at Uncle Isaac with a twisted mouth and then turned to his mother, "I have a note to give you from the principal. She said it's the rule that I have to cut my hair. Boys can't wear long hair." Everyone was stunned for a second time.

"That's discrimination," stated Nadine. Dahlia sat dumbfounded and clapped her hands.

"Lord have mercy. My kids haven't been in school a whole week, and craziness has started chasing them down the street already." She shook her head. "Go get the letter, Wilky."

Moments later, Dahlia read it out loud for everyone's ears. She and Nadine went into the living room to quietly discuss their plan of attack. Raeni cleared the table and showed Cristal how to rinse the dishes thoroughly before loading them in the dishwasher.

Late in the night, Cristal had a horrific nightmare. It had been months since she'd had her last one. In the dream, an earthquake hit the state of Georgia. Her school had crumbled, and everyone inside was trapped. At the time it occurred, she had been outside picking flowers and could hear nearby cars honking and crashing into each other. People were screaming and begging for their lives. The earth suddenly cracked, opened up, and freed prehistoric salamanders. "Help me, help me!" she cried, kicking away the bed sheets and tightly gripping Ginger. Everyone in the townhome was shaken awake in fear.

Because of her close proximity, Raeni was awakened first and screeched the loudest in response. "What is it? What's happening?" she asked, but Cristal couldn't speak. Dahlia rushed into the room, and Wilky tore behind her. Uncle Isaac sprinted up the stairs with a Glock handgun, and Aunt Nadine armed herself with a 56-degree wedge golf club that she held high in the air.

Chapter Twenty-Two:
Applause Applause

It was Friday morning, and as soon as Cristal and Wilky boarded the bus for school, Dahlia returned home to place the critical phone call to the principal. Mrs. McCallister put her on hold for over nine minutes. Before making the call, Dahlia repeated words of guidance that were often given by her previous pastor at the end of every sermon, "Treat everything and everyone with grace."

"This is Dr. Martin. How may I help you?"

Dahlia altered her voice to a higher but softer pitch to sound more professional. "Dr. Martin, this is Dahlia Duvernay. I'm calling you for two reasons. The first is regarding my daughter, Cristal. I'm angry that my child was locked entirely out of the school building yesterday. Actually, I'm furious. Do you know how dangerous that is for any kind of child, not just one who is blind?" The principal started to answer but was interrupted by Dahlia. "Anything could have happened to her. I've been listening to the news since the first day we moved to Georgia. There are murderers, rapists, snipers, kidnappers, robbers, and all kinds of weirdos walking these streets."

Dr. Martin was a well-educated, well-read individual who kept abreast of local and international news that made headlines. Her hour-long run after work on a treadmill at the gym took place only feet away from a 65" television with closed caption CNN news stories. She recalled high statistics outside of the United States where young children were being sold as part of human trafficking and forced into labor and debt bondage in places like Honduras, Thailand, Brazil, and Haiti. As if Dahlia read Dr. Martin's mind, she continued, "I'll admit that parts of Haiti are dangerous too, but Cristal never traveled far from home alone." The upset mother took a few deep breaths to calm herself down. Last night, she promised Nadine and Isaac that she would control her emotions and not cause her blood pressure to rise by getting worked up.

"Mrs. Duvernay, I deeply apologize for what happened to Cristal. I understand your anger and frustration, and I take full responsibility." Dr. Martin decided not to pull the thread on a sweater and place blame on Mrs. Trujillo and Ms. Kelsey for their lack of communication in this matter. Her teachers absolutely ignored policy and failed to email each other regarding Cristal's whereabouts when attendance was taken during the safety drill. "When I heard about the incident, I immediately began drafting an email to send to my entire staff. I will hold an emergency meeting for the faculty on Tuesday morning before the beginning of school. New procedures will be written in place. I guarantee you. Our children's safety here at Azalea Grove Elementary is our number one priority." The principal paused for a response.

"Well, alright, I appreciate your accountability in the matter," responded Dahlia reluctantly. She felt that one last admonishment was needed. "Thank goodness my child had enough sense not to wander into the street; otherwise, she could have been hit by a fast-moving vehicle! Please ensure this doesn't happen again, or I will take this to someone who sits much higher and whose pay grade is much higher than yours." Dahlia believed that that added drop of venom was necessary.

"Yes, Mrs. Duvernay. I understand."

"Now, coming to the second thing. I just put Wilky and Cristal on the bus with the forms you requested from the parent handbook.

I signed them, but I'm afraid I have to disagree with the policy regarding how my son wears his hair. Not only do I not agree with it, but I also don't understand its purpose. It feels like a form of discrimination or a stigma against Wilky's artistic style and self-expression. I believe it hints at an attack on my son's hair texture and tidiness or an implication that there is a lack of it. I keep my children clean. Wilky and Cristal get their hair washed every week. I'm sure that that's more than a lot of the other kids' parents can say. I see how they look running around these stores and on the playgrounds." Dahlia tried to think of every legitimate grievance she and Nadine listed last night. "It feels like harassment and bullying. My husband and I teach our children to embrace their identity and not hide behind the veil of artificially inflicted social norms!" she concluded.

Dr. Martin listened attentively, then responded, "I wholeheartedly agree with you, Mrs. Duvernay. Mr. Macklberg is a new faculty member, but he knows the guidelines and should have discussed this with you and your son directly during enrollment. The district's policy regarding protective styles seems unfair to me, especially to the boys. My husband wears twists and has been harassed at his job more than once. As a result, he recorded some of his coworkers making derogatory comments about his looks on tape. After filing a complaint with human resources, backed by the recorded evidence, the harassment eventually ended. It stopped because the undignified employees were dismissed."

Dahlia gasped. She was surprised at the change in tone of their conversation and how easy it was to converse with Dr. Martin. She speculated that the principal was probably only a few years older than herself. Dr. Martin was close to ending the call, but not before obsequiously reaffirming Dahlia's position.

"More and more of our young men are embracing this natural look. Trust me; you're not the first parent to complain. I believe it will take a grassroots effort to make things happen in this district and throughout the state. If enough parents complain to the school board, it might bring about the necessary change."

"Well, thank you. I may do just that. I'll try to get other parents to collaborate with me and change certain policies." Dahlia honestly didn't believe what she was saying. Other pressing concerns, like getting a job, were at the forefront. But it was something that she would have liked to have happened.

"I will get Wilky a haircut tomorrow till we can change some things around here."

Dr. Martin maintained her professionalism and ended the call. "Thank you, and I wish you a great weekend."

Dahlia returned to her boring routine of drinking coffee and watching the morning news alone. Since moving to Georgia, she hadn't the courage to wake up and sit in silence. Because the world is full of mystery, magic, and mayhem, listening to other people's predicaments made her somehow feel connected to strangers in an unfamiliar place. Dahlia felt a little better about her predicament and how she managed the situation for her children at school. Mom and Dad would have been proud of their daughter's stance, she believed. *'Maybe, just maybe, I won't find myself standing in the shower and crying for what feels like hours this morning.'*

Dahlia remembered happier times when she sang popular tunes in the shower as a teenager as well as throughout her youthful, carefree life. Now, every day was an uphill act of faith. She decided that the local television news stories were too depressing to watch, especially the one that spoke of the impending execution of Troy

Anthony Davis. He would be sentenced to death in a few weeks for the murder of a police officer. "*I can't believe that the United States' government still supports the barbaric practice of executing humans,*" she expressed out loud. "*Why can't they just make him miserable for his remaining days by serving him only bread and water and keeping him in solitary confinement?*"

Dahlia abruptly turned off the television and walked over to two CD towers to grab a musical diversion. She realized the genre to select from was primarily reduced to country artists. Once she perused a few titles, Dahlia popped in a disc by the artist Kenny Chesney, titled '*I'm Alive*'. After listening to the opening lyrics, she was pleased with her choice and started busying herself in the kitchen. The grieving mother and wife began to chop an assorted collection of vegetables and she recalled the family heirloom recipes with ease. Getting an early start to prepare dinner proved to be a great comfort. Dahlia's mindful immersion in cooking temporarily numbed her pain and directed her hands to engage in purposeful movements.

Eventually, Sudoku's internal clock ticked in and prompted some timely echolalic chatter. "You're the next contestant…come on down.... it's a brand-new car!" Dahlia placed well-seasoned pieces of pork in the refrigerator to marinate for three hours. She hoped everyone would later enjoy baked Haitian pork griot and crisp tostones. After pulling the heavy curtain back so that Sudoku could peer through the glass door, Dahlia turned the television back on. The odd pair joined a wild audience attending an upbeat and popular game show to try and guess the prices of countless merchandise.

***

Cristal was excited but a little nervous about her project. The first page of her printout contained focal points for her presentation. She planned to give it to the teacher when it was her turn to speak.

"Alright, class," said Mrs. Tubilleja. "You will each have between five and ten minutes to present. You may begin once I call you to the front of the room with your materials. I will set the timer." She then reviewed the grading rubric, reminding everyone to use descriptive words, time order words, and to speak slowly, loudly, and as clearly as possible.

Ms. Camling handed out small bottles of water to each student in case their throats felt tight and dry.

"Remember," Mrs. Tubilleja continued, "this is a lesson in which you provide your peers with information about something you know well. Feel free to use your notes and remember to turn them in when finished. Each of you is required to listen to learn. Part of your grade requires you to ask four questions to your classmates for either greater clarification or as an inquiry into something you're curious to know more about." She looked around the room as if to warn specific students in advance. "Stay on topic with your questions, and always be polite and respectful when others are presenting. Ms. Camling and I will be documenting your input. Are there any questions?" The teacher and her assistant surveyed the room for raised hands, but there were none. "You can volunteer to come up, or I will randomly call out names. Who'd like to go first?" Ms. Camling gave one last directive, "Don't forget to hold up the appropriate card for the type of clap you'd like to receive from your peers once you've completed your presentation."

Yehoon was the first to step up and present. His father had emailed the Teacher a video clip of Yehoon to upload. He was filmed using a bow to shoot arrows at a distant target. Yehoon was a skillful young archer. He signaled to the Teacher to queue it up and moved to turn off the lights. After the short clip, Yehoon talked about the bow, its parts, and how it works. His father advised him not to bring arrows to the school. Yehoon discussed the distance he typically stands from the target. He told the class that he once won $100 at a junior shooting competition during summer camp in Iowa. After passing around a copy of his certificate, Yehoon requested a rodeo clap. His classmates were highly impressed, and several hands went up with questions.

Camille demonstrated her hula hoop skills. She let one hoop spin from her waist and up to her neck. She slipped an arm inside, moved it from over her head, and let it swirl on her right wrist. Camille bent to her left and picked up a smaller hoop. This one lit up like an orange fire stick. She continued working her magic, alternating the rings to different sides of her body before tossing one and using the remaining one to jump through it as if it were a rope. One boy whistled, and she began to laugh. At the close of her performance, Camille talked about how long she had been playing hula hoops. She ended by listing games and various activities for which you could use the circular plastic toys besides actual hula hooping. Camille requested a money clap, and a few hands went up with questions.

Nevaeh demonstrated her ability to make a flying origami dragon. She said it was a geometry lesson. Then she displayed a mobile with several animals she had previously made hanging from it. Handouts with a black line drawing were handed to everyone so that they could try making their own origami frog. Nevaeh slowly read aloud detailed instructions for each step. Some students actually created an amphibian-looking piece of folded paper they were proud of.

Joshua showed an animal's horn and conch shell. He blew each one and then compared their features to his trumpet. Next, Joshua displayed some musical notes on an overhead projector and played a slightly monotone tune. He requested a DJ clap.

When Ms. Saunders walked in and took a seat, Cristal was called upon next. From the lanyard around her neck, she fanned herself for a few seconds with one painted with colorful butterflies. She then stood straight and walked a few steps to a table on her left. "I like flowers, and I like making perfumes." She unzipped her case, took out several items, and held them up high for others to see. Cristal named each one before placing them on the table, "This is made with pressed jasmine flowers, essential oils, empty bottles, a funnel, a baby aspirator, mints, chemicals, rainwater, and a block of wood." After displaying the six scented bottles, Cristal pointed to her nose and right temple just as she had practiced in front of Ms. Camling.

"The nose captures scents and sends them to your brain. You can remember over 50,000 scents. Does anyone know what scientists believe to be the most pleasant smell in the world?"

Someone yelled, "Chocolate chip cookies baking in the oven?"

"That is good," replied Cristal, "the scent of vanilla is known to be the best scent in the world."

Using delicate moves, Cristal then began demonstrating the specific steps in her perfume-making process. As required, she used time-order words to make her presentation fluid: first, next, then, after that, and finally. Raeni suggested she pass around cotton balls with a dab of fragrance on each. After that, Ms. Camling handed Cristal a tactile world globe. She held it up and let it spin. "There are perfume schools all around the world- New York, Paris, London, and Canada, and even as far away as India. I will go one day." Cristal gifted eight girls braided scented bracelets for a finale, like those she and her little cousin Mikaela made from gentle flowers with delicate stems. "Sorry to the boys," she said. The class laughed before giving black-eyed peas clap that she verbally requested. Hands shot in the air with questions. Cristal was nervous and answered only three to the best of her ability. Mrs. Tubilleja came to her aid and thanked her for a marvelous presentation.

She then called on another student, and while he was setting up, Ms. Saunders moved close to Ms. Camling, "There is something special about her; she's got the 'it' factor."

Ms. Camling bobbed her head in agreement, "You're right, she's the bee's knees."

Mrs. Tubilleja was proud of all her students and their parents for taking her assignments seriously. She believed her job as an ELL teacher was to dispel myths about children from diverse cultures and ethnicities who were often marginalized for being, as some would refer to them, 'alien citizens, refugees, or anchor babies'. Her colleagues considered Mrs. Tubilleja to be authentically 'woke' because her creative lessons inspired her children to embrace their culture and stand in their magnificent light. Mrs. Tubilleja looked forward to upcoming Fridays when parents signed up and volunteered to bring in ethnic dishes and share interesting information about their culture. Sometimes, in the teachers' lounge, Mrs. Tubilleja engaged in lively conversations with her coworkers about how the practice of acculturation can sometimes muddle a person's social and psychological well-being. Unbeknownst then, Mrs. Tubilleja would end the year as the school's celebrated 'TOTY'; Teacher of the Year.

Trevor was absent again, but Wilky tried not to speculate why. He looked forward to having fun in gym class. During the third hour of the school day, Mr. Oblinger took attendance and divided the class into groups of three. It wasn't a day of competitive sports, just an opportunity to rotate between gymnastic equipment. A few students opted to ride stationary bikes or walk on treadmills. Mr. Oblinger was glad that some boys and girls chose recently purchased rainbow-colored dance ribbons on wands. They raced to grab them from the hooks on the wall to use on the tumbling mats.

"When I blow the whistle, it will be time to rotate to the next activity center, and William Duvernay, I need to speak to you for a moment, please. Have fun, everybody!" he shouted. Mr. Oblinger blew his whistle, and students scrambled to their assigned areas. *"Oh boy,"* said Wilky under his breath, *"he's gonna hammer me again for messing around in the gym yesterday."*

Wilky walked over to where Mr. Oblinger stood, six feet and four inches tall. The teacher pulled a blue folding chair out of his office and sat down to get closer to Wilky's eye level.

"William, I wanted to talk to you about yesterday. I watched you for several minutes when you weren't aware. Little guy, you've got some serious ball-handling skills. How old are you? Do you play on a soccer team now?"

Wilky smiled, "No, sir. I'm ten years old. I used to play for the Stingrays before I left Haiti. My team got second place in a tournament."

"Have you thought about playing for a team here in Georgia?"

"Not yet. I want to, though. My daddy isn't here yet. But he told me I could play on another team again. He's gonna be moving to

Georgia, and when he does, he said he would try to get me on a team then."

"Well, William, my brother is a professional scout for youth soccer leagues. Do you know what that is?"

"No, sir."

"A scout is paid to find good soccer players for different leagues and teams. They seek highly skilled players who exhibit tactical awareness, competitiveness, specific physical attributes, and those who possess a good attitude. I want to send home some information for you to share with your mother. If she could get you to a practice game next Saturday held for boys your age, would you like that? I believe there would be some coaches out there who would love to have you on their team."

"Yes, sir. I love playing soccer. It's one of my favorite things. I even have a ball that glows in the dark!"

"Okay, then, William." Wilky twitched his mouth to the side. "Is that what I should call you?"

"You can call me Wilky."

"Alright, Wilky, let me grab some information from my office. I'll be right back."

Mr. Oblinger blew the whistle for group rotation before disappearing into his office to print information regarding youth soccer leagues in the area. He put a yellow sticky note on one of the papers asking Wilky's mother to give him a call over the weekend. Mr. Oblinger was confident that Wilky would get a spot on a team because most of the boys, according to his brother's recent account, were decidedly average. Wilky was elated. He ran to his group that just rotated to the still rings and stood bouncing in line for his turn.

Mr. Oblinger watched Wilky closely. *"Paul's going to owe me big for finding this talented kid."*

The bus ride home was strident with laughter, rumor spreading, and back and forth repartee. Everyone was excited for the long Labor Day weekend to begin. Once they stepped off the bus at their stop, Wilky and Cristal were greeted with the smell of freshly mowed grass. The budding siblings were anxious to share personal accounts of good news with their mother.

Chapter Twenty-Three:
Serendipity

Isaac released a loud, airy belch and excused himself from the table. "Thank you. I'll take that as a compliment," said Dahlia jokingly. Isaac looked back and chortled. The Duvernays and the Grangers ranked their Friday school and workday high on the imaginary scale with an eight, nine, and ten. It was a remarkable assembly around a table of good food and conversation.

"Oh yeah, momma," said Wilky after eating the last Poule En Sauce, also known as stewed chicken, from his fork.

"The lady in the cafeteria from Haiti wrote her name and number down and told me to give it to you. She wants you to call her."

Dahlia stood ready to clear the table, "What? Who is this?" she said, turning towards the sink with her dirty plate.

"No, no, no, this is a case of serendipity," Nadine demanded, stopping Dahlia in her tracks. "Such an unexpected gift of luck. I got this, Dahlia, and we agreed that when you cook, I clean. Go ahead and make that phone call."

Cristal also remembered the lovely lady named Mrs. Plaizill who stepped from behind the register and complimented her. "I went through her line yesterday. She spoke Haitian Creole and told me she liked how my hair was braided." Cristal licked the tangy sauce from her fingers before continuing, "She helped me punch in my number when I had trouble with the keypad."

Wilky ran upstairs to get a crumpled slip of paper from the front pocket of his backpack. "Here it is." Dahlia looked at the name and number and then walked to her bedroom to make the call.

"Hello, may I speak to a Mrs. Rhonda Plaizill?" Dahlia asked with uncertainty. "This is Mrs. Plaizill."

The woman on the other line seemed unsure so Dahlia continued, "Uhhh…my son Wilky Duvernay started school at Azalea Grove Elementary this week, and he gave me this number to call you. He said you work in the cafeteria."

Mrs. Plaizill took one more sip of red wine before answering, "Yes. Hello, how are you?"

"I'm just fine, and you?" responded Dahlia, unsure about the nature of the call.

"Listen, baby," said the woman, "I think that my older brother used to go to school with some Duvernays. I just thought I might know some of your family back in Haiti. Do you know a Emmanuel and Nedra Duvernay?"

Dahlia was pleasantly surprised to hear those names, "Yes, ma'am, they are my husband's relatives– his aunt and uncle! I don't think he's heard from them in a couple of years."

Equally thrilled, Mrs. Plaizill replied, "Isn't that somethin' now? I thought I might've been right. I just hadn't come across the Duvernay name in a long time." Dahlia and Mrs. Plaizill continued their conversation for more than an hour.

"Haitian immigrants account for less than two percent of the U.S. foreign-born population, though these numbers continue to increase." Mrs. Plaizill told Dahlia. The phone call ended with Mrs. Plaizill inviting Dahlia to church on Sunday morning. "There's a sizable Haitian community here in Atlanta, and many members of my church are still involved in the earthquake relief efforts. You and your family will be my guests. I think you'll like it." Mrs. Plaizill continued with words of invitation. "The people are amicable, and we always serve dinner right after the late service. That's if you're interested in staying."

Dahlia teared up, "Yes, ma'am, thank you so much, Mrs. Plaizill. We will be there on time come Sunday morning." She then searched for a pen and some paper in the top dresser drawer to write down the church's name and address.

"Goodbye, and thank you again," Dahlia repeated softly.

"And baby, call me Rhonda. I'm old, but not that old."

Dahlia chuckled, "Yes, ma'am. I mean, yes, Ms. Rhonda." The women shared a comfortable laugh before hanging up.

"We usually sleep in late on Sundays and relax most of the day, but this is a long weekend," Nadine shared. "I'll ask Isaac to drop you and the kids off at the church. I'm sure he won't mind because he'll get a chance to sleep in late on Monday since it's a holiday."

"That's good. Thank you," Dahlia responded. "I hope it won't be too much of an inconvenience. Y'all have done so much for us already, and I don't ever want to try and drive over two hundred feet away from this house in that gridlock."

"I'll get up and ride with you all. It's not a problem."

Dahlia speculated, "Hopefully, it won't be long before Jesse gets here, and we can get a little car or something to get us around. He liked being my chauffeur."

Nadine smiled, "I'm glad to be in your company, and I know Raeni is too. Isaac has been working so hard studying for an exam for his job that he needs to relax for a change and do something fun. We're meeting friends for dinner tomorrow, and I'm taking him to an action movie afterward."

Dahlia thought about it for a second, "I can't remember the last time Jesse and I went to a movie theater. I think '*Snakes on a Plane*' was the last one we saw."

Nadine laughed, "My goodness, girl, that had to be around 2006 or 2007, right?" Dahlia nodded.

"Raeni's got a sleepover this evening and won't be back until Sunday afternoon. Why don't you and the kids think about ordering a pizza or something tomorrow? Take a break from cooking; this treats on me," offered Nadine. Aunt Dahlia smiled and hugged her sister-in-law.

Nadine suggested that they go to the store the following day. "You and I can go to Super Shoppers early in the morning when Isaac takes Wilky to his barber for a haircut. He's got a golf game at 10:00 a.m. Do you think Wilky will be okay hanging out with him and his buddies?"

Dahlia smiled with gratitude, "Absolutely. He'll be fine." She then hurried to her closet to figure out what to wear to First Ebenezer Haitian Church. She wanted to make a good impression on Rhonda Plaizill. After all, Rhonda was already impressed with Wilky and Cristal. She said they looked so nice and neat coming to school and seemed to have such good manners. That made Dahlia feel she was a good mother for a change.

Before Raeni left for her sleepover, Cristal asked Dahlia if she would ask Raeni for a big favor. Cristal was glad that Tiara was becoming her friend, but she feared that if she didn't hurry up and learn more English, Tiara would get tired of having to translate for her and might start backing away. So, Dahlia addressed Raeni in a pleasing tone, "Cristal's teacher gave her some language CDs. Is it alright if she uses your computer while you're gone?" Anxiously, Cristal awaited her cousin's response. Cristal never knew what type of reaction to expect from her. Sometimes, Raeni was kind and supportive; at other times, she was aloof or just plain cranky.

During the first week of arrival at the Granger home, Dahlia told Cristal to be patient and give her cousin some time and space whenever possible. She said Raeni was a little spoiled. "She's never been required to share her things or the people she loves with anyone else."

Intentionally, Raeni delayed her response for effect. "Well, umm, does she know how to use a computer?" Dahlia bristled but calmed down a bit, although she held onto an image of her swatting Raeni on her butt with a switch for being so sassy.

She raised the CD case, "Sweetie, do you mind showing her?" Raeni reached for the CD.

"Okay," she answered, not with a spark but rather, a drawn-out sigh. Dahlia sat on Cristal's bed and watched Raeni demonstrate hand over hand what buttons to push and how and where to insert the compact discs.

"Show me; you do it now," she directed. Nervously, Cristal re-inserted the CD and took a few extra seconds to think and feel for the right buttons to push.

"Okay, it looks like you got it. But don't start clicking on all these other buttons on the side."

Dahlia's face contorted, and then she made a sucking sound with her teeth. Cristal scooted the chair closer to the desk and began to listen to her fifth translation lesson. "Oh, I forgot. Here's the volume knob on the speakers," Raeni added. Raeni walked over to the hooks on her wall and collected a couple of long ropes. The Fly Girlz Double Dutch squad made plans to practice most of the day on Saturday. She shoved the professional ropes in her overnight bag with her Winnie the Pooh stuffed animal.

"Oh yeah, can I try one of those new perfumes you made?" Raeni asked in a sweet tone. She tapped Cristal on her shoulder, and she removed the headphones. Dahlia repeated what Raeni requested.

"Yes, yes!" Cristal jumped up abruptly, almost knocking over the chair. She pulled one bottle from the case and handed it to Raeni.

Raeni dabbed some on her wrist. "Hmm, this smells so good."

Dahlia watched the smile grow wide on her daughter's face, and because of that small intentional act of kindness, she stood to kiss the moody teenager's forehead. "Thank you." Dahlia surmised Raeni didn't inherently acquire the happy-go-lucky gene from her father, but at least she tried.

Chapter Twenty-Four:
Labor Day Weekend

The Saturday morning trip to Super Shoppers went well. There was no need to worry about Wilky running off and getting lost because he was on his way to get a haircut and then to the golf course with Uncle Isaac. Dahlia and Nadine not only shopped for the weekly groceries but also purchased a few extra items to ensure that they had the necessary ingredients to bake a lemon-flavored pound cake with the praline filling. Dahlia wanted to make two of them; one would be a dessert for churchgoers. She aimed to enhance the aesthetic appeal of the cake she planned to take to church, so extra lemons were put inside the cart. They'd be used to make swirls from the peels.

In Dahlia's opinion, Nadine had limited culinary gadgets and pots and pans to cook various meals. As a result, more money than she had planned was spent on two Bundt pans, a zest grater, a glass cake pedestal with a dome, and fresh violets. She planned to cut and place the flowers in a petite vase in the center of the cake. Hanging onto her mother's cart, Cristal got to sniff and explore a plethora of flowers.

"Momma, can I use some of my money to buy a bouquet of roses?" She liked their spicy, fruity smell.

"I'll get them. Save your money for something else." At the moment, Dahlia's spirits were so uplifted that she probably would have agreed to just about anything. On the horizon, her blues would turn to vibrant violets.

Wilky hated the thought of his hair being cut and chopped, especially when he looked around the Classic Cutz Above barber shop and saw other young and older men wearing similar styles.

"It's gonna be alright, little man. I'll hook you up with a fresh new look," said Donovan, Isaacs's barber.

"Can you give me a cut like this?" Wilky pointed to a picture of a boy in a magazine with the unique unpronounceable Prince symbol in his hair. It was considered a 'Love Symbol', a mash-up of the gender symbols for men and women.

"No, I don't think your mom will go for that," Isaac professed.

Donovan voiced his opinion, too, "No doubt I can do it, but those jokers at your school might think it's a gang symbol or something," Wilky and Isaac turned page after page, looking at a few more styles for boys.

"How about this one?" his uncle asked. "You can make it your own and still let it reflect pride." He pointed to a picture of an African American boy with two thick cornrow braids in a horseshoe-like design at the crown with the rest of his hair tapered into a fade.

"Yeah, that's tope! Can you do this, Mr. Donovan?" Wilky asked with great interest.

"Yeah, that's got a fresh vibe. I'll use my clippers to go low on the sides and the back. No problem, I got you."

"Okay, I gotta ask," Isaac commented. "What does tope mean? I can't keep up with you millennials and Generation Z youngsters."

Donovan replied, "It's a mash between tight and dope, Uncle I."

Isaac shook his head and laughed.

Boys aged ten and under at Classic Cutz Above got their first cut for free, but only if they chose a book from the shelf and read it to the barber while he worked his magic. Wilky picked a picture book about a little boy who wanted to be a fighter pilot like the Tuskegee Airmen. The book was far below Wilky's reading level, but he enjoyed it and learned something new. Isaac generously tipped the barber for his artistic hands and for confidently getting his nephew involved in some eye-opening and thought-provoking conversation.

After their trip to the barber, Wilky rode with his uncle to the Green Knolls of Nottingham Golf Course. Isaac initiated a conversation with Wilky about how highly compatible team sports and life are. "You experience not only good, clean fun, but you can learn a lot about yourself when you play with others who are working towards the same goal. Just as much can be learned from your opponents. I enjoyed playing sports as a young boy but was never really good at them." Wilky was surprised to hear that because Uncle Isaac looked big and strong and seemed extra confident. Isaac continued to talk, trying not to sound too preachy.

"At a young age, competitive sports can help you mature and grow. If you stick with them, they will test your resilience and integrity. You learn to start accepting your choices and the consequences that come about because of them."

Wilky contemplated what he had just heard and reflected on his time playing soccer with the Stingrays. "I think you're right, Uncle Isaac. Thank you for taking me to get a haircut. Mr. Donovan is a solid barber. He's the GOAT."

Isaac gave vent to a gregarious laugh, "You're welcome, little man." Wilky listened for the next few moments as his uncle aptly whistled along with a country song on the radio. He was impressed.

Wilky wasn't aware that Isaac's father taught all three of his sons how to whistle at a very young age because his doctor told him that it promoted healthy blood circulation and was good for the heart and lungs. The Granger boys started playing with toy harmonica when they were three or four years old and then graduated to musical whistling.

Wilky tried to whistle along but was unsuccessful. Isaac laughed and reached into the center console of his car. He handed Wilky some Chapstick. "Here, maybe this will help."

Isaac pulled the Range Rover into the parking lot at the golf course and parked diagonally across two spots. He met with his younger brother, Ricky, and two other men from their fraternity. Isaac reached into the back seat to switch his cowboy hat for a golf cap before stepping out of the car. Ricky was anxious to try his new electronic follow/remote control golf caddy. Chloe, his fiancé, gave it to him as a birthday present right after their engagement.

"My knees hurt too much to walk 18 holes," complained Isaac.

"Mine too," said Isaac's buddy, Melvin.

"It's my back," grumbled Shane. As a result, Isaac and his friends opted to rent two golf carts. Ricky played around with his new toy, using the remote to put it in marching mode. He let the electric caddy haul his golf bag with fourteen clubs around and follow him with its electronic eye through the parking lot and up the ramp into the clubhouse. Ricky bought some balls at the Pro Shop while the electric caddy patiently waited a few feet behind.

"I think I'll walk the course," he announced. Ricky enjoyed showing off the electric trolley to onlookers. The caddy followed him towards the tree.

As Ricky and the caddy traversed a slight decline, a flock of gigantic, aggressive geese from a nearby pond chose to protect their turf at that minute. They charged at the rolling caddy. It swerved left and right, dodging the waterfowl species by zigzagging down the hill and jetting past Ricky, who stood near a sand bunker. Ricky frantically hit buttons on the remote to make it stop, but the motor of the poor *'little engine that could'* churned and sputtered. It then crashed into a Capital Pear tree before emitting a plume of black and grey smoke. The two golf carts with family and friends inside swiftly circled back around. Isaac, Ricky's fraternity brother, and Wilky cackled and hooted until their sides began to hurt.

"Where'd Chloe get that contraption from, General Dollar or Five and Under?" Melvin brutally teased.

"She spent the same amount of money on that thing that you spent on that tiny speck of an engagement ring you gave her," heckled Shane. "That's what you get for skimping on that itty bitty piece of a mineral." The three and a half men laughed so hard that two almost vomited. Devastated, Ricky gathered his clubs and bag and put them on the golf cart. He let the erratic caddy cool and then dragged it to the parking lot to throw it in the back of his jeep.

Shane passed Hemingway and Arturo Fuente cigars out before the men began their intermediate game of golf. They talked about the usual trash and discussed politics while enjoying the sport. Around the 8th hole, Wilky grew tired of sitting and watching them play from the cart. According to him, no equivalent form of entertainment brings the same amount of joy as that from a game of soccer. The sport of golf couldn't compare. Later, he told Jeremy that the slow pace of hitting a little white dimpled ball into a minuscule black hole was on the opposite end of the fun spectrum. Chasing your opponent and kicking a large black and white leather ball swiftly into a net was the ultimate sports competition. But Wilky appreciated the time spent with his Uncle Isaac. Isaac was even kind enough to order drinks and snacks for everybody by using an app on his smartphone. When the server arrived at the tenth hole with a super-sized vanilla milkshake mixed with crumbles of a Butterfinger candy bar, Wilky took his time to enjoy it. In between weighty spoonful's, he played one of Kenny's hew hand-held video games.

Cristal helped her mother prepare the lemon cake batter and poured it into two Bundt pans. While they baked, she went to her room and listened to some Haitian Creole–English translation CDs. Dahlia interrupted her.

"Cristal, what dress do you want me to iron for church tomorrow?" Cristal selected a pretty purple and gray pleated dress with a scooped collar and puff sleeves.

Before returning the headphones to her ears, she asked, "Momma, can I wear my black patent leather shoes instead of my loafers?"

"Absolutely," replied Dahlia.

For Wilky, Dahlia starched and ironed a long-sleeved white shirt and pressed a pair of slim black suit pants. She shined his shoes and placed a boy's black and yellow striped necktie on the dresser. For herself, she chose a V-neck teal-colored dress with bell sleeves embellished with a long gold zipper down the back. It stopped just above her knee. Dahlia took down beige pumps hanging from the shoe rack on the back of the closet door. She placed them on the floor. Next, Dahlia opened a small jewelry case to retrieve a dazzling pair of Marquis Csarite diamond earrings gifted by her mother on her wedding day. While in the bathroom, she examined her face closely in the mirror and decided to try something different.

Dahlia put in the work required to take down her micro braids, stopping only once to remove the cakes from the oven. She washed and conditioned her shoulder-length hair and then locked in the moisturizer by blow-drying her thick mane with a small amount of olive oil and coconut serum. Cristal heard her mother calling her into her bedroom. Dahlia wanted Cristal to brush her hair because she knew how much Cristal enjoyed the mixed scents and this intimate show of affection from her mother. After pinning her hair up and tying it down with a scarf, Dahlia returned to the kitchen to decorate one of the cakes with violets and lemon peel swirls as planned.

Later that evening, Wilky asked if Jeremy could come over for pizza and watch wrestling on the big screen upstairs. "Sure, I'll call and ask his mom." Dahlia had previously met Jeremy's mother at the bus stop, and it was apparent to both ladies by the third day of school that their boys would become good friends. Exchanging phone numbers at that time was a smart thing to do. Soon, the pizza delivery guy called from the security gate telephone. Cristal rushed upstairs to put away the weaving loom and loops and then returned to the kitchen.

"I've outgrown this. You can have it," Raeni told Cristal in a condescending tone one day, only to reinforce her elevated teenage status. Dahlia had been happy to participate in the enjoyable and uncomplicated activity of making a potholder. Many descriptive details were given to instruct Cristal on how to create a fun and crafty finished project. While doing so, Dahlia provided instructions primarily in English. She knew how important it was to immerse Cristal in the language to help her succeed in school.

"Pizzas' here!" shouted Wilky, after jerking the drawstring cord to the blinds a nanosecond before the doorbell rang. Dahlia paid the pizza guy with the money Nadine had left under a magnet on the refrigerator from Montreal, Canada. Glasses of fruit punch were filled, and a party-size bag of ranch-flavored chips was placed inside a ceramic bowl. Dahlia joined Cristal, Wilky, and Jeremy at the table. She listened to her children and their friend's cheerful dialogue between bites of extra-large cheesy pepperoni slices with mushrooms and green peppers. Cristal had already started to understand more and more conversations in English with children her age. She was even more adept at making relevant contributions that volleyed for several minutes.

Out of the blue, Dahlia asked Wilky a question.

"What happened to a student in your class during lunchtime? Mrs. Plaizill said that there was a big commotion at the table." Wilky almost choked. He and Jeremy looked at each other and burst into laughter.

Cristal chimed in, "I heard a boy got bugs all over himself and went crazy." The two boys at the table howled. At first, Wilky didn't tell a soul that he was the one responsible for dropping Suduko's live food onto Trevor's head as he slyly brushed past him when Trevor took a seat in the cafeteria. It all happened rather quickly. After committing the dirty deed, he moved on, walking calmly to his seat at the same table to eat his lunch. Jeremy didn't know the details, and Wilky wasn't sure if he should confess. He just wasn't certain how close of a friend Jeremy might earnestly become. But he owned up to it once they started chumming around and playing wrestling.

Jeremy whooped and yelped, giving Wilky a high five to validate the entire incident. Quoting in part an insulting comment he heard from one of his favorite TV shows, he commented, "That goof was playing Chinese checkers while you were playing chess. You castled on him for a checkmate, and he got what he deserved. Ever since we were in kindergarten, he's always looked for somebody different to pick on."

"No cap," Wilky shot back. "Has he ever picked on you?"

"Nope, but that's probably because he knows my big brother, Omarion. He's three years older than Trevor and four inches taller." Wilky nodded with understanding and quickly surmised that his new friend could be trusted.

"I'm surprised his own shadow wants to hang around him," Wilky deduced. Cristal was so tickled with laughter that she blew bubbles through her nose in reaction to Wilky's joke.

"And," said Dahlia, pausing and turning in Cristal's direction with a touch on her arm, "Mrs. Plaizill told me that on Thursday, you dropped a tray full of food in the middle of the cafeteria. She said you were trying to flex by balancing it on your head while using your cane to walk to the table."

"Dag, Mrs. Plaizill is snitched." Cristal claimed. Wilky and Jeremy cracked up with laughter.

In unison, the boys announced, "Snitches get stitches." Cristal repeated the phrase, articulating it emphatically while mimicking a tough gangster-like façade. Dahlia couldn't deny how funny that scenario was, especially from her sweet baby girl. Already, Cristal was learning some not-so-nice slights from her classmates. But for Dahlia, it was gratifying to sit, laugh, and connect with her children once again.

On Sunday morning, Dahlia woke early to shower and dress. After flipping through a fashion magazine the previous night, she chose a striking hairstyle. She created a glamourous halo effect by plaiting two long braids and pinning them around her head. Dahlia applied a new shade of lipstick- *Berries in the Snow*- evenly on her full heart-shaped lips. She then went downstairs, fixed a cereal bowl for her children, hurried them to eat, bathe, and get dressed.

Nadine woke up feeling awful.

Dahlia checked on her twice before leaving for church. "Is there anything else that I can do for you?" she asked.

"I'll be okay. It must have been the calamari salad that I ate at that new Italian restaurant. I checked with Tilly; she had a forkful of my salad, and she was not feeling too great either. Would you bring me some ginger ale, please?" Nadine spoke in a weak voice.

"Of course." Dahlia brought her a couple of crackers and a tall glass of ale with crushed ice. They were placed on the nightstand near Nadine. She lifted her head off the pillow just enough to take a few sips.

"Thank you. You look nice, Dahlia. Go look in my top drawer and get the embroidered silk floral scarf and tie it around your neck," she said in a raspy voice.

Dahlia did as she was directed and then looked at herself in the arched floor-length mirror. She liked how the scarf transformed her entire outfit into something elegant. "Thank you," she said, bending low to kiss Nadine's cheek.

Isaac came in to kiss his wife goodbye. "I'll pick up a couple of cans of chicken noodle soup from the store on my way back."

***

First, Ebenezer Haitian Church had almost two hundred members present on Sunday. Isaac dropped everyone off with little time to spare before the service began. Mrs. Plaizill kept an eye out for Wilky and Cristal to enter through the church's front doors.

"There she is!" shouted Wilky as he pointed to Mrs. Plaizill standing in the foyer.

"Shhhh!" said Dahlia, "lower your voice." Mrs. Plaizill walked over and greeted Dahlia.

"It is so nice to meet you." Dahlia shook her hand.

"It's nice to meet you as well," said Mrs. Plaizill as the organist began a sweeping piped prelude. "Come on, follow me. I'll take you to my pew." She ushered them in. Cristal held onto her mother's arm above her elbow with her right hand. She held Jurnee in a vertical upright position in her left hand with the tip off the floor, just like Mr. Nick taught her to do when traveling with a guide.

The Duvernays sat next to Mrs. Plaizill, and an elderly couple scooted in from the opposite side to share the same pew. Mrs.

Plaizill was proud to have such regal-looking guests standing beside her when the minister asked, "All members and their invited guests, please stand." The service was awe-inspiring, including the choir's selection of hymns.

When it came time to collect tithes, the minister reminded his congregation of the relief fund, separate from the building fund, that went towards 'our brothers and sisters in Haiti'. He cited a passage from the Bible that resonated liberal giving, "Generous people give more than just their money." Members nodded their heads in harmony as he spoke of Luke 10:25-37, the classic story of the Good Samaritan— "one who gave time, resources, and skill to meet the need of a man who had been left for dead at the side of the road."

Later that evening, Dahlia was anxious to speak to Jesse about her church experience and give him an update on their children. "Honey, I am so happy to hear your voice. I have a lot to tell you. You would be so proud of Cristal. There was an incident at the school that she handled very well. I'll tell you more about that later, but she's a trooper. Our girl is fierce and on fire! Cristal is making friends, and one of her teachers wrote me a note in her daily planner. She got an 'A' grade on an assignment, and they didn't just give it to her either. I heard her practicing. She worked hard and earned it. Can you believe it? Our baby girl is learning to speak in front of a class about something she loves to do- make perfumes."

Jesse turned his voice away from the phone's speaker and yelled, "Momma Lou, Cristal got an 'A' on an assignment." In the background, Dahlia could hear Louise praising and clapping her hands in quick succession.

Dahlia continued sharing with an abundance of cheer, "And I signed some paperwork so she can start bringing some braille technology and other equipment home."

"We don't have to buy it for her?" Jesse asked.

"No, honey. It's a loan. Cristal must keep up with it and take good care of it."

"That's alright then. It's hard to believe how fast everything is happening for our girl. It hasn't even been a whole week of school. I knew this would be a good move for Cristal and Wilky."

"Yes. They know exactly what to do for Cristal and other kids without vision. There was a big meeting and everything before she started. They've got a team of experts in this district, and the principal is aware that I plan to keep an eye on how they treat both of our children. Our Cristal is gonna be somebody!"

Dahlia then told Jesse about Wilky getting a haircut because it was district policy to wear his hair above his shoulders. "He didn't want it cut at first, and I didn't either, but he still looks so handsome, just like his daddy. I'm going to try and send you a picture soon." Dahlia talked about their visit to the church earlier in the day and told her husband about Mrs. Plaizill.

"She knew Emmanuel and Nedra." Jesse was surprised to hear his late relative's names. Both, he believed, were long deceased.

"I think the kids and I should join church next Sunday. I wish you were here to stand with us."

"That would be a good thing. I'd like to attend one of their services when I come for Christmas. But I want you to do something for me."

"Sure, what is it?"

"I want you to look into something. Find out if that church has a ministry that offers faith-based counseling or some kind of family help. We have all experienced so much external hardship, you, me, and the children. I know things are starting to look up, but Dahlia, we've been through a lot."

"Well, I'll look into it, but I think we're gonna be okay." There was an extended pause before her husband continued. Dahlia was quite wary about speaking to strangers about her past.

"Dahlia," Jesse said in an executive tone. He needn't say anything else on that topic because Dahlia knew her husband expected her to follow through with the request.

"Alright, I will."

Dahlia changed the subject at full speed after a lengthy silence. "We stayed late at church for dinner, and they served ackee and saltfish with rice and peas. It tasted just like Granny Lou's, and everyone that got a piece of my lemon praline cake loved it."

"Well, of course, honey, it's real good. You know that's why I married you, to keep the flow of succulent cakes coming. Nobody does it better."

Dahlia giggled and continued, "The secretary at the church, Vivian Stallings, said that she was pretty sure she could get me a job at the DeKalb Farmer's Market where she works. There's a waiting list for the employees who want to transfer into the bakery department, but I could probably start off in the produce section."

"You sound excited. Is that really what you want to do?"

"I think so. I'll dip my toe in the water and see what happens. Mrs. Stallings said that people from over 40 countries speaking 50 different languages work there. And this place receives global shipments of fresh foods and ethnic cuisines from all around the world. I think it could be a fantastic place to work."

"Well, okay, if that's what you want to do. Is the market close to the house?" asked Jesse.

"I don't know, but if I have to, I'll catch the bus or local train or something. Isaac said that he'd help me map it out. Honesty honey, I can't sit in this house with that nutty Einstein-like bird all day while everybody else is at work or school." Jesse heard his wife's frustration loud and clear through the phone.

"Oh yeah, I forgot to mention that Nadine's not feeling too good right now."

"What's wrong with her?"

"I'm not sure. She thinks maybe it was the calamari she ate at an Italian restaurant last night."

"Well, send sis my love and tell her I hope she feels better."

"I will. How are you doing?" Dahlia asked.

"I'm doing okay, baby. I just miss my sugar dumpling a lot."

Dahlia giggled like a schoolgirl. "I miss you too, honey."

There was much more Dahlia wanted to share with her husband, but she knew the call was growing expensive by the minute. "The church has volunteers who are also working on earthquake relief efforts, and I want to help if I can." Jesse was relieved to hear his wife's spirits lifted. He hadn't stopped worrying about his family since they left.

Dahlia continued, "Once we join the church, I will give the member who heads the relief ministry your name. I think it might help them feel more certain about tracking their food, money, and clothing donations."

Jesse agreed, "That's a good idea. Without coordination and real leadership from the top, it's like trying to build a plane in the sky here. I'll do what I can from this end and give my boss a head's up once you have more information. There's been talk about embezzlement on a grand scale. Large sums of money and tangible donations don't always reach our people in need."

Dahlia remembered something else significant. "One more thing before I put the kids on the phone. There's a teacher, a Mr. Oblinger, who is Wilky's gym teacher. I spoke to him on the phone yesterday, and he wants Wilky to try out for a youth soccer team. If he makes it, which I'm sure he will, the cost will be expensive. He said something about his brother being a scout and could see to it that Wilky gets some sort of scholarship if he's selected. They've got a Friendly going on next weekend, and they want Wilky there. But we'd still have to pay five hundred dollars for equipment and other things."

Jesse sighed long and hard. He thought about the previous conversation he had had with his son and how down Wilky was feeling. He hoped that the bullying situation would somehow improve.

"I know it would be good for him, but Dahlia, that's a lot of money. What's the financial situation like now?" Jesse inquired.

"Well, I've only spent money on groceries, a few clothing items, and school supplies so far. I do think it would be good for Wilky. If I get the job at the market, there will be enough to give Nadine and

Isaac a little something for the utilities, and I'll still have grocery money. I think we'll be okay."

Jesse hesitated, "Alright then, we'll let our little painter paint. But don't worry about the rent. As I mentioned to you before, I told Isaac I'd transfer money to him on the tenth of every month. Use the money to take care of the groceries and the everyday things that y'all need. But take your time finding work, Dahlia. It's not really urgent. As I said, you've been through a lot. Moving far away from the only home you've known to a totally different country can take a toll on the body and the mind."

Dahlia was comforted knowing that her husband's unconditional love transcended over 1,260 miles. Jesse was doing just as he had promised her father over twelve years ago when he asked permission for her hand in marriage. Her husband was still taking good care of her by putting the family front and center.

Dahlia had one more thing to say before handing off the phone. "You know, you're my modern-day Boaz, right?" Cristal and Wilky were so noisy, impatiently jumping about, making high-pitched chirping sounds and creating a rowdy scene. Sudoku became upset and confused. He began squawking up a storm. Dahlia wasn't sure if Jesse had heard her last loving comment or not.

"Are those chuck-chuck calls coming from my noisy little chipmunk?"

"Yes, Lawd. They're about to go crazy waiting to talk to their daddy."

"Well, put 'em on the phone. I need to hear my babies' voices."

Dahlia handed Wilky the phone first. "Don't talk too long. This is long distance, and it's expensive," she warned them.

Wilky nodded and took the phone, "Daddy, I did just what you said, and I used my head. I think everything is going to be okay. I'm making new friends, and I don't think it's going to be a problem anymore." Wilky hoped that he was speaking the truth. He wanted his father to be proud that he handled things well. Dahlia raised her eyebrows in question and wondered what trouble Wilky had gotten himself into.

Their Papa Jesse uttered a sigh of relief once more. He had worried a lot since he last spoke to Wilky. Could his son defend himself from a brute? He prayed that Wilky wouldn't do something foolish and get into trouble so soon after the start of a new school. "I'm proud of you, son, real proud. I know you are a smart boy and you can take care of yourself."

Wilky beamed, "Yep, Papa, and my gym teacher watched me playing around with a soccer ball and said he liked my skills. I think he wants me to try out for a real competitive team." Wilky talked about a hundred miles an hour until Dahlia interrupted and told him to give the phone to his sister.

"Hi, Daddy."

"Hey, Sweet Pea."

"Daddy, I'm learning new technology and a lot of other good things to help me read books and write at school. I got a cane named Jurnee, and my teachers liked it when I talked about making my perfumes. They said I did a good job at my work." Her father began to sniffle. Papa Jesse hoped that Cristal wouldn't recognize the emotional change in his voice.

"That is amazing, pumpkin. I love hearing good news about you and the things you're doing." Cristal's voice began to quiver too.

"Wilky wants to play the drums at church, but I'm going to sing in the children's choir." Under his breath, Papa Jesse thanked God. Cristal ended the conversation by saying, "I miss you, Daddy, and thank you for everything."

Chapter Twenty-Five:
Fishwife

The nineteenth-century Haitian ruling class was comprised of two groups: the urban elite and those with military leadership. The urban elite was primarily a closed group of educated, comparatively wealthy French and English-speaking Mulattoes. Dahlia Joseph was raised in a family of the urban elite. Her parents, Samuel, and Jean were well-respected upper-echelon community members. On the day that she saw Jesse Duvernay for the first time, Dahlia was seventeen years of age and crazy in love with a young man named Sterling Laurent. His grandfather and great-grandfather were military men held in high regard within their community.

Dahlia had known Sterling since she was twelve years old. Her mother and Mrs. Laurent didn't always travel in the same circles but were fairly good acquaintances. Samuel Joseph owned properties, including a restaurant, a small nightclub, and several commercial rental properties. He was also a business partner in a joint venture overseas with Mr. Laurent. The two men, along with other entrepreneurial investors, traveled every two years to the state of Florida to attend conventions on how to establish and grow an international business. They stood accompanied by distinguished men of the same caliber who aimed to provide philanthropic assistance to Haitians who struggled to rise above poverty.

At that time, Jesse and his work bud, Ricardo, were carpenters who helped renovate some of Mr. Joseph's properties. Later, they were commissioned to replace the flooring in the Josephs' luxury home located in the Laboule area above the hills of Petionville,

Haiti. For Jesse, it was love at first sight when he laid eyes on Dahlia. He and Ricardo were removing hardwood flooring and installing Italian marble on the second floor of the Joseph's mansion. After a few hours, the young men needed a break from inhaling toxic chemicals, so they stepped out on the wraparound terrace for fresh air.

A welcoming panoramic view of Haiti's border with the Caribbean Ocean and the Dominican Republic greeted the young men. At that time, Dahlia was relaxing at the pool wearing a blue and yellow one-piece swimsuit adorned with daisies. Her copper-colored hair was pulled up in a ponytail with soft tendrils cascading downward, framing a heart-shaped face. A pair of oversized rectangular designer Chanel sunglasses rested comfortably on the bridge of her button nose. Jesse overhead Dahlia and her older sister Mariah laughing and chatting giddily about their upcoming vacation to Athens, Greece. Dahlia's mother, Jean, made plans to take her daughters on the elaborate three-week getaway to celebrate Mariah's 21st birthday and Dahlia's high school graduation. Their trip included several guided tours chock-full of ancient history, beautiful beaches, and visits to the home of Aristotle and Hippocrates.

"Look at that goddess right there," Jesse directed Ricardo's gaze. "Her caramel-colored skin looks like one who's been kissed by the morning sun every single day. Those pouty pink lips are perfect. I bet her eyes sparkle like diamonds."

His buddy Ricardo laughed hard, "Man, you need to chill. We're here to do a job, get paid, and then get out of here. I don't think you're quite the son-in-law material for one of Mr. Joseph's daughters, but you are correct. Both of them are gorgeous. The one in the black two-piece with the belly ring looks like a beauty queen."

Jesse shook his head, "Nah, it's the other one for me. She's an angel."

Ricardo admitted, "I'm just a poor carpenter trying to make an honest living. I know I'd never have a shot at dating either one of them."

Jesse placed each hand firmly on Ricardo's shoulders, "Never say never, my man. Trust me. I'm going to marry the one in the blue swimsuit. She's a vision of rapture." Ricardo let out a deep raucous, roaring laugh, prompting the young ladies to turn and gaze up at the men standing on their balcony. Dahlia lifted her sunglasses for a better view and fastened her eyes with Jesse's for a fugitive moment. "I told you her eyes shine like jewels," declared Jesse.

"Stay calm. Those chemicals are damaging every cell in your brain, my friend. Maybe we should call it a day," Ricardo joked. The men shared another hearty guffaw and returned inside to continue their manual labor job.

After quitting time, Jesse parted ways with Ricardo and decided to ride a tap tap to *Marché en Fer*, a public market in Port-au-Prince. He picked up a few items for his grandmother, but his real reason for traveling there was to visit a vendor who was an old acquaintance of the Joseph family. Jesse was curious about the attractive young lady who seemed to have a magnetic spell on him. Her name, he discovered, was Dahlia. She was named after one of her mother's favorite flowers. Upon further research, Jesse read that the name 'Dahlia' symbolized beauty, commitment, and kindness. The foreshadowing of her personal story after the earthquake couldn't have rung truer; according to the *Encyclopedia of Flowers,* dahlias are tied to steadfastness. This is due to their ability to bloom after many surrounding flowers have died. Jesse believed in his heart that

Dahlia was a sweet and confident young lady with high energy and vitality for life.

When Jesse and Ricardo returned the following day to finish the job, Dahlia and Mariah sat lounging by the pool once more. But this time, two dashing bronzed-skinned males sat beside them. Several other young adults either swam, chatted poolside, played frisbee, and enjoyed frolic and carefree fun. A giant multi-colored decorative banner stretched across a grassy area with dozens of helium balloons tethered to each end. Jesse quickly realized that he was observing a graduation party held for Dahlia and a group of her high school friends. Somewhat disappointed, he watched only briefly as the subject of his desire giggled and screamed with glee.

A young man named Sterling chased Dahlia around the courtyard. The tall and lean chevalier then picked Dahlia up and turned her upside down. "Stop! Stop!" she chortled and skreiched breathlessly while kicking her legs crazily in play. Eventually, Sterling turned Dahlia upright, gave her a big, sloppy kiss, and devilishly tossed her into the pool's deep end. Sterling ran to the diving board, climbed up top, and bounced high in the air. With his chin tucked and knees bent, a colossal cannonball splash was achieved. The young couple continued with nonstop unabashed amusement and full-blown antics in and out of the water. Jesse turned away, dispirited. It was as if an unruly donkey had kicked him in the chest. Dahlia and Sterling's entangled joy was far too tormenting for Jesse to witness.

Ricardo recognized the dejected effect the series of tableaux had on his best friend. "Man, just forget about that girl. It ain't your turn. She's probably an obnoxiously spoiled brat anyways."

By any young lady's standards, Jesse was quite the catch himself. Suitors, since his high school days, lined up just hoping for a chance to date Rachelle and Nadine's big brother. Jesse stood 6'2" and weighed 212 pounds. His pecan-colored skin and chiseled muscular build made him quite a looker. But, his kind demeanor, commitment to hard work, and faith in God were characteristics that eventually won Dahlia over.

When Dahlia returned home from a dream vacation in Greece, her world was turned upside down, topsy-turvy, and inside and out. Her splendid childhood days, filled with rainbows and flying unicorns, screeched to an unforeseen end. Sterling, her boyfriend of two years, had fallen head over heels for a young lady named Sarik. The exotic-looking twenty-year-old, whose mother was Korean and father Haitian, was an older cousin of one of Sterling's longtime friends. She had been vacationing in Haiti from the U.S. for twelve days. Months later, rumors spread that Sarik was pregnant and that Sterling was diligently making efforts to be with her by completing and filing the necessary documents to relocate to Austin, Texas. The fairy tale with Dahlia and Sterling was abruptly halted, and there was nothing her parents of esteemed prestige could do to turn the tides.

Jesse and Ricardo returned to the Joseph estate late that summer to work on another construction project, and that's when Dahlia and Jesse officially met. She was 18 years old at the time, and Jesse was 23. Unbeknownst to him, Dahlia and Sterling's courtship had reached their expiration date months before. Dahlia was curious about the tall, handsome man who seldom looked up from his work to acknowledge and greet her with nothing more than a friendly 'hello'. She thought his broad smile and dimpled chin were the features of gods. Dahlia eventually gathered enough nerve one afternoon to offer Jesse and Ricardo a slice of her pineapple upside-down cake with a side of lighthearted babble. Almost an hour passed before she returned to clean the mess left in the kitchen. Enamored feelings conjured by Jesse's suave intellect and sarcastic but humorous nature solemnly revived the listless beat of her heart. As if fate was written in Sanskrit rule, Dahlia was powerless to change destiny. There was no turning back now.

Mr. Joseph respected Jesse's work ethic and skills for assembling and repairing almost anything on his residential properties. He practically became a fixture himself. But unfortunately for Jesse, Ricardo had been correct all along. One Sunday evening, when Mr. and Mrs. Joseph returned exhausted from a ten-night cruise in Antigua, they were appalled to see Jesse and Dahlia frolicking and splashing about in the pool. Mr. Joseph's piercing glare prompted Jesse to vacate the water immediately. He walked-ran to the pool house to change into a pair of olive-colored cargo shorts and a dark blue Polo shirt. Mr. Joseph met Jesse at an exterior side door to the main house, where he went to retrieve his tool bag. A hand placed on the chest of Dahlia's new love interest prevented him from entering.

The upset and protective father had a few curt words to share with the young man who had been stealing time with his youngest daughter. But before he could complete his monologue, Jesse interrupted and asked for Dahlia's hand in marriage.

"I'm sorry, son, but I cannot grant permission for you to marry her. I don't know how to say this without sounding cruel, but my daughters deserve to marry men in their own social class."

Jesse wasn't totally surprised by Mr. Joseph's response, but he was sickened to think that Dahlia would not be a part of his future.

He swallowed his pride and pleaded, "I promise you, sir, I will love, protect, and take good care of her for all the days of my life." Eavesdropping from around the corner of the mudroom was where Dahlia and her mother stood.

Naturally, Mrs. Joseph's convictions on so many chief principles were tied to her husband of twenty-five years. She wholeheartedly agreed with his opinions and the standards he set for their daughters. "You're too old for her," Mrs. Joseph spouted sharply into the thickness of the air. Leaning closer to whisper into her daughter's ear, she announced, "He is nothing but a rebound from Sterling. Listen to me. I know what I'm talking about. You're not in love with this man!" Her mother continued to rant, "You know nothing about how he was raised. Who knows if he even had a role model in his own life that exhibited the qualities needed to lead a healthy and supportive relationship."

Mrs. Joseph rattled on like a voice from a radio. "He may not possess the emotional maturity to be a respectable father to our future grandchildren."

Dahlia blubbered through ragged breathing and tears of hysteria, "Stop it, momma, just stop it! I am in love with him. I'm looking at this both ways like you and Daddy taught me from a very early age. I already know he comes from humble beginnings, but I sense something special in him. The Bible says, 'By humility and the fear of the Lord are riches and honor and life'."

Dahlia's mother shot her husband a questionable side glance after that unexpected religious quote, looking for help. Samuel Joseph was quick to avert his eyes down to the floor to kick back in place curled tassels on a plush Moroccan rug. Jean Joseph feared there was a slight chance that her daughter could win this argument.

"I want a life with him," Dahlia announced to everyone in earshot and yonder.

Mrs. Joseph's fuchsia pink finely manicured nails dug into her daughter's arm, leading her into the foyer, unintentionally remaining within earshot of Jesse.

"Ouch, momma. That hurts!" Dahlia winced.

Mrs. Joseph loosened her grip apologetically but continued, "He's kind to you and he's handsome. I get that. But take your time and date around. You're young and beautiful, baby. You'll have many suitors, gentlemen who are more educated, someone who can offer you financial security. Sweetie, you are blinded by love. You're not thinking rationally." The pleading was relentless and despicable. Mr. Joseph and Jesse stood motionless, locked in a mutual trance of shock. Although they stood on separate sides of the fence, neither was prepared for the rapid and brutal firing of such an appalling display of emotionalism. "I'm sorry." mouthed Mr. Joseph.

He then turned to face Jesse and look at him straight in the eyes. In one swift movement, Mr. Joseph punctured the space between them with his index finger as he delivered a stern request, "Let me say this, if you and my daughter decide to go against me and my wife's desires and proceed with marriage, I simply ask that you do the honorable thing and return her unharmed to me when love no longer resides in your heart."

"Yes, sir," Jesse answered. "I wasn't raised like that. I would never hurt Dahlia."

Dahlia sat slumped in a swanky golden-colored Louis XVI-styled armchair, fighting off the blows of verbal trouncing her mother dealt. Markedly, she rocked back and forth with her head held tight in her trembling hands. She wept like a baby. Mariah knew her role as the oldest, 'wiser' daughter required her to act or say something keen and influential at that moment. Understanding the lure and magic of young love, she was in a precarious position. She knelt to speak softly to her sister. "There will be others, Dahlia. The right man will appear one day when you least expect it. He'll treat you like a princess, showering you with love and offering more than your heart will ever desire." But to no avail was her big sister's appeal.

Mrs. Joseph made one last relentless comment before Dahlia stood to go to her room, "A woman is supposed to marry up, Dahlia-not down."

Dahlia pivoted on her ascension at the landing of a winding staircase, "I'm leaving my reputation in the arms of God. And if you and Daddy disapprove of that, I won't allow myself to be imprisoned by your feelings of superiority."

A month later, Jesse moved Dahlia out of her home with her three suitcases and two medium-sized boxes. He settled her into his sister Rachelle's spartan one-bedroom apartment. An anxious but hopeful Dahlia tried to make herself small in the crowded space until that special day arrived. It was on September 18, 1999. A gathering of Jesse's family and a small group of friends in the church where the Duvernays had been members for years assembled for a wedding. Ricardo was the best man, and Mariah was Dahlia's maid of honor. Her sister was the only Joseph family member present for the ceremony. But, to Dahlia's surprise, two of her close friends from high school were also there to give their blessings.

"You've got a beautiful new dress and a vintage rose-gold bracelet from your soon-to-be grandmother-in-law, Louise. Now, you're going to need something blue," Mariah declared as she handed Dahlia a dainty white linen handkerchief with blue embroidered flowers in the center. "And now," she paused for effect, "something borrowed." Dahlia gasped as she examined the sparkling jewels Mariah held in her hand. "These are from momma."

Tears of happiness fell from Dahlia's eyes as she slipped on a pair of pierced Marquis Csarite diamond earrings.

"They're not truly borrowed; she wants you to keep them," Mariah winked. She decided to wait until after the ceremony to give the new bride the envelope from their father that contained an embarrassingly small check written for a measly two thousand dollars.

On June 1, 2000, the newlyweds received a very precious gift named Cristal Shyana Duvernay. Their son, William DeMarco Duvernay, was born a year after Cristal on May 17, 2001.

Dahlia managed to salvage the relationship in part with both of her parents soon after Cristal was born. However, she no longer spent quality time with her mother or father like she yearned. Begrudgingly, Dahlia, Jesse, and their two babies in tow were permitted to visit the Joseph's home but never felt welcomed enough for an extended visit. Because she was truly happy and living with no regrets, Dahlia couldn't understand why her parents chose not to embrace her new family with deep love and veneration.

Those memories were in the forefront of Dahlia's mind as she stared out of a large, tinted bus window with a paperback romance novel resting on her lap. She observed the infrastructure of an inner city and its seemingly infinite brick-and-mortar features constrained by a landlocked landscape. It was so different from the island setting of rugged mountains, river valleys, and coastal plains that Dahlia had known all her life. The #102 Garland Transit bus was outbound and headed to her stop, three blocks from the Willow Wood Townhomes.

Thanks to Mrs. Stallings, Dahlia was hired to work at the DeKalb Farmer's Market.

Unfortunately, most of the open positions required her to unpack boxes or stock shelves at different departments throughout the 140,000-square-foot building. The only other option was for Dahlia to work at the massive seafood department. She chose a position in the seafood department and could now be called a 'fishwife'; a woman who sells fish.

Without a doubt, Dahlia knew if Jean and Samuel Joseph were alive, they would be profoundly disappointed in her current plight – married and selling fish for a living. It wouldn't have mattered that their oldest daughter had two failed marriages to wealthy and educated men. The union between Mariah and her first husband was supported wholeheartedly by her elitist parents. However, it was slowly revealed that her first husband was an abusive man.

He slapped her around whenever he felt that Mariah went too far with her spending. It was sinful, he believed, for her to delve into their finances for lavish furnishings for the home. After the fourth brutal encounter, her mother stepped in, "If you continue to stay, you're no longer a victim. You'll be a willing volunteer." Needless to say, that marriage was short-lived, and Mr. Joseph used his influence in city government to ensure that the vile and violent man spent a significant amount of time in jail.

Mariah's second husband, Winston Ryder Nortey, was a notorious philanderer. Life with this conceited man caused Mariah a great deal of pain, to the extent that she fell into deep depression.

It hurt Dahlia to see her sister downright miserable almost all the time. Despite his admitted dalliances and fauxpologies, Winston frequently attempted to gaslight his wife into believing their problems were all her fault. He once said to her, "To be such a beautiful woman, you're far too insecure to create a happy home with anyone."

One afternoon over lunch, Mariah confided in Dahlia, "I've stayed long enough. I plan to divorce him. I only stayed this long because he's the father of our son, and Winston Jr. adores him." Dahlia held her sister's hand, squeezing it gently as a show of support and understanding. Mariah continued, "The constant arguing and name-calling have taken their toll, and it's just too much for me to endure. I don't want my child to believe that this is a normal husband and wife relationship. My son deserves better." Dahlia was relieved when Mariah reached that conclusion because it exonerated her from responding in punitive judgment.

Sadly, days after the earthquake, thousands of Haitian citizens, wealthy and poor, were indiscriminately scattered throughout the land. There was no knowledge of Winston Jr. or his father's whereabouts. On behalf of his wife, Jesse used his connections throughout the city to try and locate them, but to no avail. Dahlia's hope for her only nephew was that he was a survivor and living somewhere in Haiti with extended family on his father's side or in temporary government housing. Mariah's day in court to finalize her second divorce was set for February 3, 2010. It was scheduled only weeks before the catastrophic quake when Dahlia promised her sister she would sit by her side in the courthouse.

***

At the market where Dahlia worked, there were over 450 varieties of whole fish, fillets, and shellfish. Wild fresh fish arrived weekly from seas as far away as Greece and New Zealand. Luckily for Dahlia the fish cutter, she was no stranger to cleaning, gutting, shucking, scaling, and filleting fish. Her children's great-grandfather, William Duvernay, had been quite the fisherman. Jesse used to take Dahlia and the children fishing with his father on weekends. Sometimes, they'd fish from a chartered boat in the Caribbean and the Atlantic. Other times, they'd spend time picnicking and fishing from a pier near the Dominican Republic. It was a fun family outing for them all. Granny Lou looked forward to cooking special meals the following days after returning from their day-long adventures. That was when Dahlia began to acquire the skills needed for her current job. It actually paid better than some of the other jobs at the farmer's market, and Dahlia was one of the few women to fill the vacant positions in the seafood department. She impressed the interviewer when they walked to the rear of the warehouse, where workers unloaded crates from numerous trucks. Dahlia could name quite a few species right off the top. "Over there," she pointed out, "are mofongo, kallaloo, coucou, pwason woz. And over here," she gestured, "are Keshi yana, sere, red snapper…"

At the end of her first day on the job, Dahlia walked inside the townhouse tired, but it was a good kind of tired. Cristal rushed to hug her mother in her 'Stay Calm and Plant a Flower' t-shirt. "Momma, momma, how was your first day at work?"

Dahlia sighed, "Oh, baby, it was okay. I guess I can say that I had a good day." Cristal wrinkled her nose, and Dahlia chuckled. "I know, I know," said Dahlia, playfully squeezing her daughter's nose and trying to beat her to the punch.

"Uhh, Momma, you smell like fish." Dahlia kicked off her shoes and headed straight upstairs to run warm water in the bathtub. She couldn't recall the last time she stood on her feet for that many hours in a single day. Under the cabinet, she found citrus-scented bath bombs and a bag of Epsom salt. Dahlia opted for therapeutic relief and proceeded to add a cup of eucalyptus spearmint salt to her bath. She looked forward to having the force from the Jacuzzi jets circulate the water and massage her body for pure relaxation and penetrating relief.

Nadine picked up fried chicken, coleslaw, baked beans, and buttery rolls for dinner.

Conversation at the table was easy and comforting. Dahlia ranked her day with an eight. "It was rather fast-paced, and there were a few loud and belligerent customers, but overall, it was a good day."

"I'd rank my day a nine," said Cristal. "Kendall was absent, but I still had fun at the afterschool nature club. We planted oregano seeds and garlic. In October, Mrs. Lovelady said we can pick some tomatoes from the greenhouse and use them to make our tomato sauce for hand-made pizzas!"

Dahlia smiled, "That's a great cooking activity."

"It does sound like fun," said Raeni. "I'd rank my day a seven. Nothing special happened. My orchestra teacher said my solo arrangement is coming along nicely, but I need to practice more."

Isaac took a bite from his extra crispy drumstick and gave Raeni a high five. "That's good, baby. Keep practicing every day after school. I want to hear you ace that solo at your next concert."

"Okay, Daddy, I will. You guys remember that student last spring who slipped alcohol into the girl's drink who played the character Rose in the musical Bye Bye Birdie?"

Isaac broke out in bellowing laughter, "Oh yeah, I remember that crazy scene. It was obviously an unexpected response after she took 'a *spot of spiked tea*' from a cup then spit it out. Isaac mocked the scene using a high-pitched voice like a regal 17th-century English woman as he took a sip from his glass with a pinky finger sticking out in the air. He sounded and looked comical, making the others laugh."

"She forgot her next lines after that debacle," Nadine noted, "and whatever happened to that kid who did it? Didn't he get suspended?"

"Yep, he got expelled and didn't come back this year. Somebody said he's being homeschooled."

"Hmmm…I know it violated school policy to have alcohol on school premises, but for a first-time offense, that seems a bit harsh," stated Nadine.

"How's that psychology assignment of yours coming along?" inquired Isaac.

"Okay, I guess. We're supposed to execute a beta testing strategy for our games. Will you all help and be my focus group in about two weeks?" Everyone around the table nodded and agreed to support Raeni on the edutainment game she created entitled *SCURRED*.

Wilky ranked his day a seven, although Trevor was back in school. He was almost certain that Trevor tried to trip him when he went to sharpen his pencil. Trevor had spent his long absence in St.

Louis, Missouri, with his mother. They had been visiting a sick relative. While eating lunch earlier in the day, Kenny told Wilky and Jeremy that he overheard Trevor tell Mrs. Collier that his cousin had gotten very sick. The sixteen-year-old high school football star was swimming in the Lake of the Ozarks over the summer and fell victim to a flesh-eating amoeba. The parasite traveled from his nose to his brain. Fortunately, after a three-week stay in the hospital, the doctors gave their young patient two thumbs up and sent him home to recover.

Dahlia glanced at Wilky's clothing. He wore a blue and yellow 'Let's Go Lego' t-shirt, and she remembered this was the first day of Cobra Clubs. "How was the Lego club?"

"It was good. Jeremy and I are erecting a medieval castle. I'm going to let him put the draw bridge wherever he wants." After Wilky's last comment, Cristal's mind again drifted back to that dreadful day she sat on the porch with Wilky and Marjon. It was abhorrent torture to hear her mother and father argue about her dismal future. Silently, she thought, '*Thank goodness momma's friend Zoe had no power at all over anybody in our house.*'

"I'm going to have to do something special for Mrs. Parker," Dahlia announced. "Maybe I'll bake her a pie or cake for kindly agreeing to bring you and Cristal home with Jeremy on Cobra Club days. That farmer's market has spices and fruits from all around the world. I may even try a new recipe for her."

"That's real sweet, Dahlia. You're a good person," Nadine remarked. Cristal reached over and squeezed her mother's hand. The gentle gesture from her daughter was validation that they both were moving in positive directions.

Chapter Twenty-Six:
Seesaw

By the end of the first sixth-week grading period, Ms. Saunders and Mrs. Tubilleja were very pleased with Cristal's progress and her motivation to achieve her goals. Mrs. Tubilleja told Dahlia that Cristal's receptive communication skills were more substantial than her expressive skills. "That's normal, and over time, while she's in a school setting, Cristal will transition naturally into speaking predominantly in English. However, I always encourage my parents to continue speaking to their children in their original language. It's so important to hold on to the richness of the unique cultural norms."

Dahlia sighed with relief before responding. "Well, I am pleased with everything you're telling me, and at the dinner table, I am requiring Cristal to speak in English as best she can."

Cristal was advancing more in writing the braille code than reading it, which wasn't uncommon for some adventitiously blinded persons. Ms. Saunders told Dahlia not to worry because they would continue working on their writing skills daily. For starters, Cristal had access to several recorded books in the auditory format. Her social studies, language arts, and science books were immediately downloaded onto her laptop so she could listen to them instead of trying to struggle with braille during the early stages of her training. Ms. Saunders told Dahlia that It would likely take about two years and maybe even enrollment in summer school before Cristal would become a fluent braille reader and writer. And like Mr. Nick, Ms. Saunders also used translation software when she thought it was necessary. Her teacher was pretty impressed with Cristal's ability to complete math assignments with the Cranmer abacus because most of her VI students didn't catch on so quickly. Some had to abandon the skill altogether.

"My Aunt Rachelle taught me to use the abacus. I learned how to add my allowance."

"Well, the next time you talk to her, tell her she is an excellent teacher!" Cristal sparkled inside. She missed Aunt Rachelle and Mikaela dearly and hoped she would get to talk to them soon.

"Cristal, if you are serious about becoming a perfumer someday, you must take several science courses, mostly chemistry."

"Yes, I will be a perfumer and make perfumes." She had no idea what the word chemistry meant.

"Well, I believe that you can do it. I will talk to your science teacher, Mrs. Lovelady, about some skills we can work on while you're in elementary school. If any talking gadgets or tools will assist you, I can order them for you now to become familiar with. Then I say, let's do it!"

"Tools?" questioned Cristal.

"I'm speaking about tools of measurement and gadgets that talk. Some devices like scales, thermometers, water level indicators, and other items will 'tell' you whatever they are measuring. Hold on."

Ms. Saunders knew her explanation was inadequate, so she walked over to a tall file cabinet and retrieved a box of new and used electronic items. She showed Cristal a talking ruler, a talking watch, and a talking compass.

"I like this," replied Cristal as she angled the talking compass from left to right.

"I'll also see if I can get permission to download a few apps on your tablet that will allow you to listen as they read aloud small print materials on bottles. Some apps can even recognize and tell the names and colors of objects." Cristal was excited and could tell Ms. Saunders was genuinely motivated to help her.

"Good!" she exclaimed.

"Next year, when you're proficient at reading Grade 2 braille, I'll introduce you to the periodic table. I can show it to you now, but it will make more sense when you're taught more about each chemical element and know their associated symbols."

Cristal understood only a smattering of the explanation her teacher provided. Still, she enjoyed spending time perusing the big chart of letters and numbers with her fingers in neat, systematic rows and columns.

Mr. Nick knocked before entering the vision resource room. A set of jingling bells sounded when he opened it.

"Hey there, Cristal. Are you ready for some O&M?"

"Yes, sir!" Taking part in O&M lessons was a favored part of Cristal's school day. In a very tidy manner, she gathered her belongings and stored them in her backpack. In the large front pocket, she pulled out her folding cane. The 'click, click, click' unfolding sound that Jurnee made when Cristal stood holding the grip of the cane high was pleasing.

"Oh, I almost forgot to give you this," said Ms. Saunders. "Give this to your mother. I would like permission to invite you back to the room on Friday for lunch and recess to attend our first Chat & Chomp session celebrating White Cane Day. We will have four extraordinary guest speakers."

"Okay, I'll give it to my mom." It wasn't until Cristal shared the letter with Tiara that she understood exactly what Ms. Saunders said about Friday's event. She didn't want to miss hanging out with her friends for lunch or recess, but she trusted that Ms. Saunders had something important in mind for her to learn.

Mr. Nick had another creative lesson planned for Cristal. First, she was required to practice traveling to three different exit doors from homeroom. Next, she reviewed the two-point touch cane technique with Jurnee held at midline. They traveled outside and down the sidewalk to the corner of an intersection. Midway, Cristal stopped and paused.

"What is it? What's wrong?" asked Mr. Nick.

"Oh, nothing. I think I felt the sidewalk go up a little."

"You've got to be kidding me! That's called the apex. Most people don't pick up on that." Cristal smiled and repeated the new word, 'apex'. They continued walking to the corner, where her O&M teacher explained the parallel and perpendicular traffic flow.

"The cars I hear are travel from east to west." Mr. Nick was pleasantly surprised. "You're correct, Cristal. But how did you know that?"

Cristal smiled, "My great grandfather taught me that the sun is over up at noon, and it rises in the east and then travels west. Lunchtime comes soon. The traffic (she pointed to her left), is east. I feel the sun here (she pointed to her cheek)."

Mr. Nick was stupefied. Most of the older students understood the concept, but he was very impressed because this was Cristal's first year receiving formal O&M training.

The last part of the lesson involved Cristal teaching one of her peers the human guide technique, including reversing directions and narrow passages. Once they walked through the school's main doors, Mr. Nick greeted Nevaeh. She was seated in a lounge chair, waiting to learn a new skill. Mr. Nick reviewed the human guide travel method with Cristal and then watched as she explained it to Nevaeh. The girls traveled as a team down the art hallway. On both sides of the hall was an exhibition called 'In Focus Throughout the World'. The famous photographer took colorful and vibrant photos of children from different cultures engaging in everyday activities. Nevaeh's role in the exercise was to describe a picture in four sentences.

Cristal was to listen carefully, repeat what she heard, and then ask at least three follow-up questions. Cristal asked several questions. "What is in the right hand? Does she wear glasses? What color are her shoes? Is he smiling? How old is the girl."

Mr. Nick told Mrs. Tubilleja about the activity and complimented her students on their excellent participation. Cristal and Nevaeh had a few minutes to talk amongst themselves and take a break before heading to the cafeteria for lunch.

During PE class on Thursday, the students in Mrs. Collier's class were given the option to play basketball or four square. Wilky and his friends Kenny and Jeremy opted for basketball with other boys and girls. They were on the green team. Trevor was on the opposing blue team. Mr. Oblinger tossed the ball in the air, which was then put into play. The tallest boy in the class deflected the ball to a girl on the blue team, and the fun began. The ball dribbled, bounced, and passed. Players were fouled, and points were scored. It was a tight game of zone defense. Within ten minutes, the green team had eight points, and the blue team had five. Trevor was becoming riled and upset because his team was losing and Wilky and his squad celebrated excessively. They gave high fives and fist bumps accompanied by hoots and hollers.

When the last basket was made, Mr. Oblinger avoided a call for a dead-ball foul. And adding insult to injury, Trevor began copiously protesting because he felt unfairly taunted by members of the green team. As a result, when Mr. Oblinger stepped away to handle a minor skirmish with the four-square players, Trevor stuck out his foot and tripped Wilky. He went down hard and came up quickly with a busted lip and blood in his mouth from biting his tongue. Wilky remembered exactly what his father told him, 'Do not run, and do not back away'. Wilky was mad. Kenny later said it looked like fiery flames were shooting from his eyes.

Trevor, standing four inches taller than Wilky and about fifteen pounds heavier, dared Wilky to hit him. "Who's the sissy now, huh, huh?"

Wilky pulled the bottle of Tabasco sauce from his pocket and flipped it open adeptly with his thumb. He used his free hand and arm to guard and block a potential blow to his face. Trevor was assailed with splashes of hot sauce simultaneously to the eyes. Then Wilky jumped up and swirled around in the air for increased momentum. One of the two kicks landed on Trevor's knee and the other in the stomach area. Trevor hit the floor like a toppled statue during a wartime victory and howled in agony. Mr. Oblinger ran to the scene and blew the whistle profusely with sharp staccato blows. Wilky stood boldly over Trevor and waited for him to get back on his feet so he could strike again.

A few students who witnessed the rackety event were temporarily traumatized. Lots of laughing unfurled, and the shouting escalated through the atmosphere within the invisible walls of the playground. After seeing the blood and a wounded student on the ground, Mr. Oblinger called the assistant principal from his walkie-talkie. Mr. Macklberg came swiftly to escort the angry boys to his office. Wilky walked holding his lip, and Trevor limped, holding his stomach. The PE teacher was sickened to think that Wilky might get suspended. It could ruin his chances for continued play in the fall soccer league. The Sundown Warriors were a solid winning team with Wilky as one of their defensive midfielders. Although he was considered a newbie to the league, Wilky was undeniably a beast on the field. Even when the team would fall a point or two behind and lose to their opponents, the coach insisted that they wear a warrior's smile with heart for a well-played game.

Mr. Macklberg had the daunting task of calling Wilky and Trevor's parents to the school for an immediate disciplinary meeting as the school policy dictated. It was already two o'clock in the afternoon. Dahlia was thankful that she had purchased a new smartphone three weeks ago. It had become an additional appendage now that she worked and was away from her children the majority of the day. However, she was not happy to receive a troubling call regarding Wilky. "I take two buses to get to and from work. I most likely will not be able to make it to the school by 3:00. I'm going to call Isaac Granger. He and his wife, Nadine, are family and are listed as emergency contacts. Please do not put Cristal on the bus," she directed Mr. Macklberg. "Cristal must ride home with Wilky and their uncle after the meeting."

As Dahlia requested, Cristal was not put on the bus but was taken to Mrs. McCallister's office to wait until Wilky's meeting ended. She decided to work on a figure-of-speech poem for language arts that required her to use at least one simile and one metaphor. Cristal titled it 'Seesaw'. It was a metaphor for when she was young and could see. She loved playing on a seesaw that her father built and painted bright yellow and orange like the radiant glow of an inviting sun. Her mother would be seated behind her on one end of the long plank while her father sat on the opposite, ensuring that Wilky, the toddler, was securely mounted and tightly held on. Cristal also remembered playing on the seesaw with her brother and cousin when she had no vision. The creative young student wanted the poem to shine a light on the ups and downs of adjusting to and living with blindness. Although she may not have expressed it as such in her poetry, the seesaw represented a fulcrum of awareness and the reaffirming identification of self. Mrs. McCallister was almost brought to tears when Cristal shared her ideas and began recording them on a handheld recorder.

Isaac arrived at the school within forty-five minutes without Nadine. She'd taken a half-day off from work for a doctor's appointment. Isaac and Trevor's mother, Ms. Irvin, took a seat in Mr. Macklberg's office. The boys sat at student desks positioned face-to-face in a confrontational arrangement. Mr. Macklberg used his walkie-talkie to summon Mr. Oblinger to his office to join the meeting.

While everyone waited for the PE teacher, they glanced around Mr. Macklberg's office to read positive and empowering words that he hand-carved from butternut and yellow pine wood. To impress his mother, Trevor read them aloud with great expression, "love, bliss, hope, smile, laugh, pray, joy, up, and blessed." Ms. Irvin smiled and patted her son's knee with gratification. Wilky looked at Uncle Isaac and rolled his eyes at the annunciation of simple one-syllable words. Isaac restrained from bursting into laughter and camouflaged it with a snort instead.

On the opposite wall were five large, deep shadow boxes labeled with items obtained from Mr. Macklberg's world travels.

"Tell us about these pieces of art you've got here," asked Isaac. Mr. Macklberg was more than happy to share.

"That child-size kimono is from a small farming village in Iwama, Japan. The ancient mandolin is from Dunhuang, China. Over there is a boomerang made by Aboriginals from the coastal area of Sydney, Australia. That Cowrie shell mask is from Abuja, Nigeria." Just as he was about to explain the hunting bow made by Eskimos living in Wasilla, Alaska, Mr. Oblinger appeared breathless at the door. Mr. Oblinger took a seat, and the assistant principal directed the initial inquiry his way.

"So tell us exactly what happened between these boys." The PE teacher cleared his throat and scooted to the edge of his chair. Nervously, he bounced one leg before speaking.

"Well, I didn't exactly witness how things transpired. I was momentarily instructing a small group of children during a game of four squares. However, I did get short written statements from several students playing the game with these boys. Three students stated that Trevor started the fight."

Ms. Irvin blurted, "Oh, no, sir! That is not acceptable. You don't get to have other kids decide what happened. For all I know, they may have something against my Trevor in the first place. You're the adult, and you were supposed to supervise all activities," Ms. Irvin chided Mr. Oblinger.

Mr. Macklberg thought the exasperated mother was going overboard with flailing hand movements and the dipping and swerving of her head. He suspected Ms. Irvin might start to take off her earrings next and escalate the situation to a whole other level. At his previous school, Mr. Macklberg witnessed two mothers engaged in a clownish argument that bordered on a possible fistfight. It was painful to watch and appallingly embarrassing for their children.

"Calm down, Ms. Irvin. We'll get to the bottom of this," he announced. Not quite ready to be pulled into the undertow of the conversation, Isaac sat with a hand under his chin and his elbow resting on the arm of the chair. His legs were crossed, and an ankle over the knee. Silent but observant, Isaac watched the boys' facial expressions and body language.

Mr. Macklberg turned to Wilky and Trevor, "Boys, let's hear the truth from each of you. Wilky, why don't you go first?" Wilky removed the icepack from his lip and began explaining in the absence of a trembling voice.

"Well, the green team was winning, my team. When Scott passed me the ball, I started dribbling down the court. Trevor left his zone and decided he wanted to play man-to-man defense. Just when I got into three-point shooting range, he tripped me."

"Uhhh, Uhhh, that ain't what happened," argued Trevor, "It's not my fault that he fell over those big feet of his. He tried to do a Steph Curry fake and spin and tripped over his shoestring. He fell and busted his own lip."

At that moment, everyone in the room looked down at Wilky's feet. Sure enough, the shoestring on his left shoe was untied.

Trevor continued, "See, then he splashed some chemicals in my face and kicked me twice."

Mrs. Irvin pulled her son close and kissed the top of his head. "My poor baby. That sounds like aggravated assault to me." She turned sharply in Isaac's direction.

Wilky shouted, "That ain't what happened, Uncle Isaac. That's a betrayal of the truth."

Uncle Isaac rubbed his hands together, leaned forward, and turned to Mr. Macklberg, "Let's see the footage."

The assistant principal looked stirred and felt a little under attack, like a cobra when it's cornered. "I'm sorry, what?"

"Let's illuminate the facts and watch the footage. I am the chief security officer for an engineering corporation, and I know that most companies have security footage. You all run these schools like a business. I'm positive that Azalea Grove has surveillance cameras. As a matter of fact, I saw some mounted on the lights in the teachers' parking lot when I pulled up. Surely, our tax dollars are vested in the security of the children. Cameras were installed on the children's playground, am I correct?"

The small group stood and followed Mr. Macklberg into the SRO's office. Dr. Martin had the custodian unlock the door because the officer left the building to run an errand. With great scrutiny, everyone present leaned forward to see the clear, convincing evidence on the tiny black-and-white screen. The truth had no defense.

"See, see, I told you, Uncle Isaac." Wilky pointed to the screen. "He tripped me and started laughing like a demon. Then I got up and defended myself before he assaulted me again."

Isaac wanted to crack up laughing. With the bottle in one hand, he watched his nephew make a Heisman trophy move before executing some serious karate kicks.

"Whatever liquid this boy splashed in my son's face is considered a weapon." Because Ms. Irvin refused to acknowledge that her son was in the wrong, Uncle Isaac thought about telling her to take a walk off a short pier but chose to respond differently.

"I would hardly call a bottle of Tabasco sauce a weapon," Isaac proclaimed in Wilky's defense.

"Yes, let's not go that far. Based upon what we've just seen, it's clear that Trevor started this incident," said Mr. Macklberg.

Needless to say, fighting was against school policy, so Mr. Macklberg was compelled to subject the boys to some form of disciplinary action. Wilky received one day of in-school suspension. Trevor was given six days of in-school suspension for his nefarious behavior. And Wilky was never allowed to bring hot sauce on the premises again.

Chapter Twenty-Seven:
The ABCs of O&M

On Friday, Mr. Nick took Cristal outside for another lesson on cane instruction. He introduced her to the touch-trail method in which she used her cane to detect the grass line that meets with the edge of the sidewalk. This technique stopped Cristal from veering and helped her remain on the sidewalk. The ability to walk a straight line without a wall was essential for increased outdoor orientation. The teacher and student stood at the corner of the 4-way intersection near the school. It was another opportunity for Cristal to analyze traffic flow.

Nick explained, using the translation program on his phone, "These bumps that we're standing on are called 'truncated domes'. Did you know that?"

Cristal smiled and shook her head, "No, sir."

He proceeded with a definition. "They are a detectable warning system, designed for the visually impaired to feel them under their feet and with their cane. These bumps were painted bright yellow. They also help and assist persons with sight by indicating where to stand before crossing a street safely."

"I didn't know that. That's good." Cristal replied.

"Yes, it is."

They returned to the school but sat on the bench near the entrance before entering. Mr. Nick discussed the X, Y, and Z concepts related to his published and well-received book, 'The ABCs of O&M'. "The 'X' represents the word 'Xenophobia'."

Mr. Nick observed a perplexed expression appear on Cristal's face. It was apparent that his translation application needed help breaking down the definition. "It means when someone is afraid of strangers or people from other countries."

Cristal nodded her head, "Oh, I get it. I'm afraid of strangers sometimes."

"You're not alone, Cristal. I've had a lot of students who were also afraid of strangers, even some of my adult clients. That's why I want to teach you a skill called the 'Hines Break'."

Mr. Nick asked Cristal to stand. He then demonstrated a systematic method of disengaging unwanted or incorrect human guide techniques.

"Someone may think that they are being of great help by grabbing you by the arm to serve as a guide. But if you don't want their help, this method teaches how to decline such advances politely. However, when you're performing this skill, Cristal, you can say something like, 'No, thank you. I am fine.' Try to avoid sounding rude or unappreciative."

The teacher and student practiced and role-played the technique twice as a team.

Next, Mr. Nick mentioned incidents where motorists make bad decisions but with good intentions, yelling at persons with visual impairments who may be seen standing at intersections analyzing the traffic flow.

"Sometimes these citizens yell, 'It's safe to go! The light is green! You can cross now!' The best practice is to ignore the comments."

This all made good sense to Cristal. She believed it would be rude to ignore adults, but in this situation, it made sense to ignore them. Mr. Macklberg continued, "You will receive some O&M training, most likely until you graduate from high school and possibly even in college and beyond if you choose it. Eventually, you will have gained the skills to cross streets at unfamiliar, complex intersections. I want you to learn to trust your training, knowledge, and good common sense. Ignore the 'yelling' from motorists or others."

She understood but couldn't imagine going anywhere far from home without her mother, Wilky, or Raeni by her side.

The final concept Mr. Nick discussed pertained to the importance of wearing proper footwear. He hoped the translation application would work as intended. "There can be unforeseen dangers when walking around the city and community with open-toed shoes, especially if there is an absence of a sidewalk or the sidewalk ends, and you take a detour and walk in the grass."

Like the good student she was proving to be, Cristal listened for clear understanding. But she didn't understand what this lesson had to do with the letter 'Z'. As if reading her mind, Mr. Nick continued to explain. "Zoysia is a popular grass that people choose to beautify the area surrounding their home. There could be snakes, broken glass, red fire ants, or a myriad of dangers found in grass. Open-toed shoes like sandals provide little protection from these evils."

Cristal got it but had one question. She raised her hand. "Is Zoysia grass only with evils, or do other grasses have them?"

Mr. Nick laughed. "You are one smart cookie. You're right. It can be any grass. It's just that many neighborhoods and communities in the Garland County School District have landscapes that are beautified with Zoysia and St. Augustine grass. For the letter 'Z', I probably should have used the word zebra in my book for 'zebra crossings'. The term applies to crosswalks marked with broad white stripes, giving it a look similar to zebra's skin and fur. The high visibility of zebra crossings exists to alert approaching motorists that there is a crosswalk and reminds them that pedestrians have the right-of-way."

"Oh, okay." It was starting to make sense to Cristal. She planned to ask Wilky if any zebra stripes were near their Willow Wood townhome.

"Now, let's go inside and make a candy land map of two routes you travel daily at school. I bought lots of candy for you to use as landmarks. We'll glue them down on a board, and you can share any candy we have left with your friends at the 'Chomp and Chat' session this afternoon."

Cristal smiled, "Sounds good. I'm ready to go!"

Chapter Twenty-Eight: Chomp and Chat

On Friday evening, Isaac decided to give the ladies a break in the kitchen. On his way home from work, he picked up some Chinese food for dinner. The menu included shrimp fried rice, wonton soup, Kung Pao Chicken, and dumplings.

"This is a real treat. Thank you, honey." Nadine smiled at all three children trying to use chopsticks to eat part of their meal.

"Who wants to go first and tell us about their day?" Isaac asked in a jolly tone.

Dahlia volunteered. "A lady at work in the seafood department got injured when she slipped and fell on some crushed ice. When it happened, she was carrying a large yellowtail snapper, which flew up in the air and almost hit a customer in the back of his head." Everyone shared a wholesome laugh, and nobody bothered to ask if the lady was okay.

"I'll go next," said Cristal. "We had a Chomp and Chat luncheon in Ms. Saunders's class. That's where she lets students bring their lunch to her classroom, and we get to listen to guest speakers. White Cane Day is tomorrow, the 15th of October, and all her guests except one use a cane to get to work. The day is about making others learn about visually impaired people with canes." Interpretation for Raeni and Isaac was needed even though Cristal used more English phrasing than Haitian Creole. Dahlia was curious and impressed. She wanted to know more.

"So, who were the guest speakers? What type of work did they do?"

"There was a man who was a radio speaker during the day and a comedian at night who told jokes. There was a 911 operator who used a dog instead of a cane to get around. One lady was a computer programmer, and another person wrote children's books."

Raeni told Cristal how cool that was. "I wish I had something like that when I was in elementary or junior high school. Maybe I'd be closer to knowing what I want to be before going to college. Did you get to tell them that you want to make perfumes when you grow up?" Raeni asked.

"Yep, the lady who works with computers told me that that was a good choice. She said I have to work hard in science and math and probably need to go to college."

Isaac added to the conversation, "That's good, Cristal. They've got you thinking about your future already. If you're serious, you'll probably need to be in college for about six years."

Dahlia nodded, believing her children would take giant steps forward and attend college. She was keenly aware of the benefits and value of a degree and had some reservations about not pursuing one of her own. "I like Cristal's teachers. I like Wilky's too. My babies got As and Bs on their report cards. I can't wait to tell their daddy."

The following week, the computer programmer at Chomp and Chat, Ms. LaFaver, emailed Ms. Saunders to thank her for the invitation to speak to her students. She then asked if she would contact Cristal's mother because she was very impressed with Cristal's energy and passion. Ms. LaFaver wanted to be Cristal's advocate. Dahlia felt honored to have her support and guidance and gladly accepted the offer. From that point forward, Ms. LaFaver sat beside Dahlia at Cristal's annual IEPs. Over time, Ms. LaFaver became an invaluable mentor and advocated for Cristal until she successfully graduated from high school and was accepted into college.

Dahlia turned to Wilky, and he shared, "I'd give my day a seven. It wasn't too bad spending time in in-school suspension. I missed playing with Jeremy and Kenny at recess, though. Everybody came to check on me to see how I was doing. Mrs. McCallister, Mrs. Collier, Dr. Martin, Mr. Oblinger, and Mr. Macklberg came to see me. I got all of my work done, too."

Dahlia told Wilky once more that she was proud of him for defending himself, but she expected that to be the one and only time he had to fight someone to resolve a dispute.

"Yes, ma'am." Wilky was grateful that his mother didn't fuss at him. He figured Uncle Isaac filled her in yesterday with all the details supporting his sleight of hand and cause of action.

"Mr. Macklberg asked how I felt about having to get my haircut. I told him I thought it was a dumb rule, and he agreed."

"Oh, really?" Nadine asked with surprise.

"Yep. He said he wasn't allowed to wear his hair long or in a ponytail either when he went to school. They made him cut it off. He said in 1902, some of his ancestors who lived on reservations got a letter from the government saying that if they didn't cut their hair, the government wouldn't give them any work and might stop sending a lot of food for their families."

Wilky decided it wasn't a good idea to share the story of Mr. Macklberg getting into fights when he was in 7th grade. A couple of bullies insisted on touching him on the top of his head after their history teacher talked about how disrespectful it was to Native American culture.

Dahlia felt better about Wilky's day of in-school suspension. Despite the isolating punishment, it turned out to be a good learning experience for him. "That's interesting," Dahlia commented, "I remember studying about Native Americans too. Some of them voluntarily cut their hair. It was a matter of showing respect to their deceased loved ones and indicated an ending, but it also represented a new beginning."

Isaac asked Raeni how she rated her day. "I'd give it a nine."

"What? Hey, now, tell us about it."

"First of all, I'm going to the homecoming game and dance tomorrow, and I can hardly wait! The other thing is that my psychology teacher looked over the draft of my edutainment game and said it was exceptional. She wants me to test it out this weekend, and then next week, everyone is supposed to turn their projects in so we can start playing our games on Fridays. She really liked it!"

"That's good, Raeni. I'm proud of you," her Aunt Dahlia stated.

Her father congratulated her as well. "I'm proud of you too! What's the name of this game?"

"It's called Scurred. Not Scared, but S-C-U-R-R-E-D. It's slang, meaning you're very afraid. My game explores different phobias – an anxiety disorder defined by a persistent and excessive fear of an object or situation."

Cristal interrupted enthusiastically and asked Wilky to interpret for her. "I know about phobia. My O&M teacher taught me xenophobia. It's fear of strangers and people from different places!"

"Hey, you're right. That's impressive, Cristal!" said Raeni.

Dahlia felt proud that her baby girl was learning big words. Raeni continued, "Any career might be jeopardized by a person hired to do a certain job but has an unusual phobia blocking their ability to succeed."

Her MaDine piped in, "This sounds very clever. Tell us more,"

"Okay, for example, the fear of money, which is chrometophobia, may be a detriment to someone who is good with numbers but prefers to be an accountant instead of a banker. So, as the game goes, you and your partner not only have to come up with a match for the tools of the trade but also, on a scale of 1-5, you decide whether or not that person would crash and burn. Or would they succeed with the help of counseling? Or succeed on their own by facing their fears. A person with ablutophobia, the fear of bathing, may discover that whatever job they take may have to be remote. They'd do better working from home." Everybody laughed.

"Yeah, I think you're right about that one," Dahlia proclaimed.

"Wow, I like that," said Isaac. My daughter is a genius! We could probably get a trademark for it and sell it. We'd be millionaires!"

Raeni chuckled and continued, "My teacher said that everybody has a fear of something, and some fears may appear to be more extreme than others. But they are of real concern to those who possess them. Can you believe that there is a phobia that exists called philophobia? It's the fear of love."

"Now, isn't that something," Dahlia interjected. "I never thought that that might be a fear for someone, but I guess juxtaposed, you'd fear getting your heart broken due to falling in love," She wisely deduced. For a lingering flash of seconds, she thought about her first and only burning heartbreak by Sterling Laurent.

Raeni made an easy request. "Can we play it later this evening if y'all feel up to it? Because tomorrow I'll be busy at the game and dance?"

"Sounds like fun to me," Wilky replied.

"Me too," Cristal replied. Everybody else agreed they'd enjoy a Friday game night playing SCURRED.

"Thanks!"

"Well, let me tell you how I'd rate my day," Isaac announced. "I'd give it a ten with two thumbs up!"

Dahlia put her fork full of food down on her plate. "What happened on your job that's got you feeling so groovy?" Nadine and Isaac laughed in harmony.

"Well," he paused for effect and gave a drum roll with his hands on the table, "Nadine is pregnant. We're going to be parents. I'm going to be a father again!"

"Get out of here!" shouted Dahlia. "What you say?"

"It's too early to know the gender, but we don't care if it's a boy or a girl," Nadine responded with an affirmative nod.

Raeni shouted, "What? I'm going to be a big sister and have a real flesh and blood walking and talking sister or brother around?"

"Yes, you are!" expressed her MaDine.

Dahlia noticed Nadine and Isaac put on a little weight, but she thought it was because of her decadent desserts and high-carb meals. And in part, it was.

"Wow. Congratulations to both of you - to all three of you." Dahlia cheered. Wilky restated the good news for his sister just in case she hadn't grasped it all.

"Yes!" shouted Cristal.

"Let's give a toast," Raeni suggests. So everyone raised their glasses of Cran-cherry punch and clinked them together at the center of the table.

The next day, Dahlia rose at 5:30 a.m. to make an over-the-top celebratory breakfast. Day-old French baguettes from the farmer's market were chosen for her recipe for Haitian French toast. On the table, she collected and placed all the other ingredients: orange juice, eggs, heavy cream, cinnamon, ground nutmeg, and white sugar. Before dusting the thick toasted slices browned in a pan of butter, Dahlia placed luscious slices of ripe strawberries on top. Plantains, fresh seafood, and spaghetti were cooked to perfection. The parents-to-be were elated when Dahlia knocked on their bedroom door with plates full of food worthy of a king and queen's palette. Pleasing smells wafted through the entire house, eventually rousing Cristal, Wilky, and Raeni.

When Dahlia called upstairs for the youngsters to come and eat, Cristal and her brother rushed to wash their hands and then eagerly bounced down the stairs in their pajamas. The Duvernay children had no idea how blessed they were to start their Saturday with such an elaborate meal.

"Where is Raeni?" asked Dahlia.

"She's getting ready to shower and get dressed for the game," answered Wilky with a spaghetti mouthful.

"Oh, I almost forgot, she's got a busy day today." Dahlia watched as Cristal drowned her slices of toast in a boatload of blueberry syrup. "That's enough, Cristal. Save some for Wilky and Raeni."

She licked her fingers and managed an 'Okay' response. Cristal passed the half-empty bottle to her brother.

"Momma, my friend Kendall is going to a pumpkin festival at a place called Cally Gardens next week. She's going to ask her mother if I can come. She said there are pumpkin sculptures and a green animal zoo made of trees and bushes cut in different shapes. There will be flowers like mums to smell everywhere. She said a lady teaches a class on how to look for plants and flowers like daisies and dandelions that you can cook and eat. Can I go?"

"We'll see. I haven't met Kendall's mother yet, but it does sound like a nice place to visit." Dahlia hadn't seen Cristal that excited since her first day at school. Her daughter could hardly contain her.

"There's a butterfly house, too, where butterflies fly all around and land on you. But you'll get in trouble if you try and grab one and take it home."

"Wow, that sounds cool!" said Wilky.

"Yeah, it is. Cristal took a breath before making one last plea, "Maybe you can come with us, Mommy, and describe the funny trees shaped like animals?"

"It's called topiary, baby. The plants are trained by clipping the foliage and twigs to grow into a particular shape." Dahlia thought it would be a good idea and wanted to encourage new friendships for her daughter. "If her mother calls, we'll see."

"Wilky, I think Cristal and I will catch an Uber to your game today. I don't want to bother your aunt and uncle, but I just have to figure out how to do it on my phone. You can ride with us." Wilky chewed and swallowed fast. Dahlia continued, "Coach Parker won't have to pick you up. I can send him a text right now."

"Awww, momma. I wanted to ride in the van with the other Daybreak Warriors. Plus, we have to be there at 9:00 for practice, and the game doesn't even start until eleven o'clock. Y'all would just be sitting there."

"Hmm…well, okay. But I want to make certain that I meet the rest of the parents when I get there. I need to know all of them, and they need to know me. Your father and I talked about how important it is for me to be involved with the parents of your teammates."

"They are nice, and they all sit together," Wilky relayed. " I think you'll like them. I know they're gonna like you, momma. You're so pretty and kind." Dahlia smiled at Wilky and thought it was funny that he was already learning to cleverly schmooze and brown-nose when he wanted something bad enough.

"And her hair smells good, too!" added Cristal.

"You two are quite the persuasive pair." All shared a merry laugh.

With Dahlia's permission, Mrs. Collier had referred Wilky to the school psychologist for testing in the area of language arts, and he qualified for the afterschool gifted and talented program. However, that program coincided with Wilky's Wednesday soccer practice. Dahlia and Jesse agreed they made the right decision to continue Wilky's training with his soccer coach after school. He was overjoyed that his parents respected his desire to continue playing and practicing with the Daybreak Warriors. The Daybreak Warriors won their third game in a row the previous Saturday due partly to Wilky's endurance and speed. He kept his head on swivel, passing and shooting with compelling athletic ability.

As Cristal had hoped, Kendall's mother did call early in the afternoon to invite Cristal and Dahlia to ride with her and her daughter to the Callaway Gardens in Pine Mountain, Georgia. And because nature used to be one of Dahlia's happy places, she accepted the offer. The all-day trip was scheduled for the following weekend. Dahlia graciously accepted the offer. And on that subsequent Saturday, she and Cristal returned home late in the evening from the gardens with a small boxwood plant. Their intentions were to cut and wire the plant in a shape resembling their dearest Cheerio.

That evening under a starry night sky during the homecoming dance three weeks shy of her 15th birthday, Raeni Granger was pulled in close for her very first kiss from a good-looking teen named Daxton Hunter.

Chapter Twenty-Nine:
Nourishment

Over time, Cristal had become increasingly more comfortable speaking in front of the class. Mrs. Tubilleja was pleased with all the significant progress she was making. Most of her assignments were turned in using voice-to-text or digital dictation software with the help of Mrs. Saunders. Sometimes, the program had difficulty with Cristal's speech pattern because of her heavy accent. So, corrections were made manually, and her work was submitted on time according to the accommodations written in her plan. Cristal's braille reading skills were improving as well.

Before the first scheduled parent conference day, Dr. Martin ensured all her teachers were trained to provide effective compliment sandwiches. Any feedback given to a parent about their child's negative performance, or the 'meat of the conversation', would be served between two sweetened slices of bread intended to leave a pleasant taste in a parent's mouth. The overall positive performance of their child's efforts needs to be highlighted. Mrs. Saunders predicted Cristal may need to attend summer school at the end of the school year. And with all her hard work, she'd most likely master reading and writing in Grade 2 braille by the end of her 5th grade school year.

"That is good news," Dahlia commented. "I am very pleased with her progress."

"So am I, Mrs. Duvernay. Cristal is one of my hardest working students."

"I'd like for her to attend college someday. I know she's informed you of her intentions to become a perfumer, and I'm now beginning to believe that she can do it."

"So do I," said Mrs. Saunders. "She's certainly got the math aptitude and the motivation for it."

"My husband and I have often said that although Cristal has a disability, she's been blessed with good common sensibility!" The ladies shared a light titter.

Mr. Nick was pleased with how quickly Cristal learned to navigate the school setting using her cane. Not only could she travel independently to six pertinent locations on campus (media center, cafeteria, clinic, central office, choir, gym) from different places of origin, but she learned to ascend and descend stairs using her cane without incident.

"She's a natural," he told Dahlia during his conference with her. "Only once did I have to reprimand her," Mr. Nick confessed.

A sudden frown with contracted eyebrows warped Dahlia's pleasing face.

"Last week, Cristal and another student were caught playing on two side-by-side elevators. They rode up and down, hopping on and off, pushing buttons for the first and second floors for quite some time. A 5th-grade teacher in a wheelchair reported the elevator broken after she waited over ten minutes for it to arrive on the lower level. It was the custodian who brought it to my attention."

"Oh my goodness," gasped Dahlia. "This is the first time I've heard of that kind of mischief from her. Cristal is a sweet girl, but I know she's not perfect. I'll be sure to let her know I'm aware of this violation and that I'm unhappy about it. My husband and I will have to come up with some consequences for her foolishness. Thank you for letting me know."

Mr. Nick nodded and continued, "Cristal has an innate ability to mentally map out her environment, naming landmarks and clues along specific routes. She attempts to strive for excellence in every O&M lesson." He showed Dahlia several tactile maps that Cristal had completed, including her favored candy land map constructed with M&Ms, Now & Laters, Pixy Stix, Starbursts, Jolly Ranchers, Life Savers, and more. "In fact, I am in the process of inventing a game called 'The Jolly Traveler' with Cristal as my muse."

Dahlia was very proud of her daughter; she wished Jesse was with her to hear all the outstanding reports.

"That is so awesome," exclaimed Dahlia. She signed papers granting Mr. Nick permission to regularly schedule Cristal and another O&M student off-campus for community-based instruction. Mr. Nick filed the papers.

"Thank you for signing this on such short notice. I meant to send it home last week, and honestly, I just remembered I need to get it done. I've actually scheduled a bus for Cristal and another student to take them on their first outing of the year today. We'll be leaving here in about an hour."

"That's fine," Dahlia replied. "I like that you're teaching her so many travel concepts. She's always eager to tell me all about her lessons with you. Thank you for helping to build my daughter's confidence."

Dahlia left Azalea Grove Elementary that day in great spirits. Despite some minor indiscretions in her book, both of her children rocked it. She believed they were just as successful as the most popular rock star. Dahlia was in good spirits and left the school to head to her first meeting with Dr. Louissaint following the parent/teacher conference. She summoned an Uber on her phone app and to the doctor's office. It was located in a high-rise building near Alpharetta. She needed to drop off confidential forms he requested prior to their first therapy session. The board-certified psychologist's website said he offered individual and family therapy. Dr. Louissaint provided services in person and remotely via the computer.

During her ride in the luxury town car, Dahlia reflected on the initial introduction Mrs. Plaizill arranged with the doctor two weeks ago after church service. Before dinner was served to the pastor and congregants in the dining hall, Dahlia had a few private moments to speak freely with the doctor. Cristal was engaged in song and lively conversation with young girls in the children's choir, and Wilky, enamored by the percussion instruments accompanying the choir, hung out with the drummer to play a few beats.

Dahlia discovered that Dr. Louissaint was a 67-year-old widow and had been a church member for fifteen years. He practiced Christian Psychology for 35 years. He explained, "Christian psychology incorporates psychological theories and theological approaches to treatment by using biblical concepts with psychotherapy practices."

Dahlia had the opportunity to share her backstory regarding the loss of her mother, father, and sister. The doctor was a trained, observant listener. The pulling of her ear was an action Dahlia repeated during their short conversation. However, Dr. Louissaint wasn't certain if such behavior was a self-soothing habit she developed at a young age or a stress and anxiety response to recent trauma. He'd have to wait and become more acquainted with her before concluding. Relying on his professional experience, the doctor was inclined to say that Dahlia most likely suffered from survivor's guilt and the anxieties that come with it. At the risk of being presumptuous, he knew it would take a few sessions to make an accurate diagnosis. Dr. Louissaint was aware that other contributing factors for someone who self-identified as depressed were likely. The kind doctor gave Dahlia his card and said he had some availability to meet with her twice a month in person or by phone.

"How does that sound?"

"It sounds wonderful, Dr. Louissaint, but I have additional concerns beyond my issues. My husband and I are also concerned about our children's mental health and well-being. They look fine watching them now, playing the drums and singing songs. But I believe they are experiencing feelings of depression as well and don't know how to express it." The doctor listened intensely, giving a nod of encouragement as Dahlia continued to speak.

"Continue," he directed.

"They've been uprooted from their home and put in a position totally out of their element. My daughter faces the challenges of structure and socialization that come with being in school for the first time. My son has to deal with making new friends and the unpleasant effects of being bullied. He was used to playing soccer and spending time on the beach all day long with his best friends after the earthquake. That was pretty much his whole world. Would it be alright if we came for family counseling in person, and then I met with you one-on-one over the phone?"

"Of course, my dear. It makes sense for me to treat the family and the individual in situations like this."

Because transportation would be an issue, Dahlia chose a plan to allow her and the children to meet for group sessions with the doctor twice a month for six months. She was scheduled to meet individually with him weekly by phone or Internet.

"Thank you so much, Dr. Louissaint. This plan sounds perfect to me. Is there a sliding scale based on a person's earnings? How much am I expected to pay?" she asked.

"We're like family at First Ebenezer. I have a lucrative private practice, but my services for members of this church come at no charge for the first three months. An affordable payment plan can be worked out. I want the individual to evaluate and embrace the benefits of my services. All of us have been somehow affected by the tragedy in our homeland. It feels good to give back the best way I know how."

Dahlia's eyes welled with tears. Hardly an audible was produced. Suddenly, a questionable smile eased over the doctor's face. He thought of something Dahlia could do to return the favor.

"Now that I think about it, there is one way that you can repay me." Dahlia hesitated to ask and prayed it wasn't a nefarious request.

"What is that, Dr. Louissaint?"

"I'd appreciate one of those fine lemon cakes you make every now and then. That cake is so incredibly delicious, it's almost sinful." She felt extremely flattered and emitted a girly giggle.

"I can do that with pleasure. Thank you so much, Dr. Louissaint." He squeezed her hand earnestly before escorting her to the dining hall for supper.

"And let me say this, young lady, you are who you walk with; continue to walk with God. Happiness cannot exist without sadness,

Dahlia. As the good bible says, '*Weeping may endure for a night, but joy cometh in the morning.*' In your future are beautiful moments, days, and years, my dear." The doctor's words of nourishment were food for Dahlia's soul.

***

Dahlia exited the Uber upon its arrival at Dr. Louissant's office just as Cristal and Kaylan boarded the school bus with Mr. Nick to travel in the community. The O&M Specialist arranged for the school bus to take Cristal and Kaylan to a semi-business area in the historic downtown city of Cottlesville. The weather was brisk that autumn morning as they stepped off a Garland bus and walked to the small, bustling café at the intersection of Culver and Pike.

"Umm, it smells like coffee in here!" Cristal reported.

"Yes, you're right. We just walked inside of '*Up a Cup Café*'," Mr. Nick explained.

A young lady approached Mr. Nick just as he sat down with his student.

"Hello there, Mr. Nick. How are you?"

"Hey, Ms. Danita, I'm fine. Good to see you here."

"Good to see you too. I'm here with my student, Chikao. We just finished a cup of hot chocolate. We've been discussing the route he needs to travel to get to the Kasper Law Firm on Locust and Harvard St."

Mr. Nick and Ms. Danita introduced their students to one another and sat down to chat briefly before each O&M specialist began their lessons.

"I want to be a lawyer one day," Chikao shared, "Ms. Danita asked me to come up with a few questions for the attorney, Allen Kasper. He works at his family's law firm and is going to let me interview him for twenty minutes!"

"That's cool," said Kaylan. What kind of device are you using to store your questions?" Chikao showed Kaylan and Cristal his latest notetaker with refreshable braille.

"Nice. I use a Perkins braille writer," Cristal volunteered.

Kaylan told Chikao, "I got an older version of that device, but I can still get on the internet with mine."

Ms. Danita interjected, "Chikao and I need to head out because our appointment is at 10:30. It was nice to meet the two of you," Ms. Danita told Cristal and Kaylan before heading for the door. She turned to Mr. Nick, "Maybe we can plan to connect on purpose next time. I want your opinion on an O&M Monopoly game I'm working on that focuses on the stores here in downtown Cottlesville."

"Hey, that sounds like a good idea. I'd like to check it out. Before the year ends, we could even plan to do a scavenger hunt or something together with our students." Mr. Nick suggested.

"That sounds like fun. Well, take care. Hopefully, Chikao and I will see you all next month." Mr. Nick watched through the large glass windows as his colleague and student stood waiting at the corner for the light to turn green.

"Ms. Danita smells nice," said Cristal, "like apricots and patchouli."

"She is nice," declared Mr. Nick. "On some Saturdays, she provides O&M services for babies who are born without sight. Ms. Danita goes into homes and works with parents to support their little ones. She teaches them how to use all of their remaining senses to move with purpose. Those little ones need to learn to explore their environments safely, too."

Cristal thought about it and announced, "I bet that's fun, teaching and playing with babies at the same time."

"I remember the early intervention specialist who came to work with me when I was little," stated Kaylan. She still calls my mom and checks to see how I'm doing in school."

Mr. Nick commented, "That's wonderful, Kaylan. Now, let's start our mobility lesson, guy and gal. Hop to it!"

Cristal and Kaylan chuckled and stood ready with their canes in hand.

Mr. Nick's lesson for his two students was to have them travel in and out of unfamiliar stores to gather information. In the process, Cristal and Kaylan were expected to independently manipulate door handles and take turns holding doors for each other. They also needed to practice safely positioning their canes while standing stationary to avoid tripping other customers.

Once inside a store, Cristal and Kaylan had to use all of their remaining senses to guess what type of store they were in and what kind of product or service might be rendered. Alternating turns, they identified a shoe repair store, a pet store, a bakery, a candle store, a paint store, and a beauty shop. Mr. Nick cued them to keep the cane tip down to recognize subtle changes in the walking surfaces. Each student took turns asking the shop owner or an employee two questions about the services provided or products available for sale. The O&M specialist and his students ended their lesson at *Up a Cup Café*. The students enjoyed cartons of chocolate milk and a divvied-up giant cinnamon roll, compliments of Mr. Nick. "Ummm…good nourishment," Cristal joked.

Chapter Thirty:
Surprise Surprise

November 5th was a day of celebration. It was Raeni's birthday, and although it wasn't a surprise party, she was very surprised during the later part of the celebration when she received an incredible gift from her father. Isaac's brother Barry and his wife Phyllis offered to host the party at their 3,089-square-foot ranch-style home. It was a beautiful, partly cloudy day with 74-degree weather. Two weeks prior, forty-five guests received animated e-invites created by Raeni's MaDine via the Internet. It was for a Kentucky Derby-themed party.

Raeni gave MaDine a list of ten girls and eight boys to invite, in addition to her cousins Cristal and Wilky. Nadine and Dahlia agreed that the guests should come in casual clothes since they would play games like horseshoes, badminton, bocce ball, Frisbee golf, and darts. Ropes were also available if the Fly Girlz wanted to perform. Upon entering the home, the young ladies would have a selection of hats, and the boys could select horse-themed clip-on bowties. A five-star restaurant catered to sweet and savory Gourmet foods. The delicacies were arranged on elevated mirrored plates in relative food groups. Isaac and his brothers wanted hearty slabs of barbeque ribs on the menu, so Nadine made sure that happened. Nobody invested time in a lot of hard work and preparations other than decorating the patio with balloons, streamers, and banners.

Raeni was ecstatic. Everyone she wanted to come came. Some guests dared to add a few of their friends and relatives to the list. The total number of attendees was higher than expected. Still, it wasn't a problem because an abundance of finger foods gave variety to an elegant layout of different food groups. After dropping off their child, some parents circled back around the circular driveway and parked temporarily to get a close-up look at the lavish spread. Raeni's grandparents from her mother's side of the family were also there to celebrate her birthday.

Uncle Isaac's brother, Ricky, was the disc jockey. Contemporary music and old-school tunes blared through the speakers for anyone feeling the urge to dance.

"I've never seen her so happy," Isaac told Nadine.

"Well, this guy Daxton seems like a nice young man. I'm glad that we got the chance to meet him."

"Yeah, me too, but I'll need to remind Raeni that there will be no one-on-one dating with him or any other knucklehead. At least not until she's sixteen, maybe not even then," said Issac.

Dahlia laughed, "You're not going to be able to keep the boys away from her forever, and you know that, right?"

"Hmmph," Isaac grunted.

"Yeah, but he'll try." Nadine laughed. "I think it would be okay if Raeni and Marsha did group dates or chaperoned dates like at the bowling alley and putt-putt golf or something like that, right?"

"Well, maybe," replied Isaac.

Dahlia and Nadine laughed again at Isaac's pouty and scrunched facial expression. Dahlia, Nadine, and Isaac tried pushing the bad news they had received the previous day to the back of their minds, at least until after the party.

When the time came, the Granger boys whistled their version of the '*Happy Birthday*' song over the mic. Successfully, Raeni huffed and puffed to blow out fifteen candles on a two-tier Kentucky Derby bonnet cake. It was an exceptional work of art decorated with multicolored fondue roses. After everyone was served a liberal slice of yellow cake with cream cheese icing, Raeni moved to the gift table. It was filled with more accouterments than a girl her age could possibly want or need. Marsha bought Raeni a pair of turquoise blue embroidered western boots with rhinestones like the ones she owned and Raeni coveted. When Daxton gave her a teddy bear with a heart-shaped locket around its neck, Raeni was overcome with joy.

Isaac grumbled, thinking the gift was inappropriate. Isaac and Nadine finally agreed that she was spoiled in a good way. Raeni wasn't a bratty kid, and she had been generous with her heart and hand when sharing her home with her cousins. Isaac knew that Raeni was used to her privacy, and it was quite an adjustment when Cristal and Wilky came to live with them. He was so proud of how she handled it all, and he liked how she managed to keep up her grades despite moments of frustration or minor bouts of depression. That's why her father was more than willing to surprise his only child with a striking Andalusian pony.

"She deserves it," said Isaac to her grandparents. Raeni's grandmother asked Isaac how soon the new house would be ready. "It's coming along as scheduled. It should be completed sometime in May, just in time for the new baby's arrival," he proudly proclaimed.

"Oh my god! Oh my god, I can't believe it!" Raeni screamed repeatedly when Uncle Barry walked in the surprise present gifted by her father from the stable. She ran, skipped, and hopped to plant a big kiss on Isaac's cheek. Raeni squeezed and hugged Nadine tightly. "Thank you! Thank you! Thank you!" she yelled. Raeni skipped back to marvel and stroked the mane of her very own pony. Nadine told Raeni that Aunt Dahlia made the elegant Garland of Roses with silk flowers that hung around the pony's neck. "Thanks, Aunt Dahlia. It's beautiful. He looks like a real prize-winning champion already!"

Cristal and Wilky helped Raeni feed the stunning stallion carrots and apples between grateful-sounding whinnies. Raeni proudly announced, "I'm gonna name him Kodály, after a sonata for a solo cello."

Uncle Barry broadcasted, "He'll stay here in our stable. I told your dad that you can come and visit whenever you want. When he gets old enough to ride, we'll make sure you get lessons from one of the best."

"I love you, daddy. Thank you!"

Isaac showed Raeni a saddle with a yellow bow. "This is from your mother. I told her you'd give her a call after the party." Hoof oil, a brush, and saddle soap were in another beautifully wrapped gift box that was handed to the birthday girl.

"How is Isaac going to top this for Raeni's sweet sixteen birthday? That's the one that's supposed to be the biggie." Dahlia asked Nadine.

"Who knows," Nadine answered with a shrug of her shoulders. "He'll probably buy her a ticket to the moon on one of NASA's heavy-lift rockets for deep space exploration."

"Now that's funny." Dahlia could hardly control her laughter.

"On her fourteenth birthday, the three of us flew to Bermuda. But I believe it was just as much of a treat for Isaac as it was for

Raeni. For bragging rights, he spent most of his time at the award-winning Turtle Hill Golf Club and the picturesque Port Royal Golf Course, while Raeni and I spent most of our time poolside or touring the island's historical landmarks."

"That sounds like a wonderful vacation. Once the kids are a little older and Jesse is all settled in, I will plan a nice trip for just him and me. After all the sacrifices he's made, he deserves it."

"You both do," Nadine affirmed.

***

Dahlia, Nadine, and Isaac decided it was best to tell the children about their grandmother's ghastly accident the day after the birthday festivities. On Sunday morning, the sisters-in-law packed clothing and a few personal longings into their roll-on luggage in preparation for the trip back home to Croix-des-Bouquets, Haiti. On Friday morning, Granny Lou experienced an unfortunate slip, a horrendous catalyst for a spiraling of negative events. The elderly woman lost her footing, stumbled, and fell while carrying Mrs. Rosie's dirty laundry down the steep hill. Granny Lou experienced an agonizing injury to her head and a badly fractured right hip. It wasn't until Aunt Rachelle and Mikaela returned home that they discovered Granny Lou lying on the ground. Cheerio's barking frenzy and swirling helicopter tail alerted them that something was seriously wrong the moment they stepped out of the car. Aunt Rachelle and Mikaela were goaded to follow the nervous dog to the trail where their loved one lay conscious but in immense pain.

When Dahlia received the call from Jesse, she was riding the bus and heading home from work. From a phone in the hospital lobby, he said his grandmother was talking and resting comfortably but highly medicated. Unfortunately, surgery was to be delayed until

Monday or Tuesday as strapped and struggling surgeons in the small hospital focused on assessing and treating patients requiring more immediate attention. Severe injuries like a heart attack and an impending kidney transplant were prioritized over Granny Lou's injuries. Due to an upsurge in violence, it also increased the demand for staff to triage innocent bystanders caught in the crossfire of gang-related activities.

Without hesitation, Dahlia told Jesse she'd take a flight out the following morning. Louise Duvernay had played a significant role in Dahlia's motherhood journey and desperately wanted to be by her side. The maternal love and support she needed as a young wife and new mother were vital to Dahlia's happiness and well-being, especially when her own mother rarely visited. A young Dahlia knew nothing about caring for a newborn. Although Jesse was a hands-on father when he wasn't working, Dahlia sometimes needed a little nurturing herself, and Granny Lou provided it. "I'll *always have flowers for Louise. Since the moment I first met her, she's been my rock,*" Dahlia poignantly said to herself.

Because of the expense and advanced detailed planning that went into preparing for Raeni's birthday celebration, Nadine wanted to be present. She wanted to ensure that everything went off without a hitch during her bonus daughter's big day. As a result, Jesse decided that Dahlia should wait for Nadine and not travel alone. Jesse's comforting and take-charge quality wrapped his wife in a layer of security she could easily submit to. Dahlia loved dearly the way her husband expressed genuine concern and demonstrated unconditional love for her. "It is safer and best that you travel home with Nadine on Sunday."

Chapter Thirty-One:
Faded Wallpaper

It felt oddly bittersweet for Jesse to pick up his wife and youngest sister from the airport late that Sunday evening. It was a different kind of homecoming. Rachelle wanted to make sure that Dahlia and Nadine's trip home was greeted with warmth and familial love. Once back inside the quaint three-bedroom house in Croix-des-Bouquets on Rue de Rivoli, the ladies' nostrils flared as from enchanting aromas dispersed and suspended throughout. Nadine's big sister put in the time and effort to prepare one of her favorite meals, lanai boukannen woma boukannen (grilled conch, grilled lobster). Rachel decided to use their grandmother's good china for the special occasion. It was taken out of the home's second most opulent piece of furniture, a mid-20th century Early America curio cabinet. Rachel wasn't concerned that pieces of sterling silver flatware needed to be mixed in with some stainless steel silverware, and no one else seemed bothered by it either.

Before everyone was seated at the dining table under an out-of-place jeweled 54" wide chandelier, one that Dahlia's sister Mariah gifted as a wedding present, Dahlia walked around opening and closing doors. She glanced inside the modestly decorated rooms she and Jesse painted with accent walls of faded textured wallpaper meticulously installed during the first year of their marriage. If those walls could talk, they'd tell a powerful tale of a tightly knit family whose love effortlessly flowed, polishing the roughest of stones between misty rains and showering storms. Although Dahlia had been away for only a short period, everything looked so different now through Dahlia's lens. The nostalgic feelings of the place where she had lived for twelve years contrasted significantly with the current promises, pulling her in a new direction. A hope-filled panoramic backdrop was on the future horizon. Dahlia realized that the place where she now stood was too small for her wings to grow and flap. The very rooms where she and Jesse lived as newlyweds, the same happy home where their two beautiful children played as infants, were now confining.

They were too restrictive for a sinking spirit that needed to soar. Her mental well-being summoned more. Dahlia glanced over at her handsome husband, whose strong hands were covered by red oven mitts. Jesse lifted hot dishes from the oven before placing them on trivets at the center of the table. *"He knew, thank God, my sweet husband knew what I needed to survive. His love is medicine for my soul."* Dahlia enjoyed listening to the siblings speak affectionately about how much they enjoyed their childhood. It was heartwarming and entertaining. There were moments of chain-linked laughter and moments of drawn-out sadness as well, especially when Jesse and Rachelle spoke about their early childhood with their parents.

"Every time I smell the smoke from a Camel cigarette, I think of Pops," said Jesse.

"That's funny, so do I," replied Aunt Rachelle.

Nadine listened as her siblings lamented and recollected their parents' misfortune and ultimate demise. She was only two years old at the time when she and her sister and brother were wrangled up to move in with Granny Lou and Papa William. But Nadine loved looking from time to time at old family photos that Granny Lou sent to her after she moved away to attend college.

The sisters and their brother remained with their grandparents until adulthood. Rachelle was the first to move out, anxious to live independently without rules and get her first apartment. She could only do so after being hired as a clerk at the same mission school Wilky later attended. Nadine was second. She left after receiving a scholarship to attend the University of Georgia. Jesse stayed at their grandparents' home a little longer than his sisters because he was saving to buy his own home. It wasn't until he met and married Dahlia that he purchased the new three-bedroom house that they were sitting in at that very moment. He moved his grandparents in with them a little over a year after Wilky was born. A heavy rainstorm destroyed the roof and one side of their own home. Jesse had assessed his grandparents' house and surmised it was indeed on the brink of decay - way beyond his ability to repair it with the funds they were willing to spend.

***

Early the following day, after a late feast on the fabulous meal, everyone ate a simple breakfast and drove to the hospital. Visitation hours at Hospital Sacre Coeur, where Granny Lou had been admitted on Monday, only allowed two visitors in a patient's room at one time. Dahlia and Jesse entered first, around nine o'clock. The nurse had just gotten the injured woman back in bed. Granny Lou had gone to the cardiology department to get clearance for her surgery. The light in the elderly woman's eyes was fading, but her pupils constricted when she looked up and saw her darling daughter-in-law. Dahlia bent low to kiss her and hold her hand.

"Oh baby, it is so good to see you. How are you and my great-grandbabies doing?"

"They are wonderful. It seems they are growing smarter every day. The teachers report that they are good students. I'm so proud of them; I know you would be too. They told me to give you a great big hug and kiss. But how are you doing?"

Granny Lou was tired and weary but didn't want to complain. "I'm doing okay, honey. They got me going into surgery in about an hour. I hope they throw this old broken hip away. I don't want anything recycled. The need to give me a shiny, brand new one with all the bells and whistles."

Jesse and Dahlia laughed. "There is somebody else here to see you, Momma Lou. Let me step out for a moment and let her in."

Tears of joy streamed down Nadine and her grandmother's faces as they held a long and overdue embrace.

"I can't believe that you came back to see me. You haven't been back here in years, Nady."

"I know, Momma Lou, and I'm sorry. I should have come sooner and under different circumstances. I just want to be here for you when you come out of surgery. I want nothing more than for you to get better soon."

"I will, baby. Don't you worry about me? How's Earl doing and his little girl, Remy?" Dahlia and Nadine giggled.

"Isaac is doing well. He's such a wonderful husband and an awesome father. And guess what?" Nadine placed her grandmother's hand on her stomach. "We're going to have a little one of our own in the spring of next year. Raeni is finally going to get the little sister she's always wanted!"

Granny Lou let out a little shriek of joy before grimacing in pain. "Oh, congratulations, baby. I'm so happy for you all!"

Dahlia stepped out of the room next so that Rachelle could enter. It was also a good time for her to sit with her husband and catch up on their children's lives in greater detail. Isaac had called earlier and left a message. He wanted permission to let Cristal and Wilky spend the upcoming weekend with his brother on their ranch. Raeni wanted to spend more time with her pony. Dahlia immediately returned the call.

"Absolutely," agreed Jesse and Dahlia on speaker.

"Thank you so much for looking out for my little ones. I appreciate you, man."

"No problem at all, you've got some well-mannered children, really kind-hearted ones."

A nurse interrupted Rachelle and Nadine's visit.

"Mrs. Duvernay, it's time for me to get you down the hall and ready for surgery."

In the hallway, the family stepped out and grabbed each other's hands to bow their heads in prayer.

The Monday morning following Dahlia and Nadine's departure for Haiti, Cristal and Wilky got themselves dressed and ready for school simply because their mother washed and ironed up enough clothing for eight days. For breakfast, Wilky enjoyed a big bowl of Cheerios for most of those days. Cristal followed suit with Raeni and filled her bowl with Cap'n Crunch. Bananas and orange slices topped off their meals. Jeremy's mother was happy to assist. She ensured Wilky and Cristal were on time and ready at the bus stop with her son.

"Have a great day at school, you two. And stay out of trouble," Uncle Isaac winked at Wilky. "We're going out for dinner this evening, so don't eat a big snack when you return home."

"Yeah! Alright!" shouted Cristal and Wilky.

As usual, Isaac dropped Raeni off at her school on his way to work before merging onto the merciless lanes of Interstate 75. It was a typical school day at Azalea Grove Elementary. After the morning announcements, Cristal worked on a language arts assignment in Mrs. Tubilleja's class. The students sat with a partner to create a short story using their spelling words. The only caveat was that before they began, Ms. Camling would walk around the room holding a jar with paper slips listing different genres: comedy, action, drama, mystery, fantasy, horror, or science fiction. As a pair, Cristal and Camille chose 'drama'. They brainstormed and decided their story would involve a driver and seven children trapped on a runaway school bus after its brakes failed during torrential rainfall. Mrs. Tubilleja was proud of her students' active involvement in the writing process. Good work was created between the giggles and laughter.

Mrs. Collier required her students to pull out their journals and respond to a narrative writing exercise as practice for the state-mandated writing test. The petite teacher slid a low bench near the dry-erase whiteboard, stepped on top, and proceeded to devise a prompt. Mrs. Collier wrote, "Discuss a time when you gave something to someone who needed it. Why did you decide to do it? How was it received, and how did it make you feel?" Mrs. Collier required that her students compose a finished product with at least four detailed paragraphs. "Be sure to begin with a strong topic sentence that leads into a well-developed arc that produces a compelling finish."

After moments of contemplation, Wilky chose to write about the time he gave someone a kick in the knee and then the stomach.

***

In the hospital waiting room, the Duvernays drank coffee and ate croquesignoles (French doughnuts). They talked quietly amongst themselves while waiting patiently to hear news about Granny Lou's surgery. Someone turned on the TV, and everyone fell hostage watching a silly comedy sketch about a bubblehead teenager who was a member of the Haitian elite. After fifteen minutes of viewing, an older gentleman had had enough of the foolish shenanigans. He scanned the room and spotted the remote near a stack of old, ruffled magazines on an end table. Without seeking a collective agreement from others, the gentleman changed the station to reruns of a popular long-running American show, '*Gunsmoke*', with a closed caption.

Three hours passed before the intercom blared in the 42-bed hospital, "Code blue, code blue." Eventually, twenty minutes later, a nurse entered the waiting room and beckoned the family to follow her into a private area. The surgeon stepped in with a mask, donning half of his face. Jesse noticed the shifty, jerky-eyed look. Once the doctor removed his mask, the grave facial expression said it all.

"I'm sorry, but Mrs. Louise has slipped away."

Granny Lou died on the operating table. Although she had received cardiac clearance for surgery, her heart was not strong enough to endure the lengthy procedure.

Five days passed before funeral arrangements were solidified for Louise Duvernay. The once most accepted funeral home in the city struggled over the past year to maintain the high level of standard customers had expected. Several employees no longer held a vested interest in such a dire state of affairs due to overwhelming losses of their own.

Zoe felt compelled to show her respect for the beloved Louise as well. But she chose to sit in a dark, recessed corner of the church instead of expressing her sympathies directly to the Duvernay family members. She was ashamed of her previous behavior and knew that her once best friend most likely had contempt in her heart for her. *'Dahlia probably wouldn't even bother to spit at me if I was on fire,'* she told herself before attempting to dart and exit undetected. The pangs of an acute gout attack prevented Zoe from escaping Jesse's peripheral view.

The repast was held immediately after the service at an adjacent dance hall. Several friends of the Duvernays traveled from different parts of the island to celebrate and honor Louise's life. Young and old church members streamed past the family to shake their hands or offer words of encouragement and hugs for comfort.

"It was a beautiful service."

"Louise and her husband were the salt of the earth."

"Her generous heart and lively spirit touched so many lives."

The healing process commenced when attendees stood at their tables or walked to the podium to share funny stories and fond memories of joyful times spent with Louise Duvernay. Dahlia and Nadine were grateful they could make the trip in time to speak with Granny Lou during the last precious hours of her life.

It was perfect timing when Dahlia's phone rang later in the evening. While everyone was back at the house, moving and piddling around in silence, Mrs. Plaizill called. She wanted to inform Dahlia that First Ebenezer Haitian Church members sent their sympathies and condolences. Three separate dinners - two pre-frozen, had been prepared for Isaac and the children. Mrs. Plaizill would be dropping them off at the townhouse that evening.

In her last will and testament, Granny Lou stipulated that she wanted to be cremated and have her ashes scattered in the Atlantic Ocean with her late husband's ashes. Many years ago, as newlyweds, Mr. and Mrs. William Duvernay shared the same vision and promised romanticism. They hoped their combined ashes would find their way to the shores of Africa - the home of their ancestors. So, the morning after the repast, the immediate family woke at dawn for a three-hour drive to Cap Haïtien. It was a port city on the northern coast of Haiti. They stopped only for freshly baked beignets, coffee, and orange juice for Mikaela. When they arrived, reservations were made for later in the evening to have a small, chartered boat take them a few miles from the coast of Haiti and the Atlantic Ocean.

With time to spare, Rachelle asked if taking Mikaela to a popular nearby attraction before lunch was okay. Everyone agreed.

"This is a special day for all of us to honor our grandmother and grandfather's wishes. I don't think either would require us to mourn and postpone a time of joy. Let us go and enjoy this day we all have to spend together," said Jesse.

The family visited the Sans-Souci palace and then the La Citadelle Laferrière fortress. Aunt Rachelle read the plaque at the entrance of the fort aloud. "The citadel, often called the Eighth Wonder of the World, was begun in 1804 and took 13 years and 200,000 former slaves to complete."

A tour of the historical sites with other tourists vacationing from faraway places was one of enjoyment and education. After a late lunch before sunset, the family set sail on the Atlantic Ocean to scatter the ashes of their grandparents. Following that devoted act of love, they elected to participate in a ritual of African tradition by pouring libations. It was a way of paying homage to our ancestors.

Mikael and Rachelle had initially planned a small, intimate wedding ceremony on December 24th, the Saturday before Christmas of 2011. But, due to Granny Lou's passing, they agreed to cancel those plans and opted to exchange their vows in the pastor's study at the church. Rachelle was glad to have Dahlia and Nadine present, so she was married just a couple of days after the funeral. Little Mikaela was a lovely flower girl who stood straight at shoulder height next to her mother. Her hair was pulled up into a perfect ballerina bun, and dressed in an adorable ivory and multicolored organza dress. No flowers were scattered on the floor, but instead, the beautiful bouquet she held was later presented to Dahlia as a gift to be given to her cousin.

"I just want Cristal to know I miss her and still love her a lot. Maybe she can use these to make something special."

Jesse and Dahlia talked until the wee hours of the morning. They reached an important decision that would change the course of their lives for the better. Jesse announced to the others during breakfast the following morning. "Now that Mr. Mikael and Rachelle Kaliff have tied the knot and decided to move to Saint-Marc, I have no reason to stay here without family by my side. I plan to sell this house and move to Georgia."

Rachelle and Nadine clapped in joyful merriment. They were so happy that their brother would find peace and happiness with his wife and children. The sisters had always delighted in Dahlia's addition to their family and knew how much joy she brought to their brother.

"It will take a while for Johan to help get my papers in order at the Embassy. I may even have to pay him a little extra to expedite the process, but it will be worth it."

Nadine and Dahlia spent the last couple of days in Haiti helping Rachelle clean the house from top to bottom. They each chose some valuable and sentimental items as a keepsake for themselves. Through memories and tears, several things were packed and ready to be donated to friends and neighbors who were still in need. That evening, Jesse drove Dahlia to the gravesite where her mother was buried. He then drove her to the location where Mariah was buried. Dahlia, the thoughtful daughter and sister at each location, said a silent prayer after laying beautiful flower arrangements from a local florist. A heartfelt message accompanied her visits, 'I love you, and I miss you terribly. The love you bestowed upon me will rest comfortably in my soul.' Before getting back in the car, Dahlia blew a kiss up to the heavens in memory and honor of her father.

Chapter Thirty-Two:
Happy Blooming

By spring 2012, the seeds of change were in full bloom. Cristal and Wilky continued progressing and flourishing during their first year at Azalea Grove Elementary. Nadine, Isaac, and Raeni moved into their new home less than thirty miles from the Willow Wood Townhomes. After luck, persistence, and an exceptional six-month job performance, Dahlia was fortunate to transfer from the seafood department to the bakery. Once the house was sold and his papers were in order, Jesse was hopeful to arrive in Georgia sometime in early summer. Everything was coming up roses.

The PTO provided funds for Naturalist Botany Club students to go on a field trip to the Atlanta Botanical Garden. It was scheduled for the first Thursday in May. In celebration of Native Hawaiians and Pacific Islanders, a special lunch was planned in the courtyard after students toured the gardens. Ms. Camling agreed to accompany club members and assist students when needed.

Cristal brought her electronic tablet and had no difficulty accessing an app Ms. Saunders downloaded. A unique mobile camera application utilized the camera on Cristal's device and allowed her to take two-dimensional and three-dimensional pictures of flowers and other objects in the gardens. Within seconds, the voice-over feature identified and described the images. Cristal was delighted to receive information about some of the plants and shrubs on display, such as pansies, creeping phlox, forsythia, weigela, and the bearded iris. One attendant even let Cristal get close and touch a few of them. The relaxing sounds of waterfalls throughout the gardens were enchanting. Cristal enjoyed taking it all in and tried to visualize the beauty of flowing water.

"My mom told me I played in a natural waterfall when I was about four years old in a city called Bassin Bleu," Cristal told Ms. Camling.

As stated in the information packet sent home to parents regarding the field trip, students were permitted to visit the souvenir shop. Dahlia gave Cristal money to buy something. Tiara named some items for sale as they traveled around the small store using the human guide method.

Over the past few months, from participating in community lessons with Mr. Nick, Cristal developed the skills and confidence to request and pay independently for purchases in various stores. "I'd like to buy one packet of sunflower seeds, sweet peas, and poppies, please."

At the educational center, students made leis from fresh jasmine, orchids, and ginger blossoms. They even got the chance to try on grass skirts and strum ukuleles. Hawaiian musicians and dancers performed Israel Kamakawiwoʻole's rendition of *Somewhere Over the Rainbow* and mele oli (sung acapella) and mele hula (accompanied by dance) songs during a lunch that consisted of Hawaiian chicken, pineapple rice, and Hawaiian coleslaw.

All was going well until a maddening raucous filled with shouting and yelling ensued. Two boys began fencing with the bamboo skewers from their fruit kabobs like swashbuckling buccaneers. One student received a superficial wound from a jab in his left shoulder. But the true harm came when the dueling two spilled over into a bed of rare flowers, causing significant damage. An employee from the garden wearing a dark blue blazer with a gold engraved badge attached spoke to the teacher in charge and jotted down names and phone numbers. "Let's hope these flowers bounce back and recover with incredible speed," she scolded the boys.

Besides that brief episode, it was a wonderful, wide-ranging field trip. The students from Azaela Grove Elementary were exhausted from all the fun, and like Cristal and Tiara, all but a few dozed off on the bus during the long ride back to school.

During the free time spent at home when she wasn't learning new features on her electronic devices, Cristal busied herself in the sunroom nursing her burgeoning flowers. She liked getting her hands dirty sometimes. As a result of time spent singing to her very own potted plants, Sudoku became less stubborn and more congenial towards others in his circle. He was willing to repeat words and short phrases when encouraged. Sudoku joined in to sing a little tune that Cristal often sang when tending to her plants and flowers. "It's a hap hap happy day, toodle loodle loodle loodle loodle ay, you can't go wrong if you sing a song, it's a hap hap happy day!"

Ms. Saunders's final Chomp and Chat for the last six weeks of school included guests from five different career fields. A massage therapist/acupuncturist, a car salesman, a Japanese language interpreter, and a pianist for the Atlanta Symphony Orchestra were in attendance.

The students had tons of questions for all of the speakers. The older students especially enjoyed listening to the civil rights attorney discuss ADA access rights for dog guides. The lively interactions conjured up feelings of pride for Ms. Saunders. Instead of everyone eating lunch in the cafeteria, Ms. Saunders let her students take orders from their guest speakers. They donned gloves to make a variety of sandwiches. There was an array of cheeses to select from, along with cherry tomatoes and miniature pickles on toothpicks. Garnishes such as lettuce, parsley, spinach, arugula, and cucumber slices were available for an added crunch to the sandwiches. No-bake cheesecakes made with biscoff cookies for the crust were made by students in Ms. Saunders's first-period class. They were placed inside the refrigerator in the teacher's lounge to chill. Small bowls of raspberries, blackberries, and strawberries were available to scoop for toppings.

Mr. Nick scheduled his final community-based lesson for Cristal and Kaylan on the last Tuesday of the school year. The bus departed the school campus right after the day's first period. A week before the final trip in the community, Mrs. Tubilleja submitted Cristal's name to Mr. Macklberg so she could participate in the morning announcements before the school year ended. Cristal stood nervously in the audio control room with three other students. Although she memorized her part, Ms. Saunders gave Cristal a braille printout as a reference. Mr. Macklberg announced her name and then handed Cristal the microphone. In Mrs. Collier's class, Wilky took a deep breath and crossed his fingers for his big sister's next accomplishment. She'd only practiced it a hundred times the night before.

"Kind hearts are the gardens. Kind thoughts are the roots. Kind words are the blossoms. Kind deeds are the fruits, by Kirpal Singh."

***

Mr. Nick and his two students met up with Ms. Danita and her student Chikao again, but instead of connecting at the *Up a Cup of Coffee Café*, they met at the county courthouse. As part of the O&M curriculum, the two specialists addressed the skills for riding an escalator - ascending and descending, while simultaneously presenting the long cane in a nonobtrusive manner. Because Chikao, the 6th grader, was interested in becoming a lawyer someday, Ms. Danita got prior approval for them to sit in on an actual trial. Mr. Nick, Cristal, and Kaylan followed inside the courtroom and sat on a long wooden bench in the rear.

A corrupt teenager on a bicycle had snatched an unsuspecting customer's food and wallet at a drive-in hamburger joint. This crime was his second offense, and the amount of money taken was forty-seven dollars and twenty-nine cents, along with two cheeseburgers and a basket of fries—the chocolate shake with mint chips splattered onto the concrete. Seconds later, the young thief was apprehended by an off-duty cop sitting in the parking lot eating chicken nuggets with sweet and spicy sriracha sauce. Because the crime was a misdemeanor, his attorney convinced the seventeen-year-old boy to address the judge directly and volunteer to perform community service.

Mr. Nick glanced at his watch; time was running short. He and Ms. Danita agreed it would be best to slip out of the courtroom and take the students to lunch. So, they purchased their meal on the first floor in the cafeteria and sat to discuss what they witnessed in the courtroom. Chikao asked about the meaning behind Lady Justice. Mr. Nick explained, "A court of law commences a trial of a dispute with no prior knowledge of it, hence the blindfold over Lady Justice's eyes." Cristal and Kaylan listened with great intent. Mr. Nick bit into a ham and cheese sandwich.

"This is designed to symbolize that justice should be rendered without passion or prejudice to ensure a fair result."

Ms. Danita added, "The scales represent impartiality or fairness, and the sword symbolizes power."

"That's interesting," said Kaylan. "I'm going to tell my big brother I know about Lady Justice and why she has a sword!"

When Cristal returned from her O&M lesson with Mr. Nick., Ms. Kelsey updated her on the particulars of a final language arts writing assignment. Mrs. Tubilleja's students were instructed to create a poem about the current season and nature, or they could write something that impacted or changed their perspective over the past year. They had to recite the poem before the class and had one week to work on it. For three days, Cristal worked on hers and found it helpful to use word prediction software. She was excited to share because it was written from the heart. Dahlia let Cristal recite it over the phone to her Aunt Rachelle and Mikaela while she listened to her on speaker.

"I like it a lot, Cristal. You are a brilliant little niece, and I always knew it."

"Thank you, Aunt Rachelle." Cristal needed some help to print out a final copy that was free of spelling errors. She obtained it using the auditory spell-check feature with assistance from Ms. Saunders.

I Remember Rainbows

"I remember rainbows arched against a sunny blue sky,

From God's artistic brush, I watched hummingbirds fly by.

With each inviting day, Caribbean winds swirled across the sea,

And I wondered what this great big world might have in store for me.

Beyond every lush green mountain, others came into view,

The triumphs and trials settled in like early morning dew.

Safely, I was guided beyond the dreams embraced each night,

And from the landscapes in Georgia, I found joy in the absence of sight.

I once desired sparkling fortunes at the end of stunning rainbows,

But in this now-familiar place, I've found them,

Where the flowery scent of love pours and overflows.

I remember rainbows."

Chapter Thirty-Three:
A Look Back

Dahlia was delighted to move to the bakery department at the farmer's market. She liked returning home smelling sweet from the aroma of fresh-baked bread instead of dead fish. Her therapy sessions with Dr. Louissaint were invaluable to her mental health and overall well-being. The quality time spent getting counseling helped Dahlia reduce her anxiety and tackle the painful causes of her depression. In anticipation of her husband's arrival, Dahlia felt ready and willing to accept new changes and challenges in her life. Transferring to the bakery was beneficial to Dahlia on several levels.

Arvetta, Dahlia's new supervisor, was from Barbados and had worked her way up the chain within the farmer's market after only four years. She and Dahlia became fast friends when they discovered more than one commonality; they enjoyed housewife reality shows and murder mystery novels. Both ladies were mothers to elementary-age children. During lunch breaks, Arvetta occasionally broke the silent rule to not co-mingle with subordinates. She would invite Dahlia into her office to drink non-alcoholic ginger beer and eat mouthwatering foods from the deli. The topic of their rapid-fire chitter-chatter took off in all kinds of directions.

One afternoon, Arvetta shared a captivating story about her journey to the United States with her parents and four siblings when she was twelve years old. She and her two sisters eventually relocated to Georgia from Texas after graduating high school. They read in a popular magazine that Atlanta was a great place to create generational wealth through real estate acquisition and entrepreneurship.

Arvetta was shocked to hear about her new friend's recent migration to the States. With all ears and an open mouth, she was entertained by Dahlia's story, especially the part about her having been the daughter of a very successful, wealthy businessman in Haiti. When Dahlia finished telling the part about her and Sterling's painful breakup, Arvetta swiveled hastily in her chair to turn to her computer keyboard and monitor. "Girl, my family and I lived in Round Rock, Texas, about 20 miles north of Austin. Let's Google and find out what Mr. Sterling, the scoundrel, is up to now. I wanna see what this man looks like."

Dahlia said, "No, don't," but admitted to herself that she was a little curious, too.

Sterling and Sarik Laurent were franchise owners of a business that sold frozen treats, '*Smooth and Silky Sorbet*'. Over the past nine years, their business grew from owning seven stores in the Austin area to preparing for a soon-to-be grand opening in the Dallas market. Dahlia and Arvetta moved closer to examine the image of the Laurent family standing in front of one of their stores. Sterling looked a lot like Dahlia had remembered him. But he stood rotund with about sixty added pounds. She had to admit the couple and their two children were handsome. Pangs of sadness inched through her body before Arvetta quickly clicked some keys to shut the computer down.

"I'm sorry, Dahlia, I shouldn't have done that. It was insensitive of me." Dahlia pulled a chain with a gold locket from inside of her black uniform blouse. She shared the engraving with Arvetta, 'Forever in My Heart', before opening it.

"It's okay. I was blessed with my own beautiful man." Arvetta scooted closer and thoroughly inspected the handsome head-shot of Jesse.

"Ohhh, chile, he is F-I-O-N-E, fine! Does he have any brothers?"

Dahlia laughed loudly, gave Arvetta a high five, and clicked the locket shut. "No girl, my Jesse is one of a kind," admitted Dahlia.

"I'm just kidding. I'm just kidding. I'm happily married too," Arvetta confessed with a dressed lie.

One Friday morning before starting her shift, Dahlia bounced into Arvetta's office and boasted, "I have highly coveted intellectual and physical property in my possession." She paused at the right inflection point to tap her temple with an index finger. "It's an inherited family recipe for one of the best cakes you'll probably ever taste. So, what do I need to do? Who do I need to talk to about putting it up front in the glass case beside our other fresh-baked desserts?" Dahlia unwrapped a small cake and handed Arvetta a fork.

"Good Lord!" Arvetta smacked her lips and erupted with a mouthful, "This cake is so good, it makes you wanna slap somebody if they get too close."

Chapter Thirty-Four:
A Gathering of Steam

In a Science, Technology, Engineering, the Arts, and Mathematics (STEAM) competition for elementary students in the Garland County Schools, Wilky won second place for his intricate Lego installation of one of the best skylines in the country, New York City. Although he had never been to Manhattan, Wilky's commitment to research within the discipline of physical science and the arts resulted in the impeccable design of the Empire State Building, the Chrysler Tower, and the One World Trade Center. Wilky stepped up on stage at the awards ceremony to receive his ribbon, and like all of the other recipients, he was encouraged to say a few words regarding his project.

"Thank you for my award. Ever since I was a little boy, I have loved building things. One day, I hope to design something magnificent to make my mom and dad proud. And what goes on inside my buildings will be just as special as how it looks outside."

Resounding applause amplified throughout the gymnasium. Dahlia's clap resonated the loudest from the front row, and Cristal gave her brother an explosive fireworks clap that made him smile. The student who won first place for building a hummingbird house with solar sun panels took the time to congratulate Wilky. Dahlia giggled when she saw her son blush for the first time in the presence of a pretty little girl. The mutual exchange of admiration combined with a soft handshake inspired an innocent spark between equally talented competitors.

Wilky was prepared to stand ten toes down and deal with Trevor in whatever the moment called for, but the bully never assaulted Wilky again after the incident on the basketball court. Trevor was too afraid that cameras existed in every nook and cranny of the school and feared they might even be mounted secretly in the lights in the boys' bathroom. After the disciplinary meeting, Mr. Macklberg spoke sternly to Ms. Irvin and directed her to reread page eighteen of the school handbook.

He warned, "According to school records, this is the third incident we've had with Trevor in which he was involved in a physical altercation. Our staff is committed to keeping all students safe, and the next step, should it occur again, is to have Trevor expelled from Azaela Grove. I would also be required to refer him for testing to determine if he would be better served in a special school for students with emotional and behavioral disorders."

Ms. Irvin looked dejected. "No. No. No. I want Trevor to remain here at Azalea Grove Elementary. This is a good school, and he likes it here."

Mr. Macklberg opened his top drawer and handed Ms. Irvin a card. "Here, take this. A friend of mine is the principal at Morning Glory Middle School. He started a bi-monthly Saturday program called C.H.A.N.G.E. It is for young men ages ten and up who might benefit from having a mentor who will motivate, embolden, and help direct students toward a path of success."

Ms. Irvin listened and read the front and back of the card, realizing that 'Creating Harmonious Attitudes - Never Giving Excuses' was just what her son needed.

"Thank you, Mr. Macklberg. I'd like to get Trevor involved in this if I can figure out some transportation arrangements to get him there." She extended her hand and said, "I appreciate you looking out for my son's best interest."

Fortunately for Trevor, with support from positive young leaders in his community, he was able to develop habits over time that determined a better future for himself.

Wilky's soccer team, The Daybreak Warriors, was rated number two in the state for their level of play. The coaches and most of his teammates credited Wilky for moving them up in the ranks from the previous year. Scouts predicted that Wilky would be selected from across the state to play in Division I Competitive 1U-19U at age eleven. It was the highest level of play within the state for that age group.

A month before his team's final season game, Wilky began feeling anxious. Following his father's suggestion, he approached his coach when he was alone to ask an important question. "Coach Parker, I'm glad that I'm a part of a winning team, but I need help with the 'V' and 'Jay-Jay' moves. And to be honest, none of my teammates can consistently perform the skills. No offense, but I believe it could take our game to a whole other level if we got more help."

His Uncle Isaac had been right, *sports make you mature and grow.*

Coach Parker was so impressed and inspired that he decided to connect with an acquaintance who was the assistant coach for a team of high school boys in their same division. He asked for a mentor-mentee practice session before the big game. In return for the favor, Coach Parker treated both teams to a new 'all-you-can-eat' pizzeria after the three-hour practice.

Raeni challenged the principal cellist in a complex piece by Edward Elgar - A Cello Concerto in E minor in mid-May before her final exam. His challenge in response was a selection from the Broadway classic *The Impossible Dream (The Quest)* from Man of La Mancha. Since the orchestra teacher announced that the drama class chose that same classic for their theatre play in the fall, Raeni immediately began practicing its most complex and prominent cello scores. She aced them both, including a difficult run, hands down.

Isaac and Nadine were thrilled that Raeni would enter her junior year as the principal cellist. Her father shared a quote he heard from a television show, "Heavy is the head that wears the crown." He told Raeni to enjoy her well-earned position. "But continue with your commitment to practice and give it your best. Being number one in anything you do sets you apart. That odd stand-alone position comes with its own rewards and encumbrances."

Raeni and Daxton broke up once and then twice after her royally celebrated birthday party in November. She had become quite popular with the boys and girls on campus once the word got out that she owned a beautiful and expensive stallion named Kodály. Raeni and her MaDine agreed that Daxton's jealousy and possessive nature were neither romantic nor healthy. He even tried to make Raeni jealous by complimenting Marsha whenever the three of them were together. "You look Gucci in that dress, Marsha. You glow like Kelly Rowland."

While passing in the halls one day, Daxton stopped at Angela's locker where she was chatting with others and announced that he thought 'she was a real "flicka," the most fly of the Fly Girlz'. Daxton knew such an inappropriate comment would eventually make its way back to Raeni.

Nadine quoted someone from a popular talk show, "If it's not right, it's wrong, Raeni. Your desire to be wanted should not supersede your desire to be respected." Her bonus daughter agreed.

Isaac was glad he decided to slack back and let Raeni figure out how to deal with the pain that arises within the confines of a first-love heartbreak. His daughter was learning that she possessed the power to walk away as opposed to staying and clinging to someone in hopes of receiving genuinely kind affection. Raeni didn't' realize it at the time, but in her later years when dating, she recognized how fortunate she was to have such a strong father figure in her life.

One Saturday after breakfast, Isaac announced, "I'm fine with you inviting Marsha, Angela, Cynthia, and a few of your other friends over, including some nice boy 'friends' to hang out with here at the pool and the stables."

Chapter Thirty-Five:
Bright Like a Diamond

As Cristal's friend Kendall predicted, students who participated in the *Karaoke Kids Club* had the best chance of getting selected to perform a song in the talent show, but they were still required to audition. Tryouts were held three weeks before the day of the program. Cristal and three other students were selected to sing solos, but only after the lyrics to their selected songs were cleared by a panel of teachers. The singers were scheduled to perform between every two acts, including a juggler, a pianist, dancers, a violinist, a magician, and a tumbling routine with ribbon twirlers. There was even a comedy skit, and Joshua from Mrs. Tubilleja's class was chosen to play his trumpet.

All participants were told to meet in the gym during recess to practice their parts. They rehearsed for two weeks before the night of the performance. Dahlia promised Jesse that she would record Cristal's performance for him. During their most recent conversation, he wished his baby girl good luck.

A month ago, after the eighteen guests left the baby shower held for Nadine, Dahlia mentioned the upcoming talent show and extended the invitation to Isaac and Raeni. But now that it was close to the baby's due date, Dahlia wasn't sure if Nadine would feel up to coming. "Don't worry if you can't make it. I plan to purchase a copy of the entire show to share with Jesse when he comes. You'll get a chance to watch Cristal perform later."

As scheduled, Mrs. Plaizill picked up Dahlia and the children early enough to get a good parking spot at the school. She told

Dahlia that the annual talent show drew such a large crowd and was a wonderful culminating event for the close of the school year. Dahlia's phone was on silent as Dr. Martin, the principal, had instructed the entire audience. But Dahlia could feel the phone vibrating in her purse near the end of the gymnasts' routine, and it was Isaac calling.

Dahlia suspected he was at the hospital, and the baby was either on its way or had just been born. She whispered to Wilky and Mrs. Plaizill, "I'll be right back." Dahlia got up and navigated the tight row of chairs in the dimly lit gymnasium. Bending low, she crept like a burglar out of someone's back door just to avoid obstructing the view of others.

Dahlia hurried into the lobby to return Isaac's call. Under no circumstances did she dare miss Cristal's performance. And that's when she got the surprise of a lifetime. Her husband was standing with Isaac, Nadine, and Raeni. Jesse was holding two bouquets of mixed roses. One was for Cristal, and the larger for his wife.

Dahlia was beyond cloud nine. She could hardly believe that Jesse had timed it all so perfectly, arriving in the States for his daughter's school performance. Later, he told Dahlia that his desire was to arrive before the talent show and surprise Cristal with a kiss and a wish for good luck, but Nadine had gotten sick earlier with a bout of projectile vomiting. Nadine and Jesse had discussed the details of the intended plan and organized his scheduled arrival a week earlier. He asked if she and Raeni would keep it a secret, and they agreed. Isaac picked Jesse up as planned from the Hartsfield-Jackson Airport before daybreak.

In advance of the comedy skit, the two couples and Raeni entered the crowded gym and stood with their backs leaning against the wall. Mr. Macklberg recognized Nadine when she entered and saw how very pregnant, she was. *'She needs a seat,'* he told himself while scanning the room. Luckily, he found a couple of empty seats in one row and politely directed individuals to scoot to the right so that two empty seats remained at the end of that row. Nadine and Isaac thanked him. Just as Isaac gestured to Raeni to sit beside Nadine, she spotted a solo chair four rows ahead. Dahlia chose to remain standing to hold hands with her husband.

Jesse observed a tall gentleman with a dirty blonde-colored man bun, a close-shaven beard, and bushy eyebrows head briskly in their direction. Jesse had a flash vision of a scene from one of his favorite American movies, *'Legends of the Fall'* and thought the man resembled Brad Pitt a little.

"Hello," he said, extending his hand to Jesse's. Dahlia proceeded to introduce Arrow Lance Nickolaus to her husband.

"Your daughter is quite a remarkable girl. She's quick on her feet and acquires new travel concepts quickly. Cristal really keeps me on my toes." Jesse laughed as he shook Mr. Nick's hand.

"Thank you for letting me know; I appreciate it. Cristal talks about you often. She thinks you're one dynamic teacher."

The fourth grader, with a red clown nose and a face painted white, wore a silver sequined hat, white gloves, and a black and white striped shirt. Red suspenders were clipped snuggly onto a pair of black pants that sat hoisted high above the ankles. Although he was a juggler, his mother insisted on dressing her fun and outgoing son like a mime. After a few entertaining moments, the young performer dropped one of five colorful hacky sack balls but still managed to get a rising crescendo of applause by the end of his routine. Dahlia pointed out Wilky's up-front location to Jesse under the dim lighting conditions.

"I like that haircut on him. My little man looks distinguished. I got a surprise for him, too."

"What is it?" asked Dahlia.

The gift of a slingshot with a laser beam that could be adjusted for distance and accuracy awaited Wilky once they returned home.

Cristal's name was announced next. After a few seconds, she stepped out on stage. She entered from the wings with a wireless microphone in her left hand and Jurnee in the other. Just as Cristal had practiced during an O&M lesson with Mr. Nick, she used a constant contact cane technique to walk to the center of the stage. After the exact number of steps as rehearsed, Cristal executed a 90-degree turn to her right. She walked forward down the center. A few guests in the audience lightly gasped when Cristal continued to step forward with her cane extended. She let Jurnee's tip detect the drop-off before her. After tactilely confirming her orientation to the edge of the stage, Cristal gracefully reversed direction, took six steps, and then made the last 180-degree turn to face the audience once again.

This fluid sequence of actions positioned her perfectly under the shining spotlight. Jesse's chest began to swell. He thought his daughter looked like a beautiful, brown-skinned porcelain doll standing poised in a sleeveless dress with blooming floral island colors. Cristal's copper-colored hair, thick and soft like her mother's, was styled into Minnie Mouse buns and embellished with one fresh-cut daisy.

Jesse kissed Dahlia on the cheek and whispered, "Thank you for always being there for me and taking such good care of our children." Dahlia squeezed his hand.

"Of course, baby. There's no other way I care to move through this life." Jesse squeezed his beautiful wife's hand.

"You know, I have no idea what she's going to sing," whispered Dahlia. "Cristal kept it a secret from me, and Wilky wouldn't tell me either," she confided.

Just then, she noticed that Cristal wasn't wearing her fan on the lanyard. "Our baby girl is feeling real confident. I believe she's gonna wow the crowd."

As practiced during rehearsals, Cristal held the microphone two inches from her mouth, skillfully avoiding loud acoustic feedback from amplified sounds through the speakers. Like no other act before, you could hear a pin drop in anticipation of her performance. It seemed that even the smallest of children halted their noisy calamity commotions. Tears began streaming as Dahlia listened to a compelling performance from her precious little girl who chose to sing '*Diamonds*' by Rihanna.

Cristal and Wilky were ecstatic that their father had finally relocated to Georgia. The Duvernays, husband and wife and their two children, were together and at peace once again with the memory of Momma Louise close at heart. Now that they had the townhouse to themselves, Cristal could have her own room for fun and rambunctious sleepovers. For once, Wilky was happy to have his own room with an actual door that closed for privacy.

Jesse got his Georgia driver's license and purchased a car a month after his arrival, and Wilky was ecstatic that his father could transport him and some teammates to soccer events. Tiara, Kendall, and Joy's parents took turns alternating the carpool drive for the girls. Although Dahlia wasn't quite ready to tackle the menacing drive-through traffic, she rode along to most activities throughout

Atlanta and the greater metropolitan area. Luckily for Sudoku, Raeni decided to leave him with Cristal and Wilky at the townhouse, where he was entertained as much as he was entertaining.

Jesse had moved to the States in time to celebrate Cristal's birthday in person, and on the fourth of June, there was another one to celebrate. It was the day that Jessica Dionne Granger was born. Nadine named her after her brother and Isaac's mother, Dionne. The Duvernays went to the hospital the day after the baby was born. Nadine and Isaac brought little sleeping Jessica Dionne to the family waiting room. She was swaddled like a burrito in a soft pink receiving blanket.

"She is so adorable," Dahlia announced.

"She's got a nose and dimpled chin like her mother and the almond-shaped eyes of her father," said Nadine proudly.

"She's got a lot of curly hair on her head, just like I had in my baby pictures," boasted Raeni.

"She's beautiful, sis." Jesse kissed Nadine on her forehead. He then shook Isaac's hand and gifted him with a humidor bag filled with thirty premium cigars dressed in elegant pink labels.

"Thank you, man. I appreciate you."

Scooting all the way back in their chairs, Wilky and Cristal waited patiently to hold their new little cousin. Dahlia bent down to keep the baby's head in place on Wilky's lap. He touched her little hands and watched her eyes open as she parted her pink, puckered lips, and yawned.

"She looks like a live baby doll," Wilky announced.

Dahlia moved next to Cristal's lap. "Awww, her skin is so soft," she expressed with sincerity. In that instant, cute little Jessica Dionne made poo poo, and Cristal inhaled a liberal whiff of the pungent dirty diaper. "Eeeww, I smell something," she announced with a crinkled face.

The Duvernays and the Grangers released a hearty and convulsive laugh.

Part III

Chapter Thirty-Six:
Merging Into Success

In August of 2014, Dahlia was triumphant in getting her 'Dahlia's Delights' lemon Bundt cakes with a crunchy praline center on bakery shelves at the farmers' market. It was such a declared favorite with those customers that she was inspired to expand and work from home while refining a recipe for a cinnamon swirl coffee cake with a thin layer of raspberry filling. Forging ahead with Jesse's encouragement, Dahlia signed two contracts for her miniature freshly baked cakes to be sold in two local coffee shops on opposite ends of historic downtown Main Street in the city of Lawrenceville.

As an active member of the ethnically diverse Garland Parent Partnership, Dahlia convinced the board to review their dress code policy to include the acceptance of hairstyles, allowing all students to embrace and express their heritage with pride. She was recognized as a woman of superb executive intellect. As a result, Dahlia recruited other supportive parents to help make positive changes to include a balanced and unbiased history curriculum.

Dahlia seldom missed attending Sunday church services, where she continued to work for the Haitian relief ministry. She discovered an uncovered hobby that brought her great happiness. Dahlia joined the handbell choir. After watching the blossoming of joy in his wife, Jesse's faith reinforced his belief in the benefits of therapy as a powerful and invisible force that could help one heal from trauma.

Jesse decided it would be at least ten more years before he could retire as a supervisor at a busy warehouse for a multinational technology company. But one Sunday, during the after-service dinner, Dahlia and Jesse approached the pastor with their dear friend, Mrs. Plaizill, by their side. They proposed an opportunity to start the church's first Krik? Krak! Festival. Jesse was willing to spearhead this captivating part of the Haitian culture and make it an annual event. Community members received invitations to hear the colorful language of amusing tales and short charades. The call-and-response formula was based on objects and details of everyday life, past and present.

Annually, Jessie received accolades for the well-attended Krik? Krak! The festival has been held yearly since he facilitated its inception in June 2015. There was music, dance, games, and an array of ethnic foods prepared by church members and others living in the surrounding neighborhood. The planning and facilitating of such an event allowed Jesse to form friendships with young and old men who also enjoyed the art of sharing folkloric trickster tales and 'why' stories. The members encouraged and pleaded for Jesse to plan and orchestrate the Fèt Gede, 'Day of the Dead', festival in November.

The Gédé symbolized the spirits of those ancestors who crossed over into another world. During the ceremonial event, participants honored the returning souls with feverish dancing and salacious speech.

Raeni Granger eventually earned a master's degree in physical therapy, and just like her father had hoped, she chose to live close to home. Raeni had become an official International Andalusian & Lusitano Horse Association member. In May of 2017, she successfully passed the Hippotherapy Certification and Hippotherapy Clinical Specialist exams. Her love for horses and her intrinsic desire to help others influenced her decision to start her own 'Ride and Shine Hippotherapy' business.

Whenever asked about her career choice Raeni explained it as, "The purposeful manipulation of equine movement. It is the natural gait of a horse as a therapy tool to engage sensory, neuromotor, and cognitive systems. It works well for persons with physical and mental disorders." Because Raeni had received a full ride to college, Isaac and Nadine were more than happy to help finance her new venture.

Little Jessica Dionne idolized her big sister. With Raeni's support and rallying inspiration, she participated in a broad range of leisure activities. In addition to learning to play the violin, Jessica participated in the Youth & Open Horse Shows. Following her sister's footsteps, she proudly displayed trophies and ribbons on floating shelves along her bedroom wall. Nadine helped Isaac put together a massive and impressive bookcase from Ikea in anticipation of their baby girl's need for more space to showcase her upcoming awards.

In 2017, Wilky's youth soccer team entered the international Gothia Cup tournament held in Gothenburg, Sweden. It was there where he connected with his old friend Endy, who was living in London at the time. Endy was recruited to play for the Purple Dragons Youth Football Academy. The locals often compared his style of play to a young Sadio Mané, a Senegalese professional footballer. After one particular match ended, spectators leaving the stadium witnessed the two young men cry, shout, laugh, and embrace with overflowing hearts of jubilation. It was a living sermon of brotherly love.

"It's so good to see you, my brother," Endy exclaimed. "How do you like living in the United States?"

"It's cool," said Wilky with a shrug. "I've gotten used to it now, but at first it was kinda rough. It's so different than home, you know. I still miss Haiti."

"I hear you. I miss it, too. I've been living in London for three years now. Hopefully, I'll get back there within the following year. How's that sister of yours doing?" Endy asked, trying to sound casual. He worked to mask his true expression in anticipation of Wilky's response.

"Cristal is doing well. She's working on a degree in chemistry. My sister still has her heart set on making perfumes," reported Wilky.

"Ahhh, that's right! She committed to making her future a reality. I remember your sister was always picking and smelling flowers. I used to love Cristal's girly giggle. There's got to be a science behind such a beautiful effervescent smile that's so beguile," Endy proclaimed.

Wilky smirked at his friend's attempt at poetic expression. They then spoke about their old friend Marjon, still living in Haiti. At 18 years old, Marjon became a father struggling to provide and care for his girlfriend and their young son. The long-time friends continued for almost two hours reminiscing about good times and not-so-good times after the 2010 earthquake struck. They acknowledge how it changed virtually every aspect of their young lives. Before Endy and Wilky parted, they exchanged numbers and emails, vowing to stay in touch.

Wilky received a scholarship to attend the university and continued playing soccer in the NCAA D1 Division. For an internship, he was given an amazing opportunity during his sophomore year to work at a successful movie studio in the southeast Atlanta area. Not only did Wilky assist in constructing soundstages on the 300-acre studio, but his creativity also earned him an opportunity to design incredibly realistic sets for popular movies with a cast of famous actors. Once the internship ended, Wilky was offered a permanent part-time position that he gladly accepted. He planned to work there at least until he completed his degree program.

Sudoku's diet consisted of fresh fruit, kale, and protein from cooked eggs and turkey, which helped him maintain healthy glucose levels at the tender age of nineteen. While sharing a home with the Duvernays, Sudoku acquired an ability to speak over seven hundred words; some were even in French. The Einstein of birds often talked in short phrases within the proper context of a conversation.

At the age of twenty-one, Cristal Duvernay graduated from Georgia State University with a B.S. in Chemistry and a minor in Botany in the summer of 2019. She contributed much of her success to supportive parents, teachers of the visually impaired in the Garland County School District, and mentors from the Lighthouse for the Blind. Although Cristal mastered a high level of O&M skills using the long cane, she chose to travel in the community with a dog guide. Mali, a large black standard poodle, was matched with Cristal upon completing the six-week training program at a training school in Michigan. Skillful dog handlers recognized that this was the best breed for Cristal, not just because poodles were one of the most intelligent dogs on the planet but also because of her allergies. Poodles were the most hypoallergenic dogs, producing less dander. If Cristal desired to live with a royal and loyal companion who would be by her side constantly, then Mali was the one for her.

Cristal's dream to become a master perfumer never wavered. "So what's next, Cristal?" Her mother and father asked after a small graduation celebration.

"Well, before I pursue a graduate degree in chemistry, I would like the opportunity to travel to France and attend one of three prestigious perfumery programs. My vocational rehabilitation counselor, Ms. Lisa, asked if she could submit my applications, but honestly, even if I was lucky enough to get selected, I couldn't afford it. It is so costly."

Dahlia spoke in a relatively firm voice, "Cristal, for the second time, I'm telling you to take the pair of Marquis Csarite and diamond earrings my mother gave me. Sell them. You could get at least thirty thousand dollars for those jewels. Indeed, that would be enough to pay for your training."

But Cristal was insistent. "No, mom. Thank you, but no. That was a special wedding gift for you. I wouldn't feel right taking something so valuable. It's an heirloom to be kept in our family always."

Her Papa Jesse offered another viable solution. "I could take out a loan with our townhome as collateral, which would certainly be enough to get you on your way."

"Thanks, Daddy. But no, thank you. I don't want you and Mom getting into debt behind me. Y'all just paid it off, and it wouldn't be right." Cristal declared, shaking her head.

Wilky made it a habit to visit his parents and his sister on Saturday afternoons for a late lunch. Rather than spend money at a laundromat, he chose that time to do his laundry. This particular Saturday was July 18, 2020, not quite a year before another catastrophic earthquake struck Haiti in 2021. Cristal sat at the kitchen table chatting away as her mother twisted Wilky's 18-inch locs. Mali lay under Cristal's chair, playing with a favorite squeak toy, and happily wagged her fluffy pom-pom tail back and forth to tickle her master's ankles. The family enjoyed catching up and discussing each other's weekly activities. They often gave advice regarding minor challenges or offered suggestions in the form of multiple-choice answers on approaching upcoming situations with the best possible outcome. Instead of rating their days on a scale of 1-10 like they did when they were younger, the clan chose to rate the previous week instead.

Jesse sat relaxing in his La-Z-Boy recliner in the bedroom, watching a baseball game. He could be heard rooting for the Atlanta Braves during their season opener against the New York Mets. The doorbell rang unexpectedly.

"I'll get it," Dahlia said after peering through the peephole. She signed for the delivery of a large, thick envelope from a global mail carrier and then shut the door. "I wonder what this is," she said while pulling the tab and ripping it open.

Jesse entered the kitchen to see who their unexpected visitor was. On his wife's shoulders, he rested his chin to peer at the cover letter from the Vincent and Wycliff Law Firm.

"I don't understand. What does this mean?" Dahlia asked. She passed it to Jesse, and he quickly reread the letter.

"I'm not exactly sure. Call Isaac."

Everyone scrambled to jump inside the teal blue Dodge Ram 1500 pickup truck. At top speed, Jesse drove his family straight to the home of Isaac and Nadine. When they arrived, Isaac's fraternity brother, Nathaniel, pulled up in the driveway right behind the Duvernays' vehicle. Nathaniel was a Family Law attorney for a large firm in Midtown Atlanta. He knew a little about wills and probate, so he was invited to help interpret the envelope's contents.

Inside the Granger's lavish, light, and airy home with vaulted ceilings, Nadine served cold drink choices of mango and lilac-infused lemonade over crushed ice from a metal bar cart on wheels. A few moments later, a charcuterie board containing cured meats, hummus, and a variety of cheeses, nuts, vegetables, and fruits was positioned in the center of the coffee table beside expensive unwrapped chocolates. The Duvernays and Grangers sat on the edge of their seats in the grand living room, munching from small plates and listening to Nathaniel. He read and discussed the merits of the cover letter and moved on to the contents and forms in the entire packet.

As fate would have it, it turned out that Dahlia's father, Samuel Joseph, had established a trust for his three grandchildren: Cristal, Wilky, and Winston Nortay Jr. Their grandfather had appointed a close business partner and friend, Augustin, as trustee. Unfortunately, Augustin had been on life-support for over a year after sustaining injuries from the earthquake in January 2010 and eventually passed away. The annual payments for the safe deposit box where the original trust documents were stored had been made from a Deutsche Bank of Lagos branch in south Florida. Just shy of five years, a financial specialist from the bank contacted Augustin Jr. as customary due to low account activity. The conscientious young man who inherited his father's unfaltering integrity and virtuous acts of service immediately contacted the Vincent and Wycliff Law Firm. Despite a few legal problems of their own, there was only a slight delay in locating the Duvernays in Atlanta, Georgia to notify them of their status as beneficiaries.

The documents specified that once each of Mr. Joseph's grandchildren reached the age of twenty-one, they were to receive in equal value a specified amount of monetary assets. Most of Mr. and Mrs. Joseph's money came from offshore investments, including the rental property of a resort in St. Kitts. It also built in payouts from the insurance company on his small restaurants and nightclubs.

After Winston Jr. received his disbursement, Cristal and Wilky became the recipients of 3.7 million dollars each.

Chapter Thirty-Seven:
Good Fortune

Three weeks later, Ms. Lisa, the Vocational Rehabilitation Specialist, arranged a virtual panel interview between Cristal and three employees from the Jalece Avant-Garde Perfumery Institute in Paris, France. The director, Mr. Beaumont, was the first to speak directly to Cristal. "We are very impressed with your credentials, Ms. Duvernay. We see that you've maintained a 3.8 in your post-baccalaureate studies. That is quite notable."

"Thank you," Cristal replied.

Mr. Beaumont continued, "As I'm sure you're aware, Jalece Avant-Garde is a leading school in the fields of fragrance, flavor, and cosmetics. Please tell us why we should select you as one of ten participants this year in our very competitive apprenticeship program to work with masters. And what consequential knowledge would you bring to Avant-Garde?"

A younger and less refined Cristal would have instantly reached for the blue silk fan in her purse before speaking under such high-pressure circumstances. But now the more mature and reassuring voice in her head began conjuring up positive self-talk. *'No, you don't need it. As Mom and Dad advised, it will be okay to speak from the heart and not the script.'* Next, it was her father's voice that took over. *'Don't shrink, baby girl. This is your time to shine, once again, brightly like a diamond.'*

Cristal cleared her throat and took two deep and slow breaths. Each panel member leaned into their computer screens and watched intensely as Cristal's heart-shaped pendant began to rise and fall with each deep breath.

Cristal and her friend Brenda were active members of a French club at a local library, and in addition to the two years of French she took in high school, Cristal had signed up for another year of advanced foreign language as an elective in college. She was a bright young lady, adequately prepared to communicate impressively at this moment. She began speaking eloquently in the predominant language of France.

"Your school has elevated others to create some of the most exquisite perfumes on the market. Since I was a little girl, years before I lost my vision, I loved picking flowers, inhaling, and analyzing each fragrance. Bouquets were always in our home, either on our kitchen table or my mother's nightstand. I studied the petals' aromas, shapes, and textures closely. I continued to educate myself on the science of scents. Since the age of nine, I've made perfumes," she emphasized with air quotes, using two fingers from both hands before continuing.

"With ingredients found in a variety of bottles and spices from the bathroom and kitchen cabinets within my home, my parents gave me the latitude to create. I, too, have a strong desire to design fragrances that can transform how one feels about themselves in moments that matter. My grandmother once told me, 'Santi bon koute che'- 'smelling good is expensive.' I believe customers are willing to pay the price for the power of a subtle but floral and elegant alchemy that gives the allure of good fortune. The right combination of top notes, such as Bergamont and Juniper berries, with heart notes like orris and pine needles, create shared spaces where the right fragrance yields feelings of euphoria. I want transformative fragrances to be available for those who could stand in adoration by simply entering into a room."

Cristal allowed all the connecting dots from her past to project an image that catapulted her to a higher level. The panel of three looked at each other with serious and agreeable nods.

"Cristal, do you have any questions for us?" Mr. Beaumont asked.

"Yes, I have two questions. Are there any concerns you have about me and my day-to-day abilities that I can clear up for you now? Also, please share the profile of someone you want to see who will exceed your expectations."

After accepting the invitation to Jalece Avant-Garde Perfumery Institute for an apprenticeship position, Cristal phoned her friends and her cousin to share the good news.

Tiara was living in Savannah, Georgia. She had one more semester before completing an advertising and digital production degree at SCAD. Tiara was thrilled for her friend. "I'm so happy for you. You've always had grit and passion, girl. I knew you could do it! As soon as I finish my classes, I will come up there, or you can come here so we can celebrate."

"Yes, we both can celebrate getting our degrees!" exclaimed Cristal.

Next, she called and left a message with three other close friends, Francesca, Brenda, and Kendall. Cristal hadn't seen Kendall since their Goalball Northeast Regional competition in early May. It seemed that Kendall and her mother were always on the move, traveling from one production studio to another. Kendall landed fun and financially rewarding parts in voice-overs for cartoon shows.

Early one Saturday morning, while Cristal aimlessly clicked through channels with the remote, she recognized her friend's enchanting voice on a cartoon channel.

Raeni was elated when Cristal announced her good news over the phone.

"Congratulations, Cristal! I'm so happy for you. It looks like your dream to design a uniquely fragrant perfume will come true!"

"Thanks, cousin. I feel so blessed, and I'm super excited. I'll be leaving for France in less than two weeks. I know this is last minute, but I was wondering if you would go with me to Paris and stay for at least the first week to assist in getting me situated?" Raeni listened intensely. "Of course, Mali will be by my side, but I could use your support for sure." Cristal hesitated briefly and then continued, "And it might be a wonderful opportunity for you to connect with your mom and brother, Colton."

A slight gasp was released from the opposite end of the phone. Cristal pushed, "Mom and I did some research last night, and we found out that the Eurostar train that travels underwater from Paris to Belgium takes around two hours."

It was an offer Raeni could not refuse. "Yes. Yes. I would love to go with you. Thank you for thinking of me, cousin. It would be an honor."

"There's something else I want to say, Raeni," Cristal's eyes began to water as her voice quivered. "I will never, ever forget how much you helped me when Wilky and I moved here. We totally invaded your space. You were kind enough to teach me how to turn the Double-Dutch rope so that I could hang out with you and the Fly Girlz. You even let me play with your chemistry set. And when I received my first cane, you said something I never forgot."

"Wow, what did I say that was so intellectually profound?" asked Raeni.

Cristal laughed, "You told me right after we named my cane, Jurnee, that it would be the exact tool to help me travel to many places all around Georgia and other places in the world. You have no idea how much that inspired me, and I love you for that."

"Awww, I love you too, cousin. Okay, I gotta let you go. I have to go shopping for my trip to Paris!"

The same year that Cristal studied abroad in Paris, Wilky's idea for easy-to-assemble prefabricated homes proved an attractive business venture for investors, especially for the movie mogul at the studio where he worked part-time. Wilky's new company, *'Hearth and Heart to Haiti'*, built tiny but durable two-story homes with quaint front porches and balconies that met international building codes as permanent housing solutions. It was Cristal's idea for her brother's tiny houses to display a signature look. Artistically painted picturesque colored rainbows would be visible on the side of his homes.

After working diligently with some of his father's well-established executive counsel back home, Wilky was fortunate to secure a contract with the Haitian government. This agreement resulted in the purchase of his tiny homes for Haiti's homeless citizens living on the streets. Because of Jesse's past commitment to the Red Cross, volunteers agreed to help citizens there erect the houses. Charitable donations from Haitian churches throughout the southern states in the U.S. supported their efforts.

After an enormous exertion of energy, Wilky finally got in touch with his old friend, Marjon.

"Hey man, it's Wilky, Wilky Duvernay." Marjon was overjoyed to hear from his old and dear friend. "I hope you, your girl, and MarJon Jr. are doing okay, especially after everything that's been happening lately. But listen, I'm calling because I got a proposition for you."

Wilky, like his father, had come to realize that after the earthquake in 2010, the young people of Haiti were never devoid of talent, just opportunities and resources. Before that hour-long conversation ended, Marjon had been hired through Wilky's foundation to establish a small crew that would oversee the ongoing maintenance of the 'Hearth and Heart to Haiti' homes. "Oh, and just so you know, I don't plan to build the homes with a murder hole."

The old friends had a robust laugh.

Cristal learned a great deal as a mentee from master perfumers while living and learning in Paris. For two years, she studied hard, critically examining the science and the craft of scent design. Endy would frequently travel to Paris from London on the weekends via the underwater Eurostar train that could arrive on the scene within thirty-five minutes. When he first showed up to take Cristal out one Saturday evening, he met her at the lobby in her dormitory. Cristal was prettier than Endy remembered her as a young girl running about on the dusty island of Earth.

"Look at you, blooming into your most elegant and authentic self." Cristal's ethereal smile and fine complimentary dimples appeared instantly. In her arms, he placed a large blooming bouquet of tulips, daffodils, and hyacinths. "I know how much you love the scent of fresh flowers," he told her.

Upon receiving the sweet-smelling flowers, Cristal reflected on a Chinse proverb she'd heard long ago, '*A bit of fragrance clings to the hand that gives flowers.*' She gave Endy an appreciative hug and decided that he felt like warm sunshine. Sure enough, Endy was still the kind and gentle person she remembered.

"These smell wonderful. Thank you for remembering, Endy." Cristal turned around gracefully and walked with Mali to the lift. "I'll be right back; I'm going to take these to my room and put these in water."

The spark and delirium of an enchanting, long-anticipated date with Endy was almost too much to contain. She managed to quell the unabashed temptation to squeal, but once the doors closed and the slow and rickety lift began its ascension to the third floor, Cristal dropped Mali's harness and reached in her purse for the fan.

Cristal and Endy's first date was to the Louvre Museum, the world's most-visited institution and a historic landmark in Paris, France. The home of some of the best-known works of art included the Mona Lisa and the Venus de Milo. Endy researched before their visit and discovered that it was entirely accessible for persons with visual impairments. The gallery was equipped with tactile ground markers and had braille booklets available for loan. Endy told Cristal to download an app ahead of time on her smartphone so that she could enjoy a guided tour with audio descriptions.

One Saturday afternoon, the two rode the Roue de Paris 200-foot-tall Ferris wheel after a joyful gondola ride. On another evening, the couple had a fine dining experience as part of a sailing tour on the Seine River. A favorite outing for the two was a tandem bike ride along the path of the famous Champs-Elysees Road. Cristal was glad to get a break from her concentrated studies and have someone from home to hang out and do fun things with. During her two-year apprenticeship, it felt good to have a friend who would check on her from time to time since she was so far away from home.

Arnessa, a young and talented lady from Vancouver, Canada, was one of the first persons Cristal established a friendship with at the Jalece Avant-Garde Perfumery Institute. Cristal, Arnessa, and two other participants accepted Endy's invitation to join him and his friends in London for the occasional weekend getaways. One of the group's favorite activities each time they met was to go rowing on the Serpentine and in south-east London on the River Thames in Greenwich Park. The self-guided audio tour at Hyde Park and Kensington Gardens was a favorite as well.

Chapter Thirty-Eight:
Bonjour Mon Amour

A month after Cristal successfully completed the apprenticeship program in Paris, she returned home to work on a business plan that included the production of a new perfume. Some of her cohorts at the institute aimed to create unusual mixed fragrances like campfire with jasmine, new books with a hint of lavender, garden dirt with vanilla, and other unconventional blended aromas. Practically all of those circled the drain on presentation. Cristal remained faithful to a particular scent, providing the school with a more than satisfactory variation of her real prize. She was clever enough to keep it guarded until she returned to the States. Her unique creation included rose notes with a concentrated hibiscus foundation and purified drops of Caribbean rainwater.

While in pursuit of a master's degree in chemistry, Cristal wrote a detailed cover letter requesting an interview with the head of a major perfume manufacturer. The young and hopeful designer included an impressive resume in a padded envelope with generous samples of her private olfactory creation. In two days, Cristal's package was hand-delivered to the CEO of a leading perfume company in downtown Manhattan. Jesse and Dahlia proudly escorted their daughter to New York seven weeks later.

For almost two hours, the Duvernays met with top executives who were genuinely impressed and intrigued by the uniquely scented perfume composition submitted by the young Haitian-born nose.

"The person who chooses to wear this exclusive fragrance stands at the complex intersection of audaciousness and elegance, ready to confidently navigate places and enter spaces unlike those that preceded them." Cristal had begun her sales pitch with poise, vitality, and more academic rigor than the senior manager had ever witnessed. In January 2021, her first designer fragrance, *Fòtin bon,* was launched worldwide.

Wilky skillfully fulfilled Cristal's wish to create an artistically sculpted glass bottle that would be the vessel for her highly coveted precious fragrance. It resembled a mountain with a 3-dimensional triangular shape at its prism base. The bottle's closure and finish were a clever replica of a reddish-orange hibiscus, the national flower of Haiti. Infused specks of gold coloring added the finishing touch. *Fòtin bon* was a top seller for those seeking the perfect Valentine's Day gift for the special lady in their life.

Cristal decided that from her first point of sale to her last, a portion of her earned income from *Fòtin bon* perfumes would go towards a crystalized vision that she had kept near and dear to her heart for over a decade. And for this, she wanted her brother's approval and support for such a huge venture. Cristal hoped that Wilky would agree to be an active partner without pay.

"He's got all the money he needs anyway," she told her friend Francesca before broaching Wilky with her ideas.

The siblings sat enjoying a delicious five-course meal on the revolving rooftop of a five-star restaurant in the center of downtown Atlanta. It was a popular hot spot with tourists who were especially eager to take selfies with the backdrop of such a magnificent skyline just before sunset. Cristal was relieved that Wilky decided at the last minute not to bring his aspiring actress girlfriend, Ember. She felt that the important topic to be discussed was a family matter.

Wilky shared a significant family matter with Cristal before she broached him with her own news, "I had a conversation with momma this morning, and she asked me to go on Facebook or another social media platform to try and find our cousin, Winston. He's not there or on Twitter, and I don't know where to start searching now. He's definitely not still in Haiti, and who knows if his father is even still living. Our cousin could be anywhere in the world, especially since he received a large sum of money, too." Wilky surmised.

Cristal made a suggestion, "What if you wrote to the Vincent & Wycliff Law Firm and explained the situation? Tell them that when mom's sister, Mariah, died in the earthquake, she lost touch with her nephew. They obviously have his contact information. If they don't divulge his personal data and whereabouts to us, perhaps we could request that they ask Winston to contact his mom."

The entrepreneurial siblings and Dahlia would later learn that Winston was living in Berkley, California, and was working as a professor's assistant while pursuing a master's degree in environmental psychology. He had found a respectable place within an open-arms community far from Haiti. It was a place where he felt loved for who he was, and it granted him the grace to live a life on his own terms.

Cristal felt a higher level of happiness from every sip of her mint Mojito. "Yeah, that might work, sis. I guess you do have a little something up there in that coconut head of yours."

"You're funny, real funny, little brother. Now let me tell you why I really invited you to this awesome restaurant."

Between her studies and outings with Endy in Paris, Cristal made strong connections with old and young members of the European Blind Union (EBU) – The voice of the blind and partially sighted people in Europe. She toured their facilities and, when possible, participated in monthly activities and events that widened her perspective on global views regarding persons with visual impairments.

At conferences, Cristal had opportunities to hear from others who were willing to address world issues such as accessibility, employment, assistive technology, and recreational interests. Remarkably close connections were established with prominent members of the EBU. They listened as Cristal talked passionately about the home of her birthplace, Croix–de–Bouquets, and her desire to one day open 'The Shyana Louis Center for the Visually Impaired'.

Cristal's new Parisian acquaintances vowed to provide her with as much moral support and guidance as they could from across the North Atlantic Ocean. Cristal even thought to appeal to Mikaela in hopes that she might be interested in some role within the center. The goal for each participant would be to increase levels of independence aimed at personal fulfillment in the area of employment and social and recreational activities. With the support of Haitian church members locally and throughout the United States, Cristal wanted to create a scholarship fund that would support students at university special education programs like the ones from but not limited to NIU, UALR, FSU, and NCCU.

It was a lofty ambition that Cristal knew could take perhaps ten years or more to come to fruition, but she was committed to a solution for recovery, reconstruction, and educational development in her homeland. With a string of supporters at home and abroad,

Cristal was prepared to rise to the challenges she'd face from the Haitian government and the existing education system for persons with disabilities. Cristal's plan for Wilky was to draw blueprints for a modest but distinctive building with several classrooms, including a gymnasium.

She told her brother, "You must include beautiful landscaping with an expansive scent garden in the front and back."

Cristal wanted the building erected far from the epicenter of the 2010 earthquake in Haiti. Sometime in the future, she and Wilky would travel there to select the exact location.

"So where would the teachers and students live, somewhere near the center?" Wilky asked.

"Well, yeah, I'll talk to you about that later," Cristal voiced. Wilky grumbled like an old man, feeling he was about to be hoodwinked into something grander.

Their Papa Jesse suggested that Cristal and Wilky consider looking for a location near Port-de-Paix, a commune in the northwestern part of Haiti on the Atlantic coast. Jesse shared a part of the port's history with his adult children. "The port was founded in 1665 by French filibusters who had been driven from nearby Tortue Island by the British. It is the site of the first black slave revolt in 1679."

"Oh yeah, I almost forgot. There's something else I want to tell you." Wilky paused before tapping his dessert spoon to crack and attack the brittle top of his crème brûlée.

"Now what?" he asked in an exasperated tone.

Cristal giggled before responding, "I forgot to mention that your friend Endy is coming to visit next month."

On a lazy mid-week afternoon under the shade of a hardwood sugar maple tree, Jesse and Dahlia sat near the small lake at their twelve-acre ranch-style home. They enjoyed the cool, sweet taste of homemade Georgia peach ice cream while swatting and shooing away a pesky trio of flies amidst the bluish-green undertones of the horizon.

"We didn't do too bad raising our babies, did we?" Jesse asked his wife.

"Not at all, and thanks to you, our little chipmunks are soaring like eagles."

He smiled and, in one romantic gesture, leaned in for a kiss. Occasionally, the couple glanced across the lake before drawing a baited line through rippling waters, hoping for a nibble under floating red and white bobbles.

Guided Chapter Questions for
Middle-Grade Readers

Chapter One: Croix-des Bouquets

Cristal discovered a hobby she was passionate about from a young age. She was lucky to have someone, Granny Lou, to cheer her on and encourage her to continue. Would she enjoy her craft just the same if there were no one to share it with? Most people have an artful side that they may or may not have discovered yet, such as music, sculpture, painting, literature, architecture, and performing (dance, singing, or acting). Have you found yours, and if so, is there someone, a family member, or a friend to encourage you to continue to do your best?

Chapter Two: Rainbows

Zoe spoke to her best friend, Dahlia, about ending the coddling and over-protection bestowed on Cristal. She felt she might be stifling her daughter's mental and emotional growth which comes with the joys and pains of growing up. Have you ever wished that the adults in your life would allow you to learn from your mistakes and become more independent? What age-appropriate daily living activities would you like to try and accomplish by yourself?

Chapter Three: Spice Girl

Dahlia struggled a great deal with her depression and, for a long time, found it difficult to carry on with the simplest of activities.

Eventually, the art of baking cakes became a hobby that kept her mind and hands busy. She was able to deflect or escape from periods of sadness. What do you enjoy doing when faced with sad or difficult times? How important was it to have a friend or family member to talk to? Do you consider yourself the type of person to be there for a friend through the good and bad times?

Chapter Four: Krik? Krak!

Cristal and Wilky's parents enjoyed sharing Aesop and African fables as a way of helping them learn about human behaviors and how to deal with challenging situations. Do you remember the fable about the Tortoise and the Hare? What was the moral of that story? A proverb is a short sentence that people often quote, giving advice or telling you about life. Cristal and Wilky's Papa Jesse shared a Haitian proverb: *"The giver of the blow forgets; the bearer of the scar remembers."* What do you think it means?

Chapter Five: Dagnabbit

Cristal's chore from an early age was to help Granny Lou do laundry. She was paid an allowance for her work. Many parents today believe that by paying their children an allowance, they are teaching them the value of work and the lifelong skill of managing and budgeting money that is earned. What chores do you do around the house and is there more than you can do to help? Write a persuasive paragraph as to why you should be paid an allowance.

Chapter Six: Cheerio and Lila

Wilky and his friends enjoyed making fun of Mrs. Rosie behind her back. Cristal never joined in because, like her Aunt Rachelle, she thought it was a mean thing to do. Cristal learned at a young age to be respectful of adults. Have you ever been around friends who spoke negatively about someone you knew or liked? What did you do about it? What traits do you look for in a friend?

Chapter Seven: Papa's Big Reveal

Parents sometimes have difficult choices to make in an attempt to do the best they can for family members. They don't always have the correct answers for all life circumstances because they are also learning and growing. Wilky didn't handle the news well when his father told him he would be moving to Georgia. What was something you had difficulty accepting, and do you think you handled it well?

Chapter Eight: Stingrays vs. Manatees

More than anything, Wilky enjoyed playing soccer with his two best friends. Besides being fun and exercising, team sports build character and leadership skills. You learn to lose and win graciously, which can prepare you for the ups and downs in life. What's your favorite team sport? Do you have a favorite professional athlete? Take some time to research a team sport and one of its best athletes. Find out how young they were when they began their athletic career.

Chapter Nine: Buckle Up

Cristal and Wilky were both sad, nervous, and excited to travel from their Haitian home and fly to the United States to live. Why do you think some people never desire to travel away from the city where they were born? How many cities have you traveled to? What places would you like to travel to and why?

Chapter Ten: Georgia on Your Mind

Cristal took deliberate action and used her remaining senses to learn the layout of the townhome where she would be living. Sometimes, people find it surprising to discover that another person's home and the manner in which they live is so different from their own. There is no right or wrong, good or bad; just different. Have you ever visited a family or friend's house for dinner and were surprised by their routines and behaviors? Did their décor reflect attitudes, values, and interests that you expected? Describe the layout of your home and then create a drawing or tactile map to reflect your living space.

Chapter Eleven: Shared Space

Raeni promised her father, Isaac, that she would politely and willingly share her home with her cousins whom she'd never met. Personal space, the physical distance between one person and another, is a boundary that allows one to feel protected and comfortable. Even standing too close to someone when you're talking to can feel like an intrusion or violation of one's preferred personal space. How difficult do you think it was for Raeni to share her bedroom with Cristal? Have you ever had to share your home with someone for a period of time?

Chapter Twelve: Table Talk

Dahlia was grateful that Nadine and Isaac provided a warm welcome and haven for her and her children. The road ahead was going to be difficult as she moved through the grieving process. She would have to learn new strategies to cope with the loss of her loved ones in Haiti. Grief is defined as a natural emotional reaction to the loss of someone or something important. It's an individual experience that affects every person differently and may be expressed in various ways. Do you think that anger is a part of grief? What are some ways that a person can try to move forward from the pain they suffer from?

Chapter Thirteen: Sweet Dreams

For years, people often held stereotypes or a fixed set of beliefs about what a person with a disability could or could not accomplish. Cristal was very hurt by her mother's conversation with her father that Cristal could possibly resort to begging as a way to earn money for the family. Why do you think Dahlia never apologized to her daughter for the low expectations she held for her at the time? It wasn't until July 26, 1990, that The Americans with Disability Act established laws to prohibit discrimination based on disability in accommodations, employment, public transportation, and telecommunications. Why do you think it took so long for these laws to be established?

Chapter Fourteen: Super Shoppers

Wilky almost missed the opportunity to go to Super Shoppers when he was sent to his room earlier that morning as punishment. Thanks to Raeni, Cristal had an excellent experience buying the things she wanted. Not only did she select trendy clothes for school, but Raeni helped Cristal purchase essential oils for her perfumes. Talk about a time when you were lost or separated from family members in the community. If given $100.00 to buy anything you wanted, what would it be?

Chapter Fifteen: Knuckleheads

The boys who threw rocks at the wasp nest made a foolish decision. Any one of them could have become seriously ill, especially if they were allergic to wasp venom. Have you ever done something that you knew was risky, but you did it anyway? Sometimes, people will do foolish things on a dare. Have you ever played the game Truth or Dare? Name a funny dare you might ask a friend to do (e.g., go to the neighbor's house and ask to borrow a cup of water or three squares of toilet paper).

Chapter Sixteen: Ready, Set, Go!

Cristal and Wilky were excited to attend school in the United States for the first time. They were also nervous because they worried, they would be treated as an outsider or someone who didn't belong. Have you ever been somewhere and felt like you were so different from the others in a group that you didn't belong? Have you ever tried to be friends with someone from a different culture? What are things you'd want to know about someone from a foreign land?

Chapter Seventeen: Introducing William DeMarco Duvernay

Wilky stood before the class at his teacher's request to introduce himself. He spoke about his home in Haiti, his favorite pastime, and even a food he liked. Wilky also made an enemy rather quickly. Have you ever been bullied, and if so, how did you handle it? List four things you would say about yourself if asked to speak in front of your class.

Chapter Eighteen: Introducing Cristal Shyana Duvernay

Cristal was never formally taught how to travel safely, independently, and efficiently using a cane. While living in Haiti, she relied on Lila to help clear her walking path. Do a little research to find out the benefits of using a long cane. Mr. Nick, the Orientation and Mobility Specialist appeared to be very good at his job. List three traits a person should have if they want to be good at something. Research the education and training required to become an Orientation and Mobility Specialist.

Chapter Nineteen: Better Tomorrows

Wilky was reluctant to tell his mother about the incident with Terrance because he didn't think she'd have a real solution. It wasn't until after he moved to Georgia that he had a serious talk with his father. During their phone conversation, Wilky learned a little more about his father's childhood and some problems he faced as a young boy. It's not easy to imagine your parents as little children. How much do you know about your parents' childhood? Think of a few questions you'd like to ask them and consider doing so at the next opportunity. You might be surprised to hear some very interesting stories about their childhood experiences.

Chapter Twenty: Tap Tap Twirl

Azaela Grove Elementary offered several after-school programs for students. What Cobra Clubs seemed most interesting to you? What club would you suggest to your principal if given the opportunity to make a decision? Wilky engaged in some naughty behavior to get back at Terrence. Do you think his behavior was justified? What might you have done instead?

Chapter Twenty-One: An Alarming Day.

Cristal was accidentally locked out of the school building during a drill. She seemed to handle it well. What could she have done to make her situation worse? How do you think your parents would have responded if you were abandoned by staff while on a field trip? Mr. Macklberg began the morning announcements with encouragement for the staff and students. Write a motivating announcement for students that you would like to read over the intercom at your school.

Chapter Twenty-Two: Applause, Applause

Mrs. Tubilleja is a teacher who likes to plan activities for students to learn and demonstrate their strengths with others. Cristal was allowed to present her craft, perfume making. What would you do if you had the chance to present a craft or skill, you're good at?

Chapter Twenty-Three: Serendipity

Serendipity can be defined as "An unplanned fortunate discovery or good luck in finding valuable things unintentionally." What a remarkable coincidence it was for the Duvernays when Wilky stood in the cafeteria line of Mrs. Plaizill, a woman born and raised in Haiti. When Dahlia received an invitation to attend her church, it set off a chain of events that would be a turning point in her recovery from depression. Talk about a time when you met someone, found something valuable, or a situation unexpectedly presented itself and set you on a positive path.

Chapter Twenty-Four: Labor Day Weekend

Your personal style includes:

- your interests

- how you dress

- the way you wear your hair

- how you speak

These are a significant part of an image you chose to curate and present to others. Wilky was devasted when he was told he had to cut his locs. His school dress code prohibited him from showing his authentic self. Why do you think schools have such a dress code? Review your school's dress code and scrutinize it to determine if there is anything you disagree with or would change if you had the power to do so.

Chapter Twenty-Five: Fishwife

Dahlia had a privileged and extravagant lifestyle before marrying. Instead of following her parents' pleadings not to marry Jess, she followed her heart. Do you think she lived with regrets about her choice? How do you think her life might have been different if she hadn't become Mrs. Duvernay? Raeni created the game *SCURRED*, which is about phobias. Everyone has something they are afraid of, but it may not be irrational. Research a list of phobias to discover if you have one.

Chapter Twenty-Six: Seesaw

Wilky was lucky that he had Uncle Isaac by his side during the disciplinary meeting regarding the fight with Terrance. How do you think Mr. Macklberg would have handled the incident if the video hadn't been available? Have you ever had someone dismiss your side of the story as fictitious or untrue? Cristal wrote about a childhood memory she had before she lost her vision. What's one of your earliest memories, and why do you think you can remember it so well?

Chapter Twenty-Seven: The ABCs of O&M

Mr. Nick was surprised at how quickly Cristal learned new travel skills, especially since she had never received formal orientation and mobility training. Why do you think Cristal was such a good student? A landmark is an important recognizable object or feature. Name some things on your school campus that would be significant landmarks that begin with the letters *L, M, and N.*

Chapter Twenty-Eight: Chomp and Chat

White Cane Safety Day is a national observance in the United States, celebrated on October 15th of each year since 1964. The date is set aside to celebrate the achievements of people who are blind or visually impaired and the important symbol of blindness and tool of independence, the white cane. Ms. Saunders invited guest speakers throughout the school year to talk to the students in her class about various careers. Have you ever attended a Career Fair? Name the occupations of three speakers that you'd like to visit your school to learn more about their job descriptions.

Chapter Twenty-Nine: Nourishment

Nourishment can be defined as food or other substances necessary for growth, health, and good condition. Mr. Nick provided his students with opportunities to build their confidence and acquire real-life skills by traveling and interacting with others in the community. This could be considered nourishment for the mind, body, and soul. Research activities available at your local library or community that might be of interest to you.

Chapter Thirty: Surprise, Surprise.

Aunt Nadine believes that her husband, Issac, spoils Raeni. For her birthday, she was given a very expensive gift. Research the definition of spoiled to give your opinion about whether Raeni was or was not a spoiled teenager. Why do you think Isaac wants his daughter to remain close to home when she graduates high school? Research the names of three colleges in your state and find out how many miles away they are from where you live.

Chapter Thirty-One: Faded Wallpaper

After only a few months of living in Georgia, Dahlia returns to her home in Croix-des Bouquets, where Cristal and Wilky were born. Why do you think it looks so small to her now? Granny Lou had been the family's matriarch for a very long time. She helped to create loving memories for each member of the Duvernay family. Think about your grandparents or older relatives and some of the special memories you have of them. If you could invite family members who live out of town to visit your city, what's a popular tourist spot that you think everyone would enjoy?

Chapter Thirty-Two: Happy Blooming

Cristal's first year in a public school went better than she ever imagined. Now and then, it's good to do something that takes you out of your comfort zone, like sitting with a different group of students in the cafeteria or trying out for a new sport. Have you ever dreaded doing something your parents wanted you to do because you believed you'd have a miserable time? What was it, and how did it turn out?

Chapter Thirty-Three: A Look Back

Sometimes, friends can persuade you to do something you're reluctant to do, but you do it anyway. Dahlia's coworker, Arvetta, encouraged her to look up someone from her past on the internet. Why do you think she did that? A famous quote says, "If you go looking for trouble, trouble will find you." What do you think it means?

Chapter Thirty-Four: A Gathering of Steam

Raeni and Daxton's boyfriend-and-girlfriend relationship was short-lived. Often, first-dating relationships bring first heartbreaks. Luckily, Raeni could confide in Nadine and discuss the importance of setting healthy boundaries when dating in the future. Although Isaac was overprotective, he understood that Raeni would eventually want to date again, so he agreed to allow his daughter to supervise group dates. Was that a good idea? What are some activities you think would be good for group dating?

Chapter Thirty-Five: Bright Like a Diamond

The talent show at Azaela Elementary was a great way for the administration to end the school year. Cristal did a fantastic job showcasing her talent. Listen to a recording of the song she decided to sing. Why do you think she chose that song? Mr. Nick met Cristal's father for the first time at the talent show and spoke very highly of her. Think about two of your teachers and what they might say to your parents about the type of student you are.

Chapter Thirty-Six: Merging Into Success

From a very early age, Cristal stayed committed to her passion for making perfumes. She received help and continued support throughout high school and college. Not every young person wants to go to college. Many great-paying jobs start from entry-level positions. Talk to teachers and family members about career options that don't require college degrees.

Chapter Thirty-Seven: Good Fortune

As the years passed, Cristal and other Duvernay family members followed their paths to success. Entrepreneurship was at the heart of their personal and professional goals. What are the risks involved in creating a product to sell and then working for yourself instead of a company?

Many people who win large sums of money from playing the lottery quit their jobs and live a life of leisure. Some winners go broke years down the road. Why do you think Cristal and Wilky continued to work for a living?

Chapter Thirty-Eight: Bonjour Mon Amour

Life can be challenging. Like a seesaw, there will always be ups and downs. But, when a person finds their gift and a passion that allows them to live with a high level of independence, joy, and happiness will come. Many successful people agree that showing kindness to others is essential for a good life. When Cristal and Wilky's father made the difficult decision to send his family to the United States, he could only hope and pray that he made the right decision. Rethink the ending for Cristal, Wilky, and Dahlia as to how their lives could have been different had they remained in Croix-des Bouquets after the earthquake.

Haiti sits on a fault line between substantial tectonic plates, big pieces of the Earth's crust that slide past each other over time. These two plates are the North American plate and the Caribbean plate. On August 14, 2021, a magnitude 7.2 earthquake struck southwest Haiti. Tsunami warnings were issued for the Haitian coast. As of September 1, 2021, at least 2,248 people were confirmed dead due to the quake and its aftermath. Approximately 137,500 buildings were damaged or destroyed.

Acknowledgment

My sisters and niece have always supported my creative endeavors and cheered me on. I am grateful and blessed to have each of you in my life.

My former students, with kind and gentle spirits, worked hard to accomplish their goals. Thank you for making teaching fun and much more fulfilling than ever imagined.

My former colleagues diligently served students with blindness and visual impairments. I've admired from near and afar the hard work and dedication you committed to everyone on your caseload. Thank you for inspiring me; you are incredible.

Made in the USA
Middletown, DE
17 September 2024

60567138R00224